Confucius Jane

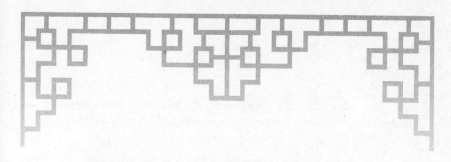

Confucius Jane

KATIE LYNCH

A TOM DOHERTY ASSOCIATES BOOK
NEW YORK

For my Jane

This is a work of fiction. All of the characters, organizations, and events portrayed in this novel are either products of the author's imagination or are used fictitiously.

CONFUCIUS JANE

A Forge Book
Published by Tom Doherty Associates, LLC
175 Fifth Avenue
New York, NY 10010

www.tor-forge.com

Forge® is a registered trademark of Tom Doherty Associates, LLC.

Library of Congress Cataloging-in-Publication Data

Names: Lynch, Katie.
Title: Confucius Jane / Katie Lynch.
Description: New York : Forge Books, 2016.
Identifiers: LCCN 2015033356| ISBN 9780765381682 (hardback) |
    ISBN 9780765383792 (trade paperback) | ISBN 9781466883529 (e-book)
Subjects: LCSH: Chinese American women—Fiction. | Man-woman
    relationships—Fiction. | Chinatown (New York, N.Y.)—Fiction. |
    BISAC: FICTION / Contemporary Women.
Classification: LCC PS3612.Y5423 C66 2016 | DDC 813/.6—dc23
LC record available at http://lccn.loc.gov/2015033356

Forge books may be purchased for educational, business, or promotional
use. For information on bulk purchases, please contact the Macmillan
Corporate and Premium Sales Department at 1-800-221-7945, extension
5442, or write to specialmarkets@macmillan.com.

First Edition: January 2016

Printed in the United States of America

0 9 8 7 6 5 4 3 2 1

Acknowledgments

I finished my first novel at age seventeen: an epically melodramatic work of fantasy, featuring a protagonist with every possible superpower and dialogue containing far too many exclamation points. My parents nurtured this hobby, and one indulgent English teacher, along with a few of my closest friends, were generous enough to help me revise and edit parts of it for inclusion in a school project. They encouraged me in what was then a nascent passion for storytelling.

Now, seventeen years later, that passion has become a profession, and I am fortunate enough to have the best possible team supporting my work. I am deeply grateful to everyone at Jane Rotrosen Agency for their efforts on my behalf. My agent, Meg Ruley, has been a tireless advocate and champion, and I cannot thank her enough. Her belief in me has been a beacon during times of self-doubt. I am likewise grateful to Chris Prestia for her wisdom and advice.

As a seventeen-year-old, my bookshelves were filled with Tor titles, and it is nothing short of a dream come true to now find myself a part of the Tor/Forge community. Kristin Sevick not only took a chance on *Confucius Jane* but also shepherded me through a collaborative and rewarding editing process. I am a stronger writer for having had the opportunity to work with her. I am also grateful to Bess Cozby for her assistance and to Edwin Chapman for his eagle eye during the copyediting process.

JUST AS I HAVE the best professional team at my back, I am also fortunate enough to have the love of a diverse family of choice: the unwavering support of my Dartmouth family, the encouragement of friends and colleagues from Wisconsin and New York, and the shared purpose fostered by the global community of LGBTQ authors. I am particularly indebted to Radclyffe for her role in helping me to develop and hone my craft.

I am also privileged to be the mother of a wonderful son, whose creativity and love of a good story will, I suspect, one day come to fruition in a book of his own. Most of all, I am deeply grateful to my wife, Jane, who is also my muse. I am at once humbled and inspired by the gift of her passion. Our love story will always be at the heart of everything I write.

CHAPTER ONE

JANE WOKE TO THE clickity-clack of her cousin Minetta's fingertips skittering across her laptop keyboard. The noise sounded like a herd of mouse-sized elephants. If there was a Hell and she ended up there, being forced to listen to this for eternity would definitely be her punishment. Gritting her teeth, she tried to burrow deeper beneath the covers and ignore the persistent sound, but to no avail. There couldn't be all that many eleven-year-old touch typists in the world. How had she ended up with one of them for a roommate?

Opening one eye, she glanced at the clock on the nightstand between their beds. Six forty-five. Jane groaned and threw one arm over her face.

"Oh, stop," Min said without a break in her typing. "You should be awake already."

"Have I mentioned that I can't wait until you hit puberty and start wanting to sleep all the time?"

"Be quiet. You're stifling my creative flow."

Jane struggled not to smile. Anyone listening in on this conversation would probably think she was the preteen and Minetta the twenty-three-year-old. An "old soul," that's what everyone called Min. And "precocious." And sometimes "annoying."

She sat up in bed and ran her hands through her short hair. "What are you writing?"

"Blog post."

"A blog post. Of course. What about?"

Minetta was what the media called a *kid-blogger*. She had even been interviewed once for an article in *The New York Times*. Jane tried not to let it rankle that Min's writing career was, by pretty much any measure, more successful than her own.

"The quality of the produce in our cafeteria. It's appalling. Not to mention the fact that we might even be eating GMOs without knowing it!"

Jane swung her legs over the side of the bed and slid her feet into the slippers waiting on the floor. How had she gotten roped into a conversation about the genetic modification of fruits and vegetables before seven o'clock in the morning?

"Aren't there laws about that?"

"The American laws suck. Europe is really strict about genetic modification."

"I see."

Jane shook her head as she padded out of their room and down the hall. Minetta was a crusader for social justice and environmentalism at the tender age of eleven. As Jane brushed her teeth, she tried to remember where she had been at that age. Italy? She paused and stared at her toothpaste-besmeared lips, counting on her fingers. No, Sweden. She had just turned eleven when her father was transferred to Stockholm, where she'd had to adjust to strange umlauts and lutefisk and seeing the sun for only an hour or two each day during the depths of winter.

"You learned Swedish at eleven," she muttered at her reflection. "That has to count for something."

When she returned from the bathroom, Min was zipping up the backpack Jane had given her this past Christmas made from recycled plastic soda bottles. Dressed in a pink-and-purple striped sweater and skinny jeans with flowers stitched along their pockets, she looked the part of a normal fifth-grader. Which just went to prove that people should never judge books by their covers.

"I'm going downstairs." She paused in the doorway. "Are you really mad?"

Jane ruffled Min's straight black hair. "Nah. Don't worry about it, kiddo."

Left alone in the room, Jane wistfully eyed her inviting bed before turning to the stack of milk crates currently serving as her dresser. As she chose her clothes for the day, she was careful to keep her head ducked well below the steeply sloping roof beams. During the first month after she'd moved in with her aunt and uncle, she had nearly brained herself far too many times.

After pulling on a pair of olive cargo pants and a vintage Joe Camel T-shirt, she pocketed her notebook and pen. When she stepped out of the room, she paused to wave to Cornelia, who was currently doing her best imitation of a zombie shuffle toward the bathroom. The poor thing had an eight o'clock lecture course this semester. There were a few parts of college life that Jane would admit to missing, but early morning bore-fests certainly weren't one of them.

As she descended the rickety stairs past the second-floor landing, the scent of *luo bo gao* made her mouth water. She would never tell her mother, but Aunt Jenny made the best turnip cakes she'd ever tasted. Upon entering the kitchen, she found Min and Uncle John seated at the wooden table, sharing the Chinese newspaper delivered daily to the doorstep of his fortune-cookie company.

"Good morning, Jane," said Uncle John.

"Hungry?" asked Aunt Jenny.

"What are you wearing?" shrieked Min.

Jane grinned. "G'morning. Smells great, Aunt Jen." She took the free seat next to Min. "This shirt is a classic. Don't knock it."

"You're a walking tobacco ad! Corrupting America's youth!"

"I think you'll do just fine. You're way too smart to take up cigarettes." Jane accepted the steaming plate of *luo bo gao* and reached for the soy and hot sauces at the center of the table.

"The tobacco industry is powerful enough," Min persisted. "They don't need your help."

Uncle John lowered his paper. "Minetta, enough. Leave Jane alone."

"It's okay." Jane patted Min's shoulder. "You're entitled to your opinion, but as far as I'm concerned, this shirt is a work of art."

Min sighed, shot her a baleful look, and went back to reading. As Jane shoveled down her breakfast, she glanced at the sea of intricate characters on the paper in Min's hand. A few familiar symbols jumped out, but mostly the page looked like a jumble of two-dimensional stick insects. By now, six months after having moved down to Chinatown, she was decent at understanding and speaking Mandarin. Her Cantonese was a little worse, though she usually managed to get by with the help of hand gestures. But reading was another matter altogether. Her natural aptitude wasn't going to help her learn an entirely foreign way of writing down language.

Maybe, she thought as she took her last bite, she should take some lessons. She would have asked Aunt Jenny, who had taught first graders before marrying Uncle John and joining in to help with the family business, but Jane didn't want to be more of a burden than she was already. At the thought, she pushed back her chair and went to the sink, waving off Aunt Jenny's protests that she would do the dishes later. After washing her plate and setting it in the drying rack, she headed toward the apartment's front door.

"Thanks for breakfast. I'm off to do the locals." She paused to glance over her shoulder at Min. "You, be good."

Min stuck out her tongue, and Jane left the room smiling. Three flights of stairs later, she turned away from the short corridor leading to the outside world and instead used her key to open the side entrance to Confucius Fortunes Company. Bypassing the main office, she walked down the hall and used a different key to access the warehouse, where boxes upon boxes of cookies were stored, waiting to go out to restaurants across the tri-state area.

Each day, she began her work by doing a circuit through Chinatown and dropping off cookies to all the venues with standing orders. By now, Jane had developed an efficient route through the neighborhood, and she worked quickly to load up the dolly with boxes. Before venturing outside, she reluctantly grabbed the company jacket with her name on it off a hook near the door. She hated jackets of any kind, but her uncle had insisted.

As she stepped outside, her gaze went automatically to the front window of the dumpling restaurant across the street, even though she knew she would find it dark and empty. Noodle Treasure didn't open until ten o'clock, and The Goddess in Glasses usually didn't arrive until the afternoon. Jane had first noticed her back in November. She'd never forget that day—it had been overcast, but as she walked out onto the sidewalk, the sun had broken through the clouds to illuminate the far side of the street. Instantly, Jane had been captivated by the sight of the woman sitting in the corner, head bent as she read something. Her honey-gold hair, tied back in a ponytail, fairly glowed in the sunlight. The woman had turned her face up to the dazzling rays, removing her glasses and closing her eyes, clearly basking in the warmth. Jane's mouth had gone dry at the sensuality of that simple, innocent act.

And then the clouds had closed back over the sun, dousing the scene in shadow. Jane had watched the woman sigh—clearly in regret—and turn her attention back to her work.

In the span of those thirty seconds, Jane had gone from resignedly single to mired in hopeless longing. Thanks to Minetta's reconnaissance, she had even discovered the woman's name. "They call her Dr. Sutton," Min had reported, "because she's getting two doctor-degrees at the same time." Sutton. It was a beautiful name, but after months of referring to her as The Goddess in Glasses, thinking of her by any other appellation didn't feel natural.

Natural? Jane shook her head and began to push the dolly down the sidewalk. Look at her, mooning over a woman who didn't know she existed. She and The—and *Sutton*—hadn't so much as exchanged two words. How much more pathetic could she get? She really was more immature than Minetta.

The streets were just starting to come alive as she turned the dolly toward the heart of the neighborhood. Her aunt and uncle lived on its northwest periphery, and as she walked south and east, Jane felt Chinatown encircle her, simultaneously embracing and threatening. Tiny stores were crammed next to and on top of each other, and she carefully threaded her way around the fruit sellers setting up their wares and the fishmongers carting bins full of ice outside of their storefronts. Later, those bins would be filled with crabs and lobster and shellfish, adding to the stench of the sea that always lingered on these streets.

Her first stop was a teahouse on Canal, where the proprietor liked to give her patrons a free fortune cookie with every purchase. Jane chatted with her briefly about the cold weather before continuing along her route. After turning right onto Mott, she stopped at two restaurants before making another right onto Mosco Street and descending the short hill to Mulberry. This section was known as Funeral Parlor Row, and Jane made stops at both of the funeral homes. The owners liked to keep cookies on hand for themselves and their clients to offset the ill luck conferred by their close proximity to death.

After two more hours of deliveries, Jane found herself approaching the last stop on her route: Red Door Apothecary. The small shop was squeezed between a massage parlor and a Chinese bakery. Hefting the last of her boxes, Jane pressed the buzzer on the doorpost. Idly, she noticed that some of the crimson paint was beginning to flake off, especially around the brass knocker, and she made a mental note to give the door a fresh coat once the weather turned warmer.

At that moment, it opened inward to reveal a petite, silver-haired woman wearing a red tunic over gold leggings. Xue "Sue" Si Ma was in her sixties, but she was often mistaken for a woman two decades younger. She bid Jane good morning in both Mandarin and English, then stepped aside to let her enter. Jane breathed in deeply as she crossed the threshold, pulling the complex, earthy scent of the shop deep into her lungs. The wall to her left was comprised entirely of curio drawers, while to her right, floor-to-ceiling shelves were crowded with glass bottles and ceramic vessels full of herbs, seeds, flowers, bark, and roots. Treading carefully so as not to bump into the shelves, Jane moved past the small lounge area where Sue did her astrological consultations. She finally set the box down on the counter next to the register.

"Did you want these underneath today, or in the back?"

"Underneath, please." When Sue smiled, the corners of her eyes crinkled merrily. "Business has been brisk this week."

Sue liked to give cookies to her customers—not only for their enjoyment, but also because discussion of their fortune often enticed them into asking to have their charts read. As Jane slid the box beneath the register, Sue edged past her.

"I'll get your tea."

Jane followed her into the back of the shop, where a small stovetop and sink shared the space with a wooden table and a narrow refrigerator. In the far corner, a rickety desk held a desktop computer and printer.

"Glad to hear you've been busy," Jane said as she fired up the PC. "Hopefully the same will be true for your online sales."

Late last year, Jane had been in the midst of delivering Sue's cookies when she'd overheard a customer ask whether Red Door Apothecary was on the Web. When Sue had answered in the negative, Jane had taken it upon herself to develop a rudimentary website for the shop. At first, she had tried to teach Sue how to download and print all the orders herself, but when that hadn't worked, Jane had taken over the task. The online orders had barely trickled in at first, but she'd seen an uptick recently. Sue had offered many times to compensate her, but filling the orders never took long, and Jane didn't mind volunteering. She had the time, and she'd listened to the complaints of more than one small-business owner in this neighborhood about increasing rents and other costs.

"*Li'huan* tea." Sue placed a steaming mug in front of her, and Jane struggle not to wince at the pungent fumes rising from the dark liquid. "Good for digestion."

"Uh, thanks."

Sue watched until Jane took a tentative sip. When Jane couldn't help but wrinkle her nose, Sue nodded contentedly. "Bitter is good. Means it's working."

Jane managed a weak smile. She'd have to drink the whole thing, too, or risk hurting Sue's feelings. "Okay. Looks like you have seventeen orders since last week. That's the most I've seen yet." After sending the documents to the printer, Jane clicked over to the word processing application. "I'll get started on these labels."

When she was finished, Jane returned to the front of the store to help Sue double-check and box up each order. As they worked side by side, Sue shared the news she'd heard over the intervening week. The manager of the massage parlor next door was pregnant with twins. One of the supervisors at the nearby market had been caught having an affair with a clerk. The gold-buyer's store two blocks away was closed while police investigated allegations of a gambling ring.

Jane worked efficiently as Sue talked, always happy to listen to her stories. Sue made her feel part of the fabric of the community, instead of a frayed thread barely dangling from the edge. That sense of never quite belonging came with the territory of being *hapa*. While most Caucasian people saw her as fully Asian, every resident of Chinatown could tell she was half-white. Many of them even knew the story of how her mother had fallen in love with the tall, curly-haired Irishman she'd met in college who had enticed her to abandon her family and follow him around the world.

After Jane had made a mess of her own education and been obliged to move in with her aunt and uncle, it hadn't taken long for her to realize that the members of this community pitied her—and that they blamed her mother for choosing the exotic over tradition.

"And how is your family?" Sue asked when she had run out of news.

"They're well. Busy preparing for the New Year celebrations."

Sue's eyes took on a faraway look. "The year of the Monkey. You must be careful to defend yourself."

"Defend myself?" Jane tried not to let her skepticism show.

"Oh, yes. Did your mother never tell you that the year of your birth sign has the potential to be very unlucky?"

"She neglected to mention that."

Sue tsked under her breath. "You must be vigilant in protecting your health, career, and love life. But for everyone else it will be a good year for innovation and creativity."

"Interesting." Jane piled the boxes next to the door. "I wonder whether Hester's ready for a Monkey-baby."

Jane's oldest cousin was pregnant with her third child. After college, she had married her childhood sweetheart and gone to work at the local elementary school. In many ways, Hester was the most traditional member of the entire family, and Jane wondered if she put any stock in the zodiac.

Sue's face lit up like an elegant paper lantern. "Remind her to bring the child here, after *zuo yuezi.*"

Sue's reference to the traditional Chinese practice of "sitting the month"—in which a new mother barely left her bed for thirty days after giving birth and was cared for by her female relatives—reminded Jane of just how Westernized she was. Being forced to lie around and do nothing for weeks on end sounded much more like a curse than a blessing, but who was she to judge? Hester clearly didn't have a problem with it. "Sure."

Sue beckoned Jane toward the sitting area. "Come. Let's look at your chart."

Jane surreptitiously glanced at her watch. She had stayed longer than she should already. Still, a few extra minutes couldn't hurt. Sue considered these astrological readings a form of payment for Jane's help, which meant Jane couldn't reject her gift without also rejecting her.

She perched on the couch and fidgeted with the tassels on its crimson coverlet. Across a small glass oval table, Sue was consulting a thick book with yellowed pages and a decrepit binding. As she flipped through its pages, she glanced up and smiled fondly.

"You are the quintessential Monkey. So easily distracted."

"Sorry."

"Don't apologize for who you are," Sue said absently as she continued to leaf through the book. "Ah. Here." After transferring her glasses from her forehead to the bridge of her nose, she peered intently at the page.

A few months ago, Sue had taken it upon herself to do Jane's birth chart. Every week since, she had consulted her mysterious book and made some sort of proclamation about Jane's immediate future. All Jane knew was that the numbers of her birth date were involved, along with the five elements: earth, metal, water, fire, and wood.

Suddenly, Sue pursed her lips. She tapped her chin, bent closer to the book, and frowned. Jane couldn't help but lean forward. "What is it?"

"Tomorrow," said Sue. "The time will be ripe."

Jane blinked. "It will be? For what?"

The phone rang. With an apologetic sigh, Sue put the book back on the table and hurried across the room to answer it. Jane leaned over to glance at the open page, but it looked like just another insect graveyard to her. Maybe, instead of reading her horoscope, Sue could teach her how to read, period.

When Sue's voice increased in volume, Jane was able to pick several phrases out of the swift syllabic river that suggested Sue was talking to her mother. The conversation probably wouldn't be brief, and it was past time to start working on the day's shipping queue. She'd have to leave without ever knowing what the time was ripe for. Pity. Maybe it would still be true next week.

After catching Sue's eye and waving, Jane slipped out the front door and pushed the dolly back to the factory. Once the warehouse orders were finished, she would climb the back stairs to the supply closet on the factory's second floor that also doubled as her office. Uncle John had pushed a small table up against the window for her, where she sat on a folding chair amongst reams of paper, stacks of cardboard, and ink cartridges. There, she would prepare for the next day's orders and jot down any pithy sayings that popped into her head. Those would find their way into the cookies being baked below.

The window looked out onto Baxter Street, giving her an excellent vantage point from which to observe The Goddess in Glasses. Not that she was a stalker, Jane thought that afternoon, as she sat tapping her pen against her chin. The positioning of her desk was hardly her fault. And surrounded by office supplies, where else was she going to look for inspiration but outside?

Her stomach suddenly dropped into her toes as she recognized the figure that walked briskly down the street toward Noodle Treasure. Sutton. There was some quality to her movement that set off Jane's gaydar, a subtle swagger that gave her a glimmer of hope. Having spent half of her college years mooning over—and then losing—her straight best friend, Jane didn't want to make that mistake again. Min claimed that in all the conversations she'd overheard, Sutton had never mentioned a significant other. Then again, why would she share details about her personal life with acquaintances at the restaurant where she came for a hot meal and a place to work?

Sutton's golden ponytail brushed against the fabric of her black parka as she hurried inside, clearly trying to beat the wintry chill.

Jane watched avidly as she chatted briefly with Benny before he left with her order. Her lips moved even after he was gone, but Jane couldn't make out the words. Was she talking to herself? If so, that was amazing. And adorable.

"You're an idiot," she muttered.

Sutton flipped open her laptop and then turned to accept some kind of drink from Mei. Probably tea. Helpless to turn away from Sutton's elegant profile, Jane found herself wishing she were a visual artist. She had yet to find any adjectives that did justice to Sutton's beauty.

After a short chat with Mei, Sutton turned back to her computer. She fiddled briefly with her glasses before focusing in on the screen. Jane sighed and laced her hands behind her head. Sutton could concentrate for hours on end. Probably because she was brilliant. Then again, some brilliant people found it quite difficult to remain focused for long periods of time. Or so Jane had heard. Maybe there was hope for her, after all.

"Oh, sure." She looked down at her notebook. "You're a real genius." She had only managed to fill half a page since lunch, and most of these lines weren't worth keeping anyway. What kind of poet had trouble coming up with pearls of pseudowisdom destined to be folded into cookies and ignored by most of the general populace? The best she could hope for on any given day was that someone would laugh after tacking on "in bed" to the end of one of her fortunes.

By the time the bell at the top of the nearby Roman Catholic church chimed five o'clock, Jane was going more than a little stir-crazy. She had forced herself to be reasonably productive, at least in terms of quantity. Whether she decided to keep anything she'd done today, though, was an entirely different question. Her writer's block had been exacerbated by the lengthening shadows of the approaching wintry dusk, which had blocked Sutton from Jane's view. For some reason, the knowledge that Sutton was simultaneously just across the street and just out of sight contributed to Jane's distraction. She couldn't bear to sit still anymore. Besides, the cacophony of the city beckoned, promising her the kind of satisfaction she would never find within these walls.

As the front door of the factory closed behind her, she zipped up her hoodie against the frozen air, glad to have escaped Aunt Jenny's badgering about not wearing enough clothing. Proper coats were too bulky. They gave her an odd sense of claustrophobia. Besides, she didn't plan to spend very much time above ground tonight.

Automatically, she turned toward Noodle Treasure. Just a glimpse, she told herself. Just one more glimpse of Sutton, and then she would go about her real work. But when she raised her head, Sutton was looking directly at her. Jane's breath stuttered. Sutton's eyes were light in color—cornflower blue, or maybe gray. Her lips were slightly parted, and as Jane watched, two spots of color bloomed on her cheeks. Helplessly, she felt herself pulled forward by the force of her attraction. What if she crossed the street? What if she walked through that door? What if she asked Sutton whether the seat next to hers was taken? What would happen then?

A cold breeze blew up suddenly to break the spell. What was she thinking? She hadn't made any sort of plan. If she went over there now, she would trip over her tongue in the worst possible way and humiliate herself—not only in front of her silly crush, but in front of Mei, Benny, Min, and who knew how many others. Sutton would never so much as look at her again, and everyone in Chinatown would know the details of her shame by morning.

No, she thought as she pulled the hood of her sweatshirt over her ears. She wouldn't do it. She wouldn't cross Baxter today. This was one situation she couldn't play by ear. But maybe, now that Sutton finally knew she existed, she could work up the courage to approach her. Someday.

Jane shoved her hands in her pockets and forced herself to turn away. For now, the city called to her, wanting to tell her its secrets. And she wanted to listen.

CHAPTER TWO

THAT'LL DO IT. Go ahead and sew him up."

From the side of the operating table, Sutton St. James watched as her advisor, Dr. Buehler, strode toward the door, his movements crisp and purposeful despite the fresh layer of sweat that had broken out on his face and neck since a nurse had last patted him dry. The four-hour procedure wasn't all that lengthy by neurosurgery standards, but it had proven more difficult than anticipated. She shifted her weight, trying to subtly ease some of the soreness that was developing in her arches.

Tom Fisher, the most senior of the neurosurgery residents, turned to look at her. "Want to do the honors?"

"Absolutely." Sutton hoped she sounded confident. She had stitched up patients before, but never after a surgery quite this complex. While watching Dr. Buehler cut away the tumor from the surrounding blood vessels, Sutton had felt her own heart pounding. But if he'd been experiencing a comparable level of stress, she hadn't been able to tell. His hands had remained steady and his focus never faltered. Now, as she switched places with Tom and asked the nurse to load the needle, Sutton exhaled slowly.

"What kind of suture are you going to use?" Tom asked.

"Running horizontal mattress." Sutton had prepared her answer hours ago in anticipation of being offered this chance.

"Good. How are you feeling about it?"

"Feeling great." There was no other possible answer. To hint at anything other than pure confidence would be to admit defeat before she had even begun. Surgeons had a saying: *God hates a coward.*

As Sutton gripped the forceps, her field of vision narrowed until all she saw was the incision. She had practiced her sutures a thousand times over the past few years, first on knot-tying boards and later on pigs' feet—much to the chagrin of her roommate, Theresa, who complained about how much space they took up in the freezer. But suturing was one of the fundamental skills of a surgeon, and Sutton knew only one way to become perfect at it. When she couldn't sleep at night, she practiced. When her mother was having a flare-up and needed a sympathetic ear, she practiced. When she couldn't stand to wrestle any longer with how to phrase a sentence in her dissertation, she practiced.

Now, she focused on making smooth and precise movements as she tied off the first stitch and embarked on the second. If she made them too tight, she risked cutting off oxygen to the healing tissue. If she didn't align them properly, she risked leaving the patient with a rough, jagged scar. But as she settled into the familiar rhythm, muscle memory melted her stress away. Her shoulders relaxed and her breathing settled, just as it did during her daily yoga exercises.

Beside her, Tom was bantering with the nurses and the anesthesiologist about some party they'd all attended over the weekend. Sutton regretted that she hadn't gone, but for the past few months, she had found it unbearable to associate socially with anyone from the hospital. They could only talk about one thing: residency applications. On the cusp of completing her M.D./Ph.D. with a focus in neuroscience, Sutton knew that the medical community expected her to be matched with a prestigious residency in neurosurgery. Some of her friends even talked as though it were a fait accompli, which is why she had taken pains to sequester herself since the start of the academic year. She didn't know how to tell them that she was no longer sure of what she wanted. To them, her waffling would feel like a betrayal. Surgeons had another saying: *better wrong than uncertain*.

After tying off the final suture, she raised her head and stepped back from the table to survey her handiwork. The row of perfectly parallel stitches marched across the pale skin like a miniature railroad track. It was a job well done, but her swell of pride was tempered by the knowledge that she had just performed the most basic aspect of the entire surgery. There was so much more to learn—if that was what she truly wanted.

"Good work today," Tom said as they scrubbed out side by side. "Let me buy you a crappy meal at the caf."

Sutton considered saying yes. Tom was one of the few people at the hospital who seemed to understand that having a father who was the former Surgeon General of the United States was not always a blessing. But before she could open her mouth, her pager went off.

"I'll have to take a rain check," she said after reading the message. "Buehler wants me on rounds."

Ignoring the ache in her feet, Sutton hurried to the locker room to grab her notebook and then jogged up two flights of stairs to the recovery ward. She found Buehler leaving the room of a patient on whom he had performed a lumbar decompressive laminectomy two days ago. Even when he caught sight of her, he never stopped moving.

"Sutton." He greeted her brusquely. "Any questions for me on today's procedure?"

She had plenty, and he answered them in between patient visits. Despite the long day, his pace never flagged. "How is the revision of your middle chapters coming along?" he asked as they approached the last room on his list. "I'd like to get that article out the door by the end of the month."

"I'm making headway," Sutton said, careful not to betray her frustrations with the writing process. "I'll have a draft to you soon."

"Good." He rested his hand briefly on her shoulder. "I know you've mentally moved beyond your thesis at this point, but a solid piece like this will help you build credibility. Especially in light of the potential controversy ahead."

Sutton struggled not to betray the anxiety his words inspired. Next month, the most prestigious stem-cell research journal in the world would include an article with her name on it. Her pride at the accomplishment had immediately been tempered by the knowledge that it would upset her parents. Her father would be doubly incensed—first, that his daughter had joined forces with the "morally bankrupt souls" who pursued such research; and second, that in doing so, she had irreparably shattered the notion that she was following in his footsteps. Keeping up appearances was vital to him, and for years, Sutton had effortlessly played the role of his faithful and obedient protégé. If he was angry enough at her departure from his core values, he could make her career path very difficult.

The only person in whom she had confided was Buehler, who had encouraged her to apply to postgraduate fellowship opportunities in several foreign countries where stem-cell research was the most advanced. A research scientist as well as a surgeon, he was in a perfect position to understand her conflicting aspirations. He was also the only authority figure in her life who had never pushed her in one direction or another, instead offering her equal opportunities in both research and medical training. Pursuing the path of a surgeon had always been a foregone conclusion, and Sutton knew exactly where it led. Once, it had been all she'd wanted. But her research belonged to her in a way that was unique and exciting. As a scientist, she paved her own road, instead of having to stand in her father's shadow.

When Buehler gestured toward the last door on the right, she reined in her wandering thoughts. "Remind me of Mr. Bartlett's case," he said, even though he didn't actually need any reminding. This was a test.

"Mr. Bartlett presented with a metastatic brain tumor in the deep left parietal lobe. He is three days' postoperative. I checked his chart this morning and he appears to be healing well, though he's apparently been badgering the nurses."

Sutton delivered her summary as concisely as possible, though "badgering" might have been too gentle a term. While checking in at the nurses' station this morning, she had heard multiple stories of just how demanding a patient Mr. Bartlett was proving to be.

"Let's—" But before Buehler could finish his sentence, his pager chimed. He looked at the number and grunted. "Trauma wants a consult. You handle this and report back to one of the residents later."

Without waiting for her reaction, he moved toward the nearest elevator. For one precarious instant, Sutton wanted to call him back and protest that she wasn't yet ready to see patients on her own. Over the past few months, he had increasingly demanded that she take the lead role on rounds, but she had always been able to count on his presence in the room. Now, a throng of all-too-familiar fears crowded to the fore of her mind: that she didn't belong here; that she was bound to make a mistake; that she had been fast-tracked because of her name and not her ability. But impostor syndrome had hounded her ever since her decision to apply to medical school, and she wasn't about to let it sideline her now. Closing her eyes, she summoned the image of the narrow closet door in her childhood bedroom and closed it firmly on every negative emotion. The familiar mental exercise loosened the grip of her anxiety enough to allow her to focus on her responsibilities.

When Sutton entered the patient's room, she was greeted by the sight of an elderly man propped up at a forty-five-degree angle in his hospital bed. A disheveled, white mane of hair fell almost to his shoulders, though the effect was spoiled somewhat by the bandage covering the right side of his head. White tufts of hair protruded from his ears and from a large mole on his chin.

"Hello, Mr. Bartlett," Sutton said as she approached. "Do you remember me? I stopped by briefly to see you early this morning. I'm Dr. St. James."

"Where's my surgeon?" he said in a raspy voice.

"Dr. Buehler was called away on an urgent case. He'll drop by to see you later." As she spoke, Sutton flipped through the chart, scanning the most recent notes rapidly. Mr. Bartlett had paged the nurses' station once this morning and once this afternoon, complaining of vague symptoms. One nurse had noted that he was "difficult."

Sutton looked up and met his rheumy eyes, automatically double-checking his pupil dilation. Difficult or not, he was her patient and deserved her undivided attention. "While I check your incision site, would you mind telling me how you've been feeling today?"

He scowled dramatically, bushy white eyebrows angling low over his deep-set eyes. "Isn't that thing supposed to tell you?"

"It's written in shorthand. I'd rather hear it from you, if you don't mind."

As he indulged in a long-suffering sigh, Sutton moved toward his head and bent to inspect his wound. There was no sign of infection, and she jotted that on the chart.

"I've been feeling like crap," Mr. Bartlett was saying. "Just . . . not right."

Sutton moved back into his line of sight. "That's disconcerting, isn't it? Can you be more specific at all about that feeling? Do you have pain? Dizziness? An ache?"

His eyes shifted between the door and back. "A few times, back in college, I got—I smoked some marijuana."

Sutton was careful to betray no reaction, even as she immediately began to catalogue and discard possibilities. "And you felt that kind of high today?"

"Sort of. Only it wasn't fun."

She held back a smile at the forlorn note in his voice. "All right. Anything else?"

"I can't see the damn TV," he groused. "Did they move my bed? I could see it fine yesterday."

"I don't think so. It's difficult to move your bed because of all the machinery. Does your vision seem blurry, or just worse?"

"I don't know! I just want to watch *SportsCenter*, damn it!"

Sutton made another note. "Who's your team, Mr. Bartlett?"

"The Rangers! Who else?"

"Did you play hockey, ever?"

He didn't answer right away, and Sutton glanced up to find him looking out the window. The desolate expression on his face was a reminder that, for him, the hospital felt more like a prison. As she waited for him to speak, she smoothed the hem of his thin blanket, wishing futilely that there was more she could do. It was a silly reaction—as useless as regret.

"All the neighborhood kids used to play on the pond at the bottom of the hill."

"Where did you grow up?"

"Flushing." His mouth tightened into a thin line. "That pond is a goddamn McDonald's now."

"I'm sorry. We don't need any more of those, do we? Is there anything else you'd like me to know?"

His scowl grew deeper. "The food here has no taste. None."

Sutton laughed. "I can empathize. It's not any better in the cafeteria, I promise." She wrote a few shorthand notes into her book and snapped it shut. "Your incision site is healing well, and you have a CT scan scheduled for tomorrow. Any questions for me?"

"If that scan-thing is clear, I can go home?"

For the first time, a note of vulnerability crept into his voice, and Sutton felt a rush of sympathy. "I can't promise you that, but it seems likely to me."

He sighed and closed his eyes. Sutton wished him a good night and left, releasing her breath on a slow exhale as the door shut behind her. That had gone pretty well. The question was, did Mr. Bartlett's symptoms amount to anything, or was he just complaining because he was lonely and uncomfortable? The strange sensation he'd felt might have been a reaction to his medication, but the loss of eyesight was more difficult to explain. Sutton had a niggling suspicion that something was going on, but she knew better than to take her hunch to the residents without any corroborating proof. That meant she had to stop at the nurses' station.

"Hi, Diana," she greeted the head nurse. "Do you have a sec to answer a few questions for me?"

From the moment she'd begun her clinical rotations, Sutton had worked hard to establish a strong rapport with as many of the nurses as possible. They were the true eyes and ears of the wards, and the glue that held the hospital together. And as a student, much further down on the totem pole than even the youngest resident, she was especially careful to tread lightly.

"No, but ask anyway," Diana said, never taking her eyes off her computer screen.

"I'm wondering if you can tell me what Mr. Bartlett said each time he buzzed today."

"Can't wait to be rid of that one." Diana stopped typing and gave Sutton her full attention. "In the morning, he told me he felt 'off.' When I pressed him for details, he said he felt like he was 'floating.' When I started asking more questions, he started yelling."

"And in the afternoon?"

"He was more focused then, but he kept insisting we'd moved his bed away from the television. When I told him we hadn't, all I got was more verbal abuse."

"Was he this cantankerous before the surgery?"

"You know," Diana said slowly, "I remember him being gruff, but not nearly this much of a pain in the ass." She met Sutton's eyes. "What are you thinking?"

"I'm not sure yet. I need to consult with one of the residents. But if he buzzes again, will you page me?"

"Sure."

"Thanks." With a wave, Sutton headed for the elevator, writing down a few additional notes as she walked. The sensation of floating. Eyesight problems. A change in mood. Instinct told her they were puzzle pieces waiting to be put together, if only she could make the connections. As she pressed the button for the third floor, her eyes skimmed over the word *cafeteria* and she smiled to herself at the memory of Mr. Bartlett's complaints. She didn't know anyone—physician or patient—who had ever praised the taste of hospital food. But Mr. Bartlett hadn't complained about how bad the food was—he'd complained that it had no taste at all.

Epiphany flared, burning away her fatigue. "That's it," she said aloud, startling the other person in the elevator—an orderly with a dolly full of boxes.

Sutton squeezed between the doors as soon as they opened. As she hurried down the corridor, she greeted everyone she recognized but didn't slow until she swerved into the residents' lounge. Tom wasn't seated on either of the couches, and she was about to turn toward the row of computers in the back when the image of her father on the television in the far corner paralyzed her. A quick glance at the bottom corner of the screen confirmed that it was just past two o'clock in the afternoon, which meant that Dr. America's daily show had just begun.

"Today, we'll be discussing one of the most hot-button contemporary issues in the medical community: stem-cell research. I'll define what stem cells are, how some scientists intend to use them, and the moral and ethical issues involved."

Her father might sound reasonable and objective now, but Sutton would have wagered everything in her wallet that, within

minutes, he would invoke the notion of "playing God." Smothering an urge to march across the room and yank the cord out of its
socket, Sutton instead turned her back on her father's glossy image and found Tom seated at one of the computers, tapping away
industriously.

"Hi again, Tom."

"Hey, Sutton. How were rounds?"

*"Stem cells are special because when they divide, they can 'dif-
ferentiate' into anything—heart cells, muscle cells, nerve cells.
There are two different kinds of stem cells, embryonic and adult."*

Momentarily distracted by her father's voice, Sutton tried to
relegate him to background noise. She had to focus. A man's life
might be in the balance. "I need to talk to you about a case. You
assisted on the brain tumor resection three days ago, right? For
Mr. Bartlett?"

"That's right."

*"Adult stem cells are most frequently harvested from bone mar-
row, and they are used in the treatment of several illnesses, including cancer and spinal-cord trauma. However, adult stem cells
are limited in terms of the kinds of cells they can differentiate
into."*

She took a deep breath. "I think he's having TIAs." Transient
Ischemic Attacks were known colloquially as *mini-strokes,* in which
the blood supply to part of the brain was temporarily blocked
before resolving without medical intervention. They were often
the harbingers of more serious and potentially debilitating strokes.

"Evidence?"

"He's reported loss of taste, loss of vision, and feeling light-
headed. The nurses have also witnessed a noticeable change in

mood since he was admitted. There's been nothing abnormal on the patient monitor, but that's not inconsistent with a TIA that's not originating in the heart."

Tom laced his hands behind his head, which meant he was going into teacher mode. As she waited for him to speak, her father's words filled the silence.

"Embryonic stem cells, on the other hand, are harvested only five days after conception. These stem cells can, under the right conditions, divide into any kind of cell in the body. However, when these stem cells are harvested, the embryo is completely destroyed."

Without looking at the television, Sutton could tell that her father had his audience spellbound. His "preacher's voice" was in full effect—inherited, so he claimed, from his Baptist minister father. By the end of the hour, stem-cell research would probably have thousands more opponents.

"Let's say you were me," Tom said, drawing her attention back to the important matter at hand. "What would you do?"

"He's scheduled for a CT scan tomorrow, but I'd have that done now. And I'd order a carotid ultrasound, just to rule out narrow blood vessels in his neck as the cause."

"And for treatment?"

"He's allergic to aspirin, and he's already taking an anticoagulant. I'd prescribe an antiplatelet medication, and frequent liver function tests to make sure his body can handle the combination."

"Sounds good, Dr. St. James. Get on it." The barest hint of a smile appeared at his lips. "I'll take this to Buehler and have him call in the CT scan, though, so it's sure to happen right away."

She nodded. The hospital hierarchy permeated every aspect of the institution, and seniority made everything easier. "Thanks. I'll take care of the rest."

". . . and even the production of adult stem cells is controversial, because it relies on cloning techniques. Is it ethical to 'play God' in this way?"

Sutton couldn't leave the lounge fast enough. As she walked down the hall toward the tiny, cramped computer lab reserved for medical students doing their clerkships, she forced her thoughts away from her father's fearmongering and focused instead on her to-do list. After placing the order for the ultrasound, she would write up her notes and send them to both Tom and Dr. Buehler. Then, she would return to the nurses' station and fill them in while waiting for the results of the CT scan. If the tests came back clear, she would look foolish and overeager.

"But better wrong than uncertain, right?" she muttered under her breath.

Regardless of the outcome, she knew exactly what she wanted once this day was over: a large plate of dumplings and a hot bowl of soup from the one place in the city where she could relax.

HEAD BOWED AGAINST THE biting wind, Sutton quickly navigated the ten-block walk to her apartment building. A converted warehouse, its high ceilings and exposed wooden beams lent a spacious feeling to her living space that was missing from many other places in the city. The only downside was the poor insulation. Sutton shivered as she stepped into her room but made no move to turn on the space heater. As much as she wanted to spend the rest of this day curled under the covers with a good detective story, she had to make some additional progress on the article for Buehler. That meant going back out into the frigid wasteland. This apartment was her sanctuary, and she refused to bring work home to it.

Mindful of the chill, she hastily stripped off her scrubs and threw on a white cable-knit sweater and jeans. After pulling her hair back in a ponytail and switching out her contacts for glasses,

she grabbed her heaviest coat. Her messenger bag was waiting by
the door, already packed with her laptop and lab notebook. Within
five minutes, she was back in the street and headed toward
Chinatown.

Until this past fall, she had done her studying and writing on
the top floor of the Ehrman Medical Library, in a carrel with a view
of the East River. But in the hubbub surrounding residency applications, the library had transformed from a refuge to a gigantic
watercooler. Her so-called friends had sought her out at every opportunity, first asking about her plans and then asking for advice.
No matter how many times Sutton tried to convince them otherwise, they assumed she had special insights into the process.
Finally, she had abandoned the library as a viable place to do her
work. After a few aborted attempts at coffee shops where the conversations around her had been utterly distracting, Sutton had
stumbled across a solution one overcast day while seeking out an
inexpensive lunch. The brightly painted façade of a small Chinese
restaurant called Noodle Treasure had caught her eye, and the
mouth-watering scent of frying dumplings had lured her inside.
A stout Chinese man had greeted her, his warm smile immediately
putting her at ease. The food was hearty and satisfying, the tea fragrant and strong. Her fortune cookie read: *Find a place to shelter
from the storm.* By the time she had finished her meal, the skies had
opened in an autumnal downpour. Sutton had laughed at the coincidence and opted to do some reading while waiting out the rain.

Noodle Treasure, it turned out, was the perfect place for her to
work. Most of the patrons were Chinese, and the cadence of their
conversations washed over Sutton without interrupting her concentration. By some mystical process, a petite woman with twinkling
eyes and salt-and-pepper hair appeared to refill her teacup whenever it was nearly empty. For once, she'd been able to focus on her
work without any interruption except her own tendency to procras-
tinate whenever she had to do any kind of writing.

The next day, Sutton had brought her laptop and asked to sit at the far corner of the faux-marble bar set against the front window. Instead of dumplings, she ordered soup and noodles. They, too, were delicious. Her fortune cookie read: *Stop and be quiet today.* Sutton had smiled, thinking that perhaps she'd finally found the perfect spot to do just that.

Since then, she had spent many an afternoon in Noodle Treasure. Now, as she pushed open the door and stepped into the warmth, she immediately felt herself relax. When a white-haired gentleman wearing a chef's jacket smiled at her from a table near the back, Sutton gave him a little wave. Giancarlo Bugiardini had been a regular much longer than she. He owned Ciao Bella, one of the nearby Italian restaurants, but ate lunch in Noodle Treasure most days. He had once told Sutton that his sister thought it heretical that he dined elsewhere than his own restaurant, but that "man cannot subsist on Italian fare alone."

"Hello, Dr. Sutton, hello!" Benny's familiar voice rang out over the scrape of chopsticks and murmur of conversation. Sutton smiled at the nickname. Over time, she had become friendly with Benny, who owned the restaurant with his wife, Mei. Once they had found out about her dual degrees, they had insisted upon using her title at every opportunity.

"Hello," she said, taking her customary seat. No matter how brisk Noodle Treasure's business might be, she always found it unoccupied. "How are your knees feeling today?"

After a few weeks of casual chatter, Benny had done what most people did when talking to a doctor—he had begun to discuss his various physical ailments. Arthritis was the main culprit, and his knees were particularly susceptible because he was always on his feet.

"Better than yesterday," he said. "The new heating pads are helping. Thank you again."

"My pleasure." Sutton's stomach chose that moment to rumble, reminding her of just how long she had been on her feet. "I'd like the hot-and-sour soup, please. And an order of pork dumplings."

Benny's smile suggested that her order was a compliment to his wife's cooking. "Right away."

Sutton retrieved her laptop from her bag, and while it was powering up, she looked out across Baxter Street to the familiar façade of Confucius Fortunes Company. She had asked Benny about it once, and he had told her that it was the oldest fortune cookie factory in the city. Their recipe was a great secret, he had insisted—passed down over generations. And Sutton could believe it; unlike the cookies she had eaten from other restaurants uptown, which tasted like cardboard, these were airy and sweet and melted in her mouth.

At that moment, Mei arrived with a steaming ceramic mug full of tea. They chatted briefly about the weather before Mei left her to her work. As Sutton inhaled the delicate scent of oolong blended with chrysanthemum flowers, she felt the last of her anxiety ebb away. Exhaling slowly, she turned her full attention to her laptop, determined to make some headway on at least one section of the article.

When Sutton next allowed herself to look at the clock, an hour had passed. As she rolled her shoulders to ease the tension that had returned to her neck, the door opened to admit a familiar face: a girl, somewhere in the ten- to twelve-year range, who came into the restaurant most afternoons to eat a snack and do her homework. Benny greeted her cheerfully in Chinese, and she answered in kind. When she passed Sutton's chair, she gave her a small wave. Sutton smiled in return. For some reason, the girl's acknowledgement always made her happy—as though she were a part of something, even if it was only the small community that patronized this restaurant.

Her introspection was broken by the appearance of Mei at her elbow, bearing a fresh mug of tea. On the saucer next to the cup was a lone fortune cookie, its wrapper bearing the familiar logo of the factory across the street. As she peeled the plastic away and turned the cookie over in her palm, Sutton made a mental note to look up how the paper strips were inserted inside. And then, with one decisive movement, she broke the shell in two.

After brushing the crumbs off the fortune, she leaned in to read its red lettering. *Love is right around the corner.* She snorted and let the wisp of paper fall back onto the counter. The idea that she had time for love right now was patently absurd. Still shaking her head, Sutton turned back to her laptop, but the screen would no longer hold her attention. Instead, she found herself staring out the window and people-watching. Tourists bundled in brightly colored jackets wandered, aimless or confused, squinting at the street signs, while the native New Yorkers walked briskly, hunching their shoulders against the cold. Sutton stroked the warm surface of her mug, glad to be inside and off her feet.

Across the street, the nondescript door next to the factory opened, and an androgynous figure in the process of zipping up a plain navy hoodie stepped out onto the sidewalk. Suddenly intrigued, Sutton leaned forward and narrowed her eyes. The individual's hair was short and dark, and their clothes were too bulky to reveal any telling physiological details. And then the person looked up, directly into the restaurant, and Sutton knew without a doubt that she had just been checking out a woman. A woman whose gaze was now locked with hers.

Her face was striking. Slanted brows drew attention to a pair of eyes slightly too round to be called almond-shaped, set above high cheekbones that lent her a vaguely exotic quality. She was beautiful. Handsome. Both.

Sutton was powerless to look away. The woman stepped forward, and for one suspended moment, it seemed as though she might cross the street. Sutton's pulse leapt at the thought. But even as she silently chided herself for her reaction, the woman pulled her hood over her hair, slid her bare hands into the pockets of her sweatshirt, and turned uptown.

Within seconds, she had disappeared around the corner, leaving Sutton chagrined by the magnitude of her response. But it was only attraction—as involuntary as it was meaningless. Nothing could come of it, and nothing would. Love wasn't waiting around the corner—love was off the agenda entirely.

CHAPTER THREE

Jane woke from a dream in which she was sitting alone at the kitchen table, surrounded by the scattered remains of what must have been hundreds of fortune cookies. Piled high all around her, the broken shells blocked her vision of all but the ceiling. And yet, she persisted in opening cookie after cookie, only to find *The time is ripe* inside every last one. Just before the dream dissolved, she'd heard a noise behind her and had turned to see Sutton standing in the hallway, wearing a floor-length, forest-green silk nightgown. And her glasses.

"Whoa." Jane rested the heel of her hand over her racing heart. The image of Sutton persisted in her mind's eye: the contrast of those thin, dark straps against her creamy white skin; the alluring half smile that had curved her full lips; the way her gold hair curled against the contours of her collarbone.

With a shake of her head, she sat up in the bed and scrubbed her palms over her face. Apparently, her subconscious had really internalized that horoscope from yesterday. And wanted her to ask Sutton out. Among other things.

"Are you okay?"

Jane turned to see Min, lying on her side and staring at her in clear concern. "Yeah, of course. Why?"

"You were talking in your sleep. It woke me up."

"What was I saying?" She tried to sound curious instead of panicked.

"No clue. It was in some language I didn't understand."

"Huh." Jane hadn't realized that she dreamt in any language other than English. "Well, I'm sorry I woke you. Guess we're even."

She glanced at the clock. Just past six. Ouch. And there was no way she could fall asleep again after that.

"What were you dreaming about?"

"Fortune cookies, of course." Jane rolled her eyes. "What else do I have to dream about?"

Min's expression turned shrewd. "Not Sutton? Because that was the one word I did understand."

Jane felt her face go hot, and she thanked her lucky stars that the rest of her sleep-talking had been unintelligible. "She may have made an appearance."

Min sat cross-legged on the bed and began to braid her hair. Great. The universal sign for girl talk. Just what she needed: advice from a preteen.

"Is this the first time you've dreamt about her?"

"It's too early for twenty questions."

Min raised one eyebrow and waited.

"To my knowledge, yes." Jane flopped back onto her pillow, lacing her hands behind her head. *The time is ripe.* The words still echoed in her brain. "Maybe I should ask her out."

Only when Min squealed, "Really?" did Jane realize she'd spoken the thought. Immediately, Min jumped up and grabbed her laptop from her desk.

"What are you doing?"

"Googling pickup lines!"

Jane choked on a laugh. "I really don't think that's necessary."

"I really do think it's necessary." Min looked over the screen at her with a stern expression. "You'll be hopeless, otherwise."

"Well, thanks for that vote of confidence. I'm a poet, remember? I think I'll be able to come up with something just fine on my own."

Min ignored her. "Okay. How about this one. 'Pardon me, miss: I seem to have lost my phone number. Could I borrow yours?'"

Jane snorted in derision. "That line has more cheese than France. Absolutely not."

"This one is kind of cute: 'Is your Dad an astronaut? Because someone took the stars from the sky and put them in your eyes.'"

"Slightly better. Only slightly. But no."

"Oh! How about, 'I know I don't look like much now, but I'm drinking milk.'"

"Thanks a lot!" Jane stood. "I'm not going to lie here while you insult me. Besides, I'm lactose-intolerant, remember?"

"No, wait," Min called as she headed toward the door. "This one's perfect! 'You must be tired because you've been running through my dreams all night.'"

Jane paused with her hand on the knob. "She wasn't running. She was standing still and smiling at me. Enough with the pickup lines. Okay?"

She closed the door firmly and breathed a sigh of relief. Min's intentions might be charitable, but being the object of them was exhausting. Maybe, when it came time for Min to date, she should get a taste of her own medicine. Jane smiled faintly at the thought of her mooning over some boy—or girl. Right now, it was practically inconceivable. Which was for the best, since she couldn't imagine a soul on earth who came close to deserving her little cousin. Even when she was at her most annoying.

As she went through the familiar motions of her morning routine, Jane couldn't stop her mind from drifting back to the dream. For about five hot seconds, she debated stopping by Sue's shop to ask what she thought. But that was silly. Dreams didn't mean anything—not objectively. Her mind had simply smashed together the horoscope, her attraction to Sutton, and her job into a brief, though remarkably coherent, narrative. All it meant was what she already knew: that Sutton was a breath of fresh air in a life otherwise defined by repetitive and rather mundane work.

"You made your bed," she reminded herself, pointing her toothbrush at her reflection as the familiar guilt kicked in. Until she

found the courage to go back and graduate, she should lie in it grate-
fully.

When she returned to the room, Min was dressed and sitting
at her desk. She swiveled in her chair, holding up both hands. "Okay,
maybe those pickup lines were tasteless—"

"You think?" Jane injected as much sarcasm as possible into the
words.

"—but you do need a plan."

"At last, we're in agreement. I suppose you have some suggestions?"

"Well, Sutton's usually there when I go after school." Min rested
her chin on her hand in the classic pose of *The Thinker*. "What if . . .
oh! What if you come in and pretend to help me with my homework? That might impress her."

"Now that is a good idea. Bravo. I could also actually help you
with your homework, you know."

Min scoffed. "I don't need any help."

"Of course you don't." Jane pulled a SPAM T-shirt over her head.
This was one of her favorites. "All right, I'll meet you at Noodle
Treasure this afternoon. It's a date. Or at least, hopefully it will re-
sult in one for me."

Min rolled her eyes. "Are you really laughing at your own pun?
Lame."

"Tough crowd around here." Jane grabbed her notebook. "I'm
going to get a jump on the deliveries this morning."

"One last thing. Don't wear any smoking paraphernalia. She's a
doctor. She won't like that."

"I suppose not." Jane tugged lightly on Min's braid as she walked
past. "Thanks for the tip. See you later."

As she descended the stairs, Jane took a few deep breaths in the
hopes of calming her erratic heartbeat. She had a plan—or at least,
the start of one. Therein lay the problem. Once she was ensconced
in Noodle Treasure, impressing Sutton with her generosity toward

her cousin, what was the next step? How would she engage Sutton in conversation? Maybe she needed one of those cheesy pickup lines, after all.

Glad to find the kitchen empty, Jane quickly slipped out the front door. She wasn't hungry this morning. In fact, she felt vaguely nauseous. What on earth was she going to do? Maybe she should just state the obvious: *Hi. I've noticed that you come here often. What is it that you're working on?* Did that sound too much like a stalker?

With a rueful shake of her head, she pushed open the side door of the factory. Unless she could come up with something better over the course of the next few hours, it would have to do.

SUTTON STARED AT THE screen and ground her teeth in frustration. She hated writing. No, that wasn't exactly true. She hated writing anything related to her dissertation. Growing up, she'd never been one of those students who had enjoyed doing papers, but she'd always been competent. Her article on stem-cell therapy hadn't been this difficult to write, but now that she was trying to revise her thesis for publication, she had hit another wall. Something about it lent itself to writer's block—perhaps because her heart wasn't really in the work. She had to deliver this draft to Dr. Buehler soon, and it was nowhere near where she wanted it to be.

In an effort to calm her rising panic, Sutton took a sip of tea, savoring the warmth as it slid down her throat. Mei steeped her green tea with pine nuts, and the distinctive flavor was always comforting in some visceral way that defied logic. Sutton closed her eyes and focused on the soothing aroma. She could do this. She really could.

As the door chimed, she steeled herself for the incoming rush of cold air. When she opened her eyes, her breath caught—not at the chill, but at the sight of the woman from yesterday. Today, she was dressed in low-slung jeans and a heavy flannel shirt. Her short hair stood up a little in the front, as though she'd been dragging her fingers through it repeatedly. Blindsided by the sudden urge to do exactly that, Sutton couldn't avert her eyes. The woman glanced her way, and one corner of her mouth curved up in a shy half smile before her gaze shifted toward the back of the restaurant.

"Hey, Min," she called softly. "What's up?"

Sutton angled her body in order to keep the woman in sight as she moved toward the back of the restaurant, waving to the people she knew.

"Jane!" Min looked up with that overly distraught expression perfected by teenage girls and daytime soap stars. "I need you! This report is killing me!"

Jane. The mystery woman's name was Jane. Sutton wouldn't have guessed that, but it suited her somehow. She hid her smile behind her mug, even as she surreptitiously continued to watch as Jane slid into the chair next to Min.

"Hey, now, relax. You'll get through it. Do you want me to take a look?"

"Yes! I give up!" Min flopped dramatically onto her open book.

"No giving up, silly." Jane looked down at Min's laptop. "Where are you stuck?"

As Min began to explain, Sutton forced herself to turn back to her own work. What a sweet thing to do, she mused, looking over her own introduction for what felt like the thousandth time. Jane had taken some precious moments out of her probably busy schedule to help her little sister. Idly, she wondered what her life would have been like growing up with a sibling. Someone who could have alleviated the boredom of so many interminable dinners with Very Important Persons; someone to play make-believe with while sequestered in the townhouse on a rainy Saturday; someone with whom she could have created a whole new language not understood by anyone else.

Of course, she thought as she caught snippets of Jane asking Min a question about the book's antagonist, that was a rather idyllic fantasy. Not everyone was so kind. What if her imaginary sibling had been cruel, or even just indifferent? Or perhaps her parents' high expectations would have made her competitive with a brother or sister. Her father might even have taken delight in two children vying for his affection.

"More tea, Dr. Sutton?" Benny's voice interrupted her musings, and she turned to the sight of him waiting near her elbow, teapot in hand.

"Yes, please," she said, setting down her cup so he could refill it. "Thank you. How are you feeling today?"

He shook his head and clucked his tongue. "My hips are very sore."

That was an ailment she'd never heard from him before. "Your hips?"

"Yes." He made a gesture along the side of his body from his waist to his upper thigh. "I woke up with a very bad ache."

Sutton flashed back to her gross anatomy course. "Were you more active than usual, yesterday?"

"After closing the restaurant, I rehearsed the lion dance. But I have been doing that every day this week."

"The lion dance?"

"For the Spring Festival." She must have given him a blank look, because he smiled and added, "Chinese New Year. The Year of the Monkey."

"Oh, of course." Sutton hated betraying ignorance. Frantically, she searched her memory for any information on the lunar new year celebrations. She didn't know much, but she'd seen the lion dance on television once or twice.

"Do you remember feeling any sharp pain last night?" she asked.

He frowned, then shook his head. "No, nothing like that."

"In that case, you may have just mildly strained your hip flexor muscles." As she gestured for him to move closer, she suddenly got the feeling that she was being watched. Had her discussion with Benny gotten Jane's attention? Tamping down a wave of self-consciousness, Sutton typed in a quick Internet search that yielded several diagrams.

"If you look here, you'll see these are all the muscles involved in moving your hips. Are you feeling some pain in your lower back, too?"

Benny seemed surprised at the question. "Yes, a little."

Sutton reached for her notebook, tore off a page from the back, and wrote *hip flexor stretches* on it. "Here," she said as she handed it over. "When you have some free time, try searching for this phrase online. You'll find photos, videos, and descriptions of some stretches that you can do to try to make those muscles more flexible. If you stretch daily, you'll be much less at risk of straining them."

"Thank you very much." Benny took the paper with a relieved smile. "And in case you were wondering, we will be open throughout the entire two weeks of the festival."

Sutton hadn't even thought to wonder. Did some businesses close for an entire fortnight? Sometimes, she realized with chagrin, she forgot just how diverse this city was. Not everything revolved around the twenty-four/seven mindset of the hospitals and Wall Street.

"You should join us this Sunday," Benny continued. "We will be serving a traditional Spring Festival meal after the parade."

"Oh yes, please do." At the sound of Mei's voice, Sutton turned to find her wiping down a table behind them. "You're very welcome to share the day with us."

Touched as she was by their thoughtfulness, Sutton was about to make her excuses when Jane rose from her seat. Instantly, the words died in her throat. For some reason, she couldn't take her eyes off the small strip of flannel brushing Jane's collarbone. Why she was suddenly desperate to feel that skin against her lips, Sutton couldn't possibly say. She wanted no part of this feeling, but it had caught her up, and she was powerless to look away.

"The whole thing can be a little overwhelming, though." Jane's soft alto voice was mildly accented in a way she couldn't place. "You might want a guide."

"Oh?" Sutton had a hard time articulating even that simple syllable. Jane's eyes were a color she'd never seen—brown and green and gold all swirling together. Hazel, her logical brain filled in helpfully. But the word seemed inadequate to describe such complexity.

"The streets are really crowded. It's easy to get turned around, even if you know your way."

"I've actually never been into the center of Chinatown," Sutton admitted. "This is as far as I've come."

Jane nodded, looking thoughtful. "Please don't take this the wrong way, but you're missing out." She extended one hand. "I'm Jane. I'd be happy to be that guide, if you decide you want one."

Her palm was very warm, and calloused at the base of each finger. Sutton felt her pulse jump as Jane's thumb brushed across her skin. When Jane's eyes widened slightly, Sutton wondered if she'd felt the same tiny shock, which had nothing to do with static electricity.

"You can't go wrong with Jane showing you around," Min piped up. "She knows this neighborhood like the back of her hand."

Jane rolled her eyes and spared a quick glance over her shoulder. "Where does that saying even come from? Who has honestly ever studied the back of their own hand?"

Sutton had to laugh. "I've never really understood it, either." Suddenly, she realized she hadn't introduced herself. "And I'm Sutton."

"Dr. Sutton," Jane corrected her, tilting her head toward Benny. Her grin carried a hint of mischief. "And the eavesdropper back there is Min."

"You were dropping just as many eaves as I was!" Min said loudly.

Jane shrugged, and with a squeeze so gentle Sutton thought she might have imagined it, let go of her hand. Was she blushing? The olive tone of her skin made it difficult to tell. In an effort to get her equilibrium back, Sutton squared her shoulders.

"Hi, Jane. Hi, Min. And outside the hospital, it's really just 'Sutton.' Please."

"All right, 'just Sutton.'" Jane sounded at ease, but she had jammed both hands into her pockets. That simple sign of nerves gave Sutton a rush of badly needed confidence. "Let me show you the Spring Festival on Sunday. What do you say? The parade really shouldn't be missed."

Sutton knew she should decline the invitation. She had more than enough to do, and besides, it made no sense for her to date— or even just make a new friend—with her future so up in the air. But as she looked from Jane to Min to Mei to Benny, she realized that she wanted to say yes. Over the past few months, they had made her feel a part of their community. Now, they were willing to share their special holiday with her. Besides, this wouldn't even count as a real date. What did she have to lose? Jane was proposing a parade, not marriage.

"I accept," she said, secretly relishing the relief that flashed across Jane's face before her insouciant grin returned.

"Great. Excellent. I think you'll really enjoy it."

"When shall I meet you?"

"How about here at ten o'clock? That should give us enough time to find a good spot along the parade route."

"I'll be here," she said, wondering what Jane could read in her own expression. Suddenly, she realized that everyone was watching as they negotiated the specifics of their not-date. The self-consciousness returned in a rush. "I'm, um, going to get back to work." She glanced quickly at Benny and Mei. "Thank you all for inviting me."

"See you soon," Jane said. "Oh, and Sutton? Wear red."

CHAPTER FOUR

SUTTON STEPPED OUTSIDE, TURNED her face up to the sun, and smiled. The cold snap had finally ended yesterday, giving way to milder air that no longer hurt every time she took a breath. True spring was still a month away, but this reprieve from the biting chill of the past week made it feel much warmer. She could only imagine how fortunate the parade marchers felt.

As she walked toward Noodle Treasure, Sutton began to feel warm enough to unzip her coat. She didn't own any red jackets, but she had put on the scoop-neck red cashmere sweater that had been a gift from her mother this past Christmas. The soft fabric clung to her body. She wondered if Jane would notice, then shook her head in annoyance at the thought. No matter how charming Jane might turn out to be, Sutton had already promised herself not to get emotionally invested. They could be friends. Not even friends—acquaintances. Casual acquaintances. She wasn't in the market for anything more.

As Sutton rounded the corner, she saw Jane standing outside Noodle Treasure. Dressed in a red track jacket, black cargo pants, and sneakers, she looked at once athletic and a little edgy. Sutton felt her stomach flip-flop as Jane smiled and raised one hand in greeting. *Casual acquaintance,* she reminded herself.

"*Gong xi fa cai,*" Jane said as Sutton approached.

"Is that a traditional greeting?" This was her first time standing next to Jane, and Sutton was surprised at having to look up. She was above average height, but Jane was at least two inches taller.

"Yes. It means, 'Congratulations, and be prosperous.' "

"Say it again, please. More slowly."

"Gong-she-fah-tie," Jane said, nodding as Sutton repeated it. "Nice. You've got it."

Sutton felt absurdly proud at the praise. Unwilling to risk betraying the emotion, she looked away down the street. "So, what's the plan, guide?"

"Well, I thought we might wander through the neighborhood a bit and find a spot on the parade route. Does that sound okay? Maybe grab some breakfast along the way?"

"That sounds great. Though forgive me if I don't eat much—I had a little something earlier."

Jane began to walk south at a leisurely pace, and Sutton fell in beside her. "Was it from a Chinese bakery?"

"It was an apple. So, no."

"Hmm." Jane's brows drew together in a frown, lending her an air of fierce perplexity that Sutton couldn't help but find endearing. "If an apple a day is supposed to keep the doctor away, but you are a doctor, what happens?"

Sutton had to laugh at the bizarre twist their conversation had already taken. "An existential crisis?"

"Then it's a good thing I'm about to show you another breakfast option." Jane shot her a sideways grin.

How, Sutton wondered, had they managed to start bantering before they even knew the very basics about one another? This not-date wasn't even five minutes old and her head was already spinning.

"What?" Jane said.

Sutton was suddenly panicked that she had unintentionally voiced her inner monologue. "I'm sorry?"

"You were sort of half smiling just then. What were you thinking?"

"That we don't know anything about each other. I don't even know your last name."

"Morrow. Yours?"

"St. James." Sutton waited to see if Jane would make the connection to her father, but no recognition flared in her eyes. That was unexpected, and nice. Maybe she had done herself a disservice by not having socialized with anyone other than medical students for the past several years. She felt oddly liberated by being "just Sutton."

"Sutton St. James. That has a nice alliterative quality."

Again, Sutton laughed. "There's a response I've never heard before."

Jane looked pleased with herself. "I like phrases that sound . . . right."

Sutton could have let the statement pass, but decided to give Jane a taste of her own inquisitive medicine. "What do you mean by 'right'?"

Jane didn't answer right away, worrying her bottom lip with her teeth as she considered the question. "I'm not sure I know. There's just a—a feel to some phrases, and even individual words. They have a good ring to them. I suppose I could sit down and try to parse it all out scientifically, but what would be the fun in that?"

"Oh? Science can't be fun?" Sutton put a slight edge in her voice, enjoying the opportunity to turn the tables in this verbal sparring match. She was gratified to see Jane's eyes widen as she realized her mistake.

"Please excuse me while I remove my foot from my mouth. How could I forget I was speaking to Doctor Sutton?"

Sutton had the urge to bump Jane lightly with her elbow, but she held herself back. *Casual acquaintance. Not date. No touching.*

"Speaking of which," Jane continued, "what's your medical specialty?"

"Guess," Sutton said, wanting to keep her on her toes.

The bridge of Jane's nose wrinkled in thought. It was cute. Damn it. "I'm going to say . . . cardiologist. Maybe even a heart surgeon."

Sutton rolled her eyes at the clear flirtation. "The heart is a relatively simple muscle. It doesn't interest me. I'm a neuroscientist."

"Impressive. What's your favorite part of the brain?"

"My favorite part of the brain?" Sutton was absolutely sure no one had ever asked that before. Colleagues always wanted to know what her specialty was, and the rest of the population tended to feel intimidated. "What kind of question is that?"

"A relatively simple one." Jane winked.

"Let me think about it and get back to you." Sutton sounded absurd to her own ears. The brain was a highly evolved and complex organ that habitually eluded human understanding, and Jane wanted her to choose a "favorite" part?

As they continued down the street, she noticed the sun glinting off portable steel barricades that had been erected along the sidewalk. She glanced up at the sign and realized that this was Canal Street—one of the main thoroughfares that bisected downtown Manhattan. Some people had already staked out places along the barricades, while others milled about, browsing through the shops.

A traffic cop waved them to cross the street, and Jane led her down one more block before pointing at a sign that read Dragon Land Bakery. "Here we are." When she held open the door, Sutton felt a quick rush of pleasure.

The bakery smelled of sugar and cream, and Sutton's mouth began to water in a Pavlovian response. To her left, several tables and chairs had been set up near the floor-to-ceiling window looking out onto Baxter Street. To her right, neatly organized rows of pastries filled a large, heated display case. A middle-aged woman dressed in a red apron stood before the case and took orders, plucking out each pastry with a clean piece of waxed paper. She smiled and waved at Jane, calling out the New Year greeting across the room.

"Do you trust me?" Jane asked once she'd returned the sentiment.

Sutton blinked at the audacity of the sudden question. "I only just learned your last name two minutes ago."

"Go on instinct. What does your gut tell you?"

"That I trust you just enough to let you order breakfast."

"That'll do for now." Jane's eyes were sparkling. "Would you mind finding us a place to sit?"

After wiping off the table in the far corner with a napkin, Sutton watched as Jane conversed with the woman operating the register. She wondered which language they were speaking, and whether Jane, with her lithe build, was an athlete—a swimmer, perhaps. When Jane turned toward her and raised one eyebrow, Sutton mentally cursed herself. She'd been caught staring. Just fantastic. She smiled briefly in response before turning to casually glance out the window, as though she'd been about to do that all along. Right.

A few moments later, Jane slid a tray onto their table. It held two round, golden buns with sugar sprinkled on top and two plastic cups filled with what almost looked like a milkshake, except that the liquid was thinner in consistency.

"Pineapple bread and bubble tea," Jane said proudly, as though she'd made them herself. "If you don't like them, I'll be happy to get you something else."

"It looks great," Sutton said, not having to stretch the truth at all. She broke off a small piece of the bun and raised it to her mouth, inhaling the delicate scent before taking a bite. The outside was flaky, almost like a pie crust, while the inside was spongy and sweet. When she caught Jane looking at her with an almost puppyish eagerness, she smiled around the mouthful.

"Delicious," she said once she'd swallowed. "But it doesn't taste like pineapple at all."

"It's called pineapple bread because of its shape and color. See what you think of the tea."

Sutton put her lips to the straw and pulled gently. The tea was mild and sweet, but her head jerked up as she felt something round and rather squishy roll across her tongue. Reflexively, she spat it out—so hard that it flew several feet before landing on the floor and rolling into the corner. Horrified by both the sensation and her reaction, Sutton grabbed her cup. Peering through the translucent plastic, she noticed, for the first time, several small dark globes clustered at the bottom.

"What—" She looked to Jane in alarm. "There are balls! In my tea!"

Jane looked as startled as she felt. "Oh, jeez. I'm so sorry. I thought you must have had bubble tea before. Those are tapioca pearls."

Sutton could feel her heated cheeks trying to match the hue of her sweater. "They're normal?"

Jane gave a tentative nod. "They're even pretty good." She started to reach across the table but then apparently thought better of it and drew back her hand. "I'm really sorry I didn't warn you."

Sutton was mortified. She wanted to disappear into the floor. Or better yet—hit the "undo" button on the last five minutes of her life. But since neither of those options was possible, she was either going to have to beat a hasty retreat from the bakery and never see Jane again, or swallow her pride. And some tapioca pearls.

"I'll try anything once." After a deep breath, she took another pull from the straw. This time, she bit down gently on the pearl, closing her eyes to focus on the flavor. It was, in fact, a very mild tapioca, and it complemented the tea perfectly. She opened her eyes to the sight of Jane regarding her intently, and for a moment, the rest of the bakery seemed to fade into the background.

"What's the verdict?"

"I like it."

Jane did a little fist pump. "All right." Her expression turned sly. "So tell me—do you carry a license for that concealed weapon?"

"You mean my tongue?"

When Jane's eyes grew hazy, Sutton knew she had won this round. The victory was heady, as was Jane's responsiveness. *Not date*, her conscience supplied helpfully.

Visibly trying to pull herself together, Jane took a long sip of her own tea. "Let me guess," she said, her voice deeper than it had been a minute ago, and slightly hoarse. "You have an older brother who roped you into spitting contests."

Sutton shook her head. "I'm an only child."

"Ah, so it's a natural gift."

Ten different suggestive replies popped into Sutton's head, but she forced herself to ignore them. "What about you—are there more besides you and Min?"

"I'm an only child as well. Minetta is my cousin."

Sutton could have sworn the name was familiar. "Minetta? Isn't that—"

"—the name of a street in the West Village." Jane grinned. "My uncle John is a thematic sort of person. My other three cousins are named Hester, Carmine, and Cornelia. It's okay—you can laugh."

"What made him choose street names?" Sutton said, glad Jane wouldn't be offended by her amusement.

"It's pretty common for a Chinese family to pick names for their children that are related in some way. He, my mom, and their siblings all have Chinese names from a famous poem."

As she spoke, she broke off another piece of the pineapple bread, and Sutton's gaze was drawn to her hands. Jane's fingers were slender and moved with an unexpected grace. Feeling her mouth go dry, Sutton quickly took another sip of tea.

"I have a theory about the street names in particular, though," Jane was saying. "I think they're sort of aspirational. Every one of those streets is outside of Chinatown, though none are very far away."

"You think they're symbolic? Of him wanting what, exactly?"

Sutton tried to work through the logic. "Something beyond this neighborhood? Why would that be the case?"

Jane shrugged. "This place is pretty insular. It has its own languages, its own rules, its own customs. And for women especially, those customs can still be limiting. Maybe he wanted them to have . . . more."

Sutton sat back and thought about that. Chinese culture was a blind spot for her—she didn't know much beyond what she liked to order at Chinese-American restaurants uptown. "Interesting," she said, not wanting to admit her naïveté. "And regardless, they're beautiful and distinctive names."

"As is 'Sutton.'"

"Also a street in Manhattan." At the moment, Sutton didn't want to divulge the fact that her own name came not from the Upper East Side thoroughfare, but from the old New York family whose scion had developed the entire neighborhood. "There's a Jane Street, too, isn't there?"

"There is. But I was named for my great-grandmother on my father's side." Jane turned to look over her shoulder. "Looks like the crowds are getting thicker. Shall we go find a good place to stand?"

They left the bakery and turned into the sea of people, almost all of whom were wearing red. As they slowly made their way through the masses, Sutton tried to soak in the sights. Streamers and banners hung across the streets, punctuated by store awnings. Most of the conversations around her were completely unintelligible. Had it not been for the occasional sign written in English, she might have suspected she'd been magically transported to Beijing.

After a few blocks, Jane pointed to an unclaimed spot along the barricades. "How about there?"

Sutton nodded and did her best to unobtrusively squeeze into the space between a family of four with two small children and a pack of adolescent girls who were popping foreign-looking candies into their mouths while pointing and laughing at those around them. But no one seemed to mind being crowded or jostled, and when the mother to her right smiled and said, "Happy New Year," Sutton felt brave enough to respond in Chinese.

"Nice job," Jane murmured. "You have a good ear for the tones."

"Perfect pitch," Sutton explained. They were pressed close together, and she felt the sudden urge to pull Jane's arm around her waist. What was wrong with her today? Was she hormonal? How could she feel this much chemistry with someone she'd spent less than an hour with?

"You'd probably have an easier time than most with learning Chinese, then."

"Not me. I'm awful at languages." Sutton flashed back to how she'd barely squeaked by with B's in the two semesters of Spanish she'd taken to fulfill her college language requirement. Her brain was a steel trap for scientific facts and formulae, but a sieve when it came to verb conjugations. No matter how many tutoring sessions and study groups she had attended, she'd never been able to achieve anything more than the most basic competence.

Beside her, Jane had struck up a conversation with the woman and her husband. The fluid cadence of their unfamiliar words put Sutton in mind of a stream bubbling over rocks. When Jane laughed, Sutton wished she could share in the joke. Finally, Jane turned back to her, eyes gleaming in clear amusement, and lowered her head to speak into Sutton's ear.

"They said we look very happy together, and wished us joy and prosperity in the coming year. They also think I'm a guy."

Sutton clapped one hand over her mouth to contain her surprised laughter. "What? You don't look like one at all."

"It happens sometimes. It's my short hair. And my clothes."

"But your face—" Sutton managed to stop herself before she blurted out something about Jane's elegant cheekbones and beautiful eyes.

"My face?"

"Is not mannish in the slightest." Sutton silently prided herself on her quick recovery.

"A lot of people don't look too closely. They see a few external signs and immediately make assumptions."

Sutton wanted to ask whether that bothered her, but she thought it might be too personal a question. "So, were you raised speaking Chinese?" she asked instead.

"No, my parents always spoke English at home."

"Where did you grow up?"

"Nowhere. Or maybe everywhere. My father works for the State Department, and I've never lived anywhere longer than three years."

Sutton was intrigued. "Where were you born?"

"Right here, while my dad was finishing up his Master's degree. When I was one, we moved to D.C. A year later, we were in Hong Kong."

"And then?"

Jane flipped her hands over and began counting on her fingers. "Thailand, Italy, Sweden, Egypt, South Africa, and Portugal. Then I came back here for college, and they went to Russia. Now they're in Brazil."

"Amazing." Sutton could only imagine what such a nomadic life must have felt like. To be completely uprooted every few years to an entirely new place with a different language and set of customs must have been so disruptive. And yet Jane didn't seem bitter at all. "Were you resentful of having to move so often?"

"You'd think that would happen, but it didn't for me." Jane's gaze grew distant as she smiled at some memory. "My parents always made each move feel like a great adventure." She homed back in on Sutton. "Did your family ever relocate?"

"Only once." Compared to Jane, Sutton felt decidedly uncosmo-politan. Annual family trips to Europe and the Caribbean couldn't compare with her experiences. "A whole two blocks away."

"Where in the city?"

"The Upper East Side." Feeling suddenly self-conscious about her privileged and sheltered upbringing, Sutton was relieved to hear noise coming down the street. "Is that the parade?"

Jane listened for a moment. "It sure is. Get ready to hear a lot of cymbal clashing today."

"Oh? Why is that?"

"Loud noises frighten away the demons."

Sutton searched Jane's face for any hint of facetiousness, but she looked serious. "The demons. I see."

"I don't believe in them, either," Jane stage-whispered. "I won't tell if you don't."

"Your secret's safe with me."

Sutton rested both hands on the barricade and focused on the oncoming procession. Sure enough, the parade was led by two men dressed in flowing, black-and-red jackets and pants, their cymbals glinting in the midday sun. Behind them danced two black-and-red lions, their massive, vaguely leonine heads bobbing up and down in synchrony. As one, their mouths snapped open to reveal red tongues and white-painted teeth. They shook their heads before charging at the barricades in a show of ferocity. The younger spectators squealed in delight.

When they drew closer, Sutton saw that each lion was controlled by two puppeteers. One manipulated the head, twisting, raising, and lowering it in jerky movements that made the creature seem remarkably lifelike. The other held a strip of cloth that looked almost like a bridal train—the lion's body, presumably.

A float followed close behind the lions, bearing a crest with Chinese characters and the word *community* in English. On the slowly moving platform, a man pounded two large, timpani-like drums. Behind the float, at least two dozen men, women, and children dressed in identical red sweatshirts beat on smaller drums of their own or shook sticks that made a loud rattling sound.

"The drums are also for the demons?" Sutton asked, having to shout to make her voice heard.

"Yes. And there will be electronic firecrackers later."

Sutton's next question was driven from her mind when one of the men suddenly broke ranks and trotted over toward them. A wiry fellow who looked to be in his late forties, he greeted Jane and conversed quickly with her in Chinese before returning to his compatriots.

"Pharmacist," Jane explained over the horns and drums. "Asking after my uncle's health. He had bronchitis last month."

Sutton nodded, marveling at just how tightly knit this community was. As the parade continued, she found herself growing more and more fascinated by the culture on display before her. Martial artists performed a choreographed series of forms, followed by a group of flag-bearers carrying a large banner of a golden monkey on a red background. Benny had mentioned that it was the Year of the Monkey, and Sutton wondered what that meant, exactly. After the flags came a marching band—by far the most Western aspect of the entire festival so far—followed by more dancing lions. When the one nearest them zigzagged toward the crowd, the head puppeteer's face was visible for a moment.

"Look," she said, pointing. "That's Benny."

Jane leaned forward. "You're right, there he is. Impressive."

Sutton could see why his hips had been bothering him earlier in the week. Even as he held the lion's head above his own, he was constantly moving—kicking his legs and spinning adroitly on his feet in synchrony with his partner.

As Benny passed out of sight, Sutton felt the way she sometimes had as a girl when, on exceptionally clear nights out at her grandparents' home on Long Island, she had floated on her back in the pool and looked up at the stars. A glimpse of the cosmos was always awe-inspiring—especially for a city girl. But what she remembered most was a sense of insignificance. Of smallness. Now, faced with the customs of a culture three thousand years old, that same sensation prickled at the edge of her consciousness. Religion had always been more a social obligation than a faith to her own parents, and they had no true family traditions outside of strategically alternating which relatives were visited during each holiday season. For an instant, as another troupe of drummers marched by, Sutton desperately wanted to believe in something bigger than herself.

As quickly as it had arrived, the moment faded. She didn't need demons or fortunes or astrology to explain the world when she had science. Exhaling slowly, she refocused her attention on the parade.

"Are you okay?" Jane asked.

Sutton smiled briefly and turned to reassure her, careful not to meet those hypnotic eyes. She would be just fine, as long as she remembered her own priorities.

JANE KEPT HER HANDS firmly in her pockets, lest she give in to the overwhelming impulse she'd had all day to interlace her fingers with Sutton's. She had nearly forgotten herself at the bakery, and then again along the barricade, when she'd wanted so badly to wrap one arm around Sutton's shoulders and pull her close. The visceral compulsions were unsettling and exhausting to fight off, especially since Sutton was full of mixed signals—warm and forthcoming one moment, cool and distant the next. But there had been several points throughout the day when Jane had caught an appreciative smile or the hint of a nervous laugh that she thought might signal attraction. And the way they'd fallen so easily into conversation— that had to be a sign of something, didn't it?

Oh, sure. It was a sign of something, all right—that she was in way over her head. *Perfect*—that was the only word to describe Sutton. Perfect eyes. Perfect hair. Perfect pitch. The perfect storm of intelligence, humor, and compassion. Sutton was way out of her league, and once she started asking the right questions, she'd be gone in a heartbeat. At this point, all Jane could do was postpone the inevitable.

The problem was, she reflected as she snuck another peek at

Sutton out of the corner of her eye, that even clumsy, unattractive moths gravitated toward the flame. Sutton was irresistible, and Jane was going to get herself burned. It was just that simple.

"How'd you like the firecrackers?" she asked, pausing to wave as she recognized the proprietor of a dumpling shop to whom she delivered cookies every Monday.

"They were fun. The dancing, too." Sutton glanced at her briefly. "It made my childhood ballet lessons look so boring."

Jane smiled, even as another alarm bell went off in her head. Ballet lessons. Upper East Side. The puzzle pieces were starting to coalesce, and the emerging picture pointed to Sutton St. James coming from a wealthy, upper-class family. That in itself didn't intimidate Jane too much—she had plenty of experience mingling with ambassadors, dignitaries, and their children. But between Sutton's social status and her multiple advanced degrees, Jane couldn't help feeling a little insecure. Maybe they were too different to find any common ground.

"So, how does Chinese culture view the monkey?" Sutton asked. "Is it a good animal?"

Jane shook off her trepidation. "It's my birth sign, so I'd like to think so. Though according to my astrologer friend Sue, whenever the year is the same as your sign, you're at risk of bad luck. More superstition."

"You have a friend who's an astrologer?" Sutton sounded intrigued.

"Mostly she's an apothecary, but she does astrology on the side." They came to the corner of Baxter, and Jane gestured for Sutton to precede her. "I bet she'll be at Noodle Treasure. I'll introduce you."

In the hours since they'd left for the parade, Mei had hung streamers and paper lanterns just beneath the restaurant's awning. As they approached, Jane heard the buzz of chatter and laughter even through the closed doors.

"Ready for a feast?"

Sutton nodded. "It smells incredible, even from out here."

Jane felt a swell of pride at Sutton's obvious eagerness, which was silly since she'd had nothing whatsoever to do with cooking the traditional Spring Festival meal. Still, the knowledge that Sutton was enjoying her adventure into the heart of Chinese culture made Jane feel as though she'd done a good job in her self-appointed role as "guide." The real question was whether she'd performed well enough to be upgraded to "date." She'd made Sutton laugh a few times, and she'd managed to hold her own during their conversational sparring. But a few flirtatious moments here and there did not a date make.

The inside of Noodle Treasure was barely recognizable. All the tables had been moved into one long row, which was covered entirely by a deep red cloth. Flower bouquets had been arranged down the centerline of the table—peach blossoms for longevity, peonies for prosperity, pussy willow plants for good fortune.

As they stepped inside, all heads turned toward them. Most of her family and many neighbors were already seated, and shouts of "Jane!" "Doctor Sutton!" and "Happy New Year!" suddenly filled the fragrant air. Sutton's face registered a mixture of delight and uncertainty, and Jane wished she could squeeze her hand in reassurance.

"We're so glad you've joined us," Mei called. "Please, sit and eat."

A seat was open between Sue and Cornelia, and another just across the table, between Min and an Italian gentleman who was another one of Noodle Treasure's "regulars." Jane could never remember his name, but when he stood to shake Sutton's hand, Sutton smiled and said, "Happy New Year, Giancarlo."

As Jane introduced herself to him, Sue rose, unclasping the gold chain from around her neck. "*Gong xi fa cai*, Jane. This is for you, to ward off your bad luck."

"You're giving me your necklace?"

"A loan. This is my Tiger pendant—do you see?" She held up the small disk where it glinted in the celebratory lights. "It will fool the spirits into thinking you are a Tiger, rather than a Monkey. Bend down and let me fasten it."

Sue's demonstrativeness made Jane glad to duck her head. "Thank you." When she looked up she found Sutton watching them in evident curiosity. "Sue, this is my friend Sutton. She has some questions about astrology. Can she sit next to you?"

"Of course." Sue stepped aside so Sutton could squeeze in. Jane took the chair on the opposite side of the table and then poured them both some chrysanthemum tea.

"Be good," she murmured to Min when she was sure Sutton wasn't looking. Min only stuck out her tongue and went back to doing something on her phone.

"What questions do you have, Sutton?" Sue asked, sounding eager to share her expertise.

"Hang on a minute, now," Jane said. "We're starving." She caught Sutton's eye as she reached for the nearest platter. "Let me explain what all of this is, first, okay? And then you can tell me what you'd like."

Sutton raised one eyebrow. "I told you I'd try anything once, and I meant it."

Jane took a sip of water to moisten her suddenly dry mouth. The woman liked a challenge. That was hot. "All right then, I'll start by giving you one of everything. First: a peach bun."

"Let me guess," Sutton said as Jane deposited one of the round, golden-pink pastries on her plate. "These don't really taste like peaches."

"You catch on quickly. They only look like peaches, which symbolize longevity. Inside, you'll find red bean paste, which tastes kind of like sweet potato."

After grabbing one for herself, Jane gestured for Min to pass her the next platter. "These are *nian gao*. Sticky rice cakes. They're sweet, and we eat them because the name sounds like the phrase 'higher year.' The idea is to raise yourself to a better place in the new year."

"I like that idea," Sutton said with a smile that set Jane's heart tripping in her chest. "I'll take two, please."

For the next few minutes, Jane continued to explain the symbolism behind each item of food: kumquats for prosperity, oranges for luck, noodles for long life. Sutton took it all in stride, and by the time the bowls and platters stopped coming, her plate was piled high with food.

"Now," she said, turning to Sue, "what were you saying, about the Year of the Monkey?"

Over the course of the next hour, Sue not only divulged everything she knew about the Monkey sign, but also began delving into Sutton's personal horoscope. Sutton had been born in a Dragon year, and as Jane listened to Sue describe the powerful ambition and drive of all Dragons, she found herself wondering whether there might be more truth to this astrology business than she had previously thought. And Sutton wasn't the only one captivated by Sue's wealth of knowledge—Giancarlo was completely spellbound as well. Even Min had stopped playing with her phone.

"Romantically, Dragons are most compatible with Monkeys," Sue was saying. "Like Jane."

Jane had been in the middle of taking a sip of tea, which promptly went down the wrong pipe and precipitated a coughing fit.

"Interesting," Sutton said. Through her watering eyes, Jane noticed that Sutton's face was flushed. Was that a good sign? Or was she simply embarrassed?

"And Roosters make a good match as well," Sue continued, seemingly oblivious to the chaos she was causing. "Like Minetta."

"Who, me?" Min's voice carried a distinct note of shock.

The musical sound of Sutton's laughter finally allowed Jane to take a deep, cough-free breath. After wiping her eyes, she looked up to see Sutton sitting back in her chair, an indulgent smile curving her lips.

"How old are you, Min?"

"Eleven."

Sutton made a show of exhaling in a deep and soulful sigh. "I'm afraid you're just too young for me."

Min reciprocated by clutching at her own chest. "I'm devastated. How will I go on?"

"Sue," Giancarlo, who until now had been listening raptly, interjected. "May I call you Sue?" At her nod, he leaned forward. "I know nothing about this topic, but I find it all simply fascinating. May I ask what animal sign I was born under?"

Suddenly, Min sat up straight and pointed at Sue, cutting him off midsentence. "You need a website."

"Min!" Cornelia said sharply. "Where are your manners? No interrupting, and no pointing."

"He interrupted me first," Min said. "And besides, it's true."

Sue looked confused. "I have a website. Jane made it for me."

Min waved one hand dismissively. "Not for the herbs and stuff—for your fortunes. That's what people really care about."

"Minetta, seriously, be polite." Jane flashed an apologetic look at both Sue and Giancarlo. Apparently, her little cousin had decided to ring in the new year by acting like a brat. How fortuitous for them all.

"It's the truth," she insisted. "Think about how many people would visit your site if they could get good horoscopes instead of having to settle for all the moronic vague ones out there that could apply to anybody."

Sue was clearly intrigued. "And you know how to do this?"

"Sure. It's not too hard." Min flicked her chopsticks together absently in a show of skill Jane envied. "I bet I could even get it to count as my project for computer class. Oh—fortune cookies!"

Jane didn't move as Mei set down a small plate in front of her on which a single cookie was encircled by thin orange slices. She could never bring herself to read her own fortune. How could it apply to her anyway, when she'd been the one to write it? Immediately, Min reached over to steal a cookie. Sutton looked between them, clearly puzzled, but ultimately decided against asking. As she broke the thin crust in two, Jane held her breath. *Please,* she prayed aimlessly. *Let it be something interesting and not lame.*

Beside her, Min laughed. "Mine says, 'Think outside the box and your new business venture will prosper.'" She jostled Jane's elbow. "I hope you're right about that."

Jane heard the words, but she couldn't take her eyes off Sutton, who was slowly unfolding the narrow strip of paper. "What'd you get?" she asked, hoping Sutton couldn't hear the strain in her voice.

"'Embrace the unexpected.'"

Jane breathed a sigh of relief. "Not one of my best, but it'll do."

It took a moment for the words to sink in before Sutton's head snapped up. "Wait—you write these?"

"I do. That's why I don't eat them."

Min elbowed her again, this time with some force. "'Respect your elders and gain wisdom'?" She waved the fortune from her own cookie under Jane's nose. "Were you having an off day or something?"

"Maybe you should take the hint," Jane replied, still unable to tear her gaze from Sutton's pensive expression.

"You write the fortunes in these cookies," she said slowly. "All of them?"

"For the past six months, yes."

"Jane's a poet," Min chimed in. "Sometimes a decent one."

At Sutton's questioning look, Jane shrugged. "It's true. The poet part, anyway. Fortune cookies pay the bills."

Their conversation was cut off by everyone else wanting to share their prognostications. From the head of the table, Benny reminded them all that unless they ate the entire cookie, their fortunes wouldn't come true, and Jane was gratified to see that Sutton immediately popped the delicate shell into her mouth. Embrace the unexpected. Jane wanted to believe that meant Sutton should embrace her.

A few minutes later, Sutton pushed back her chair. "I should be going," she announced as she turned toward Mei and Benny. "Thank you for an excellent meal and your wonderful hospitality. *Gong xi fa cai.*"

As everyone wished her well, Jane got to her feet, trying to ignore the pit that had materialized in her stomach at the thought of Sutton leaving. "I'll walk you out."

They stepped outside, and Sutton struggled with her coat until Jane grasped both shoulders for her, holding it open. Sutton slid into the jacket, then turned to look up at her. Jane had to clench both hands into fists to stop herself from sliding her arms around Sutton's waist.

"Thank you for everything," she said. "I had a really good time, and you were the perfect guide."

"You were a great sport," Jane said, watching Sutton's eyes change from light blue to gray and back again. The shifting colors reminded her of the ocean on a windy day.

Sutton's gaze darted away, then back. "Maybe we can do it again sometime."

Jane wasn't quite sure what to make of her tone. Was she getting the brush-off, or was Sutton serious? At times, she was so easy to read, but this definitely wasn't one of them.

"That might be tricky, unless you're very patient," she said, deciding to fall back on humor. "New Year only happens annually."

Sutton nudged her with an elbow. "Oh, stop. You know what I mean."

"Actually, I don't. But I'm up for anything." When she searched Sutton's face and saw uncertainty there, Jane decided not to force the issue. Instead, she reached into her pocket to grab her notebook and pen.

"Here," she said as she scribbled. "My number. In case you think of something more specific. Call or text anytime." Sutton took the paper with a rather dubious expression, and Jane decided to quit while she was relatively ahead. "I'd better get back in there. See you around."

Before Sutton could reply, Jane had darted back into Noodle Treasure. She stood just inside the door for a moment, savoring the aroma of rice and soy sauce mixed with the sweet scent of flour blossoms and the sharp tang of citrus. Aunt Jenny and Uncle John were laughing with Mei and Benny, and Giancarlo was in a tête-à-tête with Sue, and Carmine was playing with Hester's children, and Cornelia looked bored, and Min was still on her phone. As she dropped back into her seat, she felt a sudden rush of affection for them all.

CHAPTER FIVE

SUTTON TRACED A SUBTLE pattern in the immaculate white tablecloth and tried to pinpoint exactly when her father had ceased to be her hero. They sat side by side at his usual table, facing the luminescent recessed pool that lent this section of The Four Seasons Restaurant an ambience both luxurious and ethereal. At each corner of the pool flowering trees reached toward the ceiling, their slender branches and pale petals illuminated by accent spotlights.

Reginald St. James, M.D., was immaculately dressed in a charcoal suit, snow-white collared shirt, and crimson tie. His hair was still as thick as it appeared in the photographs of her childhood, though it had turned entirely to silver in the intervening years. As he smiled and waved at some corporate bigwig across the room, he radiated an unshakeable confidence that befitted "America's Doctor." He was still a heroic figure to many—from the studious young men who thought they wanted to be just like him, to the millions of women who watched his daily show and repeatedly dialed the call-in number in vain attempts to have their problems solved on air.

"So, are you getting excited? Only one month until Match Day."

Sutton shot him a sidelong glance. "I'd prefer not to talk about it, Dad."

"Why not? You have excellent prospects, and—"

"I don't want to jinx it."

This was an ironclad excuse. Perhaps ironically, most surgeons were deeply superstitious. Sutton didn't count herself among them, but in this moment, expedience was more important than the truth. If she was lucky, Reginald would take her reticence at face value.

"Fine, fine. I understand. The process is anxiety-producing, even for our best and brightest." He patted her on the back. "But you really shouldn't worry. You'll do well."

As he sipped from his water, his eyes glazed slightly, and Sutton knew he was traveling back in memory. She breathed a quiet sigh of relief. Once he began rhapsodizing about his residency experience, he could go on for hours.

"You know, when I was sitting where you are," he began, the way he always did, "we didn't have that fancy electronic matching system. We watched our mailboxes like hawks. I was just finishing up at Harvard at the time, and every afternoon I would . . ."

Only half listening to the familiar story, Sutton carefully raised a forkful of risotto to her mouth. Made with white truffles to the tune of one hundred and thirty dollars, it melted on her tongue. Savoring the bite, she had to force herself to put the fork down instead of immediately going back for more. She had only dined here a handful of times, but on each occasion the atmosphere made her extra nervous about her table manners, as though if she were to drop or spill something she would be forcibly removed from the premises.

A flash of motion drew her attention to Reginald's side of the table. He stopped speaking in midsentence and rose to greet the man now looming over them. Sutton set her napkin on the table and followed his example. These sorts of interruptions were part and parcel of lunch at The Four Seasons, where corporate moguls, Hollywood celebrities, and politicians habitually rubbed elbows.

"Hank!" Reginald clapped him on the back. "I didn't realize you were in town."

"Just for the day." The words carried a mild Southern drawl. When his gaze fell on Sutton, she plastered what she hoped was a pleasant smile onto her face. He extended his hand across the table.

"My daughter, Sutton," Reginald said. "This is Henry Phillips."

Sutton recognized the name of the CEO of one of the most powerful pharmaceutical companies in the nation. Everything about him was large—from his fleshy ears, to his protruding waistline, to the sausage-link fingers that gripped her own.

"Pleasure to meet you," she said politely.

"Sutton and I were just discussing her upcoming residency." The paternal pride saturating Reginald's voice made the risotto curdle in her stomach.

"Exciting time—very exciting time." Hank nodded like a bobblehead doll. "Once you've finished up, you should come and work for me."

"Well now, look at that." Reginald clasped her shoulder. "A job offer already."

"I'll certainly consider it," Sutton said, even though she would do no such thing. "Thank you."

"Good, good." For one fraught moment, it seemed he might kiss her hand in some misplaced approximation of chivalry. When he finally let go, she exhaled softly in relief. "Reg, I'll let you both get back to your meal. Will I see you in Washington tomorrow?"

"You will, indeed. Shall we catch up over dinner?"

Hank's jowls quivered as he nodded. "My secretary will be in touch. You both take care, now."

As he lumbered away, Sutton sank back into her seat. "What's in Washington tomorrow?"

"Hank and I—along with a few others—have been called to testify to members of the GOP about how best to counter the Democrats' latest amendments to that ridiculous universal health care bill."

"I see." Yet another conversation they couldn't continue. Reginald held the notion of universal health care in contempt, while Sutton had championed the idea ever since writing a paper on the topic for a Medical Ethics course several years ago. At least their conversation hadn't turned to stem cells. Yet.

She tried a different tack. "How is Mom? She didn't sound very well when I spoke with her yesterday."

Reginald looked up from his seafood platter. "Your mother has had a string of bad days, but that means she's due for a break soon."

Sutton's shoulders tightened. They both knew that wasn't necessarily true. So far, her mother had exhibited a textbook case of relapse-remitting multiple sclerosis, in which "attacks" were followed by periods of remission when she was entirely symptom-free. At any point, however, her condition could worsen. Sutton didn't appreciate him blowing smoke at her, especially since she wasn't just his daughter anymore—she was also his colleague.

For years, his "impeccable bedside manner" had been praised from sea to shining sea, and Sutton could still remember a time when she had believed everything he said. Now, all she heard in his words were platitudes and oversimplifications. Maybe that was what America wanted from their doctor, but did it really do them any good? Her mother's condition was unstable. That was the truth, and to run away from it was cowardly. But if she said anything more to him right now, it would sound uncharitable, and it wouldn't do to sound uncharitable here. The Pool Room was the birthplace—and the graveyard—of society gossip. Reginald had invited her here to put her on display and to maintain his public image as a doting father. Despite her annoyance, she had no desire to sabotage him. Since coming out, she had made a conscious effort to meet him halfway whenever possible. Maybe it wasn't healthy to feel a lingering sense of guilt over being a disappointment, but she didn't have time for a therapist. Besides, once her article was published, he would be much angrier about it than about her sexual orientation.

To keep from venting her frustration, Sutton ate the last of her risotto. Within seconds, a white-clad waiter had scooped up her empty plate. Reginald sat back in his chair, patted his lean stomach, and smiled at her indulgently. She had to give him credit—despite being constantly wined and dined, he kept himself in impeccable shape. In his line of work, that was particularly important as he could be called away to perform a grueling surgery at any moment. The longest had been when she was an adolescent—a twenty-three-hour procedure to separate Siamese twins conjoined at the head. Now, with so much training behind her, Sutton felt even more awe at her father's accomplishment than she had as a girl. No matter their personal disagreements, she would always respect him as a professional.

"Reginald! And Sutton, too. How lovely to see you both!"

Sutton's musings were interrupted by the arrival of a buxom brunette whose every curve was set on display by her low-cut, sapphire dress. Diamonds sparkled at her throat, ears, and wrist. As Sutton rose to accept two enthusiastic cheek kisses, her lungs were assaulted by an overdose of spicy perfume.

"Hello, hello, Beverly." Reginald's tone was jovial, and she turned to him with a coquettish laugh that forced Sutton to concentrate hard on not rolling her eyes.

Beverly Lloyd was the network executive who had "discovered" Reginald three years ago. Sutton had seen her on only a handful of occasions, but once would have been more than enough. Not for the first time, she wondered whether her father actually liked these people, or whether he was simply pandering to them. Either way, she wasn't impressed.

"Sutton, you look lovely. The hint of blue in that suit makes your eyes just pop!"

Somehow, Sutton didn't think Beverly was referring to the kind of ocular bulging produced by a neuroblastoma. She struggled not to smile at her own internal joke.

"Thank you. Your dress is lovely."

Beverly preened and name-dropped an up-and-coming designer who Sutton knew for a fact had never created anything in her size. So much for that pretense. Then Beverly leaned in close.

"So, tell me. Is there a special man in your life?"

Out of the corner of her eye, Sutton saw Reginald's posture stiffen. Aside from a few close friends, her parents were the only people she had told about her attraction to women. After they had failed to convince Sutton that her sexual orientation was some sort of stress-triggered phase, they had asked her to be discreet. Her one fling with a postdoc several years ago had ended so quickly that Sutton had never truly chafed under their passive-aggressive homophobia.

"I'm sorry to say, there's no special man," she said. "I don't have any time for a relationship right now." The latter, at least, was the truth. Unhelpfully, her brain summoned the image of Jane, eyes flashing with humor as she teased Sutton about her "favorite part of the brain." No. Just because they had spent a fun day together, and seemed to have some sort of physical chemistry, did *not* mean she wanted a relationship with Jane. Far from it.

"Speaking of time," Sutton spoke as much to distract herself as to escape the conversation, "I have rounds this afternoon and should be going. If you'll excuse me?"

"Of course." Reginald embraced her quickly. "Travel downtown safely."

After another exchange of air kisses with Beverly, Sutton headed toward the coat check. Before she could so much as step up to the window and display her token, the attendant had whisked her pea coat off its hanger. She thanked him and tipped him more than usual, the prospect of freedom making her generous.

Only when the chilly February air sluiced down her throat did she begin to relax. Fumbling for her gloves, she walked quickly to the nearest subway station. When she stepped onto the platform just as a train was arriving, she indulged in her first true smile of the day. The sooner she could be downtown, the sooner she could turn this into a productive day.

After sliding into one of the plastic bucket seats, she leaned her head back against the window and allowed her breathing to align with the rhythmic thumps of the train traversing each seam of the tracks. Slowly, she craned her neck and pushed her shoulders down toward the center of her torso, hoping to ease some of the knots that had formed during lunch. Maybe lying by omission to her father was a mistake, but as soon as he found out about her new research interest, he would fight hard to change her mind. Again. She didn't have the energy for a string of arguments right now. Why jump the gun? In another few weeks, the publication of her article would make her persona non grata. She might as well soak up her family's misguided approval while she could.

The train pulled into the station at Twenty-eighth Street, and she quickly walked the three blocks east to the hospital. After flashing her badge for the security officer, she hurried toward the locker room. She was just ten feet from the door when Travis McPhearson rounded the corner. A fourth-year medical student, he was at the top of the class and never let anyone forget it. Travis had played basketball in college, and the running joke behind his back was that he loved to look down on everyone.

"Hel-lo, Sutton." He wolf-whistled. "Look at you, dressed to the nines. Did you have a lunch date? Who's the lucky gentleman?"

"My father," Sutton said, resisting the urge to make some snarky comment about his assumptions.

"Oh." His tone shifted faster than a Maserati. "I see. Please give him my regards when next you see him."

"Of course." Sutton had no intention of doing so, and she didn't turn her head as she breezed through the locker room door. The routine of afternoon rounds and paperwork would help to calm the unsettled feeling in her chest. Maybe she would even have another chance to work individually with a patient. No matter what happened, afterward she could indulge in comfort food at Noodle Treasure. Perhaps Jane would be there again, helping Min with her homework.

If you want to see her so badly, you could always call her. That little voice had been inside her head for days now, urging her to at least send a text. But along with the text, wouldn't she also be sending the wrong impression? It really would be ludicrous to date someone right now. She would only end up hurting Jane, and probably herself as well.

No, she wouldn't call. She wouldn't text. But she also wasn't about to deprive herself of her favorite place to work. If fate threw the two of them together again, she'd just have to think on her feet.

JANE FLICKED HER PEN onto the back of her hand and walked it across her knuckles as she stared out into the night. Across the street, the brightly illuminated windows of Noodle Treasure mocked her. Sutton hadn't called, texted, or come to the restaurant in almost three full days.

"She's busy, right?" Jane asked of her reflection, dimly visible in the windowpane. "Superhero-grade busy."

There was no need to panic. Sutton came to the restaurant a few times a week, not every single day. She probably had meetings to attend or patients to see or experiments to run. She wasn't avoiding Chinatown. She hadn't decided to find a new place to do her writing. No. She was off saving the world one person at a time, and she would return once her schedule allowed it. Right.

As she glanced down at her notebook, Jane tried to console herself. At least she had been productive for a few hours. Today's prospective fortunes had started out on an anticipatory note. *Be ready to seize your opportunity. Let your happy memories empower you. Love rewards patience.* But by the time the early winter's dusk had fallen, a note of desperation had entered her work. *Don't let a chance at love slip away. The darkest hour is just before the dawn.* She'd had to look up that aphorism to be sure she wasn't violating any copyright, but it had been around since the seventeenth century. The things she learned on this job!

The sound of footsteps in the hall were a merciful distraction. She turned to the sight of Min, bundled up against the cold in her bright yellow "Lorax" hat and a puffy pink coat that had once been Cornelia's. Jane smiled as she recalled Min's stoicism at being given the hand-me-down. The Lorax would approve.

"Mom asked me to give you this." She handed Jane an envelope and then squinted at the window. "Has Sutton come back to the restaurant yet?"

"Nope." Jane tried to change the subject quickly. "How was your day? Need any homework help?"

"Please." Min's tone was dismissive. She turned, hands on hips. "What did you do to drive her away?"

"Nothing!"

"Have you been acting clingy? Sending pathetic text messages?"

Jane was about to vehemently deny both charges when she realized she was allowing herself to be baited. "No, and no. And I'm not having this conversation with you."

Min regarded her skeptically. "Maybe you should. You must've done someth—"

"Nuh-uh. No way. Out. Shoo."

"But—"

Jane worked one fingertip beneath the seal of the envelope in an effort to look busy. "I mean it. *You're* stifling *my* creative fl—"

The word died on her lips as she caught sight of the return address. Grief, all the more potent for being unexpected, constricted her chest. For one terrifying moment, she couldn't breathe.

"What happened?" Minetta leaned over her shoulder. "Who's it from?"

Jane swallowed hard, and mercifully, the vise around her lungs loosened. "Someone unexpected," she managed.

"Are you okay?" Min's tone was uncharacteristically subdued. "Jane?"

"I'm fine." The words were an effort, but hopefully they didn't sound as shaken as she felt. "I just . . . I need to read this in private, kiddo." Jane kept her eyes fixed on the blurred image of the envelope, not daring to raise her head. "I'm sorry."

"No worries." Min patted her shoulder tentatively. "I'll be across the street. If Sutton comes in, I'll text you. Promise."

"Sure." Jane blinked furiously, struggling to process Minetta's words over the riot of emotion clouding her brain. "Thanks."

At the sound of the door closing, Jane refocused on the letter. *Niles,* read the name above the familiar Brooklyn address. Anders Niles, her thesis advisor at Hunter, had been the ideal mentor. Despite being the recipient of numerous awards for his poetry, he had always treated her more like a colleague than a student. He and his wife, Sophia, had invited her to weekly meals at their cozy walk-up in Williamsburg. And he had been instrumental in helping her secure her first—and so far only—publication.

She had noticed his weight loss in the spring of her junior year but thought it intentional. By the time he confessed that he was dying, a few weeks were all he had left. She had visited him in the hospital once, where she sat at his bedside next to Sophia and tried not to feel ashamed of her tears. He had gripped her hand with surprising strength and had made her promise never to stop writing. She had given her word and was keeping it as best she could.

Wasn't she?

Jane sliced through the crease of the envelope, perversely glad when a paper cut opened along the side of her index finger. One thick, marbled sheet of paper lay inside, and her fingers trembled as she unfolded it. *The Anders Niles Memorial Fellowship for Emerging Poets* was stenciled in script across the top third of the page.

The world went blurry again, but she shook her head and scrubbed harshly at her eyes.

The more she read, the dizzier she felt. The fellowship had been created by Sophia in her husband's name. Applicants were required to submit a personal statement and ten poems by April first. Applications would be judged by the fellowship's Board of Trustees, and twenty-five thousand dollars would be awarded annually to an emerging poet—someone whose early work had promise but who was not yet established. Someone exactly like her.

At the bottom of the page, she found a brief note:

Jane,
I hope you're well. If Anders were alive, he would want this award
to be yours. I hope you apply.
All my best,
Sophia

This time, Jane didn't try to suppress her tears. They rolled down her cheeks to plink against the metal desk, tiny chimes tolling her grief. She couldn't have said how long they lasted, or how long she stared out into the darkness after her cheeks had dried. But eventually, the weight of the card stock beneath her fingertips drew her attention back down to the paper. Sophia had not only tracked down her address, but had taken the time to write a special note.

Anders would want this award to be yours.

Would he, if he could see her now: holed up in a closet, writing fragments of pseudo-prognosticatory verse? This wasn't the life Anders had envisaged for her, and it certainly wasn't the life she wanted for herself. Now, from beyond the grave, he had offered her a way out. Twenty-five thousand dollars might not be much in the grand scheme, but it would be enough to allow her to focus on her real work—at least for a little while. And the prestige of winning such a prize would be useful, in certain circles.

Suddenly energized, Jane reached for her poetry notebook and turned to the first page. As she began to flip through it, she grabbed her pen and began to mark the top corner of every piece that held a hint of promise. By the time she reached her most recent page, she had identified nine poems with potential, including her unfinished work-in-progress about Grand Central Station. Sitting back in her chair, she drummed her pen against the edge of the desk. She had to do this. It would mean splitting her free time between editing her older work, finishing her current piece, and trying to write something new, but . . . it almost felt as though Anders had been watching over her since his death and had finally decided that she needed an intervention. Laughing—laughing!—at the thought, she laced her hands behind her head and thought of what she might do with the prize money. The cautious, responsible plan involved putting it into her savings account. But the entire purpose of the award was to support her work, not maintain the status quo. Maybe she would travel for a while. After almost five years, she had lived longer in New York City than anywhere else, and claustrophobia was starting to set in. She could dust off her camping pack and sleeping roll and book an open-ended flight and—

Her phone chimed with a text from Minetta: *Sutton just walked in.*

Jane stood up so fast that she knocked her notebook and pen to the floor and nearly upended her water bottle into her lap. Her first impulse had been to make a headlong dash for Noodle Treasure, but as she returned her scattered belongings to their proper places, logic interceded. She'd had an emotional meltdown and probably looked terrible. In the tiny bathroom, that suspicion was confirmed: her eyes were still red, and tear tracks stained her cheeks. Jane shucked off her T-shirt and tucked it into her back pocket as she scrubbed her face. For good measure, she ducked her head under the faucet to restore some of the spikiness to her hair. By this time of the day, the effects of gravity always trumped her gel. Even if Sutton wasn't a fan, Jane liked the way she looked with a bit of texture, and right now she needed every drop of self-confidence she could get.

As she stared at her reflection, she felt a stab of guilt at how quickly she had gone from mourning Anders to obsessing over Sutton. But Anders wouldn't want her to wallow in grief. He would want her to live. *Write every day,* he had told her poetry workshop class one warm spring morning near the end of his last semester. *But not all day. To filter the world, you must be in the world. Learn a new language. See a new city. Make something with your hands. Climb a mountain. Fall in love.* Not that she was falling in love with Sutton, of course, but a healthy crush had to be just as good for the muse, didn't it?

After tucking the letter carefully into her notebook and shoving a stick of gum in her mouth, she hurried downstairs and nearly crashed into her aunt, who was just rounding the corner.

"Jane! Careful!"

"Sorry. I'm sorry, Aunt Jen."

"Dinner will be ready in half an hour. Would you mind letting Minetta know, if you see her?"

"Sure. No problem." Jane wanted to hug her for offering the perfect excuse to drop by Noodle Treasure. "I'm on it."

Aunt Jen opened her mouth to say something else, but Jane darted past and out the door before she could speak. When a gust of cold wind made goose bumps rise on her forearms, she belatedly looked down at her attire. In her rush to leave, she'd left her sweatshirt behind. Her crimson "Where's the Beef?" shirt wasn't exactly the sexiest of garments, but at least it was better than that Joe Camel tee. In the act of crossing the street, a pang of insecurity made her suddenly want to turn tail, but Fate intervened in the form of a speeding taxi and the momentum carried her to the front door. Resolutely, she pushed.

Sutton always sat in the corner at the window counter, and Jane forced herself not to look that way. Instead, she scanned the depths of the restaurant for Min, who was seated in the back near the kitchen.

"Hey, Min," she called. "Dinner in thirty."

Min looked up, frowning. "Really?"

"Yes, really. Your mother says so."

"Okay."

Steeling herself, Jane turned around. Sutton was looking directly at her, and suddenly, Jane couldn't breathe. Dressed in pale green scrub pants and an NYU sweatshirt, her honey-colored hair pulled back and her glasses sliding down her nose, she looked rumpled and exhausted and even more beautiful than usual.

Jane raised her hand in an awkward little wave and immediately hated herself.

"Hi," Sutton said.

Taking the greeting as permission to approach, Jane threaded her way around the tables. "Hi. It's good to see you."

Sutton took a sip of tea before saying, "Same."

Okay, so far so good. They were talking. Sutton hadn't ignored her. She hadn't spoken in anything other than monosyllables, either, but for now Jane was going to take what she was given. She rested her arms on the counter. "How was your day?"

Sutton's smile held a touch of awe. "It ended up being . . . amazing, actually."

Jane was fleetingly jealous of whatever had put that expression on Sutton's face, but she also never wanted it to leave. "What happened?"

"This afternoon, I got to assist one of the residents with an emergency ventriculostomy."

"I'm afraid I'm going to need that in plain English."

"Sorry. It's a procedure for people who have a condition called hydrocephalus, which happens when cerebrospinal fluid builds up in the brain. If the fluid isn't drained, mental disability or death can result."

"That sounds . . . terrifying. How do you treat it?"

"A surgeon inserts a shunt into the brain that drains the fluid. That's what I helped with."

Jane didn't know what to say. Sutton had spent her day saving someone's life, while she spent her day delivering cookies and writing fortunes. She felt her confidence falter. "Wow."

Sutton made a dismissive gesture. "It's not actually that big of a deal."

"Oh? Really? Saving someone's brain function and life isn't a big deal?"

"I only helped keep the field clear and then sewed up the patient afterward. I'm not allowed to do anything more complicated than that, yet."

"I still think you're remarkable." As soon as the words left her mouth, Jane knew they'd been a mistake—not because they were in any way dishonest, but because they were too much. In the ensuing awkward pause, Sutton looked down and reached for her chopsticks.

When she brought one of Mei's homemade dumplings up to her mouth, Jane forced a smile. "I love the dumplings here. Do you want to know a secret? My aunt buys them frozen from Mei by the hundred instead of making her own."

"I don't blame her," Sutton said.

"What kind are those?"

"Pork and cabbage."

"Excellent." As she watched Sutton attempt to grab another, inspiration suddenly struck. "Have brunch with me on Saturday."

Dumplings forgotten, Sutton looked up at her with a slightly panicked expression. "Jane . . ."

At Sutton's tone, Jane felt the bottom drop out of her stomach. Sutton was already using breakup voice, and they weren't even together yet. "Yes?" she asked, hoping her own voice was steady.

"I don't want you to get the wrong idea."

"What idea? I am idea-less."

"My life . . ." Sutton shook her head. "My life is just so chaotic. Soon, I'll finish my degrees and I could end up doing my residency anywhere in the country or even internationally, and . . . and I'm babbling. I'm sorry." For an instant, she allowed their eyes to meet before she looked away. "I don't have the time or energy for anything but a friend right now. And I probably wouldn't be a very good friend, either."

"Well, you'll need some sort of midday meal on Saturday, right? Why don't you join me for dim sum? Have you heard of it? Chinese dumpling extravaganza?"

"Jane . . ."

There was that tone again, and Jane furiously tried to summon a quick response that would forestall Sutton from rejecting her outright.

"Min's been wanting to go for ages. Come with us. Ten o'clock. We'll be done by eleven." Holding her breath, Jane mentally crossed her fingers that Minetta's presence would clinch Sutton's acceptance.

When Sutton continued to looked dubious, Jane acted on instinct. Looking over her shoulder, she called, "Min! Dim sum Saturday?"

"Where?" Min said, never even looking up.

"Golden Unicorn."

"Sure."

Jane turned and mustered her best carefree grin. "C'mon. You'll laugh a lot. I promise."

"Well, seeing as Min and I are so compatible . . ." Sutton said, the hint of a smile curving her lips. "All right."

"All right!" As soon as the words were out of her mouth, Jane realized she probably should have tempered her enthusiasm. She needed an exit strategy posthaste, before Sutton rescinded her acceptance. "Speaking of Min, I'm going to see how she's doing on her homework. See you Saturday."

Without glancing back, she made her way toward the rear of the restaurant and sank into the seat next to Min, who was paying no attention to her math textbook whatsoever.

"So I'll be your chaperone, I take it?" she whispered as she typed out a text message.

"More like a third wheel."

"Sounds fun." The words fairly dripped with pretended sarcasm. "I can't wait."

"Me, neither." Jane laced her hands behind her head and stared up at the streamers that still crisscrossed the ceiling. "Me neither, kiddo."

CHAPTER SIX

A S SHE CROSSED HESTER Street, Sutton felt her pulse elevate. Sometimes, being more in tune with her body than the average person was a curse. Right now, she knew that her autonomic nervous system was provoking a mild "fight or flight" response—diverting blood away from her digestive system and into her skeletal muscles while simultaneously dilating both the bronchioles in her lungs and the pupils in her eyes. And all because she was just a few minutes away from seeing Jane again. The human body truly was a miracle. Now, if only controlling attraction were as easy as saying "no" to a date.

Not that she'd actually managed to turn Jane down. If she had, she would be joining her friends for brunch at Sarabeth's on Central Park South right now, or enjoying a quiet cup of coffee at home. Instead, she was bucking the wintry morning breeze on her way back into Chinatown for another cultural experience.

Sutton shook her head. Who was she kidding? The promise of more traditional Chinese fare hadn't enticed her to say yes. Something about Jane was irresistible. Her eyes, maybe, or her laugh. Her spontaneity, or her sense of humor, or the subtle layers that Sutton occasionally glimpsed beneath her laissez-faire attitude. There was a complexity to her that Sutton found refreshing. Jane had virtually nothing in common with her friends or former crushes, and she was nothing like the driven, intensely focused woman with whom Sutton had shared a whirlwind relationship. Maybe those differences were the source of Jane's magnetism.

Since their brief chat earlier in the week, Jane hadn't appeared in Noodle Treasure, and the prospect of seeing her had made it difficult for Sutton to doze off again after waking with the sun this morning. Min's presence today notwithstanding, Sutton was getting closer and closer to date territory. If Jane kept asking, she was going to say yes in a weak moment. And then she'd regret it. Sutton hated regret. What a useless, energy-draining emotion.

Are you so sure you would?

That tiny voice was back. Sutton tried to ignore it. Maybe she was becoming schizophrenic. Schizophrenia did, after all, tend to manifest in one's twenties.

"Oh, stop it," she muttered as she caught a glimpse of herself in the window of an organic grocery. At least she looked good. The chill had dusted her cheeks with a light blush, and her hair shone golden in the sunlight. The collar of her blue turtleneck sweater—chosen because it matched her eyes—peeked out from beneath her jacket, and black jeans hugged her hips and thighs in all the right places.

Sutton took a deep breath as she approached the crooked sign for Baxter Street. As soon as she turned the corner, she saw them waiting—Min in a bright pink coat with a faux fur collar, and Jane in a dark gray zip-up hoodie. Instead of admiring her lanky frame, or the way a few strands of her dark hair had resisted her gel and lay feathered across her forehead, Sutton focused on Jane's unseasonable garb. Did she ever wear anything heavier than a sweatshirt?

"Good morning."

"Hi." Jane's smile held a touch of puppyish enthusiasm that was wholly endearing, and Sutton's traitorous heartbeat sped up in response. "Ready for dumplings?"

"I am," Sutton said as they turned south toward Canal. "But is that really all you're wearing?"

"Jane doesn't like coats," Min said. "She's a freak of nature."

"Oh, thanks." Jane elbowed her. "Maybe I just run hot. Ever think of that?"

Min and Sutton exchanged a glance, and Min rolled her eyes. "Keep telling yourself that."

"I see I'll be heckled all through brunch." Jane turned to Sutton. "How was the rest of your week?"

Sutton hesitated, not sure of how much detail to go into. She didn't have much practice at discussing her research with laypeople. "Not nearly as eventful as the first half. But I did turn in a draft of an article to my advisor yesterday."

"Congratulations. What's it about?"

"Do you really want to know, or are you just being polite?"

"Sutton," Jane said gravely. "I'm not a fan of pretense. When I say something, you can be sure I mean it."

Flustered, Sutton looked away down the street, past the goldsellers and the tiny stores selling handbags and knickknacks and T-shirts. "I didn't mean to imply that you . . . well." She watched her breath float away on the air. "This article grew out of some of my doctoral research on using surgical techniques in combination with medication to treat several common neurological disorders that affect memory."

"So like . . . Alzheimer's?"

"Yes, and other kinds of dementia."

"That sounds like a pretty big deal."

"It might be." Sutton made a snap decision to share a little more. Jane really did seem genuinely interested. "The model I've been working off of is epilepsy treatment, in which surgery is often used if medication doesn't work."

As they turned the corner, a quick series of loud popping sounds preempted whatever Jane had been about to say. Gunshots! Without conscious thought, Sutton took two quick steps to stand in front of Min in an effort to shield her while scanning the packed street. Her earlier fight-or-flight reaction felt like child's play. Why wasn't the rest of the crowd in a panic?

When Jane touched her arm, Sutton whirled so quickly that Jane immediately raised her hands in a show of innocence. "Easy. It's okay. Just someone stupid enough to set off a real firecracker."

Sutton exhaled as the relief hit home. Ahead, a small cloud of white smoke was dissipating quickly into the air, and the raucous laughter of what sounded like adolescent boys filled the street. Firecrackers. Of course. To frighten away the demons.

The high-pitched whirr of a police siren filled the air, but Sutton had a feeling the perpetrators had already dispersed into the throng. "I wasn't expecting that," she said lamely. At least Min, whose attention remained riveted on her phone, hadn't noticed her reaction.

"Throwing yourself into the line of fire goes way above and beyond the Hippocratic Oath," Jane said softly as they continued to follow Min along the sidewalk.

"Depends on your definition of harm, doesn't it?" Sutton was glad to give her brain something to do other than wallow in embarrassment. "Standing by and doing nothing can be just as bad as inflicting pain."

Surreptitiously, she watched Jane think. Her face scrunched up a little when she was concentrating hard on something. It was cute.

"I'd call that inaction,'" she said finally. "Not harm."

"What about neglect?"

But Jane shook her head. "No, neglect is when you do nothing but you're supposed to do something. You're under obligation. Nobody except the Secret Service is under obligation to throw themselves in front of a bullet, right? And then only for their protectee."

They paused at a crosswalk and Min spun to face them. "You guys are scrambling my synapses."

Jane jerked her head toward Sutton. "Blame her. She's the neuroscientist."

"Guilty as charged." Sutton glanced at their surroundings. Across the street to the east, a tall, brown brick structure towered over the nearby buildings, dominating the field of view. "I meant to ask this on New Year's," she said, pointing to it, "but what is that?"

"Confucius Plaza. It's a housing complex, built by the city. In the seventies, I think." Jane tapped Min on the shoulder as they began to cross. "Let's stop by the statue."

"But I'm hungry," she wheedled.

"Just for a second. It's practically on our way."

Sutton was about to ask what statue they were referring to, when she caught sight of the bronze figure atop a green marble base. "Is that Confucius?"

"Sure is."

As they approached, Sutton saw that the base was engraved with words in both Chinese and English. She and Jane paused directly in front of it, while Min stood off to the side, arms crossed over her chest, looking bored.

"Sue says that tracing the characters of his name is supposed to bring you luck." Jane stretched out her left hand and ran her index and middle fingers along the grooves of the golden-hued strokes. It was a surprisingly sensual act, and Sutton swallowed hard as she tried to banish the mental image of Jane's hands tracing her own lines and curves.

"Want to give it a go?" Jane asked, looking over her shoulder.

For a moment, Sutton thought Jane was reading her mind, and the sudden flood of heat beneath her skin made her body's wishes perfectly clear. But that was a purely physical response—driven by hormones, an instinctual drive to mate, and the as yet-to-be understood chemical mechanism behind attraction. Maybe she should forget surgery and stem cells and start researching pheromones instead.

"I could definitely use some luck," she said, stepping forward to touch the stone. It was cold beneath her fingertips, and as she followed the sharp angles of the characters, she marveled at how many ways humanity had found to express itself. This inscription was wholly exotic to her, but intelligible to most of the people who lived nearby. Even gibberish was just a matter of perspective.

"How do I know if it worked?" she asked as she moved back.

"Wait and see if you get lucky." Jane tried to deadpan, but the twitching corners of her mouth gave her away.

"Very funny." Sutton hoped her eye-roll seemed decisive. "I walked right into that, didn't I?"

"Pretty much, yeah." Jane extended her hand, then let it fall just as quickly. "Shall we?"

"Thank God," Min said as they rejoined her at the corner. "I'm frozen and starving."

"This is nothing. Try Sweden in the winter."

"Is she always this insufferable?" Sutton asked Min as they halted beneath a red awning.

"It's usually worse. I think she's trying to be good right now."

"Would you two like to eat?" Jane asked as she pushed open the door. "Or do you just want to stand around out here giving me a hard time?"

The blast of warm air was comforting, and Sutton quickly stepped inside. But as her eyes adjusted to the dim lighting, she looked around in confusion. There was no restaurant to be found—only a small atrium facing a bank of elevators. Sutton watched as Jane approached a woman in black pants, a white shirt, and a burgundy vest carrying a clipboard and wearing a headset. After a moment, Jane beckoned them forward.

"Third floor."

"How many are there?" Sutton asked as they waited for an elevator.

"Five. Sometimes, people will rent an entire floor for a private party."

When the doors opened, they followed a young family with two small children inside. Min said something to the little girl in Chinese that earned her a shy smile and an indulgent look from the mother. Sutton leaned close to Jane and opened her mouth to speak, only to find herself momentarily distracted by the scent of Ivory soap and a hint of cinnamon.

"What did Min say?" she whispered.

"She told the girl she had pretty hair." Jane raised her hand to gently rub a strand of Sutton's hair between her thumb and index finger. "So do you."

"Flattery will get you nowhere," Sutton warned.

Jane lowered her hand. "What about honesty?"

The doors chimed as they opened, and Sutton turned to exit, glad she had an excuse not to answer. Honesty would only get her into trouble. She followed Min, who approached a man dressed identically to the woman downstairs. He guided them to a table, set down a piece of paper that vaguely resembled a golfing scorecard, and left.

Each chair was ensconced in a gold embroidered cover, and the white tablecloth hung almost to the ground. As Sutton sank into the seat next to Min, she stared around the large, rectangular room in rapt fascination. Its décor was a visual cacophony. The wall nearest to their table was covered in upholstery, while the others were paneled with brick and faux marble in turn. Flat-screen televisions hung at each corner, tuned to CNN. At the far end of the room, red-and-gold curtains framed a low stage. Two large, golden shapes emerged from the wall behind it in bas relief. One she clearly recognized as a dragon, and as she watched, its red eyes blinked rhythmically at her. The other creature was some sort of bird, its green eyes blinking in counterpoint.

"What is that?"

"A phoenix," Jane said. "The dragon and the phoenix are another way of expressing yin and yang."

"Yin and yang." Sutton could picture the symbols, but she only had a vague notion of what they meant. "They represent opposites attracting, right?"

"It's a little more complicated than that." Jane unwrapped her chopsticks as she spoke. "Yin and yang are complementary forces. At first glance they seem contradictory, but each needs the other in order to work."

"Interesting." As Sutton unfolded her napkin, a man dressed all in black placed a teapot in the center of the table and began to fill their glasses with water. "Kind of sad that America boils that down to 'opposites attract.'"

"We're a young culture." Jane turned over the small porcelain teacups and filled Sutton's first, followed by Min's and then her own. "Everything's still black and white to us."

Before Sutton could reply, a metal cart rolled up to the table, pushed by a middle-aged woman wearing a white apron. Immediately, Min spun in her chair and struck up a conversation in rapid Chinese. On the side of the cart, a large, laminated poster displayed several different kinds of dishes, and Sutton peered at them closely, trying to make out familiar ingredients. When Min asked a question, the woman raised the lid on one of the perfectly round bamboo containers stacked inside the cart. Min nodded, and the woman placed it on their table, stamped the card, and moved on.

Min uncovered the dish with a flourish. "Chicken feet!"

Sutton blinked at the sight of a pile of golden-brown, fried chicken claws covered with a sauce that contained scallions and what looked like red pepper. As she sat staring, Min leaned forward, grabbed one with her chopsticks, and popped it into her mouth. Sutton glanced over at Jane, who was looking between her and the food and visibly cringing. Sutton squared her shoulders as her pride kicked in. Did Jane think she was that much of a baby?

"I said I'd try anything once, and I meant it." Awkwardly, she hefted her chopsticks. "How does one eat these?"

"You eat it like . . . like if you ate a spare rib by putting the whole bone in your mouth. You sort of, um, suck the skin off and then spit out the bone."

Jane's discomfort was proving more entertaining by the second. Determined to keep a straight face, Sutton watched as Min held her chopsticks up to her pursed lips and deftly grabbed the partially masticated foot. She set it on the overturned lid and went back for seconds.

"Lovely." Sutton was torn between faint disgust and amusement as she imagined what her mother would think of this meal.

Jane put her hand on Sutton's shoulder. Immediately, the heat of her palm soaked through the thin wool of Sutton's sweater, and it took a supreme effort of will not to betray her pleasure at the sensation.

"You really don't have to." Jane's voice broke the spell that her touch had woven. "We're going to order a lot of other things, okay?"

Sutton seized one of the feet and ate it, just so she wouldn't have to try to formulate words. Thankfully, the distraction worked. As she gingerly bit down, the sauce coated her tongue. It was delicious—sweet and tangy with just the tiniest hint of spice. She didn't much care for the rather gristly texture of the foot, though, and after a few moments, she awkwardly mimicked Min's extraction of the bone.

"What did you think?" Jane asked.

"Honestly, it's not really my thing. But I did enjoy the sauce."

Relief crossed Jane's face, but as she opened her mouth to reply, another bamboo container appeared next to the chicken feet. This one held a small mound of white, rubbery-looking strips. One side was smooth, while the other looked almost honeycombed.

"Tripe!" Min announced cheerfully as she reached for one.

Jane promptly buried her face in her hands. "C'mon, Min," she groaned. "Throw me a bone, here."

"A chicken toe bone?" Min asked around her mouthful, eyes twinkling mischievously.

"What is tripe?"

"Sheep stomach." Jane fixed Min with a glare. "You are the worst. Flag down some *shu mai*, will you?"

Min swallowed, then sighed dramatically. "Fine, fine. You're no fun."

"Are you kidding? I'm a barrel of laughs. I'd just like Sutton to be able to eat, so she'll want to hang out with us again."

"Relax. I'm having a great time." Sutton couldn't seem to stop herself from lightly brushing Jane's forearm with her fingers. The swift shiver she got in response gave her a rush of confidence. Steeling herself, she raised a piece of the tripe to her lips.

It tasted like soy sauce and garlic, which was fine, but when she bit down it was even more rubbery than she'd expected. After trying to chew it for several seconds, she swallowed hard and reached for her teacup. As the soothing scent of chrysanthemum washed over her, she sat back in her chair. "All right, what's next?"

Jane shook her head in clear admiration. "You are amazing."

Sutton hoped she couldn't be blamed for feeling a bit smug. "You have no idea."

Jane's eyes went wide, a swirl of green and gold materializing in their depths. Mesmerized, Sutton leaned in closer, transfixed by the desire writ plainly across Jane's features. It was addicting to know she could affect her so strongly, and for a long moment, the clatter of plates and buzz of nearby conversations faded away entirely.

"Are you happy now?"

Min's question shattered the tension. Sutton blinked and turned her head toward where another of the servers was depositing several containers full of dumplings onto the table. Immediately, her mouth began to water. This was much more her speed.

"Good work, kiddo." Jane gestured at the various dishes. "Shrimp and pork *shu mai*. And those are steamed pork buns. Mei makes a roasted version that's pretty similar."

They all dug in with gusto, and for several minutes, there was no conversation at all aside from the occasional comment about the quality of the food. Whenever another cart rolled around, Min added a dish to the mix: a plate of steaming oysters, a bowl of fragrant Chinese broccoli, a bamboo box filled with sticky rice cakes.

"We had these on New Year's," Sutton said as she helped herself. "They're supposed to be lucky, aren't they?

"*Nian gao.* And yes." Jane set down her chopsticks and looked at her intently. "When we were at Confucius Plaza, you said you could use some luck. What did you mean?"

Sutton was impressed that Jane had been paying such close attention, but she tried to wave the question aside. "I've had plenty of luck already."

"There's no quota. Are you worried about your residency? You'll find out where you're matched in a few weeks, right?"

"Oh? Have you been doing some research?"

To Sutton's delight, Jane actually squirmed in her chair. "I might have looked up how it all works. You get matched with a program on March fifteenth?"

"That's right." Sutton nibbled at one corner of her rice cake. "This may sound arrogant, but I'm not that worried about matching. I had some good interviews, and I think I'll do fine."

"What are you worried about, then?"

Sutton lay down her chopsticks and leaned back in her chair, uncertain as to how much she should say. No one knew everything—her father had no idea about the fellowship opportunities she'd applied for abroad, and Dr. Buehler knew nothing of her mother's condition. But it was safe to talk to Jane, wasn't it? Jane didn't know any of her friends or colleagues. She lived in a world that practically never intersected with her own.

"You can trust me," Jane said. "Min, too. Right, Min?"

"Sure."

Sutton doubted Min was even listening. She had her phone out and was playing some sort of game that seemed to involve exploding virtual candy pieces.

"I enjoyed the research for my thesis," Sutton began, "though the process of writing it up was a real challenge. But last year, I started to get interested in another topic when I read several studies—mostly coming out of Europe—in which stem cells were used to treat certain kinds of neurological disorders. My mother was diagnosed with MS a few years ago, and I think that made me especially intrigued."

"I've heard the name," Jane said, "but I'm ashamed to say I don't know what MS really is."

"It stands for multiple sclerosis, which is an autoimmune disease in which the body attacks the protective coverings around the neurons. Lesions form on parts of the brain and can affect coordination, balance, eyesight—pretty much anything."

"I'm sorry for your mother," Jane said. She reached out to lightly touch Sutton's hand. "That must be difficult to live with."

Sutton felt the strongest urge to intertwine their fingers, but before she could make any move, Jane had withdrawn. Probably for the best.

"It is," she said. "In most cases, the lesions will flare up and then fall dormant for a while. That's called relapse-remitting MS, and that's what my mother has. She'll feel pretty well for weeks or even months, and then suddenly she'll have an attack."

"And you're interested in seeing whether stem cells might be able to help her?"

Sutton met Jane's eyes but saw no censure—only curiosity. "I am. It's difficult to do that kind of research here, though, since stem cells are such a politically divisive issue. But I've applied to a few fellowships overseas."

"Have you heard back from any of them yet?"

"Not yet. Probably next month."

"And then you'll have to make a tough choice."

"Yes." Sutton smoothed two fingertips across the tablecloth. "Especially because my father doesn't know about the fellowships."

"Oh? Why not?"

Sutton took a deep breath and wondered whether what she was about to say would scare Jane off. She hoped not. Panic fluttered in her chest at the realization, and she spoke as much to distract herself as to answer the question.

"My father is Reginald St. James."

Comprehension dawned on Jane's face. "The former surgeon general."

"Yes. And if you know anything about his politics, then you know he's come out strongly against stem-cell research."

Jane didn't answer immediately, but when she finally spoke, her voice was soft and serious. "You have a lot of stressors in your life right now, Sutton."

It was the first time Sutton had heard her own name on Jane's lips, and she liked how it sounded. Too much. "I can manage them," she said, irritation at her own reaction making her defensive.

But Jane didn't rise to the bait. "I know," she said, regarding her steadily. "But please be sure to take care of yourself, too."

"I do. I will." Feeling more appreciative of Jane's concern than she wanted to admit, Sutton tried to steer the conversation back to more neutral territory. "And now you know why I wouldn't mind some luck, even though I believe we make our own."

Jane's gaze grew distant. "Maybe. But sometimes I'm not so sure. Sometimes I think there are bigger forces at work—that we're a part of something larger than ourselves." Their eyes met again, and Sutton must have looked skeptical, because Jane hastened to explain. "I'm not talking about believing in demons or anything. More like . . . energy." She shrugged self-consciously. "Maybe I've been spending a little too much time with Sue."

"Sue needs to get laid."

Sutton had forgotten all about Min. She couldn't help but laugh, though she immediately covered her mouth with one hand as Jane stammered Min's name in shock.

"What?" Min rolled her eyes. "It's true! She's way too wrapped up in that astrology stuff. She needs to come back down to earth."

"But . . . but do you even know what that means?"

Sutton hid her grin behind her palm as she watched Jane fumble for the right words. Min gave her a withering look.

"Of course I know. And I think we should get her together with that Italian guy. Gian-whatever-his-name-is."

"Giancarlo?" Sutton offered.

"Yes, him. He's totally into her. It was obvious at New Year's dinner."

Jane gestured to a nearby waiter for the check and immediately handed him her credit card. "Minetta, when we get home, I am going to give you a book. It's called *Emma.* I want you to read it cover to cover before you try any matchmaking."

Min exchanged an exasperated glance with Sutton, who shrugged. She'd never heard of it, either. "If Doctor Sutton hasn't read it, then I don't have to."

"Whoa, now." Sutton raised both hands. "Don't put me in the middle of this."

"You two are the literary equivalent of unwashed masses," Jane muttered as she signed the receipt.

Quickly, Sutton pulled out her wallet. "Let me chip in. Even though you just called me unwashed."

Jane immediately shook her head. "My treat. I insist."

"But—"

Jane got to her feet. "The bill was thirty dollars, including tip. Where else on this crazy island can three people stuff themselves silly during the Saturday brunch hour for only thirty dollars?"

Sutton was forced to admit she had a point. "All right. But I'm buying next time."

Jane froze in the act of plucking Sutton's coat off the back of her chair. "Next time." Her sudden smile was unguarded. "I like the sound of that."

As Sutton slid her arms into the sleeves, Jane's warm breath puffed against her neck. Suddenly, she wanted to pull Jane's arms around her waist—to know how it felt to lean back against Jane's chest and feel sheltered by her embrace. How long had it been since she had allowed herself to be held that way? How long since she had craved a lover's simple, comforting touch?

The answer, she realized as they returned to the elevator, was never. Her one actual relationship had been with a colleague. They'd been exceedingly cautious about public displays of affection, and too busy to see each other intimately very often. And then, within just a few months, it had been over. Since then, Sutton had occasionally wished for closeness and touch, but only in an abstract way. Until now. Jane gave her a face to put to the longing, a focal point for her desire.

"Are you all right?" Jane asked as they exited onto the sidewalk. "You got kind of quiet back there."

"I'm fine." Sutton tried to offer an encouraging smile. "Thanks for brunch. It was delicious."

"Except for the tripe."

"At least I can say I tried it." She fished in her coat pockets for her gloves and tried to think of the right thing to say. Better to leave it casual, she supposed. "I'm going to catch the train uptown to visit my family. See you sometime soon? At the restaurant?"

"Actually, I'm going up to Grand Central," Jane said. "Mind if I tag along that far?" She turned to Min. "You're fine getting home, right?"

"Please." Min sketched a wave in Sutton's direction, turned, and was gone.

The cold wind had picked up during their time inside, but mercifully, the station was only a few blocks away. Jane seemed content to walk beside her without speaking, for which Sutton was grateful. It was rare to find a person with whom silence didn't feel awkward.

"What takes you to Grand Central?" Sutton asked as they stepped onto the platform.

"Work," Jane said, reaching into her pocket for the same notebook and pen she'd had with her on New Year's.

"Work?"

"Not fortune cookies," Jane clarified. "Poetry."

An express train rattled to a stop, suspending further conversation until they had settled into a pair of corner seats. "Tell me more about that," Sutton said. "What kind of poetry do you write?"

"Well, I don't actually write very much, in the traditional sense." Jane's knee bounced as she spoke. For the first time all morning, she looked nervous. "Mostly I arrange what I hear."

Sutton might have let the subject drop if she hadn't sensed the opportunity to learn more about the real Jane. "What you hear?"

Jane gripped her knees with both hands and met Sutton's gaze with a clear effort. "I do found poetry. Ever heard of it?"

"I haven't. What is it?"

"The basic idea is that poetry already exists in the world. It just needs to be discovered. The way it works for me is that I listen. To everything." She smoothed her palms along her thighs. "We tend to block out all the dialogue around us, but if you listen, there's real poetry in it. I write down what I hear, and then I arrange all the pieces together."

"That's fascinating." For some reason, it was difficult for Jane to talk about this, and Sutton couldn't resist the impulse to offer comfort. Over the faint protests of logic and reason, she leaned close enough for their shoulders to touch. "I can imagine that Grand Central is a perfect place to gather . . . what do you call them? Sound bites?"

"I suppose you could. I just tend to think of them as lines. And yes, it's a great place. I've almost finished a poem that's entirely collected there, which is why I'm going back today." Suddenly, Jane sat up straighter. "You should come with me. Right now."

Sutton glanced out the window. The train was just leaving the Thirty-third Street station. Grand Central would be next. She'd been planning to run a few errands before making her weekly parental visit, but she had no set schedule. If she spent another hour—or even two—with Jane, what would be the harm?

The train rolled to a stop. The doors opened. Jane stepped out and once again extended her hand. This time, she didn't let it fall. The intensity of her stare burned in Sutton's chest.

"I've never showed anyone else what I do, but I'd like to show you."

Sutton stood. She wondered if she was crazy. She thought about regret. And then, in a burst of clarity, she realized she would only feel it if she let the doors close while she was still inside.

As the chime sounded, she touched Jane's palm with her fingers, feeling the wind at her back as the train roared away.

Chapter Seven

JANE DIDN'T LET GO as they walked up the stairs leading out of the station. Their fingers laced together perfectly, and despite the noise and press of the crowd, Jane suddenly felt as though they were the only people awake in a city full of sleepwalkers. She still couldn't quite believe that Sutton had decided to join her. Were it not for their joined hands, she might have chalked Sutton's motivation up to simple curiosity.

As they emerged into the tangle of corridors leading to the main concourse, Jane's thoughts raced. What had happened to Sutton's resolve that their outing today would not be a date? Had she come to some sort of resolution within her own mind? Had Jane done or said something to change her thinking? And if so, what?

Realizing that she was overanalyzing, she took a deep breath and tried simply to enjoy the moment for what it was. Daring to stroke her thumb lightly over Sutton's knuckles, she was gratified to receive a gentle squeeze in response.

"So, how do you do this?"

Wrenching her focus back to the task at hand, Jane cleared her throat. "Well, the first order of business is to find a good place to sit somewhere in the station."

"What counts as a good place?"

Jane thought about that for a moment. For some reason, conversations with Sutton always forced her to put words to abstract ideas she'd never had to fully explain before. "I guess . . . to me, found poetry is about movement. Either I sit in one spot and listen to the river of humanity passing by, or I move throughout the city and find sound bites wherever I go."

"So ideally you'd find a spot right in the middle of the flow of traffic."

"Exactly. Why don't you pick it out today?" When Sutton looked skeptical, Jane smoothed her thumb along the side of her index finger. "Don't worry. This is kind of like fishing. If it's not working, we can switch to another spot."

"Fishing, huh?"

Jane shrugged. "My grandfather took me a few times, when I was a kid. I liked swimming in the lake and looking at the cloud shapes, but I wasn't too wild about the flopping fish that ended up in the bottom of the boat."

A wistful expression crossed Sutton's face. "That sounds nice, flopping fish aside. My father's family are all germaphobes, so even when we went to their house on Long Island, I was only allowed to swim in the pool."

If Jane had to bet, she'd put down money that Sutton's grandparents had one of those fancy houses in the Hamptons. Trying not to dwell on the economic disparity between them, she swung their joined hands lightly. "Well, my grandfather passed away a few years ago, but my grandmother is still in that house, up in western Massachusetts. So if you ever have the urge to try a lake, you just let me know."

Sutton smiled but didn't reply, and Jane wondered whether her invitation—vague though it was—had pushed the bounds of what was acceptable on this quasi-date. Or maybe Sutton just wanted to change the subject. She was so self-possessed that it could be difficult to read her properly. Jane liked it better when her guard was down, as it had been earlier during their discussion of her career dilemma. Then again, they were still holding hands. Maybe Sutton felt too exposed right now to let any more cracks show in her armor.

"I'll probably be here for an hour or two," Jane said, hoping to put her at ease. "Feel free to stay as long as you like, or to leave whenever if you're not having fun."

"Okay."

They turned a corner and the concourse was suddenly before them. Its lofty, vaulted arches never failed to fill Jane with amazement, and as always, she felt her gaze being drawn up to the blue plaster ceiling depicting the constellations of the northern sky. If the corridors of the terminal were like rivers, then this was the sea into which they emptied. Ticket windows and kiosks lined one wall, above which the massive boards listing departures and arrivals hummed and whirred as trains arrived and departed. High overhead, a massive American flag hung, stripes down, from the center of the ceiling. Beneath it, the iconic, four-way clock face atop the information center shimmered in the light streaming through the tall windows.

"I may be a jaded New Yorker," Sutton said, "but this space always impresses me."

"It's a feat, isn't it? I heard the clock is worth more than ten million dollars."

"Are you serious?"

Jane nodded. "When I first got the idea to assemble a poem here, I did some research into the history of the terminal."

"What's the clock made out of that makes it so precious?"

"Opal."

"I'm learning all kinds of new things today." Sutton cocked her head as she regarded the vast hall before them. "So, what's the plan?"

"I usually try to find a spot on one of the benches near the main entrance to the trains." Jane pointed toward the wide corridor across the room. "Shall we?"

As they walked across the large flagstones, Jane wondered whether Sutton's presence would make it difficult for her to work. In order to do this properly, she needed to sink into a sort of trance state in which she quieted her mind and opened her ears. Being near Sutton made her want to live fully in the moment. Would the hyperawareness serve to sharpen her focus, or destroy it?

"Do you . . ." Sutton trailed off, sounding uncharacteristically uncertain. As she struggled to voice whatever she wanted to say, her fingertips caressed the inside of Jane's wrist in an utterly distracting manner. "Would you mind if I tried, also? Just to listen, I mean. To collect the sound bites—not to arrange them. I'm no poet."

The question made Jane feel warm inside, as though she'd just sipped hot chocolate on an empty stomach. It was exhilarating to know that Sutton was curious enough to want to try finding poetry herself. Her interest somehow legitimated the act. That meant more than she could possibly know.

"I wouldn't mind at all. Would you like a piece of paper?"

"Please."

Unfortunately, tearing a piece out of her notebook meant she had to let go of Sutton's hand. "I don't have an extra pen, though."

"I have one." Sutton patted her small purse as they entered the mouth of the hallway.

"I usually sit on one of these," Jane said, gesturing to the benches on both sides.

"Why don't you pick whichever one you want, and I'll sit opposite? That way we won't be hearing the same things."

Jane wanted to protest that Sutton's idea also meant they wouldn't be sitting next to each other, but she could hardly push her luck at this point. "Sounds good. I'll check in with you in a little while. Though if you want to leave at any—"

"I'm a free woman. Yes, I know." Sutton shot her a bemused smile and rested her hand light on Jane's forearm. "I think this will be fun. Relax, okay? Just do what you usually do. Forget all about me."

"Not likely," Jane muttered as Sutton turned away to find a seat on one of the benches along the left side of the corridor.

Mirroring Sutton's position, Jane pulled out her pen and opened to a fresh page. After writing down the date and location, she exhaled slowly, trying to empty her racing mind. Immediately, her attention strayed to Sutton, bent industriously over her paper, tucking her hair behind both ears with a practiced motion. Silently berating herself, Jane closed her eyes and took a few more deep breaths. Without her visual sense engaged, the sounds of the busy hallway became more distinct. As she concentrated harder, the hum of human voices began to resolve into individual words and phrases, each spoken in an intonation as unique as a fingerprint.

"Oh my god, shut up! Are you serious?"

"C'est bien, ça."

"If there's anyone who deserves to be taken care of on her birthday, it's her."

"This anger you have is not about the refrigerator. It's about everything else. It's about our life."

Jane's eyes snapped open and she gripped the pen tightly as she began to scribble down any line that leapt out at her from the cacophony. Some were instant gems. Others might seem banal at first glance, but proved essential in combination with other phrases.

"She was the one calling the shots on the meeting."

"A genuinely weird-looking person."

"He stopped answering my phone calls."

Years ago, when she had first begun to gather lines, Jane had paid too much attention to the people speaking the words. By now, she was disciplined enough not to look up from her notebook. If she did, she would risk being immediately sidetracked by the diversity of the crowd. That elusive, single-minded focus would dissolve, and instead, she would begin conjuring up stories about the people who passed her by. People-watching was useful on those rare occasions when she composed original poetry, but otherwise it was a distraction.

"They have shrimp spring roll."

"Well, I can measure it."

"I don't wanna go nowhere that I can't breathe naturally!"

When her hand began to ache from so much sustained scribbling, Jane was tempted to see how Sutton was faring. Gritting her teeth, she resisted the urge and closed her eyes again, trying to force her consciousness back into that tantalizing state of suspension in which the lines trickled through unfiltered.

"It's so rude."

"What did the other broker show her?"

But as the minutes passed, it became harder and harder to concentrate. When the first tendrils of a headache began to curl along the back of her scalp, Jane gave up. Rolling her neck in slow circles, she tried to ease the ache in her shoulders. And then, finally, she allowed herself to look over at Sutton.

She was staring off into the distance, eyes slightly narrowed, pen poised above her paper. Suddenly, her hand fell to the page like a hawk plummeting fiercely to the earth in search of prey. After writing furiously for a few seconds, she stopped as quickly as she had begun. Somehow, she must have felt Jane's gaze, because in the next moment she looked up.

Jane stood and watched the crimson spread across Sutton's cheeks as she waited for a break in the foot traffic. Not for the first time, she felt grateful that Sutton couldn't seem to hide that particular sign of her attraction. Even when she was in one of her distant or reticent moods, her blushes always gave her away.

After darting through the crowd, Jane sat next to her, not quite daring to let their thighs touch. "How's it going?'

Sutton smiled. "I think I have a few good ones."

"Yeah? Are you enjoying it?"

"I am." Sutton looked thoughtful. "I've never stopped to listen before. It's fascinating. And there's a certain meditative quality to it—similar to when I do yoga."

Jane was suddenly overwhelmed by the image of Sutton in a

matching set of skin-hugging tank top and pants, subtle muscles guiding her lithe body through a complex series of yoga poses. Swallowing hard, she clutched at her pen and notebook and tried not to betray her distraction.

"So, a few good ones, you said? Like what? I mean, if you don't mind sharing."

Sutton cleared her throat. "'I kind of feel like myself now.' I enjoyed that one a lot."

"Sounds like someone in the middle of an identity crisis, doesn't it? What else?"

"'They treat you like you don't matter.'"

"Wow. Another good one." Jane was itching to write these down herself. Would Sutton mind? "Anything else?"

"This one was my favorite: 'I'm not dating your clothes. I'm dating you.'"

Jane laughed. "Perfect!" She dared to lightly touch Sutton's knee. "You're really good at this."

She handed over the paper. "They're all yours."

"Are you sure you don't want to give it a try? Assembling your own poem, I mean?"

"Oh, no. I'm not a very good writer at all, and certainly not a creative one. I need all my writing mojo for my next article."

Jane scanned the other lines on Sutton's list and shook her head in admiration. "These are great. Thank you."

"I'm glad I could help. I'd like to do it again sometime."

Again. Twice today, Sutton had made reference to the future. Once might have been a fluke, but twice? Jane was starting to believe she really meant it. The thought made her happy—probably happier than it should have, given the facts. Sutton's life was hardly stable, after all. Within just a few short weeks, she would learn where she had matched, and whether any of her fellowship applications had come to fruition. She might find herself anywhere in the world, come summer. Logically, Jane knew, this was a terrible time to begin any sort of relationship. But the dull, monotone voice of reason held no persuasive power whatsoever.

As though suddenly realizing what she had said, Sutton changed the subject. "Have you ever had your poetry published?"

"One. In *The Iowa Review*, last year." Jane felt a little silly tooting her own horn, but on the other hand, she wanted Doctor Sutton to know she really did have some talent. "It won an award."

"That's great! May I read it?"

A rush of self-consciousness set Jane's stomach churning. "If you really want to."

Sutton leaned closer, and Jane had to clench her free hand to stop herself from reaching out to smooth away the frown lines on her brow. "Not if it will make you uncomfortable."

"I've always had trouble showing my work to people." Jane shrugged and looked away, trying to downplay her anxiety even as her nausea grew worse. "It's weird. I don't know why. But I would never have submitted my poem anywhere if it hadn't been a course requirement in college."

"I'm sure it's not easy to show people something that's so deeply personal." For a moment, she rested her palm atop Jane's. "No pressure, okay?"

"Thanks." Jane was trying to figure out how to segue to a different topic, when Sutton did it for her.

"So, where did you go to college?"

"Hunter."

"My family lives a few blocks north of there," Sutton said. "You know, we've probably passed each other in the street."

"Oh, I don't think so. I would've remembered you."

There was that blush again. Jane loved it more every time. Visibly trying to compose herself, Sutton rolled her eyes. "Right. What was your major? And when did you graduate? I just realized I don't even know how old you are."

In a heartbeat, Jane's good mood vanished. As her head began to throb in earnest, she lowered her gaze to the ground. Dimly, she noticed a discarded piece of gum less than an inch from her right foot. She'd dodged that sticky situation, but there was no escaping this one.

"I'm twenty-three. And I didn't."

"Didn't?" Sutton sounded confused. Jane didn't dare look.

"I didn't graduate. I mean, I haven't. Yet. My major is creative writing," she added belatedly, cringing as she awaited Sutton's reaction. Spoken aloud, the words sounded worse than they had in her head. And really, what had she been thinking? A college dropout, trying to kindle a romance with someone who had earned the title of doctor, twice over?

And then she felt the warm pressure of Sutton's hand between her shoulder blades. "Jane." When she didn't respond, the hand began to rub in soft circles. "What's wrong?"

"What's wrong?" Jane raised her head and stared at Sutton, not bothering to hide her surprise. "I just told you I didn't finish college."

"You did. And I was about to ask why you decided not to, when your entire body went tight as a drum."

Jane tried not to betray her surprise. She could hardly confess that she'd expected Sutton to instantly judge her. Blinking quickly, she tried to pull her wits together. "All creative writing majors at Hunter have to do a senior thesis. I was excited to do mine, and I had a great advisor—my favorite teacher of all time."

"What was she like? Or he?"

"He. Anders." Thinking of him dredged up the familiar grief, but it was tempered by the opportunity to share his legacy with Sutton. "He was this self-professed hippie who had dodged the draft by fleeing to Canada. He ended up traveling the world, teaching English and writing short stories. Over time, his fiction was well received, and he ended up settling in New York and taking the job at Hunter. Anders insisted we call him by his first name and refused to answer to anything else."

"I can see how much you admire him," Sutton said. For a moment, she looked to be on the verge of saying something else before she closed her mouth. Jane could tell she wanted to press for more details but was being patient for her sake.

"Just after my junior year ended, Anders was diagnosed with pancreatic cancer. He was gone by August." She spoke the words quickly, hoping Sutton wouldn't hear the snarl of tears in the back of her throat. But whatever Sutton had heard must have made an impact, because she gently threaded their fingers together again.

"I'm so sorry."

Jane nodded. "Me, too. It was such a shock to everyone, and just . . . so unfair." Willing herself to hold it together, she met Sutton's eyes. They were light, light blue, and shining in sympathy. "He was one of the good guys. He should have been around for another two decades at least."

Sutton squeezed her hand. "Fuck cancer."

Jane blinked in surprise at the quiet yet vehement words. The vulgarity sounded strange coming from Sutton's mouth, but all it took was one look at her face to see that she meant it.

"Well said."

"Going back for your senior year must have been difficult."

"It was. The worst part was the person they'd hired to replace Anders, Professor Ryan. He had an MFA in poetry and a few awards under his belt, and he'd just published a translation of—" Realizing she was rambling, Jane cut herself off. "The point is, he was totally full of himself. He was also young, and apparently all the straight girls found him attractive." She shook her head. "We got along about as well as oil and water. When I started describing my project to him, he went off on a diatribe about how found poetry wasn't real poetry and that I needed to be original. I felt totally paralyzed. When my first deadline came, I had nothing to turn in."

"I'm sorry he was cruel to you." Sutton gently stroked her fingers as she spoke, and Jane found herself starting to believe that reliving the most stressful time of her life in vivid detail might be entirely worth it, so long as Sutton never stopped touching her.

"He wasn't cruel, exactly. Or at least, I don't think he was trying to be. He was just totally insensitive. And I've always had trouble showing my work to other people, so when I knew I'd have a hostile audience, I just . . . couldn't. At first, I stopped writing altogether. By the spring, I was composing poems again, but I couldn't force myself to give them to him."

Jane shrugged, shooting Sutton a sidelong glance in an attempt to gauge her reaction. Would Sutton think her a coward? "So that's why I haven't finished my degree. All of my coursework is done. It's just my thesis that's left. Aunt Jenny and Uncle John have been nice enough to give me a place to live and a job while I figure things out."

Sutton didn't say anything right away, but the steady rhythm of her fingers along the backs of Jane's hands never faltered. Comforted by the soothing touch, Jane felt her tension begin to ebb away. The dull ache of fatigue moved in behind it like a cold front after a thunderstorm.

"I'm sorry you had to go through that," Sutton said quietly. "I can see it's a difficult time to talk about. Thank you for trusting me."

"Thanks for listening." Jane blinked her gritty eyes, fearing she had tested Sutton's patience. "And also, thanks to you, I think I have enough lines to finish the poem."

"I'm glad I could help. What will you do once it's done?"

"There's a fellowship in Anders' name that I'm planning to apply for, and I want to include this poem." Her self-consciousness returned in a rush. "We'll see. It'll be stiff competition."

"I'm tempted to tell you that you're a shoo-in, but I hate when people tell me that about matching." She punctuated her words with a light squeeze of Jane's hand. "Good luck."

"Thanks."

"I should make my way to my parents' house." When Sutton pulled away, Jane felt as though the world had suddenly grown dimmer. "We have a standing tradition of Sunday evening family supper."

"That sounds nice."

"It would be nicer if my father didn't usually insist on inviting one of his friends or political allies."

Jane fell into step with Sutton as she moved back toward the concourse. "Awkward conversation, I take it?"

"Not for them," Sutton said dryly. "By now, I've refined my coping mechanism. Every time I feel the urge to comment, I take a sip of wine."

"Is it good wine, at least?"

"Oh, yes, of course. Very expensive."

Sutton's frustration with her parents was clear, and Jane felt a pang of homesickness for her own family. Perhaps she would call them once she returned home. Sure, they'd had minor disagreements, but nothing like the major ideological differences to which Sutton had alluded.

"How are you getting home?"

"I think I'll walk. I don't feel like getting back into the subway." Sutton slipped on her gloves in preparation for the chill.

"Do you mind if I walk with you?" Jane held her breath, hoping Sutton would say yes. She was being greedy, but she wanted just a few more minutes.

"I'd like that."

Her shy smile sent a surge of warmth into Jane's chest and banished the lingering ache there. She jumped to hold the door for Sutton and took the outside position on the sidewalk as they turned uptown. The first few blocks passed quietly as she racked her brains for a lighter conversation topic.

"So," she said, suddenly remembering one of their exchanges during the parade. "Have you had a chance to think about my question?"

"Your question?"

"You know—which part of the brain is your favorite?"

Sutton laughed. "That's right. And this time, I have an answer: the dorsolateral prefrontal cortex."

"Gesundheit."

"Very funny. You can call it the DLPFC for short."

"I'm not sure that's much better," Jane said. "Why is it your favorite?"

"It's one of the most important areas of the prefrontal cortex, which is the most highly evolved part of our brains. It's connected to every other brain area, and it's instrumental in helping us make choices and decisions."

Jane thought about that for a while, tucking her chin into her hoodie as a particularly cold gust of wind sliced across her path. "So . . . it's the site of free will?"

"Some people think so." Sutton paused at a crosswalk and turned east when the light changed.

"Do you?"

"I suppose I do, though some neuroscientists have actually questioned the existence of the will."

"Why is that?"

As they continued uptown, Jane was treated to a lecture on the intersection of philosophy and neuroscience. Enjoying the chance to see Sutton in "doctor mode," Jane listened raptly as she explained how several recent experiments suggested that some human actions began in the unconscious rather than the conscious mind. Jane was tempted to ask how attraction fit into the picture, but decided that might be a bridge too far.

They turned east again, this time onto a cross street that practically screamed "upper crust." Large trees rose from tidy beds set into the sidewalk, their barren branches reaching for the slate-gray sky as though pleading for the advent of warm weather. Jane could picture how beautiful this block would be only a few months from now, their large leaves spreading out to shade passersby and fill the urban air with the green scent of growing things. Every building they passed was a well-kept residential townhouse, and Sutton slowed to a halt in front of the most impressive one yet. A curving stone stoop led up to a narrow porch extending the length of its cheery, red-brick façade. The black door was garnished with an elaborate golden knocker, and matching gold trim surrounded the bay windows that jutted out from the second floor.

"This is me," Sutton said. When she looked up through those long, gold-tipped eyelashes, Jane shoved her hands into her pockets to keep herself from reaching out. "I had a great time today. Thank you."

For one terrifying moment, Jane had no idea how to respond. She didn't want to come on too strong, but on the other hand, she wanted Sutton to know how much their time together had meant to her.

"Well . . . thanks for making the choice to come with me." She tried out a grin. "Or should I thank your DLPFC?"

When Sutton laughed, Jane didn't feel so bad about sounding like a huge dork. And then Sutton suddenly rested one hand on Jane's shoulder, raised herself up on her toes, and brushed her lips across Jane's cheek. The fleeting contact felt as though the ends of a live wire had skimmed her face. Every nerve stood at attention as the heat of Sutton's mouth lingered on her chilled skin.

"I'll see you." The promise in her words was almost as sweet as the kiss.

Jane managed to raise one hand in a wave before Sutton turned and jogged up the stairs. Blinking slowly, her every cell incredulous, she watched as Sutton disappeared behind the door.

"What on earth was that?" she murmured, turning her fingers to brush against the spot that still burned despite the cold. As the wind picked up again, rattling the trees, the jumble of sensations resolved into something she hadn't felt since first glimpsing the Goddess in Glasses all those months ago.

Hope.

SUTTON WANTED TO LOOK back. She wanted one more glimpse of Jane's dazed, happy expression. The knowledge that she had been the one to put it there was addicting. She wanted to see it just one more time.

Beneath the welcome confidence she'd found in Jane's reaction, a small, panicking voice was shrilly insisting that this was all a terrible mistake. Sutton tuned it out. That kiss had been instinctive—the product of a perfect storm of attraction, sympathy, and her innate desire to heal anyone in pain. She may not have planned it, but she'd be damned if she was going to regret it.

But now, as she stood on the doorstep of her parents' home, she needed to regain her composure. Resolutely, she forced herself not to turn around. It took two tries before she managed to slip her key into the lock, but when it clicked open, she pushed inside without a backward glance.

"Dad? Mom? I'm here." She turned and stopped in her tracks at the sight of her father standing before one of the front windows. By the stiff set of his shoulders and the expression on his face—as though he had sipped sour milk—she knew that he had witnessed her moment with Jane.

She suddenly felt as though she were ten years younger, and he had just caught her doing something illicit. Except she had never done anything forbidden as a teenager, and she certainly wasn't doing anything wrong now. As he turned to face her, she squared her shoulders and reminded herself that she had more advanced degrees than he did.

"Sutton."

"Hi, Dad."

He cocked his head and looked at her the way he looked at his patients—like there was something inside her he wanted to remove. "I wasn't aware that you were seeing someone."

"It's fairly new," Sutton said matter-of-factly as she made her way down the foyer. She wasn't about to confide her uncertainty in him. He would only try to use it against her. "Her name is Jane," she said as she passed him, knowing he wouldn't ask.

"Rather cruel to her, isn't it?" He followed her into the kitchen.

Sutton poured herself a glass of water and focused on keeping her cool. "What do you mean?"

"You're about to begin a surgical residency at Columbia. You'll never leave the hospital."

"She's aware of my situa—" Sutton cut herself off as her father's words finally registered. Her heartbeat thundered in her ears and she grasped the edge of the counter with one hand. "Am I to take that to mean you've heard something?"

"I had lunch with Neal today. He confirmed it. Off the record, of course."

Neal Bowers was the Chief of Surgery at Columbia University Medical Center, and one of her father's close friends. Ultimately, he was the one responsible for approving all new resident hires. Which, apparently, included her.

"He and his wife will be joining us for dinner tonight," her father continued. "So if you have any questions, I'm sure he will be happy to answer them."

"I . . ." Sutton carefully set her glass back on the counter. She had always imagined that learning her match would be a watershed moment—the ultimate relief after so much time spent building the best possible application. Residency was the true beginning of one's career, and such a prestigious match was not only a feather in her cap, but would also help her down the line.

So why, instead of triumph, did she feel a vague sense of unease? Analysis had always been her best defense mechanism, and she turned to it now, picking apart the strands of her discomfort. Once the news broke on Match Day, some of her peers would be genuinely happy for her. The rest would call her entitled and impute her match to nepotism. Most of the time, she paid no attention to the jealous whispers. But no matter how hard she tried, she couldn't shake her insecurity. Was she riding her father's coattails, or her own? She would never know. And that was part of what made her research so appealing—the certain knowledge that she had crafted every hypothesis, performed every experiment, and crunched every piece of data herself.

"Thank you for letting me know," she said finally, knowing it was a lame response. But her father didn't even seem to notice. He moved across the kitchen in long strides and gave her a brisk hug.

"We're proud of you for this accomplishment, Sutton. You should go see your mother. She's in the sitting room."

"All right."

Sutton took the stairs up to the second floor slowly. The entire world felt surreal—as though she were looking at it through a very fine mist. She had matched. The wait was over. And yet she couldn't tell anyone for another ten days. As the secret pressed in on her mind, claustrophobia constricted her chest.

And then she flashed to Jane's face and felt a surge of relief. True. She could tell Jane. Jane would understand the complexity of the situation, and would celebrate her success while also understanding how complicated the future might become. But before she could share the news, Sutton had to get through a tête-à-tête with her mother and a dinner with her prospective future supervisor.

The sitting room was one of her favorites in the townhouse. Its canary-yellow walls always improved her mood, and its scent—a mixture of pine and books—never failed to comfort her. As she took a deep breath, she turned to face Priscilla St. James, who was sitting in a Louis XIV armchair with her back to one of the inset bookshelves. Dressed immaculately in a navy skirt suit, pearls bedecking her cream-colored blouse, she fulfilled the stereotype of high society wife in every way but one.

"Hello, Sutton." With a slowness unbefitting her age, her mother rose from the chair, leaning heavily on both armrests as she stood. Sutton met her near the coffee table, and as she was pulled into her familiar embrace, she inhaled the scent of Chanel No. 5.

"Hello, Mom. How are you feeling?"

"Oh, a little tired today."

That, Sutton had learned, was code-speak for "not very well, but not awful enough for me to complain about it." She frowned and stepped back, taking in her mother's pallor and the smudges beneath her eyes. It didn't look as though she had been resting well. Mentally, Sutton worked backward. If she were having a flare-up, it had come sooner than usual. Was her condition changing?

"Your father and I are so proud of you," she was saying as she returned to the chair. "We always knew you would achieve greatness."

In that moment, Sutton wanted so badly to unburden herself to her mother—to tell her about all her professional uncertainties, her lingering attraction to Jane, her fears about the future. But she couldn't. Her mother didn't want her to be human. She wanted to have raised a success story.

"Thank you, Mom," she said quietly.

Thankfully, the sound of the front door chime obviated the need to find a new conversation topic. "That will be Neal and Agatha," she said.

"I'll show them up here." Sutton was glad of the distraction. "And see whether Dad needs any help."

"Good, thank you." She smiled indulgently.

As Sutton returned to the first floor, she heard her father's jovial laugh mingling with Neal's deeper baritone. Breathing in deeply, she closed her eyes and tried to prepare herself for what was to come. The trick to making it through these evenings, she had learned, was to stay minimally engaged in the conversation while allowing the rest of her mind to wander. And she knew exactly what topic it would drift to tonight.

Her lips tingled as she once again remembered the sensation of Jane's smooth, cool skin beneath them. Jane's cheek had been so soft. Would her mouth be even softer? If they shared a real kiss, who would lead and who would follow? Or would they fit together so well that those questions would be moot? Sutton's skin prickled at the thought, even as logic reminded her of the folly of pursuing anything other than the most casual relationship. But she and Jane hadn't crossed a line yet. She'd been honest about the chaos that was her future. As long as Jane accepted the facts, why shouldn't they make the most of what time she had left before life once again became frenetic?

While she had to live in this limbo, why shouldn't she try to enjoy it?

Chapter Eight

J ANE COULDN'T STOP SMILING, and people were starting to notice. Minetta had been nagging her incessantly since the previous night. Aunt Jenny had commented on her good mood during the morning meal. One of Jane's customers had wondered what she'd eaten for breakfast and whether there were any leftovers, while another had incredulously asked how she could be in such high spirits on a Monday.

She didn't care that people could tell she was happy, but she wasn't about to share any details. They were hers to cherish and replay, over and over, in the theater of her mind: the warmth of Sutton's fingers, the softness of her lips, the genuine compassion in her eyes.

And then there was the text Sutton had sent her last night: *Thanks again for brunch, and for letting me see you work. The rest of my day was dull by comparison.*

Of course, Sutton would be the sort of person who texted in full sentences. Jane had agonized for almost half an hour over her reply. "Thanks for taking a chance on me" sounded pathetic. "Glad you enjoyed it" sounded stilted. "Let's do it again sometime" was nothing but a hackneyed line.

Finally, after giving herself a headache, she decided that simple was best: *I had a great time, thanks to you. Good night.* ☺

She hadn't received a reply, but neither had she expected one. At least they were finally on texting terms. That had been a long time coming. Sutton clearly wasn't someone who rushed into a relationship. She needed time and space, and even though Jane didn't particularly want to give her either of those things, she knew she had to suck it up and find some patience. But it wasn't easy, especially in light of the ticking clock in the background. Sutton had been entirely up front about all the uncertainties in her life. Whatever their relationship was becoming, she clearly wanted it to remain casual.

"So don't get too attached," Jane told her reflection sternly, and returned her attention back to the open notebook in front of her.

As the weak winter sunlight slowly began to dim, she alternated between frenetic bursts of productivity and staring out the window, daydreaming. Each time she relived the sensation of Sutton's lips against her cheek, another burst of ideas took her brain by storm.

In matters of the heart, never lose hope.

Joy will catch you unawares.

When your heart is at stake, persist gently.

One kiss will transform your life.

Raising her head, she rolled her neck to ease the tension in her shoulders. That last one might be a bit hyperbolic, but that didn't mean it wasn't true. It hadn't even been a "real" kiss, but she could feel its echo in every cell of her body. Neither of her college girlfriends had ever affected her this strongly, even in more intimate moments. How was that possible?

At the buzz of her phone, all Jane's tension returned. Holding her breath, she looked over at the display. Text from Sutton St. James. The world narrowed until the screen was all she could see.

Are you free? I'll be in Noodle Treasure for the next few hours.

Sutton was across the street. Sutton wanted to see her. As the realization set in, Jane leapt to her feet, only to be swamped by a wave of lightheadedness that forced her to sit back down. Taking a deep breath, she massaged her temples. These adrenaline rushes were going to kill her.

"Casual," she reminded herself. "You have to stay casual." Clutching her phone, she typed out a quick response: *I could use a break. See you soon.*

This time, she made her way downstairs at a more dignified pace. Combing her fingers through her hair, she double-checked the collar on her rugby shirt and tested her breath against the back of her hand before venturing outside. Mei greeted her in Chinese as she entered the restaurant and gave her an indulgent look when she turned toward Sutton. Jane had a split second in which to feel bemusement at Mei's clear approval of her crush before she was once again face-to-face with the woman who had been haunting her waking dreams for the past twenty-four hours. Sutton's hair was down today, and she was dressed in earth tones—olive slacks and a dark brown cardigan over a cream-colored scoop-neck top. Jane wanted nothing more than to lean down and trail kisses along the sculpted curve of her collarbone.

"You look beautiful." Only when she heard the words did she realize she'd spoken aloud. Cursing her own idiocy, she hunched her shoulders. "I mean . . . hi."

"Hi." The corners of Sutton's mouth twitched. Even her monosyllable held a note of laughter. "And thank you."

"How are you?" Jane asked as she took the seat next to her.

"Fine. Enjoying a late lunch." She gestured to a half-eaten plate of fried noodles with shrimp and mushrooms.

Next to her mug, Jane noticed the shards of a broken fortune cookie. "Is your future looking bright?"

When Sutton reached into her pocket and withdrew the small piece of paper, Jane felt her heart flip-flop. Sutton was saving her fortunes? That was another good sign, right?

"'Don't let a chance at love slip away.'" She arched one eyebrow. "I've been getting a lot of mushy fortunes, recently. Whoever writes these is a real romantic."

Jane nodded gravely. "That does seem suspicious. Would you like to lodge a formal complaint with the president of the company, also known as my uncle? I can introduce you to him right now."

"Oh, I don't think that will be necessary." She nudged Jane's shoulder with her own. "I wasn't criticizing—only observing."

"He'll be relieved to hear that." Jane grinned, enjoying their easy flirtation and the warmth where their bodies touched. "So, how did everything go last night?"

Sutton stiffened, breaking their contact, and Jane immediately regretted the question. But before she could issue some sort of aimless apology, Sutton spoke.

"My father had some news for me. He was told by the Chief of Surgery at Columbia University Medical Center that I've matched there. For neurosurgery."

Jane rested her arm on the counter and searched Sutton's face for signs of her reaction. Columbia was a very prestigious match indeed, and if Sutton accepted it, she would be able to remain in the city with her family. *And me.* But if the frown lines around her mouth and eyes, were any indication, this news had only served to make her more anxious. Not less.

"Congratulations." Jane made her voice soft and hopefully soothing. "How do you feel about it?"

"On the one hand, I'm relieved. It's a strong match. And I'd be near my parents, so if my mother gets worse . . ." she trailed off. "On the other hand, the fact that the chief is one of my father's best friends will make the match doubly difficult to turn down if I decide to take a different route. He was the guest invited to dinner last night, and I couldn't stop thinking about how ashamed my father would be if I go elsewhere."

Jane dared to cover Sutton's left hand with her own. She wanted to tell Sutton that it didn't matter what all these overbearing patriarchal figures in her life wanted her to do. All that mattered was what would make her happy. But she knew that would be a mistake. Sutton didn't need anyone else to give her advice. She needed someone who would actually listen.

"Do you think you'd be happy at Columbia?"

"In certain ways, probably. I'd receive excellent training and op-portunities. It's the kind of competitive environment I've always thrived in."

Jane wondered if Sutton could hear herself. She hadn't said a thing that had to do with real happiness. "Okay, those are some of the pros. What are the cons?"

Sutton idly poked at her noodles with her fork as she considered the question. "For one thing, I don't know if I'm passionate enough about becoming a surgeon. There are times when it's thrilling, and I know I'd be good at it, but I don't think I'm in love with surgery the way my father is."

"Okay." Jane reminded herself to stay neutral. "Anything else?"

"I might be able to do some research there, but it certainly wouldn't be my focus. And I think I'd miss it."

"So, there are good arguments on either side. Definitely not an easy decision." She squeezed Sutton's hand. "When the time comes, maybe it will be best to trust your instincts."

The door opened, and a tendril of chill air swirled across the back of Jane's neck. "Aww," said a familiar voice. "Isn't that pre-cious."

Sutton looked over Jane's shoulder. "Hi, Min."

"Hi. Don't let me interrupt you."

"Too late," Jane said through gritted teeth.

Min raised her hands in the air. "Sorry. The words just flew out."

"Don't you have homework to do?" Jane fixed Min with her best intimidating glare.

"Whatever."

Jane let out a deep breath as Min turned away. "Too smart for her own good, that one."

"She's formidable."

"That she is. Anyway. Where were we?"

"You were just advising me to trust my instincts."

Jane quickly shook her head. "I'm not in the business of advice.

You'll have to get your chart done by Sue if that's what you're looking for."

"Oh!" In a flash, Min was back, one hand braced against each of their chairs. "Let's all go see her right now."

Jane closed her eyes briefly, trying to keep her cool. Min really was the worst matchmaker ever. How was she going to manage a serious talk with Sutton if her so-called wingman always kept cutting in?

"Minetta, you are really not helping. Homework?"

"This is homework. My school project, remember? I need to visit Sue's shop anyway."

"Which you can do on your own ti—"

Sutton laid her hand on Jane's wrist, the warmth of her touch permeating through the fabric. "It's okay. Let's all go together."

Jane searched her eyes. "Are you sure?"

"Positive."

As Sutton stood, Jane heard someone clear his throat just behind them. "Excuse me," came a masculine voice. "Did I hear you discussing Sue's shop?" Jane turned to find Giancarlo towering over Min. Dressed in black slacks and a snowy white chef's shirt, he looked the part of a restaurant owner in Little Italy. His thin mustache even had a slight twirl at the edges today.

"Hello, Giancarlo." When Sutton leaned in for one of those European double cheek-kisses, Jane felt a twinge of jealousy. Suddenly, Sutton was exchanging cheek-kisses with everyone. Had she read too much into their moment yesterday? "Did I miss seeing you come in?"

"You looked deep in thought. I didn't want to disturb you."

Sutton waved away his concern. "Please don't worry. How are you?"

"I'm well, thank you. And I apologize for interrupting your conversation, but I was trying to find Sue's shop a few days ago and couldn't. Would you mind giving me directions?"

Jane had just reached for her notebook with the intent to produce a map, when Min spoke up. "You should just come with us. We're going now."

Jane gripped the edge of the countertop tightly, suppressing the sudden urge to bang her head against it. All she wanted was to be alone with Sutton again—or as alone as they could be in a city of nine million people. Min tagging along was one thing, but playing tour guide with Giancarlo wouldn't exactly be conducive to romance.

Sutton, she felt sure, had no such uncharitable thoughts. While talking with Giancarlo, she gave him her full attention, just as she did for everyone else. Sutton's gaze was a spotlight and her smile was its warmth. Jane was willing to bet that she brought that kind of charisma to her bedside manner, too. How often were brilliant people also so empathetic? No wonder Columbia was falling all over itself to get her.

"Oh no, that's fine—I wouldn't want to interfere," Giancarlo was saying to Min.

"You won't." Jane put on a smile for Sutton's sake. "Please walk with us, if you'd like."

"Thank you." He stood and put on his coat, then reached for the fortune cookie on his plate. "I almost forgot this."

Jane turned toward the door, feeling the familiar rush of self-consciousness at the sounds of Giancarlo unwrapping the cookie. Mentally, she crossed her fingers that this would be one of her better offerings.

"What did you get?" Sutton asked as they emerged into the late afternoon shadows.

"'Be ready to seize your opportunity.'" He nodded thoughtfully. "In that case, I'll seize this opportunity to invite you to my restaurant for Easter Sunday dinner. It will be the Italian equivalent of the New Year's festival."

"Will there be cannolis?" asked Min.

"Handmade by my sister," Giancarlo announced proudly.

"I'm in."

"Sounds great," Jane said. "When does Easter fall this year?"

"It's the last Sunday of this month." Giancarlo looked hopefully at Sutton. "And you, Sutton?"

"I wish I could." Sutton looked genuinely disappointed. "But Easter is an important day for my family. I'll be celebrating with them."

"Perfectly understandable. But you will be missed."

Jane wanted to ask Sutton whether her family was religious, but that seemed like too personal a question for this group. Instead, she kept her mouth shut as she guided them around a corner and then pointed to the colorful awning of Red Door Apothecary. "Here we are."

She held the door while the others filed inside. The shop was almost entirely empty, and Sue was helping the only customers—an elderly couple who seemed to be in the market for some kind of herbal remedy. She glanced up and waved, but when she noticed Giancarlo she became visibly flustered, one hand going immediately to her hair.

"This place is amazing!" He was looking around the store in undisguised wonder.

"It smells like . . . like earth." Sutton's eyes were closed as she sampled the air, and Jane was suddenly filled with desire at the sensuality of her expression. "Rich. Loamy."

Tearing her gaze away, Jane gestured toward the rows of shelves. "All the herbs are organized alphabetically. And if you have any questions, I know a little about what some of them are good for. But I'm sure Sue will want to give you the full tour when she's done."

Giancarlo meandered off while Min began snapping photos with her phone. Jane lingered near the front, watching Sutton inspect some of the wares. Would Sue's shop seem silly to her? As she looked over the jars, drawers, and bins filled with assorted herbs and roots,

Jane felt an odd mix of protectiveness and shame. Being here with Sutton made her feel even more *hapa* than usual.

At that moment, Sutton looked over. "Do you know what this root is for?"

Jane walked to her side, standing close enough so that their shoulders brushed. When she glanced down at the label on the bin, she was relieved to see it was one of the plants she'd actually heard of. "Astragalus. It's supposed to help your immune system—or at least, that's what my mother always said."

Sutton regarded her curiously. "How does she use it?"

"It's a pretty common ingredient in the teas she makes." Jane felt her nose wrinkle at the memories of some of her mother's particularly noxious concoctions. "Some of them are preventative, but others are for specific ailments, like sore throats or indigestion."

"Do they work?"

"My father doesn't think so. He refuses to drink them. Big fan of NyQuil." For the most part, her parents' relationship was peaceful, but the merits of traditional Chinese medicine was an ongoing subject of debate.

"What about you?"

"I was always caught in the middle." Jane grimaced. "Usually that involved being double-dosed. But I was also a pretty healthy kid, so maybe all those teas actually were beneficial."

Sutton stared down along the line of shelves. "I'm almost completely ignorant about all of this." She seemed discomfited by her lack of knowledge. "There was a holistic medicine class offered during my second year, but I didn't have time to take it."

"If you ever want to learn more, I'm sure Sue would be happy to teach you." Jane looked over to see Sue handing a small bag to her customers. "Starting now, in fact."

"How nice of you all to stop by," Sue called to them after bidding her customers farewell. She bustled out from behind the counter, hands outspread.

"I wanted to pay you a visit last week," Giancarlo said, "but I wasn't able to find this charming place until I had the proper guides."

"And we're here because Sutton would like her chart done," Jane said.

"Though it's not urgent," Sutton said quickly, "if you're too busy."

"Nonsense." Sue smiled and beckoned them over to the sitting area in the far corner of the room. Every few seconds, her gaze went to Giancarlo, who seemed lost in thought as he stood contemplating a bin of dried mushrooms. Jane had to confront the evidence: Min really did know what she was talking about. Though if she ever admitted as much, she'd never hear the end of it.

"Giancarlo," she said, hoping she wouldn't have to eat her dire prediction about matchmaking, "were you interested in getting yours done as well?"

"Oh, yes, please." He turned to join them. "If that's all right."

"Of course, of course." Sue withdrew two forms from a drawer. "The first thing I'll need from each of you is basic information about your birth—year, date, and specific time. Once you fill these out, we'll be able to get started."

Sutton perched on the couch and began to write. Her body was stiff, and Jane wondered where the tension came from. Was it because she had so much on her mind? Or because she was nervous about her chart? On a hunch, she decided to make herself scarce.

"Sue, while we're here I'm just going to check your e-mail, okay? Maybe get a head start on Wednesday's work."

"That's fine," Sue said absently as she continued to gather supplies.

Jane glanced over at Sutton again in enough time to watch her slender fingers tuck a strand of hair behind one ear. The gesture was unexpectedly graceful, and Jane felt her mouth go dry as her traitorous brain imagined those fingers tracing patterns against her skin. Instinctively, she took a step backward. These flashes of desire were only becoming more frequent and intense. If Sutton picked up on how much Jane wanted her, she'd probably feel uncomfortable.

Turning decisively, Jane walked toward the back of the store. As much as she wanted to look over her shoulder, she kept her eyes facing forward. The last thing she wanted was to do anything that might extinguish the fragile spark that had been kindled between them.

AFTER WATCHING JANE LEAVE, Sutton answered the questions quickly and passed the form across the small table to Sue, who had just opened a large, hardcover book written entirely in Chinese. Sue took the paper with thanks and immediately began using it to fill out another, much more complicated-looking form that was covered in overlapping tables. While she waited, Sutton's gaze drifted up to the nearest bookshelf, which didn't have a single tome in English on it. Despite all of her knowledge and training, she felt completely out of her depth in this room. Had it been a mistake to come here?

Sue glanced up at her and smiled kindly. "Have you ever done this before?"

"Never."

"Using this information, I'll be able to tell you a few things about what you can expect in this new year, and what you should avoid."

"Okay." Sutton tried not to sound skeptical. This was part of Sue's trade, and she wanted to respect it even if she didn't believe in it.

"Next time you're here, you should bring the same birth information about anyone important to you. Family members, a significant other, a boss, a friend—it can be anyone. I'll then compare their chart to yours and shed some insight into that relationship."

Sutton nodded, unsure of what to say. Although the entire

concept sounded completely unbelievable, she almost wished she could give Sue all those details about her father right now. If there was any relationship in her life for which mystical guidance was needed, it was that one.

"So." Sue began flipping through the book. "First, the basics. You were born in the Year of the Dragon—the mightiest of all the signs. Dragons are ambitious, independent, and highly self-motivated. They are generally healthy, but sometimes they suffer from tension-related maladies, like headaches or back pain. Have you experienced anything like that, recently?"

"Yes, both." Sutton had to admit that Sue's description, while vague, was also accurate. And she had developed some nasty shoulder tension in the middle of working on her dissertation.

"The Dragon is a fire sign, but your specific year is governed by the element of earth," Sue continued. "This means that you tend to be more rational and grounded than other Dragons. You're also less likely to let your temper get out of control."

Sutton had to admit that, in this case, Sue's assessment was right on. It was all a coincidence, of course, but she did pride herself on being even-keeled, even when those around her were emotional.

Sue was now hunched over the book, glancing between the open page and Sutton's chart. "Your luckiest day of this month is actually today," she said.

"Buy a lotto ticket!" Min called from across the room.

"And this will be a prosperous year for you," Sue continued. "But the path to that prosperity is shrouded in mist."

"Mist?"

"It is uncertain." Sue glanced up. "You may have to make a difficult choice."

Sutton blinked in surprise at hearing Sue hit so close to the mark. "What kind of choice?"

"It's unclear. There seem to be many complicating factors— career, love, family . . ." Sue trailed off, frowning.

Relief settled over Sutton at the indeterminacy of the prediction. There was no strange magic here, not even coincidence. Only astrology as she'd always known it—so vague as to be applicable to anyone, in any situation.

"That's really all I can do for now," Sue said. "But please come back when you'd like to compare your chart with someone else's. That will be much more instructive."

"Thank you. This was fascinating." Sutton stood, hoping she had sounded genuine. "What do I owe you?"

"Not a thing." Before Sutton could protest, Sue focused in on Giancarlo. "Are you ready?"

"I am." He handed her his form and replaced Sutton on the couch.

"Wait, hang on," Min said, hurrying over. "Can I take a video of this? For the website?"

Not wanting to be anywhere near Min's phone when she put it in video mode, Sutton moved away. As she was about to continue perusing the shelves, Jane emerged from the back. Her wide smile was clearly unpremeditated, and Sutton felt herself return it. Jane was always so genuine. She was a breath of fresh air that Sutton hadn't even realized she craved—a welcome break from the labyrinthine politics of both home and work.

"How'd it go?"

"It was . . ." Sutton searched for the right word. "Intriguing."

"Oh?"

Sutton suppressed a smile. Jane was desperate with curiosity but valiantly trying to hide it. She glanced at her watch and made a snap decision. "There's a lecture this evening that I have to attend, and I want to stop by my apartment first. Walk with me?"

"Sure. Yes. Of course." Jane's fumbling answer made her even more endearing. "Just give me one second?"

When Sutton nodded, Jane spun toward the far corner. "Minetta! Did you create a Facebook page for the shop?"

Min glanced over her shoulder. "Yeah, and I blogged about it. Over two hundred likes in two days!"

"Impressive, but every single one of those generated an e-mail that got sent to the store's account. Change the notifications, will you?"

Min actually looked chagrined. "No problem. Are you leaving?"

"We are. Sue, see you later this week."

Sutton waved. "Take care, and thanks again."

As they emerged into the gathering dusk, Sutton zipped up her jacket. Wisps of pink and gold streaked across the western sky, while to the east, she could see one bright star above the shadowy finger of a skyscraper. When Jane fell into step beside her, Sutton reached out, then tucked their joined hands into the pocket of her coat.

"I know you're impervious to cold, but humor me."

"Gladly. Anytime." Jane flashed another broad, goofy smile that sent another rush of warmth through Sutton's chest. "So, what did you think? Did Sue tell you anything useful?"

"Well, she said that today was lucky for me, and that the coming year would be prosperous, but that that prosperity was 'misty.' So I suppose I should resist a shopping spree, just in case."

Jane laughed. "Are you sure? Because all we have to do is walk a few blocks north to find every boutique you could want."

"Don't tempt me." Sutton gently jostled Jane's shoulder with her own. "You know, what you do for Sue is very kind."

Jane seemed uncomfortable with the praise. "It doesn't take long, and her business has definitely picked up since the online storefront. I just don't want her shop to disappear. It's good for the neighborhood."

Sutton thought about that as they continued to walk north. Despite having lived in New York City all her life, she didn't feel one tenth as much a connection to her neighborhood as Jane obviously felt to Chinatown after having lived there only a few months. Was that simply because the Upper East Side didn't have as clear an identity? Or had she missed out on feeling a part of her community because she had always been too busy reaching for her own goals to live in the moment?

"This is me," she said as they drew abreast of her building. But when Jane started to pull away, Sutton realized she wasn't yet ready to see her go. "Come inside the atrium where it's warmer, at least."

Once they were inside the front door, Sutton didn't know what to say. She bent to check her mail, hoping to buy herself a few more seconds. Should she invite Jane up? A flash of heat arced down her spine at the thought of what might happen if they finally found themselves alone together. But would Jane take her invitation the wrong way? Should she initiate a "talk" about how at this point in her life, she was only interested in something casual? Or had Jane gotten that message already?

And then she saw the envelope. It was large and thick and covered in stamps, including one from U.S. Customs. The words LUNDS UNIVERSITET were stenciled along the bottom, next to the university's crest in the lower left corner. Her hands—the steady, surgeon's hands she had inherited from her father—became suddenly nerveless, and the envelope fell to the floor.

Jane bent to pick it up. "Here, you dropped—oh." She held it out, wide eyes meeting Sutton's. "Is this . . . ?"

Sutton nodded and swallowed hard. "One of the places I applied. Yes." She hugged the envelope to her chest and took a deep breath, trying to get her body and mind back under control.

"I should go." Jane took a step back. "Let me know what it says, okay? My fingers are crossed. You deserve it."

"No." Sutton blurted out the word before thinking. "I mean . . . could you stay?"

"Of course. Whatever you want."

"I want to open this upstairs." Sutton turned and slotted her key into the door. Her hands were steady now. The onslaught of adrenaline had passed, leaving her sharp-eyed and alert. The envelope was thick. That probably meant good news, but she refused to allow herself any more speculation than that.

She set a faster pace than usual up the stairs, and by the time she reached the third-floor landing, she was a little winded. Jane had kept up, and her silent closeness was a comfort as Sutton walked briskly down the corridor. Her apartment door stuck a little, as always, but she put her shoulder to it, and in another moment they were inside. She had one instant in which to feel thankful that she always kept her living space clean before the weight of the package in her hands burned all other thoughts from her brain. She shrugged out of her coat, dropped the rest of the mail on the table, and swiftly tore open the envelope. It contained a stack of printed materials, on top of which was a letter embossed with the university seal and addressed to "Dr. St. James." Her title was still new enough to seem foreign, as though she had usurped it from her father. But no—it was hers by right. She was no imposter, and this letter had nothing to do with him.

Congratulations. The Lund Center for Stem Cell Biology and Cell Therapy has selected you as one of the recipients of a postdoctoral fellowship . . .

Sutton exhaled slowly as relief rushed in to fill the void vacated by her anxiety. She had done it. She had secured her top-choice postdoc. The waiting was finally over.

As she stared down at the letter, blinking back tears, a pair of arms slid gently around her waist. Jane. Sutton leaned back, accepting the gentle embrace. Jane's chin came to rest on her shoulder, and Sutton could tell exactly when she read the first lines of the letter by how Jane's arms tightened.

"You did it," she murmured, her warm breath cascading across the shell of Sutton's ear. "Congratulations, Doctor Sutton. How do you feel?"

Needing to see Jane's expression, Sutton turned. It felt so natural to rest her hands on Jane's arms as she gazed up into her smiling face. Green and gold dominated in her swirling hazel eyes, and she looked so happy. All for her.

"I feel . . . amazing." Sutton smoothed her palms along Jane's lean biceps and across her shoulders before letting her fingers tangle in the short hairs at the back of her neck. Every touch sent a tiny jolt of electricity surging beneath her skin. For once, the sensation didn't frighten her. For once, she wanted to embrace it.

After so many years of rigorous study and laserlike focus, her plans were finally coming to fruition. For the first time since graduating college, she wanted to slow down. To take a deep breath and pause to rest, just for a little while, on her laurels. To take the time to stop and feel her own emotions, instead of pushing them aside in the name of her career. But what she wanted most of all in this moment was to feel Jane's mouth on hers. To know—to finally know—how they would fit together, and whether their connection was real or all in her head.

"You feel amazing, too," she whispered as she rose up onto her toes and pressed their lips together.

Softness. Heat. Sutton lost herself in the sensations as Jane's mouth moved over hers with tender purpose. Instinctively, Sutton pressed closer and felt Jane's hands tighten against her lower back. When the very tip of Jane's tongue lightly touched hers, Sutton gasped into her mouth.

A heartbeat later, Jane pulled away. Her breaths were quick and shallow, her eyes dark and slightly unfocused. Discontent with the space between them, Sutton stroked her thumb across Jane's mouth. Jane caught her wrist, freezing her hand in place so she could kiss the sensitive pad. When she scraped her teeth across it, Sutton shivered.

"Why did you stop?" she asked.

With one last kiss to her fingertip, Jane released her. "I wanted to make sure it was what you really wanted."

Sutton intertwined her fingers behind Jane's neck. "Your logic could use some work. I initiated, remember?"

Jane's eyes darkened. "Now it's my turn." Fluidly, she dipped her head, taking Sutton's mouth as though she'd done it a hundred times before instead of only once. But Sutton refused to let her keep the lead. Tugging at Jane's hair, she took advantage of her low moan to slip inside. Lost in the wet heat, Sutton felt the flames spreading, licking beneath her skin like wildfire. She wanted Jane's touch. Everywhere. The realization tore the air from her lungs, and this time she was the one to break their connection.

"You okay?" Jane sounded as breathless as she felt.

"Yes." Sutton nodded, not trusting herself with anything more than the monosyllable.

"You . . . I've never . . ." Jane was clearly flustered, and the pressure in Sutton's chest eased a little. "You're an incredible kisser."

"So are you." Sutton stroked the taut planes of Jane's shoulders as she looked up into her eyes. She saw her own desire mirrored there, but also something more—a tenderness that was at once wonderful and terrifying. "I'm probably going to hurt you." The words were out before she could rethink them.

But Jane's arms didn't fall and her gaze never wavered. "Well, I'm no masochist, so I hope not. But I'll take my chances."

"I just mean that I can't start something serious right now." Sutton watched Jane closely, needing to know she understood.

Jane lightly massaged her lower back. "Because you might be in Sweden in a matter of months."

"Exactly."

"Well," Jane said, her hands never stopping their soft, comforting strokes, "until then, all I want is to spend as much time as possible with you. How does that sound?"

Somewhere deep in Sutton's brain, an alarm was blaring. She ignored it. Jane's touch felt so good. She was tired of resisting. Why shouldn't she have what she wanted? Just for a little while.

"That sounds perfect."

"You have to leave soon, don't you—for your lecture? How much time do we have?"

"Enough." Sutton licked her lips and pulled Jane's head back down. "Enough for one more."

CHAPTER NINE

S UTTON'S FINGERS FLEW OVER the keyboard as she tran-
scribed her notes from afternoon rounds. Her eyes felt gritty
from lack of sleep, and her shoulders ached from her hunched position over the small corner desk. A few chairs over, Travis had cor-
nered one of the female third-years and was trying to impress her
with his description of his interview at Barrow Neurological Insti-
tute. Match Day was only a few days away, and everyone's anxiety
was at a fever pitch. Sutton kept her head down, not wanting to give
him any excuse to pull her into the conversation.

As soon as she got through these notes, she could flee this place
and take refuge in Noodle Treasure. Glancing down at her watch,
she saw that it was nearly four o'clock. All day, people had been
commenting on how fine the weather was. Sutton had yet to set
foot out of the hospital, but if it was still nice by the time she left,
perhaps she could convince Jane to go on a walk. A leisurely stroll
sounded like just the thing to clear her head. They could hold
hands and listen to the city, and perhaps she would even steal a
kiss or two.

Quite suddenly, the persistent buzz of human conversation
ceased, like birdsong in the jungle at the approach of a lion. Frowning, Sutton raised her head. Her attention was immediately di-
verted by the sight of Travis getting to his feet.

"Dr. St. James." He was up and out of his seat before Sutton had
even registered the fact that her father, immaculately dressed in a

three-piece navy suit, was standing at the door to the cramped computer lab. Immediately, dread spiraled in her stomach. This was the first time he had ever visited her at the hospital, and she couldn't imagine it boded well. She watched as he shook Travis's hand and listened to his sycophantic praise with an indulgent expression. He didn't seem angry or upset, but then again, he had an audience.

"Hi, Dad," she said, careful to keep her voice neutral.

"Hello, Sutton. I just stopped by for a brief chat. Do you have a moment?"

"Of course." As she saved her work, logged out, and grabbed her notebook, Sutton racked her brains for what might have motivated his unprecedented visit. Had something happened to her mother? But he was taking his time saying his good-byes to Travis and the others, so surely whatever had brought him here wasn't overly urgent. Her mother was probably just fine—or whatever passed for that these days.

"This way," he said, guiding her down the hallway to the right. "When I informed Rick that I needed to speak with you, he offered me his office."

Sutton's anxiety surged again. If he hadn't come bearing bad news, then why did they need to speak privately in Dr. Buehler's office? "Is this about Mom?" she blurted, unable to hold back the question.

He frowned, but in another moment the expression had transformed into the broad, trademark smile he always used in front of the media. This time, it was aimed at one of the attending physicians who was walking down the hall toward them. "Denise, wonderful to see you."

As soon as she had passed, the smile disappeared. He gripped Sutton's arm at the elbow and leaned in close. "No, this is not about your mother."

The words were spoken with a quiet vehemence that made Sutton feel like the wayward child she had never been. Over the past few years, she had respected her mother's desire to keep her diagnosis a secret, even though she didn't like the implication that MS was something to be ashamed of. Sometimes, her father seemed even more obsessed with keeping the news away from the public. But perhaps he was just being protective.

Sutton accompanied him the rest of the way in silence. Once the door had closed, he walked across the shag carpet to the dark, oak-paneled desk. For a moment, Sutton wondered whether he would actually sit in Buehler's chair. And then he rounded on her, one finger pointed in accusation.

"Do you have any idea what you've done?"

For a moment, Sutton stood blinking at him in confusion, before epiphany dawned. Her article. The latest issue of *The Journal of Stem Cell Research & Therapy* must have come out today. She'd been so preoccupied with rounds that she hadn't even realized it.

"What on earth were you thinking?" he continued. "You've stirred up a hornet's nest and made me look like a fool. When the chairman of the Medical Ethics Committee called earlier to ask if my views on stem-cell research have changed, I had no idea what he was talking about. He had to send me a link to your damn article!"

Despite the layer of sweat she could feel on her palms, Sutton refused to be cowed. She had done nothing wrong. Squaring her shoulders, she looked her father in the eyes. "And what did you tell him?"

"That, as I have always said, the use of stem cells in medical research is not only unethical but deplorable. We do not play God, Sutton."

Sutton could feel her temperature rising. Her father had never spoken to her like this before, and he had no right to do so now. She wasn't one of his political opponents or lackeys.

"I take it you didn't read one word then, did you? Because if you had, you might have realized why I published it. There's so much that stem-cell therapy might be able to do, if we study it properly."

She took a step closer to him. "It might be able to help Mom. It might be able to stop her deterioration, or cure her."

"That's entirely beside the point if we are compromising—"

A red haze settled over Sutton's vision. "Beside the point? Healing is beside the point? You may not condone stem-cell research, but there are plenty of well-respected physicians and scientists who do. This is an issue of debate in the medical community, not a political platform. It deserves investigation. We're scientists, Dad. That's what we do!"

The longer she spoke, the more mottled his face became. By the time she had finished, his cheeks were nearly purple and his upraised hand was quivering with rage. But when he spoke, his voice was eerily quiet.

"Don't you dare presume to tell me what 'we' do, Sutton. I've been a pillar of your 'medical community' since before you were born. I've shaped the direction of medicine in this country for decades, and I'll be damned before I listen to my own flesh and blood preach to me about 'what we do.' I've handed you your career on a silver platter, and this is how you show your gratitude?"

Sutton couldn't believe what she was hearing. The terrible insecurity crashed down on her, confirming her worst fears. In the space of a single sentence, he had erased her years of hard work, her struggles, her sacrifices. Nothing she had done—nothing she could ever do—would matter. All those times when she had believed herself to be in control? Illusions. He had made her, and now he could unmake her.

Despair loomed, and she wrapped her arms around her chest to ward off a shiver. The shreds of her pride demanded that she not fall apart in front of him. If only Jane were here to hold her, just as she had done as Sutton read and reread the letter from Lund.

The letter. Lund. Stem cells. Her article—the reason behind this confrontation with her father. Her research had nothing to do with him and never had. It belonged to her, and her alone. If he had pulled strings to help her surgeon's career, that was on his head. She had completed her thesis and published an article without his help. She wasn't his puppet, and he couldn't control her unless she let him.

With the epiphany, came resolve. "I don't appreciate being hauled in here like I've done something wrong. My article was published by a reputable, peer-reviewed medical journal. If you don't respect my values, Dad, then at least respect that." She turned and rested her hand on the doorknob before looking back over her shoulder. "And for God's sake, stop treating me like a child and start treating me like a professional. I've earned it."

As she stepped out into the hall, Sutton barely resisted the urge to slam the door behind her. Shaking with suppressed rage, she walked quickly toward the locker room. Suddenly, the hospital felt like a cage. She was a captive here—a prisoner to her surname and all the expectations it carried. She had to get out.

Her scrub shirt was loose, but she tugged at the neck as claustrophobia crashed over her. Mercifully, the locker room was deserted, and after yanking off her shirt she sank onto the metal bench nearest her locker. Gripping its sides tightly, she closed her eyes and forced herself to take a series of slow, deep breaths. Gradually, the feeling of suffocation receded, like floodwaters creeping back into their source.

"Okay," she muttered when the fear had finally passed. "That was pretty awful, but you survived."

After stripping off her scrub pants, she changed into jeans and a black fleece with NYU's crest embroidered below one shoulder. The fabric glided softly across her skin, soothing her frayed nerves. As she moved to pocket her phone, she paused. The only person she wanted to see right now was Jane. In her presence, Sutton felt like a real, three-dimensional person instead of Reginald St. James's daughter. In the aftermath of her confrontation with him, she needed that feeling more than ever.

Leaving the hospital now, she typed, using her phone as an excuse to keep her head down as she exited the locker room. *Are you free?*

But by the time she reemerged from the subway half an hour later, Jane hadn't texted her back. Usually, she replied within minutes. Feeling suddenly adrift, Sutton paused beneath the awning of an art gallery. The prospect of going home held no allure. She didn't want to be alone.

As she lingered, the sun came out from behind a puffy cumulus cloud. She turned her face into the rays, basking in the mildness of the day and the lateness of the light. The harbingers of spring made her momentarily forget her anger, her fear, her persistent dread about the future. Resolved, she turned toward Noodle Treasure. Someone there might know where Jane was. And even if not, she would be able to spend the rest of the afternoon with people who liked and respected her without knowing the first thing about her father.

When she stepped inside, the first person she saw was Minetta seated at her usual booth, her laptop open on the table. As Sutton looked around the room, Benny came out of the kitchen, smiling. He always made her feel so welcome.

"Dr. Sutton, hello! What can we get for you today?"

"Actually, I'm looking for Jane. Do you happen to know where she might be?"

"No, I don't. I'm sor—"

"She stopped by about an hour ago," Min cut him off. "She said she was going over to Sue's."

"Thanks, Min. I'll run over there. Take care, Benny."

Waving to acknowledge their good-byes, she quickly left the restaurant. As she turned toward the apothecary, she marveled that only a few short weeks ago, she had been wholly ignorant of how to navigate the maze of Chinatown. Thanks to Jane, these streets were starting to feel familiar. Their relationship might have begun when Jane had offered to be her guide, but she was so much more than that now. She had become a friend. A confidante. A sounding board. And something more, too—something deeper and more visceral. Not yet a lover, but almost. Did she dare let Jane that close? Could they share that level of intimacy and also remain casual?

And then all rational thought flew out of Sutton's head as she turned the final corner. Her mouth went dry at the sight of Jane, dressed in a threadbare pair of jeans and a dark gray T-shirt, putting the final touches on a fresh coat of paint for Sue's door. The muscles in her upper back were plain to see through the thin fabric, and Sutton found herself mesmerized by the way they bunched up with each brushstroke. She wanted to slide her arms around Jane's slender waist and rise up on her toes to kiss the back of her neck.

So she did. Jane was so intent on her task that she didn't react until Sutton was touching her. As she tensed, Sutton slipped one hand beneath her shirt to caress her stomach. Hot, soft skin shivered beneath her palm, fueling Sutton's desire. She wanted to—

"Dr. St. James, if that isn't you, I'm going to have to use my self-defense training from college." Jane's tone was playful, but the appellation only served to remind Sutton of her father.

"Hi," she said through a suddenly tight throat, letting her arms drop. "How's your project coming along?"

Jane must have heard a hint of distress in Sutton's voice, because instead of answering, she spun to face her. The hand not holding the paintbrush settled on the small of Sutton's back, bringing their bodies flush. Jane looked down at her intently, her eyes searching. The sensation of their thighs pressing lightly together was at once arousing and comforting, and even Jane's one-handed hug made Sutton feel safe. Tears welled up in her eyes, unexpected and unwelcome, and she looked down to break their gaze. She heard the clatter of the brush falling to the sidewalk, and her head came to rest against Jane's shoulder as she was enfolded in a gentle embrace.

"Hey. It's okay. You're all right. I promise."

Jane had no idea what she was talking about, and no authority from which to make promises. But Sutton didn't care. She pressed her cheek to the soft material of Jane's T-shirt and closed her eyes, inhaling the warm, spicy scent of her. When Jane's arms tightened in response, Sutton finally felt herself relax.

After a few moments, Jane kissed the top of her head. "How about we go inside and sit down for a little while?"

Sutton didn't particularly want to move, but it was probably a good idea to pull herself together away from the crowded streets. "All right."

Jane shepherded her inside and led her over to the couch where Sue did her astrological readings. She sat close enough for their legs to touch and lightly rested one hand on Sutton's knee.

"Do you want to talk about it?"

"My father and I had an argument." Sutton swallowed hard, hating how weak she sounded. "It's not that big of a deal. I don't know why I'm letting it get to me."

Jane opened her mouth to reply, but the sound of approaching footsteps cut her off. "Jane? Is that you?"

As Sue appeared around the corner, Jane angled her body toward Sutton's in a clear attempt to shield her. Sutton wondered whether the protective gesture had been deliberate or instinctual.

"Yes, Sue, it's me." When Jane turned her head, Sutton barely managed to resist the urge to press her lips to the column of Jane's neck. Had all the stress destroyed her inhibitions? "And Sutton's here, too. Do you think you might be able to bring her a cup of tea?"

"Doctor Sutton! Wonderful to see you." Their eyes met over Jane's shoulder, and Sue's gaze immediately turned sympathetic. "Tea. Of course. Something soothing, perhaps?"

"That would be lovely."

Once she had gone, Jane turned back to face her. "How much time do you have?"

"The rest of the day." Sutton reached up to brush away a speck of dried paint that had stuck to Jane's left cheek. "Before . . . before I saw my father, I was hoping to convince you to take a walk, later."

Jane leaned into the touch like a cat. "It's perfect out, isn't it? I think we absolutely should." Then she looked down at herself. "But I need a shower. Do you mind waiting?"

"Not at all."

Sue returned carrying a large, red ceramic mug bearing three Chinese characters painted in black. She set it down on the table and smiled at Sutton. "Lavender tea. Very soothing."

"Thank you." Sutton raised the cup to her lips and breathed in the familiar fragrance.

Jane was still looking at her intently, concern writ plainly across her face. "How about this—while you drink your tea, I'll put the painting supplies away. Then we can make a brief stop by my aunt and uncle's apartment before we go on that walk."

"Sounds great." Not wanting her to worry, Sutton managed a smile. "Take your time."

"Okay. See you soon." Jane hurried across the store, and after one final glance over her shoulder, she was gone.

Sutton took a tentative sip of the tea, and then, when she found it not too hot, another. Its warmth was comforting against the back of her throat, and its light flavor lingered on her tongue. "This is heavenly, Sue. Thanks."

"You're very welcome." Sue lingered, and for a moment it seemed as though she might say something, but then the telephone rang and she excused herself. Sutton was relieved. All she wanted was to drink this and sit quietly for long enough to regain her composure.

As she sipped, she noticed a bowl of fortune cookies in the center of the table. Wanting to know what Jane had been writing recently, she reached for one. Popping half into her mouth, she let the tender shell dissolve against her tongue as she unfolded the fortune.

Just say yes.

Sutton balanced the fortune on her knee and stared down at it. What had Jane been thinking of while composing this? Had it been written with her in mind? The notion felt more than a little hubristic. But if it were true, what did Jane want her to say yes to? Saying yes to anything in her life right now was a fraught proposition. If she said yes to Columbia, then she said no to Lund. If she acquiesced to her father's demands, then she rejected her own principles. Feeling her anxiety start to rise again, she set the mug to her lips. When the door opened, she watched Jane enter, carefully balancing buckets and brushes.

"Doing okay?"

"I am. Thanks."

"I'm just going to put these in the supply closet and wash up. Be right back."

Sutton watched her go, admiring the fit of her jeans. Desire rose in her blood like a tide, submerging her fears. *Just say yes.* Maybe, when it came to Jane, it was that simple.

As she drank the last of her tea, Jane returned. "Ready?"

"Yes." Sutton took her outstretched hand and didn't let go, even when she was standing.

The temperature had cooled a little while they were inside, but the air was still milder than it had been since November. Sutton swung their hands in a gentle arc, feeling thankful that Jane hadn't pressed her to talk as soon as they were alone. She seemed content to offer silent reassurance until Sutton brought it up. That kind of patience was so rare. Any of her other friends would have been grilling her for information by now.

"So . . . my father is even less thrilled about my article than I'd anticipated."

Jane's thumb made a comforting circle against her skin. "What happened?"

"He came to visit me at the hospital today—dragged me into

my advisor's office and told me that my article was unethical and that I'd made him look foolish and that I owed my career to his influence."

"He did what?" Jane stopped, pulled her to the curb, and gently grasped her shoulders. "You know it's a lie, right?"

The heat in Jane's voice warmed Sutton's chest, making her feel cherished. "I know he was trying to manipulate me."

"That's not what I asked." Jane took a step closer and smoothed her palms along Sutton's upper arms. "Everything you have right now, you've earned."

Too tired to argue, Sutton decided to concede the point, even if she no longer believed it. "It's not really that big of a deal. I think his reaction rattled me, more than anything. I was expecting him to disapprove, but he was just irate."

"I'm so sorry. You deserve his respect, not his anger." With one final caress, Jane moved them back into the current of humanity. "Is there anything I can do?"

"I'd like to take that walk. And maybe we can find some comfort food?"

"I know just the place." She slowed as they drew abreast of Confucius Fortunes. "I'll be quick in the shower, I promise. Would you rather wait outside or upstairs?"

Sutton was suddenly possessed of a sharp urge to see Jane's home—to have a clear picture in her head of what Jane saw before she closed her eyes at night and when she opened them again in the morning.

"I'll come up."

But Jane made no move to open the door. Instead, she shifted her weight back and forth in a clear show of anxiety. "Sutton . . . it's not exactly the Ritz up there."

"So?"

Jane looked at her feet. "I don't have a room of my own, okay? I share with Min. That was the only space they had when I moved in."

Guilt washed over Sutton that she had forced Jane into the admission. Did she truly believe Sutton was fickle enough to reject her, just because of where she lived or how much money she had? And if so, had Jane arrived at that impression all on her own? Or had Sutton done something to encourage it?

Wanting to make amends, she kissed one corner of Jane's mouth. "I understand. I'll wait here for you."

Jane searched her eyes. "Aunt Jenny's probably cooking dinner. I'm sure she'd love your company in the kitchen."

"Sounds great." For tonight, she would let Jane establish whatever boundaries she needed to feel comfortable. But she didn't intend to let them stand forever.

AFTER VIGOROUSLY TOWELING OFF and throwing on the clothes she'd brought into the bathroom, Jane swiped a dollop of gel and ran it through her hair. She paused to inspect her reflection, adjusting one stray strand before pointing at the mirror.

"Don't mess this up."

Sutton had sought her out because she was in need during a difficult time. Now, Jane had an opportunity to be there for her. But she had to keep her head. Just because Sutton was beginning to open up, didn't mean she wanted something . . . more. Whatever was developing between them couldn't become serious. No matter how much she wished the circumstances could be different.

Not wanting to dwell on that line of thinking, she hurried out the door and down the stairs. The hum of voices grew louder as she descended, punctuated by Sutton's laugh. Seated at the table between Min and Uncle John, Sutton was intently focused on the laptop screen in front of them.

"What are you watching?"

"Cats," Min said, eyes glued to the screen.

"Cats? As in, the musical?"

Min deigned to shoot her a withering glance. "No, dummy, real cats. Online."

"Will you look at that!" interjected Uncle John. He sounded more animated than Jane had ever heard him.

"So cute," Sutton agreed.

Neither of them had so much as looked up. "Really? You're all sitting here spellbound by one of the millions of videos of cats on the Internet?"

Uncle John turned toward her with a look of shock. "You mean there are more?"

Jane had to bite the inside of her cheek to keep from laughing. "Oh yeah. For sure." She looked to Sutton. "Can I tempt you away from the adorable felines?"

Her eyes glinted. "I don't know—can you?"

The teasing note in Sutton's voice, combined with her mischievous expression, went right to Jane's head. She wanted nothing more than to cross the room, lean down, and kiss her with a ferocity they had yet to explore together. The craving burned inside her, twisting and turning like a filament warping under heat. Gripping the banister hard, she held herself in place and her desires in check.

"I'm prepared to deliver that comfort food you asked for earlier," she said, trying to keep the edge out of her tone.

Sutton frowned and tapped her chin, making a show of making up her mind. Jane watched Min hang on her every movement, and even Uncle John had stopped watching the cats.

"Well, in that case . . ." She stood and pushed in her chair. "Thanks for the laughs, Min, and for the hospitality, John and Jenny. It was wonderful to see you all."

"Enjoy your night," Uncle John said simultaneously with Aunt Jenny's "Have fun." But as Jane allowed Sutton to precede her down the hallway, Min simply had to weigh in.

"Don't do anything I wouldn't do!"

"For goodness' sake, Minetta." Aunt Jenny's chiding voice followed them down the stairs.

As they emerged into the night, Sutton caught the hem of Jane's hoodie and tugged her close. When Sutton's arms came around her neck, Jane was beset by twin surges of relief and desire.

"I just wanted to say thank you." The teasing note had left Sutton's voice, and her eyes were serious.

"For what?"

"For being such a good listener, earlier. For welcoming me into your home." Her fingertips caressed the nape of Jane's neck. "You're a very nurturing person."

Jane had known the kiss was coming, but the sensation of Sutton's lips sliding against her own was still miraculous. The soft heat of Sutton's mouth seeped into her blood, spreading warmth beneath her skin. It ended all too soon, leaving Jane breathless. She wanted to memorize the way Sutton looked right now—her expression soft and unguarded, her golden hair illuminated by the red neon letters of the Confucius Fortunes sign in the window.

"You feel good," she said, daring to smooth her palms along Sutton's rib cage.

The low rumble of Sutton's stomach broke the moment, and she pulled away, laughing. "I think that's a sign. Where are you taking me?"

"It's a surprise. You'll have to follow my lead." Jane stretched out her hand. "Better hold on."

As they walked north, her breathing slowed to match the cadence of their footsteps. The air was crisp but not painfully cold, and the promise of spring invigorated her, even as she steadfastly ignored the ticking clock in her head. This was not the time to fret about the future. She could do that when she wasn't holding Sutton's hand.

"I should tell my parents about the postdoc at Lund," Sutton said after a few blocks of silence. "Especially now that my father knows about the article."

The trepidation in her voice made Jane want to turn around, walk Sutton back to her apartment, and hold her for the remainder of the night. But that wasn't what she needed. Sutton wasn't asking for her comfort right now—she was asking for a sounding board.

"Okay. How do you want to tell them?"

"I don't really care, just as long as I do. But I think I'm in serious danger of losing my nerve."

"What if you set yourself some kind of deadline? That might help you feel less anxiety about it." Jane shrugged, not wanting Sutton to feel pressured. "It's what I did when I was tying myself in knots over coming out to my family."

"How did that work?"

"I finally just gave myself a week to do it. This was during my senior year of high school, while we were living in Portugal." Jane felt a sharp pang of nostalgia at the memory. "On the fifth day, we were eating at this cute little café in Lisbon that my mom had discovered while shopping, and the sun was setting over the water as we sat drinking our coffees. I just remember feeling like the world was so at peace in that moment. And I wanted to feel the same way, you know? At peace with myself and my identity. So I told them."

"That's beautiful. How did they react?"

"They were great. I think my mother might have been a little disappointed that she wouldn't get to see me married off to some dashing, exotic bachelor, but that's just a feeling I get. They've never been anything but supportive to my face. I'm one of the lucky ones."

"Yes." Sutton's expression was pensive. "Everyone should be so lucky."

The note of pain in her voice tore at Jane, and she detached their hands to slide her arm around Sutton's waist. "You don't have to tell me. But I'll listen if you like."

"There's not much to tell. My parents have always had a very clear picture of what my life would be like, and that picture did not include me eventually settling down with another woman. I think they still hope it's a phase."

"I'm sorry." Jane hugged her closer. "I hate that they made it difficult for you. You deserve to be cherished, not guilt-tripped."

"It's only been a few years. I'm hoping they'll come around yet."

Jane was just considering whether to ask what had motivated her coming out to her family, when they turned a corner and found themselves at the edge of Washington Square Park. Before them, the fountain's basin was entirely dry, still awaiting the advent of true spring. She could remember playing in it once as a child, on a hot summer's day, during one of her family's visits to the States. Beyond the fountain, floodlights illuminated the ornate façade of the Washington Arch.

"Let's go underneath," she said, pointing.

Sutton smiled. "All right, tourist."

"Hey, now. Just because I'm not a lifer like you doesn't mean—" The sound of a trumpet made Jane break off her argument, and she searched out the musician as a jazz riff filled the air. He was sitting on the edge of the basin and playing, instrument case open at his feet.

As they approached, Sutton extracted a dollar bill from her purse. "Thank you," she said, bending to deposit it on the black velvet. The man never stopped playing, but he dipped his head in acknowledgement.

"He sounded good," Jane said as they walked away.

"Very. I wonder what made him have to busk."

"Maybe he doesn't have to. He might just want to play for a different audience. Or maybe he just doesn't want to practice inside on a night like this."

"Good point." Sutton sounded thoughtful, and Jane wondered whether that was a new notion to her. There were plenty of impoverished artists in New York City, but not all of them needed to beg to eke out an existence. Some of them simply wanted to perform for the joy of it.

Their pace slowed as they meandered through the park. The

chorus of human voices filled the mild air with a soft buzz, and Jane reached for her notebook as words and phrases jumped out from the cacophony like fish from a river.

How many times are you going to stand there and argue with him?

Is it called 'Some Greek God Café?'

But I'm not going to eat, so I don't know if that will bother you— me sitting there and watching you eat.

"That would totally bother me," Sutton murmured.

"Me, too," Jane said as she finished scribbling. "I don't trust people who don't like food."

As they drew abreast of the fountain, they passed a skinny, Mohawked young man under a street lamp whose cardboard sign read, ONE DOLLAR JOKES. MONEY BACK IF YOU DON'T LAUGH.

Jane nudged Sutton. "Want to risk it?"

"I'll save my money this time, thanks. But I have to admit I'm intrigued." She nodded toward a bearded fellow standing next to a placard advertising TAROT READINGS BY KYLER. "Oh, look. Maybe he and Sue should compare notes."

"Maybe he'd be a better match for her than Giancarlo."

Sutton's laugh sounded as musical as the jazz. "Or maybe they'd be hopelessly at odds. Do Chinese astrology and tarot have anything in common?"

"No idea. Have you ever had your cards read?"

"Never. You?"

When Jane shook her head, she noticed a slender woman perched on a bench near the arch, her hand resting possessively on a piece of poster board. Her inner arm bore a script tattoo that Jane couldn't quite make out, but her sign was clearly legible. HI. I'M COLLECTING YOUR STORIES. STOP BY AND SHARE ANONYMOUSLY OR ASK, "WHAT FOR?"

"That's an intriguing project," Jane mused.

"Do you want to go talk to her?" There was an unexpected edge to Sutton's words that aroused Jane's curiosity. Sutton was frowning as she looked at the woman, and the muscles in her chin were tightly bunched. She seemed almost jealous—only that was crazy, wasn't it? Crazy, but intoxicating. If Sutton were jealous, that meant she cared. That her feelings were more than simply casual.

Careful to keep her tone nonchalant, she shrugged. "No, I want to feed you comfort food."

"Oh, really?" The teasing note was back in Sutton's voice.

Blindsided by the mental image of sharing a pint of ice cream in bed, Jane hurriedly tried to pull herself together. "Not that . . . I mean . . . obviously you can feed yourself."

"Mm." Sutton sounded positively smug.

As they passed beneath the arch, a man, holding a copy of what Jane presumed was a Bible, spun in a slow circle. "You'll be crumbling in the ground while Satan scorches you," he ranted. "That's what happens to those who think God is a joke!"

"Lovely." Sutton picked up the pace, and Jane was happy to match her.

"The hellfire-and-brimstone ones are the worst." She glanced over. "Are you religious?"

"Only on Christmas and Easter." Sutton's mouth twisted wryly. "My parents' real church is the Metropolitan Club. Yours?"

"My dad's a lapsed Irish Catholic and my mother believes more in the power of medicinal herbs than in any sacred deity."

"No wonder you feel so at home in Sue's shop."

As Jane steered them further east, the age of the passersby noticeably decreased. The East Village was dominated by NYU students, lending the neighborhood an atmosphere at once Bohemian and bourgeois. As they crossed Astor Place, she felt a pang of nostalgia for her college days, followed by guilt that those days weren't exactly over yet. Taking a deep breath, she focused on the hum of the crowd and the sensation of Sutton's fingers intertwined with her own.

She doesn't want him in her house.

Yeah, I can hear you. You sound very obese. Can you hear me?

Well, I was made in a Petri dish . . .

"You're getting some good ones tonight, aren't you?" Sutton asked as Jane unlaced their hands to write down a few more lines.

"I am. You must be good luck." Jane blinked as she realized she had paused mere feet from their destination. "And here we are."

"Pommes Frites?" Sutton sounded a little dubious, and Jane mentally crossed her fingers.

"Is there any better comfort food than Belgian fries smothered in the sauce of your choosing?" She pulled Sutton toward the tiny hole-in-a-wall restaurant. "C'mon. Trust me. I'm getting the parmesan peppercorn, and if you're nice, I'll let you have a bite."

"If I'm nice?" Sutton sounded affronted, but when Jane glanced over, she was already perusing the menu above the restaurant. "Vietnamese Pineapple Mayo? On French fries?"

"On Belgian fries."

"Is there really that much of a difference?"

"Light-years. Belgian fries are thicker, and they're always served in a paper cone. Usually with mayonnaise and ketchup." When Sutton continued to look skeptical, Jane shook her head. "Seriously, just trust me. And if you ever find yourself in Belgium, go to a friterie."

A few minutes later, Jane watched as Sutton took a tentative bite from a large, golden-brown fry slathered with a sauce called "Honey Mustard Mayo." She chewed, swallowed, and frowned.

"Uh-oh." She shook her head gravely.

"Uh-oh?" Jane couldn't believe it. Sutton had enjoyed her first dim sum experience despite chicken feet and tripe, but she wasn't sold on the best fry stand in New York?

"Uh-oh." A slow, teasing smile bloomed across her face. "I think I'm addicted."

Jane couldn't believe she'd fallen for Sutton's acting. "You suck!"

"Only if you're nice." With a wink, Sutton popped the rest of the fry in her mouth.

Totally flustered, Jane felt her own jaw drop. When she tried to speak, she only managed to stammer. Finally, she took a deep breath, looked away from Sutton's lips, and forced her own to work properly. Two could play at this game.

"Was that a promise?"

"Maybe." Sutton took a few steps toward the curb. "Let's find a place to sit."

"How about somewhere near St. Mark's?" Jane pointed toward the illuminated façade of the church, which turned into a popular loitering spot by night.

They found an empty bench, and Jane watched in delight the blissful expression on Sutton's face as she savored another fry. As she licked her fingers clean of the sauce, Jane felt a little dizzy. But when she paused with her next fry in midair to ask what was the matter, Jane quickly took a large bite, not wanting to answer.

"So, I've been thinking about your advice," Sutton said a few minutes later. "About setting a deadline to talk to my parents."

"Oh? What's your plan?"

"I want to do it by the end of the week. Which probably means telling them at dinner on Sunday."

Jane propped the paper cone between her legs and smoothed one palm over Sutton's knee. "Is there anything I can do to help?"

"What would you think about coming with me? To keep me honest." Surprise must have been plain on her face, because Sutton quickly continued, "I know it's a lot to ask. But if you're there, I won't let myself get away with being cowardly."

The prospect of meeting Sutton's parents was terrifying, but Jane wasn't about to betray her anxiety. If Sutton needed her to be there, then she would be. She might not have a college degree or spend her day saving lives, but she could damn well be supportive.

"'Cowardly' is the last word I'd use to describe you. But if it would help for me to be there, then I will be."

"Really?"

"Of course." Jane mustered a grin, hoping to disguise her unease. "Just tell me what I should wear, okay? I have a feeling the dress code at your family's Sunday dinner might be different from mine."

Chapter Ten

I N HER PERIPHERAL VISION, Sutton caught Jane tugging at the collar of her pale green shirt for the third time in as many minutes. A black blazer and gray slacks completed her outfit, accentuating the crisp lines of her lean legs and long torso. Her expression was one of intense concentration, and her almost military carriage gave her the air of someone preparing for battle. The clear evidence of her nerves only increased Sutton's guilt. Jane was walking into the lion's den of her own volition, all because Sutton had asked her to. Ever since they had parted earlier in the week, she had been second-guessing the selfish impulse that had prompted her to ask Jane for her company. She had even offered an out during their brief phone conversation last night. But Jane had remained adamant about joining her.

As she continued to fiddle with her shirt, Sutton realized something was missing. "You took off Sue's pendant."

"It didn't match my outfit." Jane's smile was a bit forced. "And I don't believe in spirits, remember?"

"You look great," Sutton said, hoping to reassure her.

She squeezed Sutton's hand. "I think that's my line."

Sutton glanced across the train to catch a glimpse of her reflection. Her burgundy Dior suit would be flimsy armor against her parents' disappointment and prejudice, but it helped her feel competent and in control. As the train hurtled toward their stop, Sutton gently extricated her hand and got to her feet. The elevation of her pulse was a reaction to cortisol being released by her adrenal cortex, but that didn't make the biological imperative any less compelling. Even as she tried to center herself in the moment and regulate her breathing, Sutton felt the train begin to slow. Time was inexorably marching forward, bringing her ever closer to confrontation.

A cool breeze greeted them as they emerged from the station, and Sutton paused to button her pea coat. The day had been mild, but clouds had arrived with the dusk, pushing colder air before them. The wind whipped at her hair as she bent her head and turned into it. All too soon, they were standing in front of the brick townhouse. The dull roaring in her ears was another byproduct of the cortisol spike, but she could no sooner control it than she could the weather.

"Ready?" she asked, picking a tiny piece of lint off one arm of her coat.

Squaring her shoulders, Jane nodded. "I am."

But Sutton didn't move. She had to try one more time. "You don't have to do this. I asked you to come with me in a selfish moment. This is my fight, and it might get ugly." She tried to smile. "I promise I'll tell them, even if you're not there."

Jane began to shake her head before she had even stopped talking. "My DLPFC is fully functional. I'm here of my own free will." She extended one arm in a sweeping gesture. "After you."

Sutton didn't care if her father was watching from the front window. Bracing one hand on Jane's shoulder, she raised herself up to place a quick kiss to the corner of Jane's mouth. "Thank you."

As she led the way up the stairs, gravity pressed in close, tempting her to turn around. This felt like coming out all over again, and in a way, she supposed it was. Letting her momentum carry her forward, she inserted her key and pushed open the door. There. It was done. No turning back now.

Her father was waiting in the foyer, his mouth compressed in a tight line.

"Hello, Dad."

"Sutton." His voice and face were equally impassive, but if he had hoped to intimidate her, he was going to be disappointed. Was he really so prejudiced against her sexual orientation that he couldn't so much as act happy to see her for their weekly meal? Thankfully, the anger burned away some of her trepidation.

"This is Jane."

Jane immediately stuck out her hand. For a moment, it seemed her gesture would not be reciprocated, until finally, he met her grip with a cursory shake.

"It's a pleasure to meet you," she said. The words were clear and steady, and Sutton felt a rush of pride at Jane's grace under pressure.

"Likewise." The word held a chill more potent than the wind.

He moved past them to lock the door. The sound of the bolt catching made Sutton feel for the briefest of moments like an animal caught in a trap, before she reminded herself that this was her childhood home.

"I'll fetch your mother from the sitting room," he said. "Supper is nearly ready."

Once he had gone, Sutton reached for Jane's hand and led her down the corridor. "Doing okay?"

"Absolutely. You?"

"I'm fine," she said automatically. But she must not have sounded very convincing, because with a light tug, Jane stopped her forward progress, leaned in, and kissed the nape of her neck.

"How about now?"

Jane's lips were soft, and the solicitude of the gesture gave her strength. "Definitely better."

The scent of garlic, dill, and fish filled the air as they moved toward the kitchen. Its marble countertops gleamed under the fluorescent overhead lights, and the woman responsible for its pristine condition stood at the stove, tending to several pots and pans.

She turned with the wide, genuine smile that had always warmed Sutton from the inside out. "Sutton!" After exchanging cheek kisses, Maria held her at arm's length. "You look beautiful."

"You always say that," Sutton said, feeling oddly self-conscious at being praised in Jane's presence. "Maria, this is Jane. Jane, Maria has been part of the family since I was very young. I can't remember life without her."

"Something smells delicious," Jane said after shaking hands. "Is there anything I can do to help?"

Maria laughed and shook her head. "Go ahead and sit. The meal is almost ready."

"This way." As Sutton turned into the dining room, she wondered whether Jane thought her horribly spoiled. The idea was disconcerting, especially because it lined up with Jane's reluctance to show Sutton her own living space. But then her father appeared in the doorway, arm in arm with her mother, and Sutton could think only of what she had to do. Battling anxiety, she met them halfway across the room.

"Hi, Mom." Sutton embraced her carefully, wishing it weren't so easy to feel the outline of her mother's shoulder blades against the thin material of her cardigan. "This is Jane. Jane, this is my mother, Priscilla St. James."

"It's nice to meet you, Mrs. St. James. You have a beautiful home."

"Thank you, Jane." Her mother's voice was carefully modulated, and Sutton felt a pang of gratitude that she could be counted on to remain polite, no matter what she was actually thinking.

"Let's sit," Reginald said brusquely.

Sutton took her customary place across from her mother, and Jane sat to her left, directly across from him. Immediately, Maria appeared with a bottle of white wine in hand. As she moved around the table, Sutton reached out to skim her palm over Jane's knee and was gratified to see the corners of her mouth twitch.

And then her father raised his glass. "Jane, would you like to propose the toast?"

Caught off guard, Sutton's first instinct was to protest, but she managed to swallow her angry retort. Instead, she looked to Jane, who had dared to meet her father's challenging gaze.

"I'd like to toast Sutton's success, both as a physician and a scholar." She held her glass aloft in a grip as steady as a surgeon's. "To Sutton."

His expression remained impassive. "To Sutton."

"To Sutton," her mother echoed in her reedy soprano.

Sutton wanted to kiss her. Instead, she tried to telegraph her gratitude while maintaining her distance. "Thank you."

At that moment, Maria reentered the room bearing a large silver tray. Sutton smoothed her napkin across her lap as the Caesar salad was deposited in front of her. Discreetly, she watched her father, who seemed almost disappointed at the familiarity with which Jane reached for her outside fork. His expectation that Jane would fail to meet the demands of polite society made her blood boil, and she quickly took a bite in order to force herself to stay quiet.

"I saw a fascinating case today," her father said into the silence, and then proceeded to explain it using all sorts of medical jargon that neither Jane, nor her mother, could possibly follow. When Maria returned with the main course, Sutton tried to turn the conversation to a more accessible topic, but her father quickly circled back to surgery. The more he spoke, the more tightly her nerves ratcheted, until she was fairly vibrating. Jane must have been able to sense her tension, because under the guise of retrieving her napkin, she brushed her fingers against Sutton's leg.

As Maria cleared the dinner plates, Sutton prepared to deliver the news she had come here to reveal. Sweat broke out on both palms as her vision telescoped, the rose-colored walls hung with the oil paintings fading away until all she could see were her parents, seated before her like a tribunal. But before she could open her mouth, her father spoke into the silence.

"So, Jane. Tell us about yourself."

Sutton didn't know whether to scramble to Jane's defense or allow her to fend for herself. If she did the former, would Jane appreciate the intervention? Or would she think that Sutton believed her weak and incapable? Paralyzed with indecision, she tried to gauge Jane's psychological state.

After dabbing at her mouth with her napkin—presumably an attempt to gain some time to think—Jane met Reginald's gaze without blinking. "Well, right now I'm working at my uncle's fortune cookie factory."

Sutton watched her father lean forward slightly, eyes gleaming, as though he were a shark sensing blood in the water. "Doing what, exactly?"

"I'm responsible for deliveries, and I write the fortunes that go into the cookies."

He settled back in his chair, looking smug. "I see."

Feeling her temperature rise, Sutton struggled to maintain her composure. Deliberately, she rested her palm on Jane's leg. Through the layer of her slacks, her muscles were taut and flickering.

"Jane is also a very accomplished poet," she said, her tone brooking no arguments.

Reginald's brows lifted. "Oh?" He seemed vaguely amused. "Well, congratulations. What sorts of career options are available for poets these days?"

A wave of pure fury burned away her fear, but even as she took a deep breath to retaliate, Jane trapped her hand in place. Beneath her anger, Sutton felt a surge of pride that Jane wanted to handle her father's passive-aggressive behavior on her own.

"Right now I'm working on my first collection of found poems and on pulling together the materials for a fellowship application. Hopefully, that will come through for me so that I can focus on pursuing publication opportunities. But if I haven't gotten anywhere as a poet by the time I'm thirty, I figure I'll start reevaluating my career options. My father works for the State Department, and he thinks I should join the Foreign Service. I'd be good at it, and I like traveling, but I think I'd rather travel on my own terms, you know? I mean, what if they send me some place like, like Saudia Arabia or something? I like sand fine when it's on a beach, but when it's everywhere, well, that's just uncomfortable. It gets places. Anyway. So that's my plan."

As she watched her parents react to Jane's rambling monologue, Sutton was in danger of breaking into hysterical laughter. Her mother seemed completely taken aback, but her father was looking at Jane with a mixture of scorn and disgust—almost as though she were an insect he wanted to squash.

He cleared his throat. "What on earth are found poems?"

This time, Jane didn't ramble at all. "Found poems are a form of art in which the poet acts as compiler rather than composer. I find lines of poetry everywhere—in signs or graffiti, for example. But mostly in conversations. Then, I assemble all the found lines into a poem."

"Are you serious?"

"Yes, sir. And as Sutton mentioned, I've had one poem publi—"

But Reginald cut her off. "Honestly? This is what passes for poetry in twenty-first-century America? Eavesdropping on people and then plagiarizing them?"

Jane went rigid in shock, and Sutton felt her fingers tremble. "I can assure you it's not—"

Reginald leaned forward, and Sutton's gaze was drawn to the visible pulse throbbing in his neck. "Will this conversation be making it into one of your little poems?"

"Of course not," Jane said through gritted teeth. "That isn't how it—"

"I'm sorry, Jane. I need to interrupt." Sutton had had quite enough of her father's bullying tactics. "Dad . . . how dare you? Jane is my guest in our home. She doesn't deserve to be interrogated and

insulted. She is a published, award-winning poet, and you can respect her work even if you don't understand it."

Crimson suffused her father's neck and cheeks, but when he
opened his mouth to speak, she forestalled him. This was it—the
perfect moment. So far, Jane had taken all the risks. It was time for
her to be brave.

"I also need you to respect me and my choices. I've been offered
a postdoc by Lund University in Sweden to study stem-cell therapy. It's fully funded for two years, with the option of a third." She
took a deep breath. "And I'm going to take it."

Her father recoiled as though her words had been a physical
blow. "Excuse me?"

"But, Sutton," her mother chimed in. "What about Columbia?
Neal has a place for you there."

"I don't want to go to Columbia, Mom. Not right now. I want to
take this opportunity in Sweden. If I decide I want to do a surgical
residency at some point, I can always reapply later." She extended
her free hand across the table, palm up. "Stem-cell therapy might
be able to help treat or even cure certain neurological conditions.
We just don't know enough yet. I want to find out what it can do. I
want to see if it can help you."

Sutton remained focused on her mother, hoping the appeal
would have its desired effect. But for the first time, her polite mask
fell away to reveal the frightened, angry woman beneath. Pressing
her lips together, Priscilla drew back from Sutton's outstretched
hand.

"How dare you discuss this now!"

Her animosity snapped the last strand of Sutton's frayed patience.
"What is the matter with you, Mom? So you have MS. You know
what? Plenty of other people do, too. Hiding a disease—making
it less visible—only makes progress less likely. Stem-cells have
such potential. I'm going to Sweden to try to turn that potential
into reality for you and everyone else who is suffering."

"Quiet!" her father barked. "Sutton, this is ridiculous. You're not going. I won't allow it."

"Oh, really?" Sutton pushed back her chair and stood, refusing to listen to his ultimatums. All her life, he had tried to control her. When her own goals had aligned with his ambitions, she hadn't even noticed his manipulation, but now, it was all too clear. "Just you try and stop me, Dad. I am your daughter. Not your marionette. You can't control me. This is my career and my decision."

Jane scrambled out of her chair to stand at Sutton's side, and in a final show of defiance, Sutton reached down to lace their fingers together. "Let's go."

AS SUTTON PULLED HER toward the front door, Jane rhythmically stroked the soft skin below her knuckles, wishing the touch could convey what she was thinking—that Sutton, in all her strength and intelligence and conviction, was her hero. Reginald's manner had been cold enough to burn, and even Jane's pity for Priscilla didn't outweigh her anger at the way she had lashed out against the daughter who was trying to heal her. Sutton was too good for them. They didn't deserve her.

Maria was waiting in the foyer, Sutton's coat in hand. "Congratulations," she said softly as she held it open. "I will miss you, but I am glad you are following your heart."

"Thank you. Dinner was delicious, as always." Sutton's face softened. "I'm sorry about the drama."

Maria shook her head. "You have nothing to apologize for. I'm glad you finally stood up to him." She embraced Sutton lightly, before stepping back and including Jane in her smile. "Good night."

Once they were outside, Sutton set such a brisk pace that despite Jane's longer legs, she struggled to keep up without breaking into a jog. As they hustled down the sidewalk, she forced herself not to speak. Sutton's main priority at the moment seemed to be putting as much distance between herself and her parents, as quickly as possible. For now, Jane would stick with her in silent solidarity.

A downtown train pulled up to the station within moments of their arrival. As they settled into a pair of seats in the corner, Sutton linked their arms and rested her head on Jane's shoulder. That simple gesture of affection triggered a wave of relief so strong that she shivered. Sutton tightened her grip, but said nothing. Only as they emerged onto Spring Street did she finally speak.

"I'm sorry you had to go through that."

Jane glanced down at her, but Sutton was looking straight ahead. "I wanted to be there. If I had to do it all over again, I'd still want to be there."

The tense set of Sutton's jaw relaxed slightly when she finally met Jane's eyes. "You're amazing. Thank you. I'm not sure I could have done it without you."

"Sure, you could have." As they paused to wait for a car to pass, Jane rolled her shoulders in an attempt to dislodge the tension that had settled there. "You know, I think someday I'm going to look back on that conversation and laugh."

"But not today."

"No, not today."

All too soon, they drew abreast of the door to Sutton's building. The full emotional impact of the night hadn't yet hit her, and Jane didn't want to let her go. Then again, some space might be exactly what Sutton needed.

"Do you want me to . . . I mean, you probably want to be alone right now."

"I really don't." Her eyes shone, reflecting the halo of the nearby street lamp. "Come upstairs with me."

Her throat suddenly dry, Jane simply nodded. Sutton didn't mean it like that, of course. She just wanted company. Maybe once they were alone, she would actually open up about what she was feeling. But even as she tried to rationalize Sutton's request, her skin hummed with need. If Sutton gave her the chance, Jane knew she could make her forget all about the evening's unpleasantness. Jane would have given the world to see inside her head at that moment, and she watched her closely as they climbed the stairs. But Sutton betrayed no clues as to her mental state. Did she want comfort? A sounding board? A distraction? If only Jane could tell what she truly needed, she would move heaven and earth to provide it.

After wrestling with the door, Sutton held it open. Jane took a few steps across the hardwood floor and paused, wondering whether she should take off her shoes. The sound of the door closing, followed by the soft snick of the safety chain sliding home, made her turn. Sutton stood with her back to the wooden surface, arms crossed beneath her breasts. The expression on her face remained introspective, even as her gaze moved slowly up Jane's body.

Paralyzed by Sutton's scrutiny, Jane even held her breath. Her gaze was drawn to the triangle of pale skin and hint of cleavage revealed by the cut of her blouse. Jane needed to touch her tongue to that spot so desperately that she took one step forward before she could check the impulse. The last thing she wanted was to make Sutton feel uncomfortable in any way, especially after the emotional abuse she had just endured. Swallowing hard, she tried to rein in her desire. Whatever was about to happen, she had to let it progress at Sutton's pace.

Sutton's hands fell to her sides. "Come here," she called softly.

In three long strides, Jane was across the room, mere inches separating her from the woman who had somehow managed to so completely bewitch her after only a few short weeks. The urge to touch her was irresistible and she raised one hand to Sutton's face, fingers lightly cupping her jaw as she traced the curve of Sutton's cheekbone with her thumb. When Sutton's eyes half closed and her lips parted slightly, Jane thought her heart might leap clear out of her chest. Her hand trembled as she fought her need to crush their bodies together.

"You're shaking," Sutton murmured.

Caught by the flecks of blue swirling through her stormy eyes, Jane could only tell the truth. "I want you so much." Ruefully, she shook her head. "And that's not what you need right now. I should go."

"Don't." Sutton trapped her hand against her cheek before she could pull away. "Ever since our first kiss, I haven't been able to stop thinking about your mouth." She reached up, threading her arms around Jane's neck and finally closing the space between her bodies. Jane's head spun at the sensation and she tentatively rested her hands on Sutton's hips.

"Kiss me again," Sutton whispered, tugging her down.

With a soft groan, Jane surrendered. Not wanting to break the spell between them, she held her passion in check and brushed her lips ever so lightly against Sutton's. Immediately, Sutton's grip tightened, holding her closer. When Sutton rose up onto her toes, Jane let her hands slide around the curves of Sutton's waist. And then the world spun as Jane found herself with her own back to the door, skin tingling at the assertive force of Sutton's desire. Their other kisses had always kindled a spark, but this—this was an inferno.

Jane lost herself in the warmth and softness of Sutton's mouth against hers. Dizzy with need, she sucked Sutton's bottom lip between her own, then scraped her teeth gently across it. At the sudden sting of Sutton's fingernails digging into the nape of her neck, Jane's control snapped. She pushed her tongue deep into Sutton's mouth and pulled Sutton firmly against her thigh, reveling in the breathy gasp that greeted her actions. But Sutton battled for dominance, sucking hard on Jane's tongue before twining her fingers through Jane's hair and tugging sharply. The small spike of pain fused with the pleasure to send a bolt of white heat slashing down Jane's spine. The ache grew unbearably sharp, and her knees buckled under the sensual onslaught. Gravity restored her conscience, and with a gasp, she broke the kiss.

"Are you sure this is okay?"

Sutton's eyes, dark and intent, held no sign of uncertainty. "It was more than okay, until you stopped."

Relief made Jane feel even dizzier. "I . . . I don't think I can do this standing up anymore."

Sutton trailed her hands along Jane's waist and hooked a finger through one of her belt buckles. She took one step backward, and then another. "Let's lie down, then."

"I'm not so sure that's a good idea." The words were out of her mouth before she could take them back, but Sutton never stopped moving.

"I am." Her smile was bewitching. "It's only kissing. We can stop whenever you want to."

Jane's arousal increased exponentially with every step. "That's the problem," she murmured hoarsely. "I'm not going to want to."

Deftly, Sutton guided Jane down a short hallway and into the first room on the left. Its walls were painted a light blue and were tastefully decorated with several watercolor paintings. A queen-sized bed filled the far corner, its white coverlet looking soft and inviting. She wanted to topple Sutton onto it and watch her golden hair spill across the lace-fringed pillows. Instead, she forced her arms to hang loose at her sides.

After a few more steps, Sutton planted her free hand in the center of Jane's chest. "Stay."

Jane wanted to make some sort of joke about how she was a Monkey, not a Dog, but the words simply wouldn't come. Her eyes tracked Sutton's every movement as she closed and locked the door, then bent to turn on a space heater. Disbelief warred with her desire. Was this really going to happen? And if so, was Sutton initiating it because it was what she really wanted, or because she wanted to distract herself from thinking about the earlier unpleasantness?

As warm air began to circulate, Sutton returned and tugged at the hem of Jane's shirt. Without speaking, she moved them both across the room, and Jane hurriedly racked her brains for a way to voice her concerns without breaking the moment. When the backs of Sutton's legs touched the bed, she sat and looked up with an expression equal parts desire and longing. Bringing her hands to Jane's hips, she rubbed her thumbs in slow circles. Unable to suppress the whimper that rose from her throat, Jane had to grasp Sutton's shoulder to keep herself upright. Smiling triumphantly, Sutton scooted back on the bed and beckoned.

No longer able or willing to fight her instincts, Jane rested one knee on the mattress before gradually lowering herself to cover Sutton's body with her own. Finally, Jane pressed her lips to that tantalizing spot just above Sutton's breasts that had been tormenting her all night. At Sutton's breathy sigh of encouragement, Jane flicked her tongue against the flushed skin. When Sutton's hips shifted restlessly, Jane kissed her again, and then again. Slowly, she moved up along her collarbone to her jawline, peppering kisses across it until she reached Sutton's earlobe. Closing her lips around it, she sucked gently.

Sutton gasped and pulled her closer, one hand clutching a fistful of Jane's shirt while the other came to rest on Jane's lower back. When Jane swirled her tongue, Sutton's fingertips scraped against her skin, setting her nerves aflame. Suddenly breathless, Jane pulled back just enough to look into Sutton's eyes. Only the thinnest ring of blue encircled her pupils.

"Sutton." Jane didn't know what to say, only that she felt she had to say something. "You're so . . . you feel so . . ."

And then Sutton's hand was cupping the back of her head and pulling her down, down until their lips met again in a surge of softness and heat unlike anything Jane had ever felt before. The kiss went on forever as their tongues tangled in a passionate give and take. Wanting to be even closer, Jane reached down to cup Sutton's hip, her fingers instinctively dipping below the waistband of her slacks. Hot skin seared her fingertips as Sutton's abdomen trembled at her touch. More. She had to have more.

Deepening the kiss, she slid her hand up to the first button on the blouse and prayed her fingers wouldn't fumble. Thankfully, it gave way. As did the next. And the next. When her knuckles brushed against the side of Sutton's breast, all the air left her lungs and she suddenly had to pull back. Breathless, she looked down to behold the pale strip she had just revealed. The edge of a black bra was barely visible.

When Jane looked up, needing to be certain, all she saw in the depths of Sutton's eyes was a need that seemed to match her own. Slowly, she flicked the right half of the shirt aside and then the left, baring Sutton's torso to the cool air. Her mouth began to water as she stared down at the taut expanse of skin framed by her rib cage, now rising and falling with Sutton's quick breaths. She reached out to trace the lower edge of one breast, delighting in Sutton's swift inhale and the smooth sensation of silk beneath her finger.

"You are exquisite." Jane let her palm rest lightly against Sutton's abdomen and stretched out her fingers. Under the soft skin, muscles flickered. Thrilling at Sutton's responsiveness, Jane dipped her head and claimed another long, deep kiss.

Only when Sutton whimpered into her mouth did Jane realize her hand had moved up. Pulling back, she looked down in awe at the sight of her fingers cupping Sutton's left breast. It fit perfectly in her palm, and when she brushed her thumb against the tip, Sutton's nipple pebbled instantly beneath the thin fabric.

"Oh, Jane."

The sound of her own name, whispered in passion, unleashed a storm of desire that frightened Jane with its intensity. She wanted to push that bra up and wrap her tongue around Sutton's nipple. She wanted to rid Sutton of the skirt and slide her hand into the wetness she knew would be waiting. She wanted to crush their bodies together and kiss Sutton hard as she made her come.

Too much. She wanted too much. Her desire would frighten Sutton. And no matter what she might want, she needed never, ever to make Sutton feel afraid. In the next heartbeat, she tore herself away, sitting back on her heels so their bodies were no longer touching. The separation was physical pain, and she clenched her fists against it.

"I . . . I have to stop."

Sutton's glazed eyes sharpened. In the next moment, she fluidly raised herself up, mimicking Jane's position on the mattress. Without blinking, she reached out to touch Jane's cheek with two gentle fingertips. "No. You don't."

"Sutton . . ."

"Shh." Sutton's fingers stroked her jawline with infinite tenderness. "I need you to trust me tonight. Can you do that?"

Jane hesitated. How could she? She didn't even trust herself. But Sutton had used that magical word, *need*, and it made Jane want to try. "All right."

"Good." Her smile was gentle. "Watch me now."

As Sutton reached behind her back, her breasts brushed lightly against Jane's. Even through several layers of fabric, it felt so good that Jane barely managed to hold back a moan. She watched in awe as Sutton pushed her skirt down her hips to expose a black bikini that hugged the juncture of her thighs. Her mouth suddenly dry, Jane raised her hands to her own shirt. She was getting left behind.

"No, let me." Sutton hurriedly kicked off the skirt and knelt before her, easing Jane's hands away and slowly freeing each of her buttons.

As she worked, Jane felt a new surge of anxiety. She hadn't done this, or even anything close, in a long time. She wanted so much to make Sutton feel good, but what if she couldn't? What if she failed? Sutton knew more about the human body than Jane did about anything. What if she couldn't keep up?

When Sutton peeled off Jane's shirt and then pushed her bra over her head, Jane gripped the blanket with both hands, suppressing the urge to cover herself. She felt exposed, and the sharp rush of panic caught her off guard. What if Sutton didn't like what she saw? Or worse, what if this didn't mean to Sutton what it meant to her?

"Jane." The voice was as soft as the fingertips stroking her shoulders. "Look at me."

Sutton's eyes were dark, dark blue—almost black—and swirling with flecks of gold. They held a promise she'd never seen before, and she wanted to fall into them.

"You're beautiful," Sutton whispered, leaning forward to join their lips again in a kiss as soft as the last one had been fierce.

Her hands came up to cradle Jane's face, fingers lightly caressing Jane's cheekbones in synchrony with the slow strokes of her tongue. Instinctively, Jane reached out in return, her hands sliding beneath the parted edges of Sutton's shirt to cup her waist. When Sutton gasped into her mouth, Jane pulled back, dragging her thumbs up and down.

"I want to see you," she said hoarsely, barely recognizing her own voice.

Mutely, Sutton lowered her arms, allowing Jane to rid her of the shirt. Once she had tossed it aside, Jane drank in the sight of Sutton's elegantly sculpted torso, her skin broken only by the black satin bra that cupped her full breasts. Leaning forward, she slid both hands up Sutton's back, fumbling with the clasp as she pressed light kisses to the column of Sutton's neck. When she gently dragged the straps down Sutton's arms, a shiver greeted her touch.

"Are you cold?" she whispered.

"No." The syllable didn't tremble. "I want you."

At the quiet admission, Jane finally let her gaze drop. Sutton's breasts were in perfect proportion to the rest of her body. Pale and full, tipped with dusky pink nipples, they pebbled beneath her admiring stare. When she reached out one hand to brush her fingertips across them, Sutton shivered again. Jane wanted so badly to press her into the mattress and feast on both her mouth and her skin, but she held the impulse firmly in check and looked up, wanting to see into Sutton's soul.

Her eyes held a heat that burned away the last of Jane's doubt. But as she moved to close the remaining space between them, Sutton met her halfway and grasped her shoulders, urging her down. Jane fell willingly, hips surging against Sutton's as they tumbled onto the sheets. Immediately, Sutton loomed over her, hair brushing against her collarbone as she bent to join their lips again.

Beyond pretense, Jane plunged her tongue into Sutton's mouth, needing to be inside her. When Sutton battled back, Jane pulled her hips closer and moaned at the pressure of their bodies grinding together. And then, quite suddenly, Sutton pulled away. Blinking through the haze of her desire, Jane looked up in confusion only to feel her racing heart shift into a higher gear at the sight of Sutton undoing the first button of her slacks.

"Lift your hips."

Jane obeyed, transfixed by the intensity of Sutton's gaze as she eased the trousers down. Once they were off, Sutton trailed her fingers slowly up along Jane's legs. This time, the moan escaped before she could hold it in. But before she could pull Sutton into her arms, Sutton straddled Jane's waist and flipped her hair over her shoulder. Her lips curled in a sensual smile as her gaze roamed down Jane's torso. Spanning her hands across Jane's rib cage, Sutton slowly moved up her body, before finally closing her fingers around Jane's aching breasts.

"Oh, God." Jane struggled to keep her eyes open. She didn't want to miss one millisecond of Sutton gently kneading her skin, looking down with an expression equal parts hunger and delight.

"Mm. You like that, don't you?" Sutton sounded immensely pleased with herself.

Forcing herself to concentrate through the blizzard of desire, Jane skimmed her hands up Sutton's sides. "You're driving me crazy," she said hoarsely. "I need to touch you. I need you to let me."

Sutton cocked her head, regarding Jane thoughtfully. "Oh? You need to?" Falling forward, she rested her palms on either side of Jane's shoulders. Her breasts swayed at the motion, and Jane surged up to capture one nipple in her mouth. It pebbled instantly as she swirled her tongue around it and began to suck. Wanting to tease Sutton into abandon, she fluttered her tongue and was rewarded by sharp gasp. As she continued her light caresses, she raised her hands to sift her fingers through glossy golden hair that had formed a curtain around them.

The longer she teased, the faster Sutton moved against her thigh, and Jane gloried in the clear evidence of her desire. Gradually, she increased the pressure of her mouth against Sutton's breast before daring to bite down gently. When Sutton cried out, arms trembling, she did it once more. And then she switched to the other and began all over again. Sutton's frustrated moan quickly became a soft keening sound that went straight to Jane's head. Resting one palm in the small of her back, Jane urged Sutton's hips down to press more firmly against her leg. As she licked and sucked, she cupped Sutton's free breast, sliding her thumb in slow circles around the sensitive tip. Sutton's responsiveness was beyond anything she could have imagined. Every concern, every insecurity, turned to ash in the conflagration of her desire.

Sutton's movements became even more urgent. "Oh, I . . . I'm—"

Jane pulled her mouth away and surged up, wrapping her arms around Sutton's back and rolling them over. When Sutton's legs opened beneath her, Jane groaned at the sensation of her stomach pressed snugly against the juncture of Sutton's thighs. The need to taste Sutton, to feel her come apart under her tongue, was all consuming. As Sutton shivered beneath her, Jane kissed down the centerline of her body, forcing herself to go slower than she wanted, teasing Sutton and testing herself.

When she reached the boundary of her underwear, Jane hooked her fingers beneath the edge of the fabric. "I want to take these off."

Sutton arched to allow it, and the sensual sight nearly caused Jane to fumble. The last barrier gone, Jane inhaled slowly, pulling Sutton's warm, musky scent deep into her lungs as she settled her shoulders between Sutton's legs. Her pulse leapt again as she took in the delicate beauty of Sutton's sex. Pearls of moisture clung to her rose-colored lips, and at their apex, the tiny, swollen knot of nerves was visibly begging for her touch.

"Please," Sutton whispered brokenly. "Oh, please."

Ducking her head, Jane dipped her tongue into Sutton's opening before sliding it up through her soft folds and ending with a gentle flick. Galvanized by her wordless cry of pleasure, Jane did it again, increasing the pressure. When Sutton began to writhe beneath her, Jane clamped down on her thighs, pushing them even further apart as she willingly lost herself in the act of worshiping Sutton's body.

More than anything, she wanted to make Sutton feel cherished and desired. Wanting to draw out her pleasure, Jane forced herself to be patient. Only when Sutton's pleas reached a fever pitch did Jane finally stop her teasing. She worked her tongue in slow, firm circles, and Sutton clutched at her hair, pulling her even closer. Groaning at the sensation of Sutton's nails digging into her scalp, Jane had to hold on even more tightly when Sutton's hips bucked at the vibration.

"Jane, oh God, I need you to—"

Need. There was that word again. Sutton needed her. Pride filled her chest, along with something else—something deeper and stronger that tugged at her thoughts like a riptide. Suddenly desperate to see Sutton come apart, Jane hollowed her lips, sucking gently while she continued the swirling motion of her tongue. Beneath her palms, Sutton's legs tensed, the muscles growing hard as iron. And then she shuddered violently as the ecstasy found her, and Jane thrilled to the soft cries that accompanied her passion.

Raising her head, Jane met Sutton's pleasure-glazed eyes and fell into them. Wanting her to feel safe and cared for in the aftermath of her release, Jane moved up the bed and gathered her close. The sensation of Sutton curled against her, still shivering, dissolved her pride into awe. Sutton had turned to her, not only for pleasure and comfort, but also for strength. Jane stroked her hair and listened as her gasps gradually resolved into the slow rhythm of sleep. Despite her unfulfilled desire, Jane felt only contentment. Rubbing her cheek lightly against Sutton's hair, she luxuriated in the sensation of Sutton cradled in her arms. Jane wanted to hold her all night, until she had to get up to go to the hospital.

Her grip tightened. Despite her parents' opposition, Sutton had been firm in her conviction to go to Sweden. As proud as Jane was of Sutton's accomplishments, the idea of being an ocean apart from her after all they had shared over the past few weeks—and especially after tonight—filled her with an anxiety to which she was unaccustomed. Why couldn't they have just a little more time to solidify what was happening between them before they were separated?

"Jane." Sutton's murmur brought her out of her thoughts, and she loosened her arms as Sutton struggled to raise her head.

"Hi." Jane's heart thumped painfully when their eyes met. "You're so beautiful."

"And you're amazing." Sutton blinked sleepily even as her hand began to trail down Jane's side.

Every cell in her body lit up under the purposeful touch, but Jane trapped that hand against her ribs before it could descend any lower. "You're exhausted," she said. "And it's been a crazy day. And you have to get up early for rounds. I'm okay."

The bridge of Sutton's nose wrinkled as she frowned. "You don't want—?"

"Believe me, I want." Jane tried to shove aside the ache of desire Sutton had reawakened. "But I also want you to rest."

Sutton opened her mouth to reply, only to be overcome by a yawn. Burying her face in Jane's neck, she was silent for a few moments before she shifted so that her mouth was poised next to Jane's ear. The light puffs of her warm breaths were incredibly distracting.

"Touch yourself for me."

Jane's body jerked at the unexpected and visceral words. "Um. Really?"

"Yes." Sutton kissed her earlobe. "I want to watch you. And feel you."

The sensual command burned away what was left of Jane's self-consciousness. Never breaking Sutton's gaze, she slid her right hand down her belly and beneath the waistband of her briefs. Sutton's hazy eyes bored into hers as Jane followed the curve of her own thigh.

"Tell me how you feel," Sutton whispered.

"Wet. From touching you." Jane swallowed convulsively as she moved her fingers up. Had she ever been this sensitive? She struggled to focus. "I don't think . . . I can last very long."

"You don't have to." Sutton lowered her head to kiss down the column of Jane's neck. "Just keep going."

As Sutton continued to trail kisses along her collarbone, Jane obeyed. Pressing harder, she groaned involuntarily as the motion sent sparks skittering under her skin. The familiarity of her own touch collided with the newness of Sutton's lips brushing random patterns across her sternum.

"I love seeing you like this," Sutton whispered between kisses. "It's even better than I imagined."

Jane dimly realized that Sutton was admitting to having fantasized about her. But then Sutton's mouth was on her breast, and the sensation drove every thought from her head. Pressure coiled in her abdomen, coalescing into a tight knot deep inside.

"Sutton," she groaned, circling faster. "I can't . . ."

Suddenly, Sutton cupped her hand between Jane's legs, pressing down on the fabric covering her fingers. The extra pressure was all Jane needed, and with a hoarse shout, she tumbled over the edge into oblivion.

Only when the last of the aftershocks had passed did Jane feel Sutton lift her head and move her hand. Settling back into the curve of Jane's side, she wrapped one arm around her waist.

"Thank you for trusting me with that."

"So good." Jane licked her own dry lips as she struggled to focus through the haze of endorphins and fatigue. She wanted to say so much more, but the right words eluded her. "Sutton, I—"

"Shh." Sutton cuddled closer. "Sleep now. Hold me. Okay?"

"Okay." Smothering disappointment that Sutton hadn't let her finish, Jane focused instead on curling her body around Sutton's smaller frame.

Sutton had asked her to spend the night. For the moment, they were together. As she closed her eyes and inhaled the scent of lilacs, Jane tried to convince herself that nothing else really mattered.

CHAPTER ELEVEN

SUTTON WOKE THE WAY she always did—abruptly, without any transition from sleep to wakefulness, five minutes before her alarm. But this morning, something was different. She could feel it beneath her skin, even before she looked to her left and saw Jane sleeping beside her, one arm curled around her head and the other hand splayed across her stomach. Affection rushed through her at the sight, and she felt a smile curve her lips. Asleep, there was an air of vulnerability about Jane that Sutton had never perceived before, and it made her feel protective even as the sight of her nearly naked body rekindled Sutton's desire.

Their chemistry last night had been incredible—far, far beyond anything else Sutton had ever experienced. Her face flashed hot at the memory of Jane pleading for the chance to touch her. In granting that wish, she had given Jane the power to turn the tables, and that wasn't like her. In her previous sexual encounters—not that there were all that many to speak of—Sutton had always preferred to be in control. But something about Jane made it easy for her to let down her guard and relax. And the way Jane had touched her, at once gently and possessively, had driven her absolutely wild.

Mesmerized by the steady rhythm of Jane's breathing, she couldn't help but focus in on her breasts, compact and topped by dark brown nipples. If she concentrated, she could remember exactly how they had hardened beneath her tongue as Jane grew closer and closer to release. Her field of vision narrowed, and her throat convulsed in a swallow as arousal burned away the last of her fatigue.

With a rueful shake of her head, she disentangled herself from the sheets and padded toward her bathroom. Jane needed to sleep, not to be jumped before the sun even came up. And she had to get to the hospital, where a busy morning of rounds awaited. With thoughts of work came thoughts of her father, and in an attempt to put him out of her head, she splashed cold water on her face more vigorously than she had intended.

After putting in her contacts, Sutton stared at her reflection. Aside from the lingering blush, she looked no different than she had yesterday. And yet, over the past twelve hours, she had chosen a career path, stood up to her parents, and had the best sex of her life. The thought gave her pause. Calling it that—even only in her thoughts—felt wrong, somehow. She and Jane had shared a night of intimacy. It had been beautiful as well as pleasurable, and she didn't want to cheapen it.

When she reentered the bedroom, she found that Jane had turned over in her sleep. She was clutching her pillow with both hands, and the sheet had bunched up around her waist. Sutton's mouth went dry at the sight, and before she could stop herself, she was kneeling on the bed. The alarm clock taunted her with its large red numbers, and she did a quick mental calculation. If she skipped her morning yoga and grabbed breakfast on the go instead of at the cafeteria, she could buy herself an extra forty-five minutes. And she knew exactly how she wanted to spend them.

She placed her first kiss on the nape of Jane's neck, and her second just a few inches lower at the top of her spine. From there, she swept her lips first to the right and then to the left, covering the entire width of Jane's shoulders. The comforting scent of Jane's warm skin washed over her, and she inhaled deeply, wanting more. Her kisses became haphazard: one on Jane's shoulder blade, one on her flank, one next to a small mole in the center of her back. Only when she lightly rubbed her cheek against the soft skin at the base of Jane's spine, did she finally stir.

"Sutton?"

Hearing her name spoken in the low, gravelly tones of Jane's early morning voice only increased Sutton's arousal. She pressed one palm between Jane's shoulders and leaned in close to whisper in her ear.

"Don't move."

Replacing her lips with her hands, Sutton slowly massaged her way down the length of Jane's back. Soft groans of pleasure egged her on, and she luxuriated in the sensation of firm muscles yielding beneath her fingertips. When she reached Jane's hips, she hooked her fingers beneath the waistband of her underwear and tugged.

"Lift up."

Once she was naked, Jane tried to roll over, but Sutton kept her in place with a firm hand on the small of her back. Slowly, she ran her palms along the curves of Jane's buttocks and down the backs of her thighs.

"So good," Jane groaned.

"What's so good?"

"The way your hands feel on me."

She laughed softly. "Just you wait." With a gentle push, she eased Jane's right leg up, teasing her inner thigh with light touches that provoked her hips into restless movement. Her responsiveness was like a drug, demolishing Sutton's restraint, and she finally gave in to the urge to brush her fingertips across Jane's most sensitive skin.

"Oh, God." The tortured whisper that greeted her caress sent an electric charge through Sutton.

"Shall I do that again?"

"P-please."

This time, Sutton slid two fingers through Jane's folds, finding her wet and swollen. Intoxicated by the clear evidence of her desire, Sutton bent to kiss the nape of Jane's neck as she made her touch firmer, rubbing slow circles around the tiny knot of hardness in the midst of so much softness. When Jane cried out wordlessly, her every muscle tightening, Sutton eased off on the pressure. Jane whimpered and Sutton kissed her again, intoxicated by the sensual power she possessed in this moment. Never had she felt so present, so connected, so alive.

Suddenly desperate to see Jane's face, Sutton moved her hand away. "Turn over."

Jane rolled onto her back, craning her neck and clutching the sheet in her fists. Her stomach rippled as she held herself up, and her chest rose and fell rapidly with her quick, shallow breaths. Planting her hand between Jane's breasts, Sutton pushed lightly.

"Lie back. Relax."

Jane let her head fall back to the pillow. "Can't."

Sutton claimed a gentle kiss before trailing her lips down to Jane's ear. "Yes, you can. Just feel me, touching you."

Her words elicited a shiver, and she pulled away just enough to look down into Jane's wide, dark eyes. They pleaded with her silently and she acquiesced, kissing a path down Jane's body, lingering briefly on her breasts and on the soft, pale skin around her navel. By the time she reached the apex of Jane's thighs, her every other breath emerged as a moan.

Sutton traced a slow line down Jane's center, ending at her opening. Dipping one finger into the moisture that had gathered there, she looked up along the curves and planes of Jane's torso. Her hips arched in a clear effort to pull Sutton inside. Suddenly desperate to be there, Sutton made herself go slowly. She wanted to savor this.

"Please, oh please." Jane's head thrashed against the pillow as she begged.

"Tell me what you want."

Jane's eyes snapped open. "Be inside me. Please. I need you."

I need you. Alarm bells sounded deep in Sutton's brain but the sweet rush of desire drowned them out. Carefully, she pushed the very tip of her finger inside, watching in fascination as the space between them became nonexistent. Jane's body clutched at her. When she set up a slow, steady pace, Jane's knuckles turned as white as the sheets. Mouth watering, Sutton dipped her head, dying to know Jane's taste.

As soon as she flicked out her tongue, the smooth muscles clenched hard around her finger. Jane was so close already, and Sutton suddenly couldn't wait any longer. Gliding more quickly, she felt Jane throb against her mouth as she increased the pressure of her lips. Jane pulsed beneath her, around her, and Sutton exulted in the rush of wetness that accompanied her sharp cry of release. Slinging one arm over Jane's abdomen, Sutton held her thighs open as they tried to close against the pleasure. Determined not to stop until Jane was entirely sated, Sutton coaxed every last tremor from her body until her muscles went limp.

When she finally raised her head, she smiled triumphantly at the sight of Jane, eyes closed, her glistening torso rising and falling as she gasped for air, her fingers still gripping the sheets. At once handsome and beautiful, she was a study in sensual abandon. As Sutton admired her, Jane pried one hand from the sheets and reached out blindly. Touched by the gesture, Sutton laced their fingers together and moved up to stretch out alongside her. Gold-flecked eyes blinked up at her, completely unguarded. Sutton felt her heart turn over in her chest, even though she knew that was medically impossible. The feeling should have been frightening, but as she gently traced the contours of Jane's rib cage, she wasn't scared at all. She only wanted more.

"You're amazing," Jane said hoarsely.

"I'm sorry I woke you."

"Don't you dare be sorry."

Sutton had to smile at Jane's earnestness. "I know it's early, but you were irresistible." She rested her hand over Jane's heart, automatically cataloguing the slowing of her pulse.

"How long before you have to go?"

"Ten minutes." Sutton settled her face against Jane's neck. "Hold me for five?"

"Of course." Jane rubbed her cheek against Sutton's hair. "Whatever you want."

Sutton sighed and closed her eyes. Whatever she wanted. She didn't want to think about that too hard. What if she was starting to want more than she should?

"Five more minutes," she whispered, cuddling even closer. "I just want five more minutes."

THE DAY HAD TURNED blustery, and raindrops spattered down haphazardly from the ominous gray sky above. Jane walked faster, hoping the clouds decided not to open up. But even a downpour wouldn't dampen her spirits today. After the brief good-bye kiss she had shared with Sutton outside her building early that morning, she had wandered the few blocks home in a daze. She felt as though she had emerged into an entirely new city. Despite the dreary weather, the streets seemed cleaner and the air brighter. Even the pedestrians, hustling to the nearest subway station to begin their morning commutes, looked happier.

Since then, she had managed to accomplish her morning duties while focusing with only half her brain. The other half had been reliving every second of the time she'd spent with Sutton, relishing each sensual detail. At times, her memories felt like dreams, and at one point she had paused halfway through taping up a box, wondering whether she had hallucinated the entire interlude. But if she closed her eyes, she could feel Sutton's surrender and hear her soft cries of pleasure.

She hadn't dreamt it. They had made love. And every moment had been amazing.

As Jane rounded the corner toward Red Door Apothecary, she tried to compose herself. If she didn't, Sue would be able to read her like an open book, and Jane wanted to keep her newfound intimacy with Sutton as close to the chest as possible. Her entire extended family might know that she hadn't slept in her own bed last night, but hopefully, they would respect her privacy. Composing herself, she opened the door, stepped over the threshold, and immediately drew up short.

The store was more crowded than she had ever seen it. Previously, the apothecary had been patronized mostly by Chinese Americans, but this afternoon, the customers were almost as diverse as New York City itself. Sue looked harried as she tried to answer a young woman's question while ringing up a purchase for an elderly gentleman. And then, to top it off, the phone rang.

Jane darted across the room to grab it before it could go to voicemail. Sue shot her an appreciative look as she hefted the receiver. Only when she raised it to her ear did Jane realize it was connected by a cord. What was this, the Dark Ages?

"Red Door Apothecary. How may I help you?"

"Good afternoon," said a male voice. "My name is Dan Wong from News 4 New York, and I'm hoping to speak with Ms. Xue Si Ma."

Jane blinked down at the countertop. The local NBC news affiliate wanted to speak with Sue? "I'm Jane, her assistant," she said, claiming the title she had long since earned. "Sue is busy at the moment, but I'd be happy to take a message if you'd like."

"Great. Let her know that News 4 would like to do a brief piece on her store for a special-interest feature on thriving small businesses in the city. If she agrees, we'd like to set up a time to shoot some footage next week."

"Will do." Fumbling for a pen, Jane looked around for a scrap of paper, found nothing, and hurriedly wrote Dan's number on the back of her hand. As she returned the phone to its cradle, she looked up to see that the line at the register had grown even longer, and the young woman was still waiting—now impatiently—for Sue's help. Instead of trying to pose as an expert apothecary, she side-stepped around the counter and tapped Sue on the shoulder.

"Let me take care of the register. You handle the questions."

"Oh, thank you."

Sue looked completely drained, and as Jane began to ring up the next customer's purchases, she thought back to the last time she'd been in the store, one week ago. It had been busier than usual, but nothing like this. Later today, she was going to have to find Minetta and figure out what on earth she had done for her school project that had managed to raise the apothecary's profile so extremely in the past week. Cringing at the thought of how many unchecked e-mails were waiting in Sue's inbox, she made fast work of the queue.

Once the store's congestion had eased, Sue leaned heavily against the countertop. "Thank you so much, Jane. I don't know what I would have done without you."

Jane waved away her gratitude. "You would have managed. But I think it might be time for you to hire someone who can be here more than I can."

"You may be right." Another customer walked into the store, and Sue greeted the person briefly before turning back to Jane. "Who was on the phone?"

"News 4. They want to do a special-interest piece on the store." When Sue's jaw dropped, Jane smiled. "I know, right? Pretty cool. Just think how much business you'll have after that."

Sue paled. "I'm not sure how much more I can handle."

"You'll be fine." Jane patted her shoulder awkwardly. "Especially once you hire someone." But when Sue only continued to look sick with worry, Jane realized she was going to have to do a lot more than simply offer platitudes.

"Okay, how about this. I'll go check out your volume of online orders. You stay here and keep the customers happy. If you run into another traffic jam, just come and get me."

"What about the reporters?" Sue was actually wringing her hands. Jane didn't think she'd ever seen someone do that before.

"We'll worry about them later." She flashed what she hoped was an encouraging smile. "Trust me. It's all going to be okay."

Leaving Sue's skeptical expression behind her, Jane sat down at the computer in the back room. Just as she'd suspected, Sue's inbox was overflowing. Even after weeding out the spam and printing the messages containing questions Sue would have to answer herself, the number of orders was daunting. Suddenly overwhelmed, Jane leaned back in the chair and closed her eyes, taking momentary solace in her memories.

Two hours and one mug of foul-tasting tea later, Jane had processed and boxed half the orders. Twice, Sue had called her out from the back to help with additional customers. The store was finally empty for the first time, and Jane took the opportunity to collapse onto the couch. Her lower back was starting to ache and her eyes felt like sandpaper. The rest would have to wait until tomorrow.

"Are you all right?" Sue hovered above her like an anxious butterfly. "Let me get you more tea."

"No! No. Thank you. Really." Jane pried open her eyes. "I'm fine. But I think I need to be done for the day."

"I cannot thank you enough." Sue hurried back toward the register. "Here, let me pay you something."

"No way. Absolutely not." Jane sat on her hand and shook her head while Sue brandished several twenty-dollar bills at her. "Save them for whoever you hire."

Sue's face fell. "How should I find someone? How can I be sure they're trustworthy?"

"Go with someone local. Someone whose family you know. They'll have more accountability that way. And—"

The sudden chime of her phone made whatever else she'd been planning to say fly out of her head, and she grabbed it from her pocket before the display could grow dark. Text from Sutton St. James: *I'm in Noodle Treasure. Join me when you're free?*

There was nothing Jane could do to hide her smile. The text might not scream hearts and flowers, but it clearly demonstrated that Sutton was thinking about her and wanted to see her. She'd take it. Fatigue forgotten, she jumped to her feet.

"I have an idea." She quickly checked her watch. "It's almost five. I know you're normally open for another hour, but let's close the place early today and grab a bite at Noodle Treasure."

"But—"

"You've done at least twice as much business as usual today, right? And have you eaten a thing since breakfast?"

"Well, no, but—"

Jane tried to look stern as she pointed toward the door. "That's it. Out."

Sue must have truly been exhausted, because she didn't put up any more of a fight. Within a few minutes, they were walking north. Jane turned her face toward the sun, soaking up what warmth she could, thankful for the extra hour of daylight. The promise of spring filled the air, making her feel buoyant inside. This really was the perfect season for falling in love.

She stopped short as she caught herself, prompting a muffled obscenity from the person walking behind her and a concerned glance from Sue. Her heart was suddenly pounding in her ears. Falling in love? Where had that come from?

"Are you all right?"

"Sure. Of course. Sorry." Jane lurched forward and spent the remainder of the walk lecturing herself about how falling in love was not on the agenda.

Even so, when she didn't see Sutton in the window, she began to worry. Had she been called into the hospital? Jane was just about to flag down Benny and beg an explanation when she caught sight of Sutton sharing Min's table. Their heads were bent over some kind of textbook, and Sutton was tapping her finger on the page as she explained something.

It was hard, now, to remember a time when she hadn't been a regular at the restaurant. She had so easily charmed Jane's entire family, not to mention members of the broader community like Sue and Mei. She'd become a fixture in their lives within a matter of months. And soon, she would be gone. Poof. Just like that. Trying to ignore the tightness in the back of her throat, Jane concentrated on soaking up the moment.

"Sue, how wonderful to see you." Giancarlo rose from his seat near the door and bent to deliver two cheek-kisses.

Jane didn't pay their cuteness any mind. She couldn't take her eyes off Sutton, who was dressed more casually than usual today in a purple sweatshirt and scrubs. Her hair was down, and as she flipped it over her shoulders, Jane flashed back to the sensation of the silky strands brushing against her collarbone.

She shivered, and that was when Sutton looked up. A slow smile bloomed on her lips, and her light blue eyes grew several shades darker. Jane suddenly couldn't pull a deep breath into her lungs. This was crazy. She had never felt anything like this before. These feelings happened to the characters in the romance novels in her mother's nightstand that she'd read on the sly as a teen, not to real people.

And yet.

"Hi." When Sutton spoke, Jane realized she had crossed the room without being aware of it. Tracing the edge of the table, she tried to think of something to say that wouldn't sound inane.

"Hey."

The monosyllables hung in the air between them, and Jane silently cursed everyone else in the restaurant. If not for them, she would have leaned down and shown Sutton exactly how much she'd missed her. Compared to one of their electrifying kisses, all words— even poetry—were paltry.

"How was your day?" Not the most original line, but she really was curious. And she had to say something.

Sutton's lips twitched. "My morning was spectacular. Everything else paled in comparison."

Jane flashed hot, every muscle in her body suddenly paralyzed by the onslaught of memories. "Um." She swallowed hard. "Glad to hear it."

"Oh my god."

Blinking, Jane glanced over at Min, who was shaking her head and starting to pack up her books. "What?"

"I'm getting out of here. And you guys need to get a room."

"Minetta. Knock it off."

Min must have heard the note of real anger in Jane's voice, because she sighed and glanced at Sutton. "I'm sorry."

Sutton waved off her apology. "You're sure you're feeling okay about the cell nucleus? Because we can go over it one more time if you'd like."

"I'll be good. Thanks." She turned to Jane. "See you at home. Or . . . not." And then she darted out the door before Jane could open her mouth.

"That kid." Shaking her head, Jane settled into the vacated seat. She hoped Sutton wasn't upset. "Even if her apology was insincere, mine isn't."

Sutton's hand slid over to cup her knee. Such a simple touch, but the intimacy it signified felt so, so good. When Sutton began to slide her thumb back and forth, Jane felt a profound sense of relief even as her pulse jumped.

"I wasn't insulted," Sutton said. "She's just trying to get a rise out of you. She loves you, and she wants your attention."

"And she's too perceptive for her own good."

Sutton laughed softly. "That too." She leaned in closer. "You look exhausted."

"That reminds me." Jane looked out the window, but Minetta

had completely disappeared. "I meant to ask Min what she did on-line to turn Sue's shop into a madhouse. It was a zoo in there. I'm completely beat."

"And you were up early this morning."

Jane wanted so badly to plant a kiss on that tantalizing spot be-hind Sutton's ear. She loved the subtle, vaguely floral fragrance of her skin, and its flower-petal softness. "Believe me when I say I'm not complaining."

Her eyes glinted. "I'm happy to hear that." Slowly, her hand moved higher, tracing the inner seam of Jane's jeans. "I have an idea. Would you like to hear it?"

At that moment, Jane would have happily listened to her read the phone book. Though come to think of it, did they even print phone books anymore? "I'm all ears."

"Since we're both tired, why don't we go back to my apartment and order a pizza?"

"O-okay." Jane didn't even care that she was stammering. Her brain was overloaded with visions of the two of them lying in Sutton's bed, twined around each other, a half-empty pizza box forgotten on the nightstand.

"As soon as we're alone again," Sutton whispered, "I want you to tell me exactly what popped into your head just now."

"Why is that?"

"Because your eyes got all hazy, just like they did this morning."

"Oh." For the second time in ten minutes, Jane cursed her in-ability to come up with an eloquent response. She was a published poet, yet Sutton had the power to reduce her to grunting monosyl-lables.

Sutton smiled knowingly. "Come on. Let's go."

As they approached the front door, they had to pass Giancarlo's table. Jane momentarily hoped that he and Sue would be too caught up in each other to notice them, but as they walked by, Sue called her name. Her color was high and an excited smile brightened her face.

"Giancarlo is being such a help!" she said, patting his hand where it lay on the table next to a pair of unused chopsticks. "He thinks his nephew may want to work in the shop."

"A trustworthy boy," Giancarlo added, nodding sagely. "Very serious. Good head for business."

"That's great," Jane said, even as she began inching toward the door.

"That must be a relief," Sutton echoed, keeping pace with her.

"Jane." Sue suddenly became serious. "If he does want the job, would you mind teaching him how to do . . . everything you do?"

"No problem. Happy to." Jane flashed a quick smile that she hoped didn't betray her eagerness. "Okay. We're heading out. See you around. Tomorrow. Sometime."

Giancarlo smiled indulgently, and Sue gave them a little wave. Just before she turned, Jane realized their hands were clasped on the tabletop. That was a step forward. They were so sweet together. *Love can find you at any time,* she thought. She should remember that line. It would make a good fortune.

"You're smiling," Sutton said as they emerged into the gathering dusk. "Tell me why."

"Because I'm happy." Jane reached for her hand, feeling so light inside. So free. "It's that simple. You, us, them, this . . . this whole thing. All of it makes me happy."

When Sutton's expression grew pensive, Jane realized she might have said too much. "But do you know what would make me even happier?"

"What?"

"Going back to your place and ordering that pizza."

CHAPTER TWELVE

SUTTON PERCHED ON A stool near the register, sipping a tea made from some kind of root that she still couldn't pronounce despite the fact that Sue had repeated the name twice. It smelled pungent and tasted awful, but she was determined to finish the whole thing.

"You're really part of the family now," Jane had said, her nose wrinkling as they clinked mugs.

Part of the family. The warmth in her chest somewhat mitigated the bitterness of the tea. When she sat back and thought about it, the way in which Jane's friends and relatives had embraced her was truly remarkable. Despite the many cultural differences, she felt more at home with them in many ways than with her own parents.

Today marked one week since her announcement about Sweden, and she still hadn't spoken to either of them since. Jane had invited her to dinner with her aunt and uncle tonight, even going so far as to promise that Min would be on her best behavior. Sutton knew exactly what Jane was doing—trying to provide a distraction so she wouldn't feel upset during her family's habitual Sunday night family time. She was so considerate that way. And not only to her, of course—Jane's generosity clearly permeated the entire community. She helped Min with her homework. She donated her time to Sue's shop. Today, as soon as the news crew arrived, she had jumped up to lend them a hand. Sutton didn't think she had ever met a more selfless person.

Right now, Jane was helping Giancarlo's nephew, Giovanni, move the couch so that it could be better illuminated by the hot, bright lights the crew had brought. Over the past few days, Jane had been busy teaching him how to help manage Sue's inventory. Tall and lanky, with a shock of red hair that was constantly falling into his eyes, he wore wire-rimmed glasses and his Adam's apple bobbed precipitously every time he swallowed. Today he sported a blazer that was slightly too large and slacks that were slightly too short. He and his dark-haired, debonair uncle looked about as related as an ostrich and a sparrow.

Sutton glanced at Min, sitting a few feet away. She had her phone out, but was holding it idly against her knee, its screen dark. Ever since Jane had introduced them both to Giovanni, Min hadn't been able to take her eyes off him. By all indications, she had the beginnings of a crush, and it was adorable. Sutton couldn't wait to hear Jane's reaction.

Of course, she thought as she watched Jane conversing with Dan, the reporter, it wouldn't be fair for her to poke too much fun at Min when she was nursing a crush herself. A few weeks ago, it would have frightened her to admit such a thing, but at this point there was no use in denying it. Unexpectedly, Jane had become an important person in her life. As long as she didn't lose her head completely, where was the harm in admitting it?

Perhaps, just to be safe, she shouldn't invite Jane home with her this evening. They hadn't spent a night apart since their first time together, and maybe that was a little crazy. But it felt so good to fall asleep each night curled into the curve of Jane's body, one arm slung around her waist, luxuriating in the aftermath of their shared pleasure. She couldn't remember ever having slept so well.

The door opened to admit Giancarlo, and Sutton watched as Sue looked up from her conversation with a customer to wave shyly at him. They were adorable. Romance certainly seemed to be in the air at the moment, and Sutton found herself wondering whether

anyone had ever tried to scientifically study why so many relationships blossomed in the springtime.

"Doctor Sutton!" Giancarlo's jovial voice pulled her out of her
thoughts. He leaned against the counter and stroked his mustache
as he smiled. "And Minetta. How are you both?"

"Fine, thanks," Min said, quickly returning her attention to his
nephew.

Sutton struggled not to laugh. "I'm well. And you?"

He mimed wiping sweat from his forehead. "Sundays are always so
busy at the restaurant, but I wanted to see how everything is here."

"Fine so far. I think they're about ready to start filming."

"Good, good." He patted her on the shoulder. "I'll be back in a
moment. Excuse me."

As he headed in Sue's direction, Sutton's attention was caught
by Jane. She had tied her plaid flannel shirt around her waist, and
the white tank top beneath accentuated the swell of her breasts. As
she approached, Sutton had to grip the edge of her stool to stop herself from smoothing her palms along Jane's waistline and dipping
under the hem of her shirt. Just last night, she had pressed her hand
firmly against the soft, hot skin of Jane's abdomen, holding her in
place as she drew out her desire with gentle, teasing strokes. If she
concentrated, she could still hear the needy sounds Jane had made
in response.

"Penny for your thoughts?"

Sutton blinked and focused immediately on Jane's broad smile.
Whatever her expression had been, it must have given her away. But
she wasn't about to let Jane have the upper hand so easily. "A penny?
Seriously?"

"It's an expression."

"Mmhmm."

"So you're not going to tell me what you were thinking?"

"Not until you give me a clearer picture of how much that would
be worth to you."

Jane's eyes—mostly brown today, with just a touch of green—grew darker, and she leaned down so that her mouth was close to Sutton's ear.

"I'll give you anything you want," she murmured, her breath ghosting against Sutton's neck, raising goose bumps in its wake. "Anything. Really."

"Really."

Sutton turned her face slightly, not wanting her words to be overheard. "I was thinking about the sounds you were making last night."

When Jane pulled back and jammed her hands into her pockets, Sutton smiled up at her sweetly, loving the clear effect of her words. The muscles in Jane's arms stood out in sharp relief, and her jaw was tightly clenched. She was vibrating with tension, and Sutton wanted nothing more than to drag Jane back to her apartment and allow all that passion to be unleashed.

"All right, everyone, let's begin!" Dan's raised voice cut through the room, curtailing all conversation. "We're going to start by filming a few astrological consultations. So, I need some volunteers." He glanced around the shop and suddenly pointed at Sutton. "How about you? The camera loves you."

"I guess that runs in my family," Sutton murmured.

"You really don't have to." Jane said.

Dan beckoned her forward. "It won't take more than ten minutes."

Sutton was possessed of a sudden urge not to just sit on the periphery anymore. This little community had given her a second home. The least she could do was to give back ten minutes, even if they were in front of a camera. She might be incapable of pleasing her own parents, but she could do this much for Sue.

"All right. I'll do it."

"That's the spirit!" Dan gave her one of those kilowatt smiles that media people always seemed to be able to summon at will. "Come on down. We'll get you and Sue hooked up with mics."

As one of the technicians clipped a small microphone to her shirt collar, she smiled reassuringly at Sue, who was starting to look a little green. "Don't worry," she said. "We've done this before, remember? Let's focus on that and forget all about the cameras."

Sue took a deep breath as she sat down on the couch and rested her hands on the large book she had consulted last time. "Of course. Yes. Thank you."

"Okay," Dan said as Sutton sat beside her. "We're rolling. Go ahead and start. Don't worry about any gaffes. We'll be editing this down quite a bit. Just pretend we're not here."

Sutton angled her body toward Sue, trying to ignore the heat and light of the lamps beating down on her shoulders. Just behind the cameras, Jane was watching avidly. Tuning out the media was one thing, but ignoring Jane was much easier said than done.

Sue flipped open her file folder and extracted Sutton's chart. Her fingers were trembling slightly, but as she met Sutton's eyes, she grew visibly calmer. "Since we've already discussed your basic chart, and what it means that you were born in the year of the Earth Dragon, we can move on to answering some of your more specific questions. Is there any aspect of your life that has been particularly on your mind, recently? Your career? Family? Love life?"

"My career," Sutton said, thinking it would be the safest to discuss.

"No, no, no," Dan interjected. "Careers are boring. No one wants to hear about that. Talk about her family and love life instead!"

When Sue raised her eyebrows, Sutton reluctantly nodded her assent. It wasn't as though she believed in astrology anyway. If the conversation became uncomfortable, she could always ask Dan to edit part of it out.

"Very well. We'll focus on your family and love life today." Sue glanced down at the book and then back up to Sutton. "When did you have your last menstrual cycle?"

Sutton could only hope she wasn't blushing. It was impossible for her to tell under the heat of the lamps, but she hoped her flash of discomfort wasn't obvious. She was a physician, and periods were a fact of life. "Let me check," she said, pulling her phone from her pocket.

"You keep track on your phone?" Jane's voice sounded incredulous, and Sutton had to force herself not to look up and glare.

"Shhhhh!" someone said.

Sutton tried to focus. "When did it last start, or when did I begin ovulating?"

Sue looked up from what she was writing. "Oh, both would be wonderful."

As Sutton read off the dates, she heard Min whisper, "Is there an app for that?"

"Probably," Jane said.

"Shhhhh!"

"When were your parents born?" Sue asked. At Sutton's reply, a frown creased her brow. "And you have no siblings, correct?"

"No."

"This will likely be a year of conflict for your family," Sue said. "As you know, the year of the Monkey has just begun. The Monkey is a sign of cleverness and inquisitiveness, and the years that it governs are full of epiphanies. These revelations may create tension between you and your parents."

Sutton struggled not to betray surprise at the accuracy of Sue's prognostication. Surely it was a coincidence, wasn't it?

Sue's frown deepened. "Also, this is not a good year for you to conceive a child. In fact, you must avoid doing so at all costs. See?" She stabbed her finger down on the page. "The Monkey child tramples the Dragon mother!"

Taken aback, Sutton shook her head. "Don't worry. That's not going to happen for a long, long time. If ever."

Sue's expression turned wistful. "Oh, I hope you do decide to become a mother. You would be wonderful. But not right now." She looked back to the page. "And after—let me just do a quick conversion—May first, you should not enter into a new relationship for the remainder of the year." She raised her head and wagged her index finger. "Very bad idea."

Relief that she had met Jane before that deadline was trumped, moments later, by logic's insistence that their relationship was casual and temporary. The emotional seesaw made her feel a little dizzy, and she leaned back against the couch as she struggled to regain her equilibrium.

"However," Sue continued, "if you do begin a relationship before May first, it has the potential to grow into a powerful and durable connection."

"Okay." Sutton forced her thoughts away from Jane. How could they build something powerful and durable when both their lives were so up in the air? "Is there anything else?"

"Not at the moment." Sue extended her slender hand. "Best wishes as the year continues."

"Thank you," Sutton replied.

"And, cut." Dan stepped forward. "Thanks. We should be able to use some of that. Now let's see if we can get footage of someone new to the process. A customer, maybe?"

"I'm new," Giovanni said, moving into the circle of light.

Dan looked him up and down critically. "But are you legal?"

"I just turned eighteen."

"All right, have a seat."

Sutton surrendered her microphone and rejoined Jane, who immediately reached for her hand. "Are you doing okay? Some of that hit a little close to home."

As much as Sutton appreciated her concern, she didn't feel like having a serious conversation right now. "You mean the part about being sure not to conceive a child?"

Jane's shoulders hunched as she tried to keep her laughter quiet. "'The Monkey child tramples the Dragon mother?' What on earth is that supposed to mean?"

"I don't know, but it sounds ominous." She leaned her shoulder against Jane's. "Good thing you can't get me pregnant."

"Mm." For a moment, it looked as though Jane wanted to say something more, but then she apparently thought better of it. "Do you want to get out of here? We can hang out at my aunt and uncle's until dinner's ready, or we can stay. Up to you."

"Let's go." Sutton tapped Min on the shoulder. "Coming with us?"

"I'll stay," she said, never taking her eyes off Giovanni. "Text me when dinner's ready."

"Sure thing, Your Highness." When Min didn't so much as react, Jane looked to Sutton. "What's gotten into her?"

"I'll tell you, but not here."

Sutton led her toward the door and out into the night. The temperature was mild for late March, but still too cool to be wearing only a tank top, even for Jane. Once she had shrugged back into her shirt, Sutton linked their arms together.

"How old is Min again?"

"Eleven. Why?"

"You're going to need to have a talk with her."

"About?"

"About the fact that she has a crush on an eighteen-year-old."

Jane's expression was the very definition of incredulous, and Sutton wished her phone was handy for a snapshot. "You're kidding me. Giovanni?"

"From the moment you introduced him, she became a homing beacon."

"Really?" Jane shook her head. "I've never seen her behave that way. Or even talk about boys. Which is good. She's so young!"

"Stop panicking. It's just a crush." When they paused at a stoplight, Sutton rested her head briefly against Jane's shoulder. "Besides, I'm pretty sure he didn't notice her existence on the planet."

"But that's not good, either. She'll get her heart broken! You know Min—she's incredibly bright and annoyingly snarky, but deep down, she's still just a kid who can get her feelings hurt as easily as anyone else. What should I do?"

Sutton had to bite her lip in order to keep herself from laughing. Jane, who was one of the most laid-back people she had ever met, was acting like an overprotective sibling and a hapless matchmaker all at once. She had quite suddenly become neurotic. It was completely endearing.

"Just listen if she wants to talk to you about it."

"That's it?"

"Well, you could always give her the full court press and see how well that works."

"Point taken." Jane let out a sigh as she unlocked the front door to Confucius Fortunes and held it so Sutton could pass by.

The sensation of her phone buzzing brought her up short, and as she fished it out, she looked down at the display. Mom. For a moment, her thumb hovered over the ACCEPT button, but then she slid the phone back into her pocket. Her mother hadn't reached out all week, but had decided to call during their usual dinner time? That seemed like a guilt trip, and Sutton wasn't about to indulge her.

"Sure you don't want to take it?" Jane asked quietly.

Sutton shook her head. "I want to spend an enjoyable evening with your family. I'll call her back later."

Jane kissed her gently. "Okay."

As they ascended the stairs, Sutton tried to put her mother out of her mind, at least for the next few hours. She wanted to learn more about Jane's family, and perhaps even coax an embarrassing story or two out of them. They probably hadn't gotten to see Jane much while she was growing up, but surely they had something on her.

When Jane unlocked the door to the apartment, the first thing Sutton heard were the children's voices. High-pitched and raised in some kind of screeching exclamation, they echoed down the hallway to pierce her ears. She shook her head wryly as she thought of Sue's admonition not to conceive in the coming year. There was truly no danger of that. Her maternal instinct hadn't remotely kicked in yet.

Jane turned to her with a grin. "Sounds like Hester's brood is here."

"How old are her kids?"

"Four and two." Jane must have seen a hint of panic in her face, because she patted her on the back. "Don't worry. No one will make you change the little one's diaper."

"Excuse me, do you have any idea how many times I've sutured surgical incisions? And you think I can't change a diaper?"

"I didn't say that. Did I say that? No." Jane held up her hands as she moved down the hall. "Come on. Before you kill me."

As they moved down the hallway past the now-familiar photographs, Sutton debated asking whether Jane wanted children to be a part of her future but then thought better of it. The question seemed too intimate.

"Min, is that you?"

"No, Aunt Jen, it's Jane. And Sutton."

They emerged into the kitchen, which was at least five degrees hotter than the corridor and smelled heavenly. Sutton recognized soy sauce and garlic, but there were a few other scents she couldn't quite place. A very pregnant woman with long, glossy black hair was sitting at the table, and Sutton was struck by how much her facial features resembled Jenny's. A slender man sat beside her, one hand encircling her shoulders. His kind, weary smile welcomed them inside.

Jenny set down her spatula on the stovetop and hurried over. "We're so glad you're joining us tonight, Sutton," she said as she leaned in for a quick hug, careful to keep her bespattered "I <3 NY" apron away from Sutton's shirt. "Have you ever met my oldest daughter, Hester? And this is her husband, Allan."

But before Sutton could shake anyone's hands, another chorus of high-pitched shouts erupted from the adjacent room. Seconds later, two small boys, one a few inches taller than the other, careened around the corner and into the kitchen followed by John, who was looming over them, pretending to be a monster. He stopped as soon as he saw Sutton.

"Dr. Sutton! So good to see you."

"And these are their rabble-rousing kids," Jane said over the hubbub. Sutton turned to the sight of her kneeling on the floor, each arm wrapped around a wriggling small boy. "Allan Junior and Sam."

As the boys shrieked in pretend terror, Jane deposited a loud, smacking kiss on each forehead and then released them. They immediately crowded around Hester, while Allan Senior tried in vain to quiet them down. Sutton watched Jane look after them, a fond smile on her face. Of course she was a natural with children. She had the perfect temperament for them.

"Boys, boys, boys," Jenny called, clapping her hands. "Don't you have pillow forts to build with Gong Gong in the family room?"

"'Gong Gong' is the Chinese phrase for maternal grandfather," Jane explained.

"We're all done!" Allan Junior said.

"Then it's time to build Lego forts inside the pillow forts. Right, Gong Gong?" Jenny gave John a look that clearly indicated his sole purpose in life right now was to get his grandkids out of the kitchen.

"Right. Boys, you heard Po Po. Let's go!"

"'Po Po' is Chinese for—"

"Let me guess. Maternal grandmother."

Jane caressed her lower back with a light touch. "You're a quick one, Double Doctor."

As John led the boys back into the adjoining room, Sutton moved toward the stove. "It smells fantastic in here. How can I help?"

"You should sit. Relax."

"No, really, put us to work." Sutton smiled. "Do you have anything that needs chopping? I have good hands."

"In that case, you can slice the mushrooms into narrow strips. Jane, you can cut the cabbage. And where is Minetta?"

"At Sue's. I'll text her."

After being supplied with a sharp knife and a cutting board, Sutton carefully began chopping the black mushrooms. Jane stood next to her, and every once in a while, their hips bumped lightly. Min walked in the door a few minutes later, and Cornelia came down from her room where she had been studying for an exam the next day. Carmine was the last to arrive, and the only sister Sutton had yet to meet. She had her father's eyes and nose, but the outgoing disposition and businesslike mannerisms of her mother.

"Carmine's going to take over Confucius Fortunes one day," Jane said as she introduced them. "She's in business school right now at Stern."

"I take classes at night," Carmine clarified, "and help Mom and Dad during the day."

"You sound busy," Sutton said. "And if you're the heir apparent, does that mean you know the secret recipe?"

Carmine laughed. "If I say yes, will you hold me hostage for it?"

"I might. Those are honestly the best fortune cookies I've ever tasted."

"Dinner's ready!" Jenny's shout produced a stampede for the table, and Sutton pressed her back against the counter to stay out of the way. "Cornelia and Minetta, go get some extra chairs," Jenny added when it became clear there weren't nearly enough.

Jane grabbed a stack of plates from the cupboard and began handing them to her aunt, who scooped a generous serving of noodles mixed with pork, cabbage, and mushroom onto each. Sutton moved to Jenny's other side and began dispensing the loaded plates around the table. The boys wanted to start eating right away, and Hester was patiently trying to explain the concept of waiting politely. When everyone had been served, Sutton finally squeezed in next to Jane, proud that she'd had a hand in creating the meal.

"There's plenty more, so don't be shy," Jenny announced as she sat down at the table's head.

"Pass the dumplings, please," John said from the other end.

Sutton lifted a forkful of the noodles to her mouth and chewed slowly, savoring them. They were just the slightest bit crispy, and the combination of flavors was delicious. "This is wonderful, Jenny," she called out over the buzz of conversation. "Thank you."

"Oh good, I'm happy you like it. Thank you for the help."

"Try it with some sriracha sauce," Jane said, handing her a red squeeze bottle labeled in Chinese characters. "But not too much. It's hot."

As she continued to eat, Sutton looked around the crowded table, marveling at the controlled chaos. Allan Senior was giving his namesake pointers on how to use chopsticks, while Hester cradled Sam on her lap, helping him eat without dropping too many noodles. John was asking Allan's advice on some kind of investment, and Hester was chatting with Min about school. On the surface, Sutton's family and Jane's family had the same tradition: Sunday night dinners where everyone gathered to share their news from the previous week. But the atmosphere in her parents' townhome was positively stale compared to this.

"So, what's your exam on tomorrow, Corny?" Carmine, who was sitting on Sutton's left, directed the question across the table at her younger sister.

"Don't call me that. And it's for my twentieth-century poetry class."

"Poetry? What use is poetry?"

"Don't knock it, Carm," Jane said. "Someday you'll need a poet to write the fortunes in your cookies."

"Can someone pass the *kai-lan*?" asked Jenny.

"The Chinese broccoli," Jane translated. "Want some?"

"You know me. I'll try anything once." Sutton tasted the leafy green vegetable and smiled. "I think I like this better than the other kind of broccoli. What's in the sauce?"

"That's oyster sauce," Jenny chimed in. "Junior, hold your milk glass nicely, please."

"You can buy it in any Asian grocery store," Min said.

"That depends what you think will happen with the European debt crisis," said Allan to John.

"Do you know anything about e.e. cummings, Jane?" asked Cornelia.

"Born Edward Estlin Cummings, fought in World World War I, loved experimenting with poetic forms. Quite the original guy. Except that he fell in love with Paris while he was stationed there. That's unoriginal—everyone falls in love with Paris. What do you need to know?"

"I'm sure Sutton will make it into the clip they show on TV. She's so pretty."

Sutton felt herself blush at Min's praise, which had been delivered wholly unprovoked to Hester, who turned to smile at her. Sutton raised her water glass and took a long sip. She felt a little dizzy, but in a good way.

"Are you flirting with my girlfriend again, Minetta?" Jane asked.

Girlfriend. Sutton's heartbeat sped up at the epithet. She liked it. Maybe too much.

"Does anyone know the forecast for next weekend?" asked Allan. "We want to take the boys to Coney Island before the crowds get too bad."

"Hang on, I'll check my phone," said Carmine.

"So, Hester," Sutton said, deciding to dive into the bedlam. "Do you know the sex of this child, or are you going to be surprised?"

"Who needs more noodles?"

"Why do people care whether he wrote his name in uppercase or lowercase letters? I mean, really. Who cares?"

"Oh, we want to be surprised. We didn't know with either of the boys, either." Hester smiled again. She was one of those pregnant women who seemed to radiate a soft frequency of light. "I love surprises. You?"

"Not especially." Sutton laughed and set her fork down so she could rest her hand on Jane's knee beneath the table. She was always so warm. For the past week, Sutton hadn't had to turn on her space heater at all. "I was born and raised to be a surgeon. We like to be in control."

Jane leaned in close under the pretext of reaching for the broccoli. "Not all the time," she murmured.

Her words sent an electric charge through Sutton that made her shift restlessly against the chair. When she dared to glance over, Jane's lips were curled in a smug smile even as she continued to listen to Cornelia bemoan her exam.

The remainder of the meal passed in a conversational whirlwind. Eventually, Sutton stopped trying to pay attention to every little detail and allowed herself to relax into the chaos. All her life, family dinners had been formal, stilted affairs. Decorous, of course, but also lifeless. She'd never realized that before, but she could see it now. Jane's family was vibrant. Organic. Alive.

When Jenny began to clear the dishes, Sutton stood to join her, only to be waved aside. "You and Jane helped with preparation. Minetta? Cornelia? Carmine? Dishes. Now."

"What about Hester?" whined Min.

"Hester is seven months pregnant. Apologize to her now, and when you find yourself in the same condition someday, apologize then, too."

"Sorry, Hester."

Sutton suddenly realized this was her golden opportunity to see Jane's room. "I'd like a tour, please," she said, arching one brow in a silent dare.

Jane's eyes shifted left, then right. Realizing she was trapped, she sighed. "All right. Follow me."

Sutton trailed her into the adjoining room, where an array of couches and chairs faced the large tube television hulking in the far corner. "This is the family room," Jane said blandly.

Sutton looked over her shoulder, and when she realized they were alone, she slipped her arms around Jane's waist. "You know this isn't what I want to see."

"You asked for a tour."

"Let me be more specific, then." Sutton stood on her toes and gently nipped at Jane's chin. "I want to see your room."

"If I show you, what do I get?"

Sutton drew back, frowning. "Oh, let's see—to come home with me tonight?"

"You weren't going to let me anyway?"

"Well, I was—but now I'm not so sure."

"Fine. Let's go upstairs."

Sutton batted her eyelashes. "I thought you'd never ask."

Jane sighed again, though Sutton could tell she was fighting back a smile. After leading her up two staircases, she pushed open a creaky door and gestured for her to enter. "Et voilà, as the French say. My room. Which I share with my youngest cousin. Which is humiliating. Okay. Now you've seen it. Let's go."

"No, wait."

Sutton turned in a full circle, taking in the loft space beneath the roof. It was amazingly tidy for a room shared by two people—one of them a preteen. Min's bed had to be the one with the pink coverlet, and the desk looked to be mostly used by her as well, if the bottles of nail polish arranged along one side were any indication. Jane's bed was covered with a blanket stitched in the pattern of the Brazilian flag, and her clothes were arranged neatly inside a set of stacking milk crates. A few cardboard boxes tucked under the eaves likely held the rest of her possessions.

"Come here." When Jane approached, Sutton wrapped her arms around her neck. "You have nothing to be ashamed of. Do you understand?"

Jane nodded but wouldn't look at her. So Sutton moved both

hands to cup her face. "I mean it. I want you to trust me. Trust me with this. Okay?"

After a moment, Jane nodded. "Okay."

Her eyes were greener than Sutton had ever seen them. They reminded her of a forest refuge, dark and peaceful after the perpetual freneticism of the city. And then Jane looked away, severing the moment. Sutton watched her throat work as she swallowed hard, and wondered what she was thinking. Far more than a penny's worth, she was certain.

"We should probably go back downstairs," Jane said. "Did you want to stay a while? Or no?"

"Will you come home with me?"

Thankfully, she smiled. "Of course. I kept my end of the bargain, didn't I?"

As they descended the stairs, Sutton decided they needed a return to lighter matters. "So, now that I've experienced your family dinner, you have to tell me how you do it."

"Do what?"

"Have five conversations at once."

Jane laughed and reached back for Sutton's hand. "You just have to relax. Go with the flow. Listen."

"I'm a good listener."

"You are. But you're also hyper aware of your surroundings. You have to be willing to miss something, once in a while. To see the whole forest, instead of just trees."

Sutton didn't quite know how to reply. Jane's verbal echo of her internal metaphor was rather eerie, but more importantly, she was right. She saw so much. Was that what made her so difficult to resist? That she was the only person who had ever looked at Sutton and seen the whole picture?

Suddenly wanting no barriers between them, Sutton gripped Jane's hand. "Let's say our good-byes and go back to my apartment."

Jane paused and turned. "Okay," she said a moment later, leaving Sutton to wonder what she had seen in her face.

The sound of the television led them back into the family room, where they found everyone gathered watching the local evening news. The boys were sitting still for once, mesmerized by someone's smart phone. Jenny and John sat close together on the couch, holding hands, and Sutton smiled at the sight. She didn't know many older couples who still shared such easy affection. Certainly, her own parents had lost it, if they'd ever had it in the first place.

"We're going to head out," Jane said over the sound of the news anchor, who was just introducing a new story from the Upper East Side.

"Thank you all for a wonderful evening," Sutton said. "Dinner was delicious, and—" The words froze in her throat as she suddenly heard the anchor say her father's name.

"What's wrong?" John asked loudly.

"Shh!" Jane hissed. "Quiet."

Sutton couldn't look away from the television. In the hush that had fallen over the room, the newscast came through with crystalline clarity.

"The allegation emerged this afternoon from a woman asserting that Dr. St. James coerced her into an affair when she was his patient. St. James, who has been married for thirty-five years and has one daughter with his wife, Priscilla, has made no comment. It is unclear at this time as to whether the medical licensing board will investigate the matter."

"Oh my god." Sutton couldn't feel her fingertips, and her cheeks were tingling. Her rational brain recognized the signs of hyperventilation. Slow, deep breaths. She had to take slow, deep breaths. But when she tried, her lungs wouldn't fill and she began to cough.

"We'll be in the kitchen," Jane said sharply.

The words sounded as though they were coming from far away. But then warm, gentle hands were on her waist, guiding her through a doorway. And then, moments later, she was enfolded in a familiar embrace. Jane. She always smelled so good. Why was that?

"Hey," she was saying. "I've got you. Breathe with me, okay? In and out. That's right."

Gradually, the heat of Jane's body permeated her skin, thawing her paralyzed lungs and freeing her from the stupor of shock. With a shudder, she pulled away just enough to meet Jane's eyes. A patient? Her father had had an affair with a patient?

"My mother. I have to go to her."

"I know, baby. I know. Do you want me to come with you?"

"Yes." And then Sutton shook her head. "But that's not a good idea. She must be so overwhelmed. She's going to have a flare-up, if she hasn't already."

Jane nodded. She leaned down to gently kiss Sutton's cheek, and then stepped away. "I understand. You'll call me if there's anything you need, right? I want to help however I can."

"Okay." Sutton pulled out her phone, wanting to call her mother as soon as she was outside. She had to be so angry. So sad. So frightened. How could he have done this? To her. To their family. To the reputation he cared so much for. How? "I'll send you a text when I can."

"You know . . . it might not be true."

Sutton looked up, feeling her mouth twist into a grimace. "I wish I believed that." She took another deep breath, forcing her expression to soften. "But you're right. Thank you. For everything."

She made her way quickly down the hallway, feeling suddenly claustrophobic. She had to get out. Had to get home. Had to fix this, or at least try. That was what she did. Who she was. Who she had trained to be, all her life. The one who fixed what was broken.

"Sutton!"

Jane's voice followed her, and she forced herself to turn. Backlit by the kitchen lamp, Jane was a tall, slender shadow at the mouth of the corridor. Her face was invisible.

"Anything. Anytime. I mean it."

Sutton nodded. She couldn't think in here. She had to get out. "I'll call you later," she said before spinning to open the door.

By the time it closed behind her, she was halfway down the stairs.

CHAPTER THIRTEEN

AS SOON AS HER feet hit the sidewalk, Sutton lurched into motion. While she ran, she fumbled with her phone. Her thumb slipped, accidentally selecting Jane's name. Cursing, she backtracked and finally touched her mother's grainy photograph, making the call.

The line rang once, twice, three times before Maria picked up. "Sutton?"

"Maria. Where's Mom?"

"She's lying down in the guest bedroom." Usually unflappable, Maria sounded positively sick with worry. "She complained of a headache. Sutton, your father . . ."

"I saw on the news," she said quickly, not wanting her to say the words out loud. "Is he there, too?"

"He's locked himself in his office. I heard him talking on the telephone."

Sutton dashed across the street, where she managed to flag down a cab. "I'm coming home," she said, yanking open the door. "Just make sure Mom stays in bed until I get there, okay?"

"Be careful."

She watched the cityscape pass in a smear of light. Could it be true? Was her father capable of doing that to her mother? Of seducing—no, *coercing*—another woman behind her back while she was sick? Her father was as selfish and entitled as he was skilled at saving people's lives. But just because the allegation could be true didn't mean it was. While she could imagine him having an affair, the charge that he had done so with a patient was hard to swallow. He had always taken medical ethics very seriously. Perhaps this woman was lying. Perhaps her father had spurned her, and she was trying to bring him down out of spite.

Closing her eyes, she focused on her breathing. Right now, no matter what she might be feeling, she had to stay calm and strong for her mother. In an effort to center herself, she flashed back to the memory of Jane holding her only minutes earlier. Miraculously, as she relived that gentle, comforting embrace, her nausea began to ebb. If only Jane could be here with her right now. Should she have allowed it? But she had been selfish enough where Jane was concerned, and her mother wouldn't want a stranger seeing her during such a vulnerable time. Sutton would have to navigate these fraught waters alone.

As the cab turned onto her block, she sat up in alarm. Several white news vans were parked further down the street, and a crowd had gathered in front of her parents' townhouse.

"Stop here! Please," she added belatedly. All the major networks appeared to have sent someone to cover the story, and their numbers were likely swelled by random passersby who had stopped to gawk. She was going to have to push her way through to get home. Just perfect. If only her father hadn't insisted on keeping such a high profile in the media, he might have spared their family this madness.

Gritting her teeth, she exited the car and moved forward briskly, leading with one shoulder as she reached the edge of the crowd. "Excuse me. Excuse me."

Thankfully, no one seemed to recognize her. But when she turned onto the short brick path leading up to the stairs, she instantly became the focus of every single reporter in the mix. Shouts went up like the baying of hounds at a foxhunt.

"Miss, Miss!"

"Are you the daughter?"

"Do you live here?"

"What do you think of the allegations against Dr. St. James?"

"Did you know your father was having an affair with a patient?"

Sutton kept her eyes trained on the front door. But when she pulled her keys out of her pocket, her fingers trembled and they fell to the second step. Before she could lean down, one of the press darted in and grabbed them.

Red tinged her vision as she spun to face the perpetrator. "Give me my keys. Now."

He stuck a microphone in her face. "Give me a quote."

Sutton narrowed her eyes, looking from the keys, dangling just out of reach, to the reporter's smug face. For the first time in her life, she wanted to hit someone, Hippocratic Oath be damned. Right now, nothing was more important than getting to her mother's bedside.

She held out her hand, palm up. "I don't know what's going on. Just leave us alone."

After a moment, the man dropped the keys into her hand. "You're the daughter, right?"

Sutton turned without replying, and this time, she kept a tight grip as she fit her key into the door. After slipping inside, she closed and locked it as quickly as she could, then leaned back against it, inhaling deeply. If only she could feel safe here, but this was just another version of the lion's den outside.

"Sutton? Is that you?"

Maria's voice filtered down the stairs, and Sutton pushed herself away from the door. "It's me. I'm coming up."

Moments later, she knocked on the guest room door, then slowly pushed it open. The room was illuminated only by the lamp on the desk where Maria sat knitting. Sutton's gaze went immediately to the bed, where her mother lay covered by a blanket.

"How's she doing?" she murmured.

"I'm awake, Sutton." Priscilla's voice was thin and reedy.

"How are you feeling, Mom?" As Sutton approached the bedside, she saw the cool compress on her mother's forehead. Her eyes were barely open, as though even the dim lighting pained them. Dropping down to one knee, Sutton gently touched the back of her hand. She could make out a faint age spot near one knuckle that she had never noticed before.

"My head is throbbing, and when I sit up, I feel dizzy. Do you think I have vertigo?"

Sutton squeezed her hand. "I think this was probably caused by stress, and that it'll pass in a little while. Did you take anything?"

"Just some ibuprofen." She closed her eyes and turned her head away.

"Okay." Sutton settled back on her heels, hoping that if she waited patiently, her mother might start talking about the real problem. But as the minutes wore on, she realized that wasn't going to happen. Closing her own eyes, she tried to find the right words to ask the questions that needed answers.

"Mom . . . I know you're not feeling well, but we should talk about what's happening."

For a long moment, Priscilla didn't move. Then, finally, she sighed. "Maria, will you bring me a new compress, please?"

"Of course, Mrs. St. James."

Sutton peeled the cloth off her forehead and passed it back to Maria, who left the room. Once the door was closed, she waited for her mother to speak again. Still, she said nothing. Battling back her irritation, Sutton focused on maintaining an even keel.

"Did you hear what they said on the news about Dad?"

"I heard it, yes." Her words were clipped.

"Do you think it's true?"

Finally, Priscilla met Sutton's eyes. "Does it matter?"

Sutton felt her jaw drop. The question was inconceivable. "Yes! It matters!"

Priscilla sighed. "Of course it's not true. It's a fabrication invented by someone trying to ride the coattails of his celebrity. Or get some of his money."

She sounded so certain that Sutton actually experienced a surge of relief before she realized that her mother's theory was exactly that. It might be right, or it might be wishful thinking. No one except her father knew for sure what had happened.

"Unfortunately, as long as the media believes it's true, they're going to make our lives difficult." Sutton grimaced as she imagined her mother interacting with the reporters outside. Their invasive questions would bewilder and fluster her.

Suddenly, she had an idea. Their country home, on several acres of land in Southampton, would be the perfect place for her mother to weather the storm. Reporters would still be able to find them there, but it would be out of their way. And since her father would no doubt remain in New York, they might choose to focus on him and leave them alone entirely. She would have to take time off from the hospital, of course, and she hated having to leave suddenly. But there were plenty of other students to pick up her slack. And if she didn't take care of her mother right now, who would? Even if he was innocent of the charges, her father would be terribly distracted.

"I have an idea. What if we go out to the house?"

Priscilla blinked slowly and sat up in the bed. "For how long?"

"However long it takes for this to blow over." Sutton stood and pulled aside the curtain of the nearest window. The throng outside looked as though it had increased. "At this point, it's only getting worse."

As Maria returned with the compress, Sutton's phone rang. "Don't answer that," her mother said sharply.

"We had to disconnect the house phone earlier," Maria said fretfully. "It wouldn't stop ringing."

"Who called?"

"The first time it was one of those reporters, asking all kinds of inappropriate questions." Priscilla shuddered delicately. "Then it was my brother. And then the neighbors phoned to complain about the noise outside."

"What did you tell Uncle Phillip?"

"I assured him there had been a misunderstanding, and that we would have it resolved soon."

Sutton couldn't quite believe what she was hearing. Her mother truly didn't seem worried about her marriage at all. She wasn't even admitting the possibility that the rumor might be true. All she seemed to care about were the consequences of a scandal to the family's public reputation.

"I called the police about all the people outside," said Maria, "but they said no one had broken any laws and they couldn't do anything."

Sutton wasn't surprised. "We should go, Mom. Really. At least in the Hamptons, the press won't be able to camp out five feet from the front door. I think you'll feel much better out there."

Her mother was silent for a long moment. "We would leave tonight?"

"Yes." Sutton had no idea how much worse the situation might become, and she wanted her mother tucked safely away behind the high walls of their estate by the time the morning news cycle began. "You don't have to do anything, okay? While I call for a car, you tell Maria what you'd like to pack. She and I will handle it."

"Very well."

Relieved to be taking action, Sutton hurried into the hall, pulling up the number of the car service as she went. She ducked into her childhood bedroom as the line connected and she was placed on hold. Perching on her bed, she tried to focus her swirling thoughts into a mental to-do list. On the wall above her desk, the orderly columns and rows of the Periodic Table of the Elements seemed to mock the chaos that had suddenly infiltrated her life.

After arranging for the car and calling the hospital to let them know she wouldn't be coming in for the next few days, Sutton climbed the stairs to the third floor. She hesitated when she reached the landing, before turning toward her father's study. While she might have significantly less faith in his innocence than did her mother, he hadn't been proven guilty yet. He didn't deserve to find them mysteriously gone, without so much as an explanation.

The door was closed, a sliver of light leaking out onto the hardwood floor from beneath the crack. She raised her hand to knock, only to pause at the sound of his voice.

"Where is this coming from? Who leaked it?" The cold fury in his voice made the hair on Sutton's neck prickle. She had never heard him sound so angry. "Then who has those? What do you mean, you don't know? I pay you a great deal of money to know these things!"

Sutton lowered her hand and backed away from the door. She wasn't about to interrupt that conversation. Besides, he didn't exactly sound like an innocent man. An innocent man wouldn't be talking about leaks. Anger flared in her chest, hot and sharp, urging her to barge inside and demand answers. Instead, she forced herself to walk away. Now was not the time for a confrontation. She had to focus on keeping her mother safe and making her comfortable, two things that were obviously nowhere near the front of her father's mind right now. Guilty or not, that said an awful lot in and of itself.

"How are you doing?" she asked as she entered the master bedroom to find Maria transferring clothing from the boudoir to a large valise open on the floor. "Can I lend a hand?"

She looked up briefly. "I'm fine. I'll be ready to help you, soon."

"No need." Sutton headed toward the bathroom, squinting at the brightness of the white tiles reflecting the fluorescent overhead lights. "I'll get Mom's medicine."

The cabinet revealed several prescription bottles, and Sutton examined each in turn. The beta interferons were a long-term medication, taken daily in an attempt to stave off a flare-up. The corticosteroids, on the other hand, were only meant to be used during a relapse. Sutton also reached for the anti-anxiety medication. Better safe than sorry.

The only vial with her father's name on it was a prescription for some antihistamine eye drops. But as she looked through the drawers beneath the sink for her mother's toiletry kit, she found another bottle tucked away beneath his shaving supplies. Viagra. Grimacing, she hastily covered it back up. That didn't prove anything, of course. But either way, she didn't want to think about it.

"I'm sure we are forgetting something," Maria said anxiously as she surveyed the suitcase.

"Don't worry. If so, we'll just pick it up out there." Sutton knelt to zip the case, then paused and looked up as a thought suddenly occurred to her. "Maria, do you want to come with us? Or would you rather stay here?"

"I will stay. That way, if you need something here, I can help."

"You're sure? You feel safe? The press will try to talk to you, too, you know."

She smiled a little. "If they try, I will pretend I don't speak English."

Sutton wasn't sure how well that tactic would work, but she let the subject drop. She had one more question to ask. "Do you think it's true? What they're accusing him of?"

Maria looked toward the door and then back to Sutton. "I don't know," she said quietly. "But I will watch and listen."

"No, you don't have to do that," Sutton said. "Just take care of yourself. The truth will come out, one way or another."

As they descended the stairs, she caught a glimpse of the large family portrait hanging over the mantel in the sitting room. Her father had commissioned it just before she left for college, from a photographer who had been recommended by the Secretary of the Treasury. Briefly, she met the eyes of her glossy, younger self. Her smile had been genuine that day. Anticipatory. Flanked by her parents, she had been sheltered by their pride and just free enough to feel exhilaration.

Once upon a time, she had been the perfect daughter. Once upon a time, they had been the perfect family. A wave of nostalgia washed over her, even as she shook her head at the thought. Like the photograph, that perfection had been only skin deep. She had been so naïve at seventeen. Despite the many ways in which she had disappointed her family since that day, she wouldn't go back and rewrite any chapter of her journey, even if she were magically given the chance.

As she continued down the stairs, she suddenly remembered Sue's words from their session in front of the cameras. Had that really been only this afternoon? It felt like years ago now. *This will likely be a year of conflict for your family,* Sue had said. How right those words had turned out to be.

Thoughts of Sue led to thoughts of Jane, of course. Her chest ached at the prospect of leaving New York so quickly, even though she knew that was silly. Instead of being disappointed, she needed to think of it as a warm-up to her departure in the summer. The Hamptons were at least in the same time zone as the city. But still, if only Jane could come with them. Her mere presence would lighten the load Sutton felt pressing down on her shoulders. Jane comforted her. She made her feel strong and capable and beautiful. She made her laugh. They could talk about anything candidly.

Well, no. That wasn't quite true. Not anything. They never discussed their relationship, and where it was going. There were a few occasions on which she'd thought Jane had been about to bring it up, but something had always held her back. Probably for the best.

Pausing outside the guest room door, she pulled out her phone and tapped out a quick text message. *I'm taking my mother out to our house on Long Island. Not sure how long I'll be there. I'll call when I can.* Thumbs hovering above the cramped keyboard, she frowned down at the screen. *I miss you,* she typed. And then immediately deleted it. *Sorry I had to leave so abruptly,* she wrote instead.

Before she could second-guess herself, she pocketed her phone and turned the corner. Maria was helping her mother sit up in bed, and Sutton schooled her features into what she hoped was a semblance of calm.

"Okay, Mom. Are you ready to go?"

JANE LAY ON HER stomach, arms curled around her pillow, left leg bent slightly and her face turned toward the small window. This was her favorite way to doze off, and she was exhausted. But despite the long day behind her, and a restless sleep the night before, her brain refused to quiet.

Flipping onto her back, she sighed into the rafters. What was Sutton doing right now? Was she asleep, or also lying awake? What was she thinking about? Was she completely embroiled in the drama that was unfolding around her father, or did she spare a thought for her, once in a while?

They had exchanged only a handful of texts since Sutton had left on Sunday night. Her messages were always short, and always somewhat formal in tone. That wasn't new, of course—her texts had never been warm and fuzzy. But until now, Jane had always been able to supplement them by reading her body language and the intricate patterns in her expressive eyes. A few stilted words in a text bubble only left her frustrated and wanting more. Sutton was barely two hours' drive away on Long Island, but she might as well have been in Sweden already. Or on the moon, for that matter.

Grimacing, Jane sat up and leaned over to check her phone on the nightstand. Just past one o'clock in the morning. The light from the screen illuminated the tabloid paper beneath it. "Dr. America's Daughter in the Dark," read the headline. Beneath it was a

photograph of Sutton outside her apartment, one hand outstretched, looking furious. And beautiful. The article had been
brief, and Jane had ground her teeth the entire time while reading
all about how Dr. America's extramarital liaison had blindsided
both his wife and daughter. What on earth had he been thinking
when he decided to bully a patient into having an affair? And how
dare he preach to Sutton about her choices, when he had betrayed
not only his family but also the ethics of his profession?

Silently fuming, Jane sat up and propped her pillow behind her
back. Her renewed anger had set her heart to racing, and now she
needed to find a way to keep from stewing in her own indignation.
If she wasn't going to sleep, then damn it, she could at least be productive. She hadn't yet begun to sift through the new lines she and
Sutton had found together in Grand Central. If she could finally
finish the poem, her application for the fellowship would be complete. At least then she would have accomplished something.

Thankful that Min was a heavy sleeper, Jane turned on the
lamp and angled the shade toward her bed. Pulling up her knees,
she propped her notebook onto them and opened the front cover.
She had tucked Sutton's paper just inside, and she took her time
unfolding it, savoring the memory of that afternoon. Something
had shifted between them that day, like tectonic plates sliding
subtly beneath the earth's crust. It had begun with a not-date
and ended with a kiss on the cheek that still pierced Jane with its
sweetness.

With one fingertip, she traced the compact strokes of Sutton's
lines. Her handwriting was elegant yet efficient. Just like her. Jane
smiled and flipped to the pages she had set aside for her work in
progress. But almost immediately, she found it impossible to concentrate. Closing her eyes, she tried to picture Grand Central's main
hall—to see and hear and smell the press of humanity in perpetual
motion along the floor of the cavernous space. But try as she might,
she couldn't seem to project her consciousness back into the station.

Sutton's image kept pulling her away, back into her own body. Aching to comfort her, Jane sat paralyzed in the cone of light from the lamp.

I miss you, she wrote on the empty page. It felt good to write down the truth. And where was the harm? Sutton would never see it. This scrap of paper, bound into the notebook she kept on or beside her always, was safer than a confessional box.

> *Sleep left me when you did.*
> *It takes all my strength, every moment, not to go to you.*
> *Every train station gapes as I pass, tempting me.*
> *Every overheard conversation between lovers reminds me of us.*

Suddenly inspired, Jane flipped back through her notebook, picking out appropriate lines. Fatigue forgotten, her eyes roamed each page for the gems she had yet to mine.

> *"When I'm with you, I feel safe. So relaxed."*
> *"Your body is 150% amazing."*
> *"Remember what you told me? You said with me, you don't want anyone else."*
> *"Everyone will always find their soul mates."*

For a moment, Jane leaned her head back against the wall. Soul mates. Was there a more overused phrase? And yet, when she thought about how she felt in Sutton's presence, it seemed to fit. Which was the whole point, wasn't it? They fit together—two halves of a whole, bound by irresistible chemistry. Perfect complements. Yin and yang. Could Sutton see that? Or was she too blinded by the bright lights of her own future?

Staring back down at the page, she raised her pen and held it just above the paper. Words rushed through her brain like butterfly wings, fragile and transitory. Under normal circumstances, she would never think of capturing them. But this wasn't normal. This was once in a lifetime.

> *They speak for me, these anonymous voices.*
> *I wish they could speak to you on my behalf.*
> *In whispers, they could show you what we are together.*
> *Imprisoned on two islands, we drift apart.*
> *The sun rises a heartbeat sooner for you than for me.*
> *Do you see the world more clearly for it?*
> *You say what we share is casual, but it's not.*
> *You think you have to carry your pain alone, but you don't.*
> *Trust in the harmony of our shared laughter.*
> *Trust in the secrets we dared to confess.*
> *Trust in the heat that burned between us in the dark.*
> *Trust yourself. Trust me.*

Slowly, Jane lowered her pen. The butterfly wings had quieted, and she felt strangely empty inside—hollowed out, like a jack-o'-lantern. Her hand ached from the frenetic scribbling, and as she scanned over the words, her eyes began to burn.

She hadn't written any original poetry in well over a year, and she had no doubt that every line she'd just committed to paper was awful. But that didn't matter. No one would ever see it. This had been an exorcism of emotion. Catharsis. Nothing more.

Suddenly drained, Jane reached over to turn off the light. Burrowing back under the blankets, she tried to ignore the persistent ache beneath her skin. Withdrawal. One week of Sutton sleeping in her arms and she was an addict.

Turning her face toward the east, Jane closed her eyes and hoped her dreams would be kinder than reality.

CHAPTER FOURTEEN

THE FIRST TENDRILS OF gold were shimmering on the edge of the horizon as Sutton stepped out onto the deck, coffee mug cupped in both hands. The chill seeped through her bulky sweater immediately, but she welcomed the fresh, salt-scented breeze against her face. She took a tentative sip of her coffee, sighing in pleasure as it slid down her throat and into her empty stomach, warming her from the inside out. Fatigue hovered behind her eyes, ready to swoop down and plunge her into exhaustion. Even so, she had awoken before the dawn, just like always.

For a moment, she allowed herself to wish that Jane were here—to imagine the scratchy sound of the screen door opening and the slow beat of footsteps crossing the deck. She felt Jane's arms slide around her waist, and when she breathed in, she could almost taste the comforting scent of her. Jane's embraces always made her feel so cherished. Sutton took another sip of coffee, imagining the heat of Jane's body cradling her against the railing. She dipped one hand into her pocket, fingertips brushing her phone. She hadn't heard Jane's voice in days. The last words they had exchanged were too-short texts wishing each other a good night. Sutton always spent forever composing those messages, and they never turned out the way she wanted them to. Writing down what she was feeling had proven impossible. She could think the words in her head, even whisper them aloud, but as soon as she tried to type them, her courage failed. *I miss you. I wish you were here. I can't sleep well without you.* All of it was true—every syllable. But writing them down just seemed so . . . permanent. She and Jane didn't have a future. What good would it do to complicate their present? Shivering in a sudden gust of wind, she gripped her mug more tightly. Sometimes, her logic felt like cowardice.

A fat drop of rain landed on her cheek. As it slid down to her chin, another plunked into her coffee. Glancing up as she hurried back indoors, Sutton noticed for the first time the dark clouds gathered overhead. Hopefully, the storm would quickly move out to sea. She wanted to be sure her mother got some fresh air today. Left to her own devices, Priscilla would never leave the house, and that wasn't healthy at all.

As the rain began to fall in sheets, drumming heavily against the roof and the windowpanes, Sutton double-checked the bus schedule. Maria would arrive in a few hours, having decided to join them after Reginald had checked into a hotel to try to escape the press. Sutton felt her temples begin to throb as she flashed back to their brief, stilted conversation yesterday. He had called to inform them of the move and to check on Priscilla, who had already been asleep. When Sutton had tried to talk to him about the allegations, he had put her off immediately with platitudes about how it was all a misunderstanding and that his "people were handling the situation." He had followed up those vague statements with an admonishment not to say a word to the press, and then cited another incoming call before hanging up quickly.

After downing two aspirin to nip her headache in the bud, Sutton poured another cup of coffee and opened her laptop. She alternated between checking her e-mail and watching the rain, assiduously avoiding all news sources. After skimming a few articles yesterday, she had seen enough. Everything the press put out was speculative, and most of the media seemed determined to heap aspersions on her father's character despite any new information. The only consolation was that her mother hadn't relapsed. She had complained of more than the usual fatigue, and her hand tremors had been more pronounced than usual. But she had lived with those symptoms for well over a year now, and their presence didn't indicate the formation of a new lesion in her brain. Hopefully, by leaving the city and avoiding the news, she would avoid a flare-up.

"Sutton?" Priscilla walked slowly into the kitchen, slippers scuffing against the hardwood floor.

"Good morning, Mom." Sutton rose from the table and embraced her gently. "Can I make you some breakfast? Toast and tea, maybe?"

"Yes, please."

Sutton made sure to keep the conversation light as she prepared the food. They discussed an article Priscilla had read recently in a fashion magazine, and worked together on a grocery list. Sutton wished she dared do the shopping herself, but she didn't want to risk being recognized by any members of the press who might be hanging about. Maria would be the perfect person to do a little reconnaissance.

Priscilla welcomed Maria with a smile and an embrace that Sutton might have envied once. Now, she was simply glad to see her mother's face brighten, especially during such a stressful time. Thankfully, Maria said not a word about Reginald or the reporters, though she did whisper to Sutton that she had seen what looked like a news van parked down the street.

By the time Maria had settled in, noon was approaching. "Let me do that shopping now," she said. "And then I'll fix us some soup and sandwiches."

"That sounds lovely," said Priscilla, who was acting as though civilization itself had returned along with their housekeeper.

"Mom, let's go walk a little in the garden while Maria runs errands." Sutton gestured toward the bay windows. "The sun has come out and everything will smell so fresh."

"It isn't too cold?"

"No, Mrs. St. James, it's turned into a beautiful day," Maria said as she shrugged back into her coat. "You would look even lovelier with some color in your cheeks."

Again, that beatific smile. Sutton hadn't made her mother smile like that in years—not since she had come out. Squelching the familiar disappointment, she grabbed their jackets from the front closet. "Just for a little while, okay? This is the perfect chance to inspect the garden to see whether you want to make any changes."

When Priscilla nodded, Sutton helped her into the coat and laid her shoes beside her feet. "I'll be right back. I'm just going to walk Maria to the door." As soon as they turned into the foyer, Sutton lowered her voice. "While you're out, would you mind looking for more signs of the media? I'd like to have a sense of just how closely they're watching us."

"Of course." Maria looked worried. "How long do you think this will last?"

"I wish I knew," Sutton said as she opened the front door. A black car idled at the base of the short flight of stone stairs, waiting to carry Maria into town. The gravel drive culminated fifty yards away in a tall, wrought iron gate that was the only break in the wall encircling the estate. Today, Sutton was glad of the barricade between herself and the rest of the world.

She returned to the kitchen to find her mother staring out the windows, her expression melancholy. But when Sutton knelt at her feet and rested one hand on her knee, Priscilla shook her head and plastered on a smile.

"Ready to go, Mom?"

"Of course."

Sutton preceded her down the deck stairs, vigilant in case a tremor caused her mother to stumble and lose her footing. At the sight of Priscilla clutching the railing as she descended, Sutton felt a rush of sympathy. Her mother's life was defined by fear. She was so afraid that her body would betray her at any moment; that her social circle would treat her like a leper; that society at large would judge her for her gay daughter. Now, Sutton imagined, the fear ran even deeper—that her marriage would fail, and that she would live out the rest of her life alone. She wanted to reassure her mother that even if she did end up getting a divorce, she would never be alone. But offering that reassurance meant opening a conversation in which her mother refused to participate. At this point, wasn't it kinder to let her keep her head in the sand, insofar as she was able?

Taking a deep breath of the crisp, rain-scented air, Sutton tried to put her own fears out of mind and focus on the immediate present. "The earth smells like it's waking up," she said, linking her arm with Priscilla's.

The garden formed a ring around the periphery of their yard. They walked along the brick path that separated it from the lawn, past the skeletal rosebushes and the bare patches of earth where bulbs prepared their shoots for an upward assault on the loosening soil.

"I was thinking," Priscilla began as she paused to examine the naked branches of a hedge, "of mauve and gold as the colors for this year's Memorial Day party. Belinda was in Paris over New Year's and she said that combination was all the rage."

Sutton froze in disbelief. How could her mother be thinking about the annual St. James family party, when her father was facing not only public humiliation but also the loss of his medical license? If the accusations were true, would she even want to present a united front to the high society vultures?

"What is it?" Priscilla asked, looking over her shoulder.

Sutton wanted to fall to her knees and beg her mother to open her eyes. Instead, she forced her voice to remain evenly modulated. "Maybe it would be best to cancel the party this year."

Priscilla waved one hand dismissively. It trembled slightly in midair. "Oh, surely this misunderstanding will be resolved long before then."

"Mom . . ." Sutton closed her eyes briefly in an aimless prayer for patience and strength. This was as much of a conversation-starter as she was likely to get. "I think we have to face the possibility that it's not a misunderstanding. That it's true."

Priscilla stiffened and began to move away. "It's the liberal media lashing out against your father in retaliation for his conservative political views. They've always hated him, and they finally found someone who would be willing to accuse him. Who knows how much they paid that misguided wretch of a woman to say those terrible things?"

Before Sutton could even take the breath needed to reply, a loud rustling sound drew her attention up to the top of the nearby wall. Adrenaline flooded her bloodstream as she caught sight of a man wearing a dark blue windbreaker, balancing between the tree and the parapet with the clear intent to jump down into the yard.

"Mom!" Stepping in front of her, Sutton protectively spread out her arms as the man's feet hit the ground. Priscilla shrieked and clung to her, trembling. Had she been alone, Sutton would have run for the house, but as it was, the phone was her only recourse. She yanked it out of her pocket, holding it between them like a weapon.

"Who are you?" she demanded, focusing on her anger instead of her fear.

"Calm down," said the man, holding up one hand. "I just want to ask you a few questions."

"We're not going to answer any questions." Sutton jammed her thumb against the touch screen. "You're trespassing, and I'm calling security."

The man looked unconcerned. "While we're waiting for them to show, why don't you tell me how you feel about the allegations from the other women who have stepped forward?"

"Other women?" Priscilla sounded dazed.

Sutton struggled not to betray a hint of surprise or distress. She refused to give this reporter anything—not even a meaningful facial expression. Over the pounding of her heart in her ears, she wanted to tell her mother not to pay attention to a word he said. But at that moment, the call went through. Never in her life had she been so thankful that her father kept a twenty-four-hour security staff to watch over the estate.

"How can I help you, Dr. St. James?"

"Someone just climbed over our wall and jumped into the garden. Please hurry!"

"Stay on the line. We'll be there right away."

She tightened her grip on the phone and stared down the reporter. "I don't think you want to be here when our security arrives."

But he ignored her. "Don't you watch the news, Mrs. St. James?" The man took a step closer. "Four more women, all former patients of your husband, have admitted to sexual liaisons with him."

"Lies."

The ragged whisper broke Sutton's heart. She wrapped one arm around her mother's shoulder and glared at him. "Stay back. We have nothing to say to you. This is a private matter, and you're on private property."

"There's no such thing as privacy anymore." His eyes narrowed. "You really didn't know about the other affairs. Are you not on speaking terms with your husband right now, Mrs. St. James?"

Sutton glared. "I told you: we have nothing to say."

"You've said plenty. And others will say more. When you want to tell your side of the story, find me." He dropped a business card into the grass and then turned back toward the wall. Only then did Sutton notice the rope he had tied to a tree branch high above, which he deftly climbed even as faint crunch of gravel beneath speeding tires sounded from the front of the house. Moments later, two men in dark suits raced toward them across the lawn. At their approach, Priscilla sagged against her in relief.

"He went over the wall by rope," Sutton said, hugging her mother even closer. "And dropped a card there."

The older man nodded crisply and gestured for his colleague to take a look. "I'll escort you inside."

As they walked slowly back toward the house, Sutton felt as though she had vertigo. Her brain was in free fall, unable to settle long enough on any one topic to gain traction. A reporter scaling the walls of the estate just for a quote. New accusations of her father's infidelity. And now her mother seemed near catatonic, clinging to her arm with a death grip as tears streamed down her face. She didn't even make an effort to wipe them away.

"Let's go sit down on the couch," Sutton murmured as they stepped inside. She glanced at the guard as he closed the door behind them. "You'll stay here with us?"

"Yes, ma'am."

Priscilla was shivering as she sat, and Sutton hurried to the hall closet for an afghan. After propping up a pillow against the armrest, she urged her mother to lie back. "I'm going to make you some more tea. Okay?"

At Priscilla's faint nod, Sutton bent to kiss her forehead and went into the kitchen. But as she watched the water come to a boil, her anger at her father bubbled over. Snatching up her phone, she called him before she could change her mind. But his voice wasn't the one on the other end of the line.

"Hello, Sutton."

She watched her reflection bristle in the dim mirror formed by the microwave window. "Who is this?"

"Bertram Goetze."

Her father's personal attorney—a bulbous, bombastic man who got outrageously drunk at their annual Christmas party—was answering Reginald's phone. Wonderful. Biting back an acerbic response, Sutton tried to strip all trace of emotion from her voice. "Bertram, I need to speak with my father."

"I'm afraid that's not possible, Sutton."

"What are you talking about?"

"The team feels it's best to control all communication at the moment. Until we have this situation under control, your point person will be your father's secretary, Diane."

"My point person?" Sutton could hear her own voice growing louder. Her self-control was slipping away. "This is my father we're talking about! What if there's an emergency?"

"Diane will know how to reach him at any moment. What's most important right now is that everyone play by the script. Later today, she'll send you some talking points in case you're approached by the press, and—"

"Approached by the press?" Sutton gripped the edge of the counter so hard her knuckles cracked. "I just had to call security because the press invaded our yard, Bertram!"

"What?"

"That's right. A man climbed over the wall and started asking—"

"What did you tell him?"

Bertram's anxious question was eclipsed by a wordless shout in the living room. It held a note of true terror, and Sutton was moving even before the guard managed to call her name. She rounded the corner to the sight of her mother convulsing on the couch, white foam bubbling at the corners of her mouth. The guard was holding her shoulders down, but her head flopped with each successive seizure as though she were a ragdoll.

A wave of pure terror sluiced down her spine like ice water, but in an instant years of training took over. "Call 9-1-1!" she snapped, darting forward. Bracing one hand between her mother's shoulder blades, she turned her onto her side, then held her firmly and watched for signs of choking.

"I'm right here, Mom," she murmured. "I'm right here. You're going to be okay. I promise."

JANE PERCHED ON THE stool in the corner of Noodle Treasure, tapping her chin with her pen as she watched the wind worry at the crimson awning over Confucius Fortunes. Clouds swirled ominously above the rooftops, and every once in a while the unsettled sky let loose a brief salvo of raindrops. The blustery day matched her mood. She had exchanged a few texts with Sutton early this morning but had heard nothing from her since then.

For about the thousandth time, she wondered whether Sutton's radio silence was related to the breaking news she'd seen on the local news station during one of her deliveries. Apparently, four more women had come forward reporting affairs with Sutton's father while being under his care. All morning, Jane had vacillated over whether to text Sutton with the news. Surely she had known before the press. But if so, why hadn't she said anything? Was she ashamed?

Jane shook her head, then bent to scribble in her notebook. *You don't have to carry your burdens alone.* Maybe, if that made it into a fortune cookie, someone else would think twice before not letting their significant other help them through a difficult time. Then again, maybe Sutton would have allowed a "significant other" to help. Maybe she didn't think of Jane that way. Staring into her empty teacup as though the dregs might hold some clue or comfort, Jane forced herself to admit the truth.

She had fallen in love with Sutton St. James.

Thinking back over the course of the past few months, she saw that it had been inevitable. And if she were really being honest, she'd known that all along. She had never been one to date casually, and Sutton was irresistible. That wasn't exactly a recipe for keeping things light.

Love is a cruel mistress.

A wave of guilt washed over her when she remembered just how much Sutton was dealing with right now. So what if she wasn't letting Jane help? Her father was at the center of a media storm, and her mother was sick. Not to mention the fact that she was still reeling from that blow-out argument with her parents from a few weeks before. Sutton had bigger fish to fry than contemplating this nascent relationship. Her entire world was topsy-turvy.

Things fall apart.

The very least Jane could do was to be patient, and as supportive as Sutton would allow her to be from a distance. *Weather the storm,* she wrote, silently vowing to put aside her own selfish concerns. And then her phone buzzed, and her heart lurched into a gallop.

Text from Sutton St. James: *Sorry for not replying earlier. I'm at the hospital. Mom had a seizure.*

Jane felt the bottom drop out of her stomach. *Oh, no. How's she doing?*

She's disoriented. They want to observe her overnight.

"Damn it," Jane whispered. How much more did Sutton have to take? *How can I help? I can be on a train within the hour.*

I'm fine. Maria's here with me. But thanks.

Jane stared down at that text for several minutes. When she caught herself grinding her teeth, she forced her jaw muscles to relax. Patient and supportive. This was not about her. This was about Sutton. *Okay,* she typed. *Hoping to hear good news soon.*

The sanitized sentence tormented her, and she stabbed at the display button so she wouldn't have to look at it anymore. Propping her elbows on the counter, she buried her face in her hands. Maybe she should go home and try to nap. She hadn't slept well in days. But as her brain continued to rev, all she could picture was Sutton witnessing her mother's seizure. Even for a trained medical professional, that must have been so scary.

Lifting her head, she typed a quick search into her phone. Moments later, she had confirmation that Priscilla's seizures were most likely related to her multiple sclerosis. Apparently they often indicated an acute flare-up—the kind of relapse that might point to a worsening of the patient's condition. That wasn't good at all.

"More tea, Jane?"

Startled, Jane spun on the stool and nearly elbowed the teapot out of Mei's hands. She stammered an apology as she held out her cup, but Mei waved her words aside. "How is Dr. Sutton?" she asked. "Have you heard from her?"

Jane paused, considering her answer. Over the past few days, it felt like the entire neighborhood had been asking after Sutton. She loved that Sutton had become such an important part of the community, but she didn't want to betray any confidences.

"Her mother isn't doing very well," she said finally. "She had to go to the Emergency Room earlier."

"Aiyah." Mei sounded almost exactly like Aunt Jenny when she delivered the traditional Chinese expression for dismay. "Is she going to be all right?"

"I hope so." Jane cupped her hands around the warm ceramic. "I just wish I could help somehow."

"She knows you care. That helps." Mei patted her gently on the shoulder. "This too shall pass."

As she walked away, the front door opened to admit Min, phone clutched in her right hand. She looked uncharacteristically worried, and Jane half rose from her stool before she realized what she was doing.

"What's wrong? Are you okay?"

Min spared a moment to roll her eyes. "Chill. I'm fine. But you need to see this."

After quickly thumbing through her phone, she handed it over. Jane found herself looking at an article from one of the New York tabloids, emblazoned with the header "Dr. America's Daughter Consults Psychic." Her stomach twisted as her gaze dropped to the photograph of Sutton sitting next to Sue on the couch in Red Door Apothecary. As she skimmed the article, the sensation of free fall only grew worse. It was a melodramatic piece, of course, spinning Sutton's consultation with Sue as an attempt by the young doctor to seek guidance about her family's plight. The author had twisted everything and everyone. Sutton was made out to be weak and indecisive—a desperate daughter who had sought answers from the stars when reason failed to explain her father's behavior. Sue was portrayed as a shrew businesswoman out to make a quick buck off the fears and insecurities of her clients. The author even suggested that Sue had supplied Sutton with "Eastern medication" to treat her depression. The only saving grace was that the actual footage of the consultation belonged to News 4, so the tabloid couldn't edit it to fit their agenda.

As Jane continued to read, her nausea gave way to a hot, throbbing headache. By the time she returned the phone to Min, streaks of red tinted her vision. How dare they do this? How dare the opportunistic media treat Sutton so callously when her family was collapsing before her eyes? And how dare they misrepresent Sue's apothecary—the business she had built from scratch over decades?

"What do you think?" Min asked anxiously, shifting back and forth on her feet.

"It's bullshit!" Jane didn't care that several heads turned at her vulgarity. "Total bullshit."

Min was shaking her head. "The guy who wrote that doesn't know anything. I mean, Sue isn't a psychic. She's an astrologer!"

"Does Sue know about this?"

Min shot her a withering glance. "What do you think?"

"We have to tell her."

"She's not going to be happy."

"I know that, Minetta, but—" When Min's eyes widened and she took a step backward, Jane realized she was letting her anger get the best of her. "I'm sorry. Look. You know New York. People are going to read this stupid article, and then they'll go looking for Sue's shop. When they find it, they'll have expectations. We need to warn her."

Min thrust out her chin, suddenly the picture of determination. "I'll go."

For the first time all day, Jane wanted to smile. For all her snarkiness, Min was fiercely protective of her friends and family. Pushing off her seat, Jane closed and pocketed her notebook, then drained her tea.

"I'll come with you."

Chapter Fifteen

UTTON ARRIVED AT THE hospital at nine o'clock on Sunday, as she had been doing all week. By now, the nurses knew her not only by association with her father, but by her diligence at her mother's bedside. They had been kind to her, and for that she was grateful.

"How is she this morning, Mary?" Sutton asked the nurse at the on-call station.

"She had a restless night." Mary's tone was professional, but her eyes were sympathetic. "They're doing another CT scan now."

Sutton nodded, unsurprised. Her mother had gone through an MRI upon being admitted, which had confirmed the presence of new lesions in her brain. Since then, Priscilla had suffered two more seizures, which had left her alternately confused and anxious—sometimes so anxious that she required medication to calm down. Sutton was glad the attending physician had ordered another test, even as she feared that it might confirm that her mother had crossed over to the more serious "secondary progressive" stage of the disease.

"I'll just sit in the waiting room, then. You'll let me know when she's out?"

"Of course."

Sutton perched on a hard plastic chair and stared absently at the television. It was easy to tune out the drone of the talk show when her mind was in such turmoil. The past few days had only increased

her desire to pursue the opportunity she'd been offered in Sweden—
to devote her life to finding a cure for this insidious disease that
was laying waste to her mother's mind and to her quality of life.
Only two short weeks remained before she had to make a choice:
Columbia or Lund. She knew what she wanted. But could she in
good conscience make plans to go overseas right now, when her
family was in crisis? Definitely not until her mother's physical
condition was at least stable—and then, of course, there was her
mental state to think of. If all these new allegations were true, would
Priscilla want a divorce?

Sutton wouldn't blame her mother at all if she did want to separate from her father. Maybe she should even encourage her to do
it. He called every evening like clockwork, but to Sutton, what
looked like dedication smacked of showboating. Was she being perceptive, or overly critical? When she thought about what he was
accused of doing, the anger welled up so hot and fierce that it hi-
jacked her intellect. Sutton removed her glasses and massaged her
temples in an effort to stave off a rising headache. When he called
tonight, she was going to have to do more than pass the phone to
her mother. They needed to decide whether to keep Priscilla out
here on Long Island or risk having her transported back into the
city. Hopefully, she would have a lucid period later today, so Sutton
could actually ask what she wanted. The question was, did she
have her own best interests at heart anymore? Was she in her "right
mind" at this point?

The television had switched from a talk show to a news segment,
but Sutton couldn't focus enough to follow the anchor's report. She
glanced down at the bag containing her laptop. When she wasn't
sitting at her mother's bedside or conferring with the physicians,
she was reading everything she could lay her hands on about the
latest theories in the treatment of multiple sclerosis. Much of it
she already knew from writing her postdoctoral proposal, but since
then, a few new medications had come onto the market. The first

problem was that they had terrifying side effects. The second problem was that even if she believed an experimental drug was the answer, she didn't have the power to make decisions for her mother. Only her father could make that judgment call.

Deep in her pocket, she felt her phone buzz. Grateful for the distraction, she reached for it and did an internal twirl when she saw Jane's name. Immediately, logic asserted itself, trying to censure her reaction. This was not the time to indulge in a romance. This was a time for pragmatic action.

Good morning. ☺

The smiley face made the corners of her own mouth twitch, despite everything. *Hi.*

How's your mom?

Sutton shrugged even though no one would see. *Nothing much has changed. How are things with you?*

I'm fine. Worried about you. And then, a moment later, another text came through: *I miss you.*

Sutton bit her lower lip. Should she return the sentiment? It was true, wasn't it? She missed Jane's unfettered smile, her chameleon eyes, her solicitous touch. But how could she encourage her, when the present was chaos and the future totally uncertain?

The words stared at her from inside the brightly colored text bubble, silently chastising her. Shouldn't she be honest? Didn't Jane deserve that much from her? She had never pushed to define their relationship, or to turn it into something more than Sutton had wanted. She had kept Sutton's secrets and offered her comfort and support. Why should Sutton withhold the truth when it was so simple? "I miss you" wasn't a protestation of love or a marriage proposal. Writing those words back to Jane wouldn't shift the fulcrum of their relationship. Would it?

Her thumbs hovered over the keypad. *I-m-i-s-*

"The cast of *Saturday Night Live* weighed in on the Doctor America scandal last night." The news anchor's words sliced through her brain like a scalpel, and she looked up so quickly that for a moment, the screen blurred. "The skit has gone viral on social media. Take a look."

Mired in shock and disbelief, Sutton watched as the title, ON SET WITH DOCTOR AMERICA flashed onto a black screen, which faded into a familiar scene: a pair of armchairs nearly identical to the ones on the set of her father's television show. One was occupied by an actor who was clearly meant to be a caricature of her father—dressed in a lab coat over a suit, his hair was slicked back and a stethoscope hung around his neck, its ends dangling down past the tight Windsor knot at his throat. Other actors depicting the members of the crew milled about—some holding clipboards, others manning cameras. A young woman half sat, half reclined in the other armchair, her eyes at half-mast as she smoked from a tall, ornate hookah standing on the floor. As Sutton watched, a harried-looking woman hurried across the field of view to pause before fake-Reginald. The neckline of her blouse plunged sharply downward, displaying ample cleavage, which he ogled in an exaggerated fashion.

"Dr. St. James," the woman began, "would you mind asking your daughter to extinguish her pipe? The smoke is making it difficult for us to set up proper camera angles."

Sutton felt her mouth fall open. The woman in the chair was supposed to be her? The dread already swirling in her stomach magnified exponentially.

"Now, now, Danielle—" fake-Reginald began, his gaze still riveted on his assistant's breasts.

"It's Denise."

"Denise, of course." Her fake-father's voice oozed sleaze. "Sit on my lap and let's discuss this." With a long-suffering sigh, she sat on his knee and endured his arm snaking around her waist. "I've invited my daughter onto my show to discuss Eastern medicine with us. Opium is a very important part of that discussion. Isn't that right, Sutton?"

"Confucius say, those who get too big for their britches will get exposed in the end."

"Well said, well said." He ran his hand up and down Denise's side. "She's very wise, don't you think?"

"Um . . ." Denise managed to pull out of his grasp. "Excuse me."

As she hurried off, her fake-father's mournful expression was replaced by one of rapacious desire as a buxom brunette woman approached, holding a makeup palette. He looked her up and down and licked his lips lasciviously.

"Why, hello, Maxine."

"It's Michelle," the artist said brusquely, maintaining as much of a distance as she could while simultaneously powdering his face.

"Michelle, of course." His hands reached out to cup her waist. "Don't you think you should come a little closer, Michelle?" But she pulled away from him abruptly, spinning on one heel and barging out of the scene.

Again, the camera panned to fake-Sutton, whose face was nearly obscured by a growing cloud of smoke. "Confucius say, vitamins are good for what ails you," she slurred. "Viagra is good for what fails you."

Fake-Reginald began to cough as the insistent mist coagulated around him. Waving his hand, he sought to clear a gap in the cloud. "Quite right, my dear."

Through the smoke, a shaggy-haired man approached him, holding out a wireless microphone. "Okay, Dr. St. James—time for your mic check."

When he leaned in to adjust the device, fake-Reginald stroked the man's shoulder. "I don't recognize you. What's your name? And what are your plans later tonight?"

The man recoiled, his face stretched in a comical expression of horror. "My name is Anthony and I quit!"

Fake-Reginald pulled his arm back, lips pinched in distaste. Fake-Sutton cackled gleefully. "Confucius say, the useless skin around a penis is called a man."

A wave of dizziness swept over Sutton, and the muted light of the waiting room turned a jaundiced yellow before her eyes. Automatically, she leaned forward to put her head between her knees. But even when she could no longer see the television, she could hear the awful dialogue as her fake-father flirted with anything that moved. The nauseating sense of vertigo persisted into the newscaster's brief analysis of the skit and the "ongoing scandal." Never in a million years had Sutton thought that phrase would ever be used to describe her life.

As she began to regain her composure, disbelief set in. Her family—her self—had just been the laughing stock of *Saturday Night Live*, and by extension, the nation. What's more, the skit had completely misrepresented her. The cast and writers had used that idiotic tabloid article about her in Sue's shop as the basis for their parody, and Sutton's dizziness returned as the implications came crashing home. How dare they? Thanks to the show, the entire country would know her not as the daughter of a man who cheated on his wife while she was ill, but as a drug-addled enabler of that betrayal. And what would Columbia think? Or even Lund? What if they believed the media's portrayal and rescinded their offers?

Inhale, exhale. Inhale, exhale. Slowly, the fresh panic faded enough to let her think. At least her mother hadn't seen the skit. Yes. Sutton could focus on that. The backlash against her family was intense right now, but would probably be short-lived. The video would go viral, but perhaps by the time Priscilla was out of the hospital, the Internet would have forgotten all about it. In the meantime, Sutton would stay at her mother's bedside and avoid the media at all costs.

But even as reason and logic marched their solutions along her neurons, bringing order to her roiling brain, the nausea lingered. Despite it, Sutton reached down for her bag and pulled out her computer, where the latest issue of *The Journal of Neuroscience* was on her hard drive. She couldn't control her father's behavior or change his past actions, but she could control herself. She would not let this time go to waste. She would not allow that ridiculous skit to torpedo her mission. Her priorities were clear: to protect her mother in the present, and do the best she could to heal her in the future. Nothing else was more important.

JANE SQUINTED AT HER phone, mechanically spooning congee into her mouth as she skimmed the list of alerts in her inbox. Every mention of Sutton's name on the Internet generated a new message, and Jane forced herself to skim each article, no matter how awful it might be. Ever since Sutton's mother had been hospitalized, story after story had emerged about Priscilla St. James's "nervous breakdown." Others speculated that her heart had quite literally broken at the news about her husband's lengthy list of conquests. Meanwhile, Reginald was being investigated by the American Medical Association for a breach of ethics. Jane hadn't been able to muster even an ounce of sympathy for him. After the way he had treated his wife and daughter, he deserved all the hard knocks the media could offer. But over the weekend, things had grown astronomically worse. *SNL* had every right in the world to lampoon Reginald, but Sutton was an innocent bystander. The writers had taken that ridiculous article about her as a blueprint, and their portrayal had made Jane want to throw her uncle's television across the room. She still didn't know if Sutton had seen it. Would it be crueler to bring it up or help to maintain her ignorance?

Only when her spoon clanged against the bottom of the bowl did Jane realize it was empty. She hadn't tasted a bite. She hadn't wanted breakfast at all, actually, but Aunt Jenny had refused to let her leave the house without eating something. Under normal circumstances, Jane would have savored every spoonful of the salty porridge, but right now she was too preoccupied. As the days had passed, Sutton's texts had grown few and far between. The lack of details only fueled Jane's speculation as her imagination tried to fill in the gaps. Was Sutton's mother improving? Had her father joined them on Long Island? Had the press continued to hound her, or were they backing off? Had she made any kind of decision about her career? Did Sutton ever miss her?

Shaking her head, she pushed back her chair. Work would at least partially distract her from the storm of questions. But just as she was getting to her feet, her phone lit up with an incoming call. Sue. As she reached out to answer it, alarm prickled the back of her neck. It wasn't even seven o'clock yet.

"Hi, Sue, is everything o—"

"Jane, Jane the store—" Sue's voice was high and thin with panic, and she suddenly switched into Mandarin. The hurried syllables made only sporadic sense to Jane. Something about broken glass, and thieves? And money?

"Sue," she said, trying to make her voice steady. "I can't follow. Slow down, please, okay? What happened?"

Instead, Sue switched to English. "Someone broke in! The front window is shattered and there's glass everywhere and they took all the money."

Adrenaline brought her to the balls of her feet. "Have you called the police?"

"No, I . . . you were the first person I thought of."

"Are you sure the store's empty?"

Sue was silent for a long moment. "I haven't gone in the back yet," she whispered fearfully.

"Okay. Here's what you're going to do." Jane braced herself on the table as her brain spun wildly. "Don't stay in the shop. I want you to walk over to Dragon Land Bakery right now—they'll be open already. When you get there, dial 9-1-1. You'll tell the dispatcher exactly what you just told me, except with even more details if you can. I'm coming over right now and we'll wait for the police together. Do you understand?"

"I walk to the bakery," Sue said, her voice trembling. "And then call 9-1-1."

"That's right. I'll be there very soon. Okay?"

"Okay."

As the dial tone sounded in Jane's ear, she faced her aunt, who stood clutching a frying pan in one hand and the countertop with the other, frown lines wrinkling her brow. "Sue's shop was robbed. She says it's a mess. Send anyone you can."

With that, she spun away, hurrying toward the front door. "Be careful!" Aunt Jenny shouted after her.

Jane ran. Her sneakers thudded against the pavement and the crisp morning air burned in her lungs, but she didn't slow down before skidding to a halt underneath the sinuous crimson sign of the bakery. Immediately, Sue stepped out onto the sidewalk.

"The police are coming. They told me to stay here until they arrived."

Jane looked her up and down. She was pale and trembling, and Jane reached out to rub her shoulders gently. "Are you hurt anywhere?"

"No. But the shop . . ." Her eyes filled with tears. "They smashed so much. Why would someone do such a thing? Why not just take the money and leave?"

At that moment, the wail of approaching sirens rose up into the sky, sounding strangely mournful even as they trumpeted the alarm. Like a pack of hounds baying, Jane thought as she hooked her arm through Sue's and led her slowly back toward the store. They turned the corner in time to see a pair of cops enter, pistols drawn. Two more flanked the door, listening intently. Only at a distant shout of "Clear!" did the backup lower their weapons.

"Um." Jane swallowed hard when her first attempt at speaking failed. The sight of those guns, out and ready to be used, made her quail inside. "Officers? This is Sue. She's the one who called."

At a nod from his partner, the man on the near doorpost walked forward to greet them. Jane stood by Sue, sometimes helping her answer the questions, but mostly offering silent support. A crowd was beginning to gather, and Jane recognized many of the faces. She was oddly comforted by the fact that these people weren't random tourists hoping to be titillated by New York City crime, but neighbors who would support Sue as she and her business tried to recover. Red Door Apothecary was her life's work, and now it was in ruin.

"Are you ready to go inside, ma'am?"

When Sue nodded, the cop turned and led them both over the threshold. Jane couldn't help but feel irony at walking across the doorstep when the entire window to their right was shattered. When the sun broke through the clouds, the long glass shards littering the sidewalk gleamed fiercely, looking for all the world like prismatic knife blades as they scattered the light. Trying to escape the sinister image, Jane turned away and moved into the shop.

And gasped. The destruction was even worse inside. Almost every jar had either been upended or smashed, and the cabinets stood with their doors flung open, contents spilled out on the floor below. Herbs and roots lay strewn among the scintillating bits of glass, and the couch cushions and pillows had been sliced open, their white, fluffy guts festooning the sitting area.

"Who would do something like this?"

She hadn't meant to speak the words aloud, and when Sue buried her face in her hands and began to cry softly, Jane regretted her outburst. As she wrapped one arm around Sue's thin shoulders, she wished she'd brought tissues. Swallowing against nausea, Jane focused on the officer standing beside her. She could at least try to get some answers.

"Do you have any suspects?"

"Not yet, ma'am."

At a gesture from one of his colleagues, he moved away to confer quietly with a few more uniformed police and what looked to be two detectives in dark suits. Even if the police did have their suspicions, he probably wouldn't be able to tell her. Squinting down at her shoes so she didn't have to see the mess, Jane tried to think back. Had she heard of any other similar robberies in the city recently? Was this related to something bigger, or was it an isolated incident?

A new thought dawned. Forcing herself to look up, she took in the ransacked store with fresh eyes. It had quite literally been torn apart—as though the perpetrators had been looking for something. But what had they been hoping to find?

Beside her, Sue was wiping delicately at her eyes, clearly determined to pull herself together.

"What happens now?" she asked tremulously.

"I imagine they'll ask you to give a statement," Jane said. "They might want you to go to the station for that."

Sue looked alarmed. "Will you come with me?"

"Of course." Jane glanced around the room again. "Do you remember seeing anyone suspicious recently?"

"Difficult to say. I used to know everyone who came into the store, but for the past few days, it's been so busy." Sue shook her head wearily. "Everyone has come in wanting 'Eastern medicine.' They think I have opium!"

Jane froze. Suddenly, the scene before her made perfect sense. This hadn't been an act of vandalism or even a simple robbery. "That's it. They were looking for drugs."

"Who?"

"The people who did this." The realization burned away her queasiness. "We have to mention that to the police, okay?"

Sue nodded slowly. Her eyes looked a little glazed. Clearly, she was still in shock, and Jane wondered if the police would let her remain with Sue while they took her statement. Just then one of the detectives approached—a woman, whose brisk gate and alert expression conspired to lend her an air of competence that immediately made Jane feel much more at ease.

"Good morning. I'm Detective Hoffman." She looked to Sue. "And you're the owner?"

"Yes." Sue had to choke out the monosyllable, as though identifying herself had reminded her of just how much she had lost.

"This is Xue Si Ma, Detective," Jane said, when it was clear Sue wasn't able to continue. "And I'm Jane Morrow. I help out around the shop."

"I'm sorry that this happened." Despite her efficient mannerism, Hoffman's eyes were sympathetic. "I'd like to take you over to the station to get your statement. Our people here will secure the scene."

"May I come along?" Jane asked.

"Yes."

But when they emerged onto the sidewalk, a male voice immediately called out Sue's name. A moment later, Jane located Giancarlo waving urgently from behind the garish crime scene tape. When Sue's face brightened and she turned aside, Jane started after her, fearing the detective would be angry.

"Sue. We need to go."

"I . . . but . . ."

"This won't take long," Hoffman reassured her.

Sue's indecision turned to obstinance. "I want Giancarlo to be there."

Jane watched Hoffman's internal debate—the frown, the flick of her eyes back toward the shop, the glance at her watch. And then she sighed. "Fine." Striding forward purposefully, she beckoned for Giancarlo to step beneath the tape.

As he and Sue embraced, Jane suddenly felt like a third wheel. At a crime scene. Shaking her head, she trudged in their wake, suddenly overwhelmed by fatigue. In that moment, she missed Sutton so fiercely that it hurt to take her next breath.

But Sutton was miles away, embroiled in her own crisis. And if Jane told her what had happened, she would probably feel respon-

sible. Best to keep it to herself for now. She would find out soon
enough.

THE AMBULANCE JOLTED OVER a pothole and immediately
slammed on the brakes, probably in response to a red light. Strapped
into one of the jump seats in the back, Sutton kept her hands in her
lap and tried to look calm even as she glanced over to the monitor
recording her mother's vital signs. Not so much as a blip in her
heart rate. Good. At first, Sutton had been hesitant about having
her sedated for this trip. But ever since the seizure, Priscilla had
experienced intermittent bouts of intense disorientation and even
some paralysis in her extremities. It was better, the attending physician had argued, for her mother to make the trip unconscious
than to risk triggering additional anxiety that might lead to an even
more significant relapse.

Sutton had insisted on riding in the back of the ambulance. The
EMT who joined them looked as though he had just graduated
from high school, but he had watched over her mother like a baby-
faced hawk for the duration of the drive. She had tried not to scrutinize his every move throughout the three-hour trip, but giving
up control had never been her strong suit.

Except with Jane.

The thought seared through Sutton's mind, leaving her resentful of the heat prickling her skin and the dull ache in the pit of her
stomach. Shifting uncomfortably on the hard plastic seat, she closed
her eyes and took a deep breath, trying to will away the surge of
unwelcome arousal. She didn't want to want Jane while she was sitting in the back of an ambulance with her mother lying unconscious a few feet away.

Her fingertips strayed to her right pocket and traced the hard
edge of her phone. Since receiving the news early this morning
that her mother would be immediately transferred to New York

Presbyterian Hospital, Sutton had had plenty of chances to text Jane with the news that she was coming home. But every time she reached for her phone, something stopped her from typing out a message.

Maybe it was that when she saw Jane again, she would have to explain everything. Jane would be gentle and solicitous, wanting to hold and comfort her while she shared the story of the past two weeks. But Sutton didn't want to go back there in her head. She had lived under the cloud of her father's infidelity long enough, and at this point, she just wanted to move forward. To escape. Sweden was looking better each day. And even though Jane would probably understand if Sutton said she didn't want to rehash everything, what sense did it make to go running back to her when she would have to turn around and leave again in a matter of months?

And yet. The desire was a hot coil in her belly, twisting tighter at the memory of Jane moaning her name. If she concentrated hard enough, she could taste the salt-cut sweetness of Jane's skin, feel the magnetic heat of her body, picture the brilliant ring of gold that always encircled her irises when they were making love. Such distinctive, expressive eyes—the very attribute that had first caught Sutton's attention months ago.

As the ambulance bobbed and wove in and out of traffic, the rush of desire began to cool, cracking like dried lava floes to reveal the layers beneath. She didn't just want Jane's body—she craved the banter they had swapped, the laughter they had shared, the peace she felt in her embrace. Whenever she was around Jane, she felt more herself and less what everyone else wanted her to be. But that was dangerous, wasn't it? She couldn't rely on another person to bring her serenity. Another person might break a promise. Another person might leave, or life might separate them by thousands of miles. She needed to find contentment in herself.

"ETA five minutes."

The driver's voice cut through her musings, and she watched as the EMT began to ready her mother for transport. She had yet to speak with her father. Shortly after visiting hours had begun this morning, the order had come down from on-high, sudden and swift, that her mother was to be moved to the city. The decision had caught Sutton completely off guard, leaving her angrier than ever. She wanted a say in her mother's treatment—she deserved it. But her father had the power to cut her out of the loop completely if he wanted.

The ambulance pulled to a stop and the driver flung open the back doors a few seconds later. Quickly and efficiently, they worked together to lower the stretcher onto the waiting gurney. Intending to follow them, she hopped out onto the pavement.

"Dr. St. James!"

Sutton looked around for her father before suddenly realizing the greeting was meant for her. A young, harried-looking woman in pale green scrubs waved as she approached. Probably an intern, if her bloodshot eyes were any indication.

"Your father asked me to look out for you. He's in his office and would like to speak with you right away."

Sutton glanced between her and the gurney. Best to get this confrontation over with while her mother was being admitted. "Thank you. I'll go see him now."

Her legs wanted to lag, but she forced herself to hurry through the maze of corridors. The familiar glare of the fluorescent bulbs and the scent of antiseptic anchored her racing thoughts. Right now, she didn't want to deal with what her father had done to their family. Right now, she wanted to talk to him, professional to professional, about Priscilla's case. Steeling herself, she pushed open the door leading to his office suite.

"Good afternoon, Sutton." Diane had her hair pulled back in a bun so tight it gave her eyes a slightly slanted look. Her black-and-white checkered suit was as dizzying as an Escher painting. "He's expecting you. Go right in."

"Thank you." Sutton made her voice as frosty as she knew how.

His door opened before she could touch the handle, and then he was there, dressed as always in a dark Armani suit, looking perhaps a little thinner than he had been but still radiating charisma. He loomed over her, welcoming her inside with the solicitous tone that always put his patients at ease. When, Sutton wondered, did that tone begin to change from solicitous to seductive? The thought made her want to vomit.

With new eyes, she took in the dark, polished wood of his desk, the high-backed leather chair behind it, the sculpture of a caduceus, carved in jade, that sat across from his computer. In addition to his diplomas, photographs adorned the wall—framed snapshots of his political career. They showed him hobnobbing with presidents, vice presidents, even some foreign dignitaries—highlighting the range of his influence. An influence he had abused for years now.

Sutton tried to imagine what they had felt, those women he had fooled. They had come to him frightened and in pain, betrayed by their bodies and minds, seeking answers. They had sat in that low, plush chair before his desk and stared up at him with almost religious adoration as he charmed and reassured them, making them feel safe for the first time since diagnosis. After he had outlined their treatment, they had trusted him with their lives. Would it have felt like a small matter, then, to offer him their bodies? How could he have taken advantage of them that way? Not to mention the betrayal of his wife!

As soon as he closed the door, she rounded on him. "Dad—"

"Wait." He crossed the space between them in just a few long paces and enfolded her into an embrace. Sutton remained stiff, taking only shallow breaths in an effort not to fill her nose with the cloying scent of his aftershave. After a moment, he stepped back and grasped her shoulders, holding her at arm's length.

"I've been a terrible father to you."

Sutton blinked, nonplussed. She had expected denial or excuses, not frankness and candor. In the next moment, anger returned to burn away the initial flash of surprise. But when she opened her mouth, he shook his head.

"Please. Let me finish. I've been a terrible father to you, and a terrible husband to your mother. I allowed my success to go to my head, and I've been so selfish. But all of that ends now. I am going to give your mother the best possible care. She'll have everything she needs."

He was saying all the right things, and that made Sutton even angrier. "You hurt her so badly." She forced the words out before he could keep talking. "Do you have any idea what it was like, to see that? To watch her start to seize? To know exactly what was happening to her, and why?"

He tightened his grip on her shoulders. "I'm sorry, Sutton. I'm so sorry you had to go through that. That I wasn't there, where I should have been."

"It's not about you not being there! It's about what you did! And what that did to her!"

His eyes closed, then opened. "I will never betray her, or you, again."

Sutton felt herself start to tremble. She hoped he knew it was from rage, not fear or exhaustion. "How can I believe anything you say? Now, or ever?"

"This is a healing process. It's going to take time. All I ask is that you be open to the possibility of reconciliation."

Sutton crossed her arms beneath her breasts and held his stare, biting her lip against the retort that wanted to escape her mouth. This much, she could control. She wouldn't malign him anymore, but she wasn't about to lie or issue platitudes.

Finally, his hands fell away from her. "I know that it's going to take a long time to rebuild the trust between us. That's why I'm hoping you'll reconsider your next steps and decide to take the residency at Columbia."

"Excuse me?" A renewed surge of fury sliced through her. Was he actually trying to bully her in this moment? Under the guise of an apology?

"Stay in New York, with your family. Help me mend what I've broken."

His tone was almost beseeching, and it gave her pause. If her parents didn't reconcile, her mother would need to be cared for. Even if they did, it would be a precarious situation for a while. More than once, the thought had crossed her mind that it would be nothing but selfish to go to Sweden in the midst of a family crisis. Maybe her first impulse had been wrong. Maybe his plea was an honest one. Or maybe he was fooling her as he had so many other women.

"How do you intend to do that?"

He sat down behind his desk and rested his folded hands atop the polished surface. "I've lost my way. It began when I lost sight of my priorities. You and your mother should always be first in my mind. That hasn't always been the case, but it will be now." The implication was clear. If family was most important to him, then it should be to her as well. "Some of the choices I've made have hurt you deeply, but I have the power to change my behavior going forward. We all do."

"What is that supposed to mean?"

"Do you think it's been easy for your mother to watch you drift away from us? To watch you choose the kind of lifestyle that's antithetical to how we raised you?"

Sutton's vision went red. "Excuse me? Are you referring to the *fact* that I am a lesbian? It's not a lifestyle, Dad—it's who I am!"

"We can all change who we are, Sutton. To say otherwise is to imply that we are predestined, predetermined, trapped by our genetics."

"Dad, there is nothing wrong with me. Nothing. I'm not the one who lied, cheated, and abused my professional status. *You* are." Even as Sutton debated his logic, a separate part of her brain couldn't believe that they were having this argument right now. How had she become the focus of this conversation?

"I'm not excusing my actions. But try to look at this from my perspective." He leaned forward in his chair. "How do you think it felt to watch your mother growing more and more sick as she fretted over you?"

Sutton was so stunned that she actually took a step backward. "Are you blaming me for Mom's illness? Because that is the most nonsensical, ridicul—"

"Of course not," he snapped. "But you are well aware of how multiple sclerosis works. Your mother is extremely sensitive to stress. We have both caused her too much anxiety. Going forward, we both must do our best to help her remain happy and at peace. Whatever it takes, Sutton. No matter the sacrifice."

For the first time since she had walked through his door, doubt prickled her skin. It was true, of course—stress did trigger relapses. But how could he lay even part of the blame for Priscilla's illness at her feet? Was she supposed to suppress her true self, just because of her mother's diagnosis? His unfaithfulness was morally and ethically wrong. He might try to say the same about her sexual orientation, but they were in entirely different categories.

As she was taking a deep breath to respond, the phone rang. He reached for it quickly, issuing a clipped "St. James" into the receiver and then listening for several seconds. "One moment." He put his hand over the mouthpiece and turned back to her. "I'm afraid I need to take this."

"I can wait."

He shook his head. "Go to your mother, Sutton. She should be in her room by now. I'll join you shortly."

For a moment, she thought about arguing. How did he expect her to trust him when he wouldn't even take a phone call in front of her? Then again, if the call related to a patient, he was obligated by law to see that the information remained confidential. Physicians were, she reflected as she made her way toward the door, secret-keepers by necessity.

As it closed behind her, she felt herself begin to crash, exhaustion rushing in to fill the spaces abandoned by adrenaline. Ignoring Diane's syrupy farewell, she left the suite and walked slowly back down the corridor. Her legs and arms seemed heavy and wooden, and she could feel herself beginning to dissociate in response to the stress. What a pathetic sight she must be—trudging down the hall after being summarily dismissed by her father. Had he meant anything he'd said about changing his ways? Or had every word been merely lip service? His passive-aggressive comments made her want to board the first flight to Stockholm. But was her anger making her overreact? Was she supposed to give him a second chance? Did he deserve an opportunity to prove himself?

Two weeks ago, everything had seemed so clear. Now, her life was spiraling out of control. She could feel her psyche mimicking the body's response to shock—curl up, turn inward, protect the heart. Reaching any kind of decision in this state of mind would be a mistake. But it might be one she was forced into making.

CHAPTER SIXTEEN

A S SOON AS SUTTON boarded the downtown train, she slid into a corner seat, wrapped her arms around her messenger bag, and closed her eyes. She had never felt so tired in her life—not even during one of the many all-nighters she had pulled while trying to juggle her clinical rotations and her research. This fatigue was more than physical—she felt it in the sluggishness of her mind and the unrelenting tightness in her chest. It was barely past six o'clock, but she wanted to go home, fall into bed, and sleep for years. Or at least until her alarm went off in the predawn, summoning her to rounds. The idea of having to play catch-up at the hospital made her honestly want to cry. She hadn't shed a tear throughout this whole debacle, and now her body wanted to break down?

Thankfully, after a little while, the rhythmic cadence of the car rattling on the tracks coaxed her off the mental ledge, and she even managed a shallow doze until the train pulled up at Spring Street. But instead of turning toward her apartment, she found herself walking in the direction of Noodle Treasure. Mei's soup and dumplings would be the perfect antidote to having barely eaten all day. Once she had fortified herself, maybe she could find Jane. To talk, Sutton reminded herself sternly, not to fall into bed together.

As she turned the corner and the cheery façade came into view, an odd sense of reluctance overcame her. How much did Mei and Benny know? And the regulars? Had they followed her father's scandal in the news, or had Jane needed to explain her absence to them? Steeling herself, she pushed open the door and stepped in-side, breathing deeply of the warm, fragrant air.

"Dr. Sutton!" Mei's eager cry spread that warmth throughout her body, and she smiled in surprise as Mei hurried over to em-brace her. "How are you? How is your mother? We have all been so worried."

"Thank you. That means so much. I just returned to the city a few hours ago. She's been moved to a hospital here. Her prognosis is still uncertain, but she'll have the best care."

Mei nodded gravely. "I'm glad you are back."

"Me, too. I've missed you and Benny. And your soup and dump-lings." But as she spoke, Sutton realized the restaurant, usually bustling, was entirely empty except for one Caucasian couple in the back booth. "I was hoping to get caught up on the news here. Where is everyone?"

Mei's face fell. "They are still at Sue's. Cleaning up. Benny took some food to them a short while ago."

"Cleaning up?"

"Oh, I'm sorry. Of course you haven't heard. There was a break-in late last night at Sue's shop. So much damage."

As Mei shook her head, Sutton's heart lurched. Late last night, Mei had said. Surely Jane and Sue and Min had been asleep. Still, the panic clawed at her insides. "But no one was hurt?"

"No, no. Everyone is fine. No one was in the store. But Sue lost so much. Money, and inventory, and—"

"Do you think they're still cleaning up now?"

"Oh, yes. They've been there all day."

"In that case, may I have my order to go?"

"Of course." Mei smiled. "They will all be very happy to see you. Like I said, we have been worried."

As she hurried back into the kitchen, Sutton sat in one of the chairs near the register. Seconds later, she got to her feet and be-gan to pace. Who would break into the apothecary? And why? She couldn't even imagine how Sue was feeling right now. She had built her business so painstakingly over the course of many years, only to have criminals invade and vandalize her life's work in a matter of minutes. Anger pierced the dense fog of her fatigue, but despair was close behind. Was everything falling to pieces?

Mei returned carrying two brown paper bags. "Here is your supper," she said, handing Sutton the smaller of the two. "And these are some roasted pork buns. I forgot to send them with Benny. If you are going to Sue's, would you mind dropping them off?"

"Not at all." Sutton felt relieved to be able to do something. "I'll go right away."

She hurried out into the night, her steps automatically retracing the familiar route. But as she turned the corner to approach the apothecary, she froze. The scene before her was awash with light and motion. People swarmed busily around the outside of the store, and probably inside as well. A large piece of plywood crisscrossed with crime scene tape extended across the gap where the large window had once boasted artfully arranged displays of books and teas designed to attract curious passersby. One curb was piled high with a wall of trash bags, and as she watched, someone came out of the shop carrying two more. When he crossed into a pool of street lamp light, she recognized his face.

"Giancarlo."

He peered at her in confusion until she grew closer. "Dr. Sutton! I didn't know you were back in New York." He heaved the bag to the top of the pile, then brushed off his hands. "Forgive me for not greeting you properly. I'm filthy."

"I just heard what happened from Mei," Sutton said. "I'm so sorry. How is Sue holding up?"

"She is devastated." Giancarlo shook his head. "If someone ever did that to my restaurant, I would be inconsolable." He glanced back toward the shop. "But she is strong. And it has been so good for her, I think, to see the community respond like this."

Sutton fleetingly wondered whether a similar catastrophe in her neighborhood would lead to the same swell of support. "I'm glad there are so many people here. Do they have any idea who did it?"

"The police have not said anything yet. But I have a friend with a brother on Vice, and he told me earlier that they suspect it's drug- or gang-related." His voice grew rougher in frustration. "Apparently there is some rumor that Sue's shop was a front for a drug cartel? Ridiculous! These idiot gangbangers will believe anything!"

The epiphany struck like a rattlesnake. Beneath the sudden roar that filled her ears, Sutton could feel the tremor in her legs and the color leaching from her face. The skit. She saw it again in her mind's eye—the thick plumes of smoke that had wreathed "her" head, blocking out the sight of her father's infidelities. Eastern medicine. Opium. That was the rumor. It may have been started by a sensationalist reporter, but he would never have come up with it if she hadn't agreed to be filmed for that news feature. In trying to help, all she had done was to set in motion the chain of events that had led to this—this tower of garbage bags, this glass-salted stretch of sidewalk, this loss of property and inventory and precious time.

Sutton looked between the shattered window and the curb, feeling as though an invisible pair of hands was trying to strangle her. She should never have come here. Not today, and not all those months ago, back when she needed a quiet place to escape the scrutiny of her friends. The watchful eyes had followed her, and their gaze had turned sinister. She should never have come. She didn't belong. She had to leave. Now.

"I wish I could stay and help," she said, not quite meeting Giancarlo's eyes, "but I have to get back to the hospital. Can you drop these off for me? Mei gave them to me when I stopped by. They're for everyone." Realizing she was babbling, Sutton pushed the larger of the bags into his hands.

"Of course. But don't you want to see—"

"Sutton!"

Minetta's unmistakable soprano felt like a knife to the chest. In the next instant, she was nearly knocked to the ground by the force of Min's embrace.

"You're back! We were so worried! How's your mom? We wanted to do something to help but no one could figure out what." Suddenly, she let go, visibly censuring her public display. Smiling sheepishly, she finished with a meek, "Are you all right?"

"I'm all right," Sutton lied. She wasn't all right at all. Her skin felt too tight, and if she had to stay for even one more minute, she thought she might shatter into a million pieces. But she couldn't just turn her back on Min and walk away without so much as an explanation.

"Okay. That's good. Jane is going to be so happy to see you!" Min rolled her eyes. "Ever since you've been gone, she's been a huge pain in the ass."

As Giancarlo chuckled indulgently, Sutton forced her lips into a crude approximation of a smile. The only thing she knew for certain was that she couldn't face Jane. Not right now, not like this. "I wish I could stay," she managed, "but I'm due at the hospital. Will you tell her . . ."

The words crowded her throat, choking off her speech. *Tell her I miss her. Tell her I want her. Tell her I'm sorry. Tell her I lo—*

"Sutton?" Min was looking at her apprehensively. Giancarlo's expression was troubled.

"Tell her thanks. For being so sweet about my mother."

Before their kind, earnest faces changed her mind, she fled. Her heart pounded against her ribs like a wild animal demanding freedom. Moisture flooded her eyes but she dashed it away with one sleeve. She was doing the right thing. She was. She was a surgeon. When she found a problem, she cut it out. When she was the problem, she cut herself out. Her leaving was the best possible thing for this community. All she had to offer them was chaos. All she had to offer Jane was sadness.

But the closer she got to the border of Chinatown, the harder it became to move forward. Crossing Canal felt like fighting against a buffeting headwind. Every step up Baxter was like a slog through sucking mud. Tears slid down her tingling cheeks, but she refused to acknowledge them now. Why was this so hard? Losing a patient on the operating table was hard. Standing at Dr. Buehler's side while he delivered bad news to a family member was hard. Watching her mother go into seizures had been hard. Turning her back on a month-long romance shouldn't be hard. She had no right to feel like this. None. None at all.

By the time she arrived at the hospital, her eyes were dry. Hopefully, her colleagues would attribute their puffiness to lack of sleep. While out on Long Island, she had occasionally wondered what they were saying about her, but now, as she slid into the rhythm of the revolving door, she found no room in her thoughts for self-consciousness. Heartache had made her numb. They could say whatever they liked. She wouldn't feel a thing.

CHAPTER SEVENTEEN

SUTTON CLUTCHED HER STYROFOAM cup and shuffled forward in line. She kept her gaze trained on the steam rising like mist from dark lake of her coffee. Through the haze of her fatigue, she wondered whether it, like the incense in her childhood church, would carry prayers to heaven. She had stopped praying a long time ago, but maybe it was time to start again.

Her life was a waking nightmare. Since returning to the hospital, she had been alternately ignored or teased by the majority of her colleagues. Dismayed to find herself less numb than she had hoped, Sutton poured every ounce of her energy into work in an effort to escape. The hours blended together into a dizzying collage of patient charts and paperwork. Worse still, the uproar over her father had yet to die down. After a few close calls with the press, she had taken to wearing a Yankees hat and sneaking into the hospital through side entrances. At home, alone in the bed that now reminded her of Jane, she had barely slept for days.

Jane. Sutton took a deep breath against the flutter of panic that filled her chest every time Jane's face appeared in her thoughts. She had answered only one of her increasingly anxious texts: the first one, sent less than an hour after her encounter with Min and Giancarlo.

Just heard you're back in the city. Can I see u 2night?

At first, Sutton had planned on not replying at all. But as the evening dragged on, pain and guilt had eaten away at both her resolve and her focus. Finally, she had locked herself in a bathroom stall and laboriously tapped out a reply.

I'm sorry. I'm so overwhelmed right now. I can't.

Solicitous as usual, Jane had texted back immediately, and then again the next day, and the next. Each time, Sutton made no reply. People who broke up with someone via text message were selfish cowards, and now she was one of them. Maybe the whispers in the hallways were right. Maybe the apple hadn't fallen far from her father's tree. Not an hour passed when she didn't want to break the silence she had imposed, but what good would it do? Anything she said would only invite discussion, and discussion was pointless. Entering into that relationship had been a terrible idea. She had known the only possible outcome: that she would be the one to hurt Jane. The part she hadn't bargained for was how much pain she would cause herself in the process.

The cashier snapped her out of her reverie, and Sutton mustered the dregs of a smile as she handed over her money. But when she turned toward the locker room, she came face-to-face with Travis McPhearson. Once her father's most ardent sycophant, Travis was now his loudest detractor. His perfect smile broadened as he approached, and once he was close enough, he threw one arm around her shoulders.

"Dr. St. James!" he said, drawing the attention of a cluster of nearby interns. "What a pleasant surprise."

"Hello, Travis." She tried to keep walking, but his grip was too strong.

"Where are you off to in such a rush? Your opium den?" He looked around with a smirk.

Sutton fought the urge to throw her coffee in his face. Setting her jaw, she shifted her stance. "If you don't let go of me, Travis," she said, too softly for anyone else to hear, "I'll make you."

His jaw thrust forward stubbornly, and for a moment, it seemed he might test her threat. Sutton's skin tingled with the desire to lash out, and when he finally backed off, her disappointment was stronger than her relief. What on earth was happening to her? What kind of person was she turning into? Shoving down her self-castigation, she walked away. As much as she wanted to blow up in his face, any hint of instability would feed into the image of her constructed by the media. Ice. She had to be like ice. It was the only way to rebuild her professional reputation.

After putting on her "disguise," she hurried into the subway, slouching beneath the prominent brim of her hat. As luck would have it, a corner seat was free in the next train, and she curled up into it facing the wall. Despite her recent influx of caffeine, she almost drifted off on her way downtown.

Climbing the stairs to Spring Street felt like tackling Everest. When she finally gained the summit, a warm breeze tugged at the brim of her cap, bringing with it the faint scent of roasting chestnuts from a nearby street vendor. For a moment, she closed her eyes, basking in the unlooked-for caress. At least Mother Nature was treating her kindly.

She couldn't go on like this much longer. Maybe it was time to start taking sleeping pills, or at least something for the anxiety. Weighing her options, she turned the corner toward her apartment complex.

"Hi."

Jane.

The sound of her voice burned and soothed in a dizzying riot of emotion. Adrenaline lit up Sutton's every cell at the sight of her standing near the entrance to her building. Washed-out jeans hung loosely from her hips, and on her faded blue T-shirt, the Tootsie Roll owl sat on top of a rainbow. The text beneath the image, of course, was How Many Licks? and for one precarious instant, hysterical laughter threatened to burst from Sutton's throat. But if she started laughing, she would also start crying, and if she started to cry she might never stop. Jane would offer her comfort, as she always did, and Sutton would selfishly accept.

No. Ice. She had to be ice.

With a Herculean effort, she forced herself to remain still. "Hi."

Jane was looking at her intently. As though she could sense Sutton's internal conflict, she kept her distance. "How's your mom?"

"She's in good hands. They're working on getting her back into remission." Sutton clutched her coffee tightly. "How is Sue?"

"She's hanging in there." Jane cleared her throat. "I've been worried about you."

Her voice held a hint of accusation, but Sutton couldn't blame her. As she struggled to find the right words, Jane took one step closer. Her gaze felt like a spotlight. The bustling activity around them seemed suddenly to grow less distinct, and for one insane moment, it felt as though they were the only inhabitants of the city. Dropping her eyes to Jane's feet, Sutton saw them rocking back and forth against the pavement—a clear display of nerves.

"I needed to see you." Jane raised one hand but let it fall just as quickly. "I hope you're not angry."

Sutton swallowed against the pressure of all the unsaid words sticking in her throat. Never had she seen Jane so uncertain, and she hated knowing she was the cause. All she could do was to shake her head.

Jane took another step closer, her expression softening. "How are you?" she asked. "Really."

"Exhausted." It was the first word that came to mind.

"I can only imagine." Suddenly, her face brightened. "Oh! I though you might be hungry." She extended a small paper bag. "Mei's dumplings. She sends her regards."

Sutton was careful not to touch Jane's fingers as she accepted the food. A distant part of her brain wondered whether this had been Min's idea. It smacked of her influence. "Thanks."

Silence descended between them, awkward and suffocating.

Now that she was over her initial shock, Sutton began to notice details she had missed. Jane was thinner than she had been, and the shadows under her eyes were almost as deep as the ones Sutton saw every day in the mirror. "You must be exhausted, too."

"A different kind, I think." Jane's hands hung loosely at her thighs, fingers twitching. "I . . . it's not just me. Everyone has been really worried. About you."

"So I've heard. Thank you." The longer this conversation went, the more stilted it became. Claustrophobia rose into her throat, making it difficult to swallow.

She needed to tell Jane the reasons behind her lack of communication. Her apartment would be empty, but she couldn't do it there. As though it had already happened, Sutton could picture that future unfolding. The moment they were alone together, she would forget her resolve and push Jane gently against the door, frantic kisses replacing the words she needed to say. She would lose herself, let the heat of Jane's body catch her up in a conflagration that would burn away reason and logic. And then, once the fire had shivered down to embers, her guilt would be unbearable.

"Can we walk a little?" she asked. "Find a place to talk?"

Wariness stole over Jane's features, narrowing her eyes and compressing her mouth. "Sure." After a second's hesitation, she turned south toward Chinatown. A block passed in silence while Sutton struggled to find her courage. Finally, Jane spoke first.

"So . . . what brought you back to the city?"

"My father had my mother transferred to New York Presbyterian. He's taking over her treatment."

"How do you feel about that?"

"I don't know. I mean, I believe he wants to help her, of course. And I'm glad she's at one of the best hospitals in the world. But I worry that her seeing him every day might be stressful. The more stressed she is, the more likely it is that she'll get worse."

"Have you talked to him?"

"Briefly. He . . . he asked me to stay in New York. To take the internship at Columbia instead of going abroad." Sutton purposefully skipped the rest of what he'd said. Telling Jane about her father's homophobic comments would only make this more difficult.

"He did what?" Jane sounded affronted. "How can he ask that of you? You're not going to do it, are you?"

Her moral outrage spiked Sutton's irritation, and she quickly latched on to the emotion. It was a relief to feel something other than loneliness and pain. "Why shouldn't I? My family is falling apart, my mother's condition is getting worse, and you think I should blithely jet across the ocean? What kind of daughter would I be if I abandoned them like that?"

"Whoa." Jane held up both hands. "I'm sorry, okay? I just . . . I want you to be able to fulfill your dreams. You worked so hard to earn that postdoc."

Her tone was conciliatory, but Sutton didn't want to let go of her anger. Bright and hot, it filled up the hollow places inside and banished the fog of her exhaustion. Under its influence, the contours of the world were sharp and crisp again.

"Do you honestly think I *want* to let go of Lund? That I want to stay here and deal with the shit storm unleashed by my father?" When a few passersby turned to look at them curiously, Sutton lowered her voice. "I don't! But I'm not going to be selfish."

"No one could ever accuse you of being selfish, Sutton." Jane finally dared to touch her, then, pressing her fingers ever so lightly to the small of Sutton's back. "But do you have to make a decision right now? You'd leave for Sweden over the summer, right? That's still months away."

Her touch felt so good, so comforting, and Sutton had to remind herself to stay angry. She quickened her pace enough for Jane's hand to fall. But before she could come up with a retort, a blare of trumpets echoed beyond the curve in the road ahead of them. At first,

Sutton looked for the source of the sound in the park to their right, but Jane pointed across the street.

"It's a funeral."

A group of musicians in dark suits moved into view, marching slowly in the center of the road. The first man beat on a snare drum, while the other three played trumpets. An open car trailed them, the gold-framed portrait of who Sutton assumed was the deceased individual displayed prominently between the front and back seats. Behind the car, the hearse lumbered solemnly, a Chinese flag flying from its antenna.

"The music is to—"

"Let me guess." It was so easy to connect the dots. "Keep the demons away." As the group drew closer, she leaned forward, peering into the gloom. "Is that Benny?"

"The drummer? Yeah."

As they walked on, Sutton couldn't stop watching the procession. Benny set the pace, his arms churning and his legs steady. She wondered how his hips and knees were feeling. Suddenly, she realized that walking away from Jane tonight also meant walking away from Benny and Mei, and the sanctuary she had found in Noodle Treasure. Was she ready to turn her back on this entire community? To renounce the narrow, crooked streets of Chinatown for the broad, airy geometry of Midtown and Uptown?

Jane inclined her head toward the open gate leading into the park. "We can sit on a bench if you want."

"All right." Sutton chose one facing the street, and Jane sat beside her, close but not touching. Sutton could feel her anger dissipating as the sounds of the funeral faded away, and vainly, she tried to gather the shreds of emotion around her like armor. She had to do this. Now, before she lost her will. "So, there's something—"

"Have I ever told you about my mother?"

Sutton blinked at the interruption. Jane's knee was bouncing, and she was looking at her out of the corners of her eyes. Quite suddenly, she seemed manic. "No, but—"

"She was born here, in New York. And she did most of her growing up in that same apartment my aunt and uncle are in now. Where we had dinner, remember? Before . . . your mom called that night."

Sutton was confused. Did Jane really think she couldn't remember dining with her family? How warm and friendly they had been toward her? "Of course."

"Well, my mom has two sisters and two brothers, and she was the only woman in her family to go to college. That's where she met my dad." Jane shook her head. "Apparently her family hated that she was dating a Caucasian. Her parents tried to convince her to leave school and settle down with a suitable Chinese man. But she refused. Even after they stopped paying her tuition. She got a loan and a job and paid it herself."

"That's really impressive," Sutton said. She meant it. But where was Jane going with this story?

"My mother graduated with honors and my parents got married right after college." Jane took a deep breath and met Sutton's eyes. "My maternal grandparents were so angry at first, on so many levels. They hated her husband. They hated her life—all that traveling. My mom almost stopped talking to them a few times. At least, that's what she's told me. But she never gave up on them. She called them once a week and we visited once a year and now they've retired to Ocean City and my dad goes fishing with her father every time we're there."

Jane had run out of air again, but her eyes pleaded with Sutton as she caught her breath. "So . . . I mean . . . I just wanted to tell you that you don't have to give up what you want. You can follow your dreams, okay? Who knows—maybe someday you can even have it all. Just like my mom."

Unable to bear witnessing Jane's hopeful expression, Sutton

looked down at her hands, folded properly on her lap. She wasn't just facing her parents' disapproval—she was facing her mother's illness and probable legal action against her father. And she was their only child. She couldn't afford to go haring off after her dreams when they needed her so much, no matter how badly they made her feel. Squeezing her fingers together tightly, she finally forced herself to begin the sentence.

"Jane, I—"

"Don't." Jane's voice, so animated a moment ago, was now a low monotone. She leaned forward, elbows braced between her legs, looking out toward the street. It seemed so desolate in the wake of all that noise. "I get it, okay? Don't say anything."

Sutton's heart felt like it was trying to claw its way out of her throat. She imagined it flopping rhythmically, red, like a dying fish on the asphalt. Swallowing hard, she forced it back down where it belonged. It didn't know the whole story. It didn't have all the facts. She couldn't afford to grant its wishes. "I want you to know that I care about you. I do. It's not about that. It's just that I don't feel capable of doing this anymore. I'm not good for you. I can't give you what you really want."

Finally, Jane turned her head, eyes bright and piercing in the light of the street lamp. "Have I ever said that? Don't put words in my mouth." She reached out to touch Sutton's knee, only to draw her hand back and clutch the edge of the park bench. "I've fallen in love with you. Okay? *You* are what I want."

The fence rails swam before Sutton's eyes. "Don't say that."

Jane laughed harshly. "I guess turnabout is fair play tonight."

"No." Sutton shook her head, as though by doing so, she could dislodge the roaring sound in her ears. "You're not in love with me. You're in love with some version of me that only exists in your head."

"If believing that makes this easier for you, be my guest."

The bitterness in her tone drove another spike of pain through Sutton's chest, but now that she had begun this, she had to finish.

"Think about it pragmatically. You have your aunt and uncle and Min and Sue—a whole community pulling you one way. And I have my family and my profession pulling the opposite way. I think we should just give in."

Jane stood, spun, and pointed one finger down at her. "Bullshit. That's the biggest pile of bullshit I've ever heard."

"Excuse me?"

"Give in? You have to fight for the things you want!"

A shadow of Sutton's previous anger returned, and she grasped at it with all her strength. "I can't fight my ailing mother and my disgraced father."

"So you're just going to give up."

"No!" Sutton looked up into Jane's face, backlit and haloed by the street lamp. She wasn't a quitter. This wasn't about giving up. This was about ethics. Duty. "No. It's more complicated than that. I just . . . can't."

Jane clenched both fists. "You won't," she whispered.

And then, unsteadily, she turned and walked away. Tears blurred Sutton's vision as she watched her go. For one single, insane moment, Sutton wanted to run after her—to beg her forgiveness, to press her cold palms to Jane's warm cheeks and kiss away the pain she'd just inflicted.

But no. No. She had done what was necessary: eliminated what didn't belong. But when, she wondered as she sat clutching her paper bag as though it was all that anchored her to reality, would it stop feeling as though she had excised her own soul in the process?

Alone, she waited for the sharpness of the pain to fade. But instead it grew worse and worse, flaying her open, until the tears were running silently down her cheeks to drip, drip, drip onto the slats of the bench. Thankfully, the park was deserted and only the street-light bore witness to her breakdown. Surely this was to be expected, wasn't it? She would grieve her loss—not only tonight, but for many days in the future. It was logical. It made sense.

And yet, deep down, she knew that if Jane were to come walking back into view right now, that logic would disappear like a popped balloon. In that sickening moment, Sutton would have given anything to see her again. Her grip tightened so hard that she tore a small hole in the bag, her finger brushing against a crinkly piece of plastic inside.

Her fortune cookie.

Suddenly desperate, she made the hole wider and brought the cookie into the dim light. After ripping through the wrapper, she snapped the golden-brown shell in half. Her fingers trembled as she unrolled the tiny strip of paper.

Things fall apart.

Only after reading the message did she realize she had subconsciously wanted this last communication from Jane to provide some sort of escape clause or glimmer of hope. But no. It was honest—brutally so. Everything was falling apart. The fortune forced a mirror in front of her face. Whether her motivations were selfless or not, noble or not, in the end, she was this—a hypocrite on a park bench, alone in the dark.

JANE FLED.

She had tried to fight, and now flight was the only option left. The sidewalk passed by in a gray blur beneath her feet, punctuated by crosswalk lines that swam before her blurred vision. Her head throbbed and her eyes stung and the cool air burned in her lungs. The heat spread across her chest and down into her stomach, searing her insides, parching her throat. Turning into a bodega, she bought a bottle of water and forced herself to drink it all in large gulps. But it did nothing. The thirst was in her mind, not her body.

Gradually, her scattered thoughts resolved into one word. Fool. She had been such a fool—for thinking she would be able to hold Sutton's interest; for believing herself capable of a casual relationship; for granting Sutton the power to break her heart. Fool.

Even so, how could Sutton turn her back so easily, after everything they had shared—the laughter, the revelations, the intimacy? They had celebrated the New Year together and braved her parents' dinner table. They had collected poetry and eaten tripe and confessed their hopes, their dreams, their insecurities. Sutton was the first person who had seen Jane the way she wanted to be seen.

But no. That was a lie. Sutton hadn't seen her as worth fighting to keep.

"Yeah, well, maybe I'm not."

She spoke the words aloud, startling an elderly woman out walking her puggle. Ducking her head in apology, Jane quickly passed her by. For the first time since leaving the park, she took stock of her surroundings, squinting at cross streets and numbers to get her bearing. TriBeCa, near the river. Had she been operating on animal instinct—seeking out a water source in a time of pain and suffering? It seemed as good a plan as any.

Within a few minutes, she was leaning against the railing, looking out across the churning Hudson toward the lights of Jersey City. Lady Liberty's torch burned brightly in the distance, a spark hovering before the dark mouth of the harbor. It was a beautiful scene, and Jane wished Sutton could—

No. She had to stop thinking like that. It was over. Sutton had been clear, and firm in her conviction. She had left no room for ambiguity.

Gripping the railing tightly, Jane released a long, shuddering breath. When the tears came, she didn't wipe them away, but let them run slowly down her cheeks to be dried by the wind. Only when her hands were numb and her eyes dry did she turn away from the water. But she couldn't go home. Not yet. The thought of breaking the news to her family made her feel sick. She didn't want to tell them she hadn't been good enough for Sutton after all.

Instead of turning east, she walked north toward the Village, hoping to lose herself in the charm of its cobblestone streets and quaint little shops. The city had always been her solace, but now it turned against her. She saw Sutton everywhere—in every beautiful blond woman who passed her by; in every couple sharing a kiss while waiting at a stoplight; in every street performer's corner serenade.

Finally, head and heart aching, she turned into a twenty-four-hour diner on Bleecker Street and sat with her back to the window. She ordered a beer and sipped it slowly, tracing patterns in the condensation on the glass. What was she going to do now? How could she possibly go back to her life before Sutton? Working a dead-end job, writing poetry no one would ever read . . . what use was it all? What use was she? To anyone?

Feeling unbearably pathetic, Jane reached into her pocket for her notebook. Maybe she could write down a few fortunes. At least then, the night wouldn't be completely unproductive. At least she would be worth something. *Love is a disease,* she scribbled. *Happiness is an illusion.* Pouring her sorrow and grief into the page didn't make her feel any better, but at least it gave her something to do. *Falling in love is like sliding on rough cement.*

After her first beer, she ordered a second. And then a third. The waitress looked at her sympathetically but never said a word. Jane watched her own handwriting grow sloppier under the influence of fatigue and alcohol, but only when predawn light began to filter through the windows did she switch to coffee.

As the caffeine banished some of the haze from her head, she tried to figure out what to do. Sober up for another hour, maybe, before walking home? Better yet, she could spend the early hours of the morning helping out at Sue's before slipping into her aunt and uncle's apartment during the middle of the day, when they would both be working. She couldn't avoid them forever, of course. She'd have to tell them sometime.

But telling them would make it real. True. Final. And that was the last thing she wanted.

CHAPTER EIGHTEEN

JANE BIT INTO A dumpling as she watched two workmen struggle to raise the large pane of glass into the empty frame of Red Door Apothecary's front window. Outside, tourists looked into the store with mild curiosity as they passed. They probably thought this was a normal renovation—something the shopkeeper was doing to improve her window display. They had no memory of destruction to fall back on—of the shards that had been scattered across the floor and the pungent aroma of herbs crushed underfoot that had filled the air.

What a day that had been. And she still didn't understand why Sutton had made a point of stopping by the store, only to leave before seeing her. Ruthlessly quashing the memory of her, Jane focused on chewing and swallowing.

"Oh, I hope they don't drop it," Sue murmured, her spoon poised halfway between her mouth and the plastic carton of miso soup. She had been busily restocking one of the wooden cabinets until Jane made her take a break, but she'd barely eaten any of the lunch Benny had delivered a few minutes ago, free of charge despite their protests. Jane was glad he didn't mind dropping off their food, even though Noodle Treasure didn't have a delivery service. She hadn't been back in the restaurant since Sutton's declaration, and she doubted she'd be able to force herself to go inside anytime soon.

"They'll be fine. They're professionals." She looked at her watch.

"You know who is not a professional? Giovanni. He should have been here half an hour ago."

Sue frowned. "That's right. I lost track of time. And he is usually punctual."

Jane watched as Sue finally ate another spoonful. She had clearly lost some weight over the past several days. Jane wasn't the only one who had noticed—Giancarlo had pulled her aside yesterday to confess his concern.

"Good soup, isn't it?" she said, hoping the reminder would encourage Sue to eat a few more bites.

"Yes, always."

She was just dipping back into the carton when the door opened to reveal Giovanni. "I'm so sorry for being late," he said urgently, revealing his uncle behind him as he limped inside. Each step made him wince in pain.

"Oh no," Sue said. "What happened to you?"

"I fell off my skateboard on my way to school."

"We've been in the emergency room all day, waiting." Giancarlo's baritone was scratchy, and he sounded exhausted.

"What did they say?" Jane asked.

"It's just road rash. They cleaned it up and put bandages on. I can work."

Giancarlo shook his head. "He has one large patch on his left shoulder and the other on his thigh. But he refused to go home without coming here first."

"I can work. I mean it. I know how much there is to do."

Sue patted him gently on his good shoulder. "It's all right. Go home and rest." Her face fell. "There is a poultice I could make for you, but the thieves destroyed my entire supply of linseed flax."

Giovanni looked at her blankly, and Giancarlo quickly jumped into the silence. "There's something else. While we were waiting at the hospital, I asked a nurse about this rash on my neck." He gestured toward an angry patch of red skin that hadn't been there yesterday. "She says it might be shingles."

"Shingles!" Sue's eyes went wide. "Oh, dear. Let me see."

He held up one hand. "Have you had the chickenpox?"

"No, but—"

"Then you have to stay back."

"But I want to help!" Sue sounded genuinely distraught.

"I'm going to the doctor in a few minutes. The nurse said there is medicine that will make it go away quickly, if I get it soon enough."

Sue looked to Jane. "When will the new inventory arrive?"

"Tomorrow or the next day, I think."

"Good. I feel so helpless without all my herbs."

"Feel better, both of you," Jane said as they turned to leave. "Cornelia woke up with a cough this morning and had to stay home from class. I guess it's just that time of the year."

Once the door had closed behind them, Sue turned to face her. "How are you feeling?"

"Me? Healthy as an ox."

"That's not what I meant."

Jane set down her half-full container of dumplings. "Sue . . ."

"I know you said you didn't want to talk about it. But it's been over a week now. You need to talk. You can't keep it bottled up forever."

"Yes, I can." Jane felt her temples begin to throb.

"That isn't healthy."

"Look." Jane paused and took a deep breath, trying to keep the frustration out of her voice. "It's over. It's done. That's what she wanted. I'm trying to put the whole thing behind me, okay?"

Sue shook her head and clucked her tongue as she unwrapped the fortune cookie that had come with her soup. Jane glanced at the remainder of her lunch, but she had lost her appetite. If she finished the portion for dinner, she could also avoid eating with her family. Aunt Jen's pitying looks and Min's uncomfortable questions had been driving her crazy.

"'Love is a disease.'"

Jane glanced down as Sue read her fortune out loud. Feeling stubborn, she shrugged. "I was having a bad day."

"It's more than that." Sue smoothed the paper between her fingers, looking up with an almost fearful expression. "Everything is connected. Now I understand."

Jane didn't have the mental fortitude to patiently endure Sue's cryptic comments. "Understand what?"

"You are upset. Justifiably so. But you must be careful. Your chi is very powerful, creating ripples that echo throughout the community."

"What does that mean?" Jane packed the food and her chopsticks back into the delivery bag, intending to use the excuse of putting her meal in the fridge to escape Sue's extremely odd mood.

"You wrote about love being a disease and then Giancarlo and Cornelia took ill."

The bag almost slipped from Jane's fingers. "What? I'm sorry . . . what? You think they got sick because I wrote that fortune?" She couldn't believe what she was hearing. "In what universe does that make sense?"

Sue stood and put her hands on her hips. "In this universe! You are a poet. A smith of words. And when you bend your will to writing the future, who can say what will happen?"

"Sue." Jane closed her eyes and took a deep breath. "Viruses make people sick. Not my writing." She indulged in a humorless laugh. "Not like that, anyway."

"You are a contributing factor." Sue stepped forward and took Jane's free hand between hers. "Which is why you must be cautious."

"In that case, I'm going to cautiously put my lunch in the refrigerator. Excuse me."

Jane sidestepped her and walked quickly toward the back office, struggling to keep her temper in check. Sue's life had been plunged into so much turmoil—it was no wonder that she was grasping at straws to explain the vicissitudes of recent events. The problem was, Jane didn't have her usual reservoir of patience right now. She needed to get that back. Pronto. Sue didn't deserve to be snapped at, no matter what crazy things she believed.

"Jane?"

She turned around to find Sue standing in the doorway, clearly hesitant—as though she didn't belong in her own store. Guilt moved in like a summer storm front, blowing her irritation out to sea.

"I'm sorry. I didn't mean to snap at you."

Sue waved off the apology. "It's been a difficult week for everyone. Maybe you're right to try to put Sut—her . . . behind you. A change of scene, perhaps? A change of pace?"

Jane managed a weak smile. "Trying to get rid of me?"

"Of course not. But sometimes we can't find peace where we are."

"Yeah. That's true." Suddenly feeling like an interloper, Jane gestured toward the back door. "Speaking of which, I was thinking I might take a walk. Clear my head. But I can stay if you think you'll need me."

"Go ahead. I'll be fine." Sue sounded almost relieved, and Jane didn't know whether to feel amused or wounded.

"All right. I'll see you later."

As soon as she stepped outside, she took a deep, grateful breath. The temperatures had been mild all week, and some of the trees were beginning to bud. Even so, she shivered when a light breeze ruffled her hair. The cold was inside her—a band of deep freeze around her heart that remained unthawed by the advent of spring. For the first time in her life, she found herself wishing she had worn a jacket.

As she reached the corner of Canal, the crossing signal flashed white. Maybe that's what she would do—take whatever path through the city fate provided. It was easiest, she had found, to look up at the façades of buildings as she walked, keeping her eyes focused just high just enough so that she didn't fixate on people who looked like Sutton or notice awnings of restaurants that seemed like they might be perfect date spots. True, she had tripped over an uneven curb once or twice, but that was a small price to pay for her relative sanity.

Instead of flashing back to Sutton's kisses, she concentrated on the conversations around her, waiting for a gem that would demand to be written down. Instead of wondering where Sutton was at each moment, she brainstormed possible themes for her next piece. One additional poem would make her fellowship application complete. She was determined to work, to produce, to transform her pain into something . . . else. Something positive and real and enduring. Unlike her relationship with Sutton.

So preoccupied was she in admiring the architecture, that she somehow glossed over the sign informing her she had turned onto Second Avenue. The POMMES FRITES placard, however, was impossible to miss, and the sight of it punched the breath from her lungs. That night returned, flashing before her mind's eye like a strobe. Walking through the park holding hands and listening to the city; Sutton's blissful expression as she savored her frites; the mix of pride and panic she'd felt when Sutton invited her to family dinner; the tender good-night kiss shared in front of Sutton's building. The memories split her open like a surgeon's knife. Suddenly dizzy, she stumbled toward a place to sit, only to find herself on that very same bench in front of St. Mark's where they had cuddled together just a few weeks ago.

Maybe Sue was right, she thought dimly as her heart pounded and her breaths whistled. The city was conspiring to remind her of Sutton at every turn, and her emotional response to those reminders was off the deep end. Trying to heal from Sutton's rejection in

New York felt like trying to free herself from a pit of quicksand—each effort only mired her more surely than the last. She was losing her mind. Maybe she did need to get away. If she put herself in a setting that didn't resonate with memories of Sutton, she might finally be able to find some peace.

Pulling out her phone, she scrolled through her contacts list and tried to ignore the jolt in her chest when she bypassed Sutton's name. Her parents were always saying she didn't visit them enough. Maybe it was time to take them up on their standing offer of a plane ticket. Rio de Janeiro would be nothing like New York. With any luck, the hot sun and warm sand would melt the ice inside her.

BY THE TIME JANE returned home, her parents had used their stockpile of frequent flier miles to purchase a ticket to Rio in her name—leaving tomorrow night with an open-ended return. She felt terrible for inconveniencing her aunt and uncle, especially without any warning. But instead of resenting her sudden departure, they reacted with sympathy and understanding, extracting a promise that she would rest and enjoy her time in the tropics.

Min was off at a sleepover, for which Jane was thankful as she threw clothes into her faded duffle. Since the breakup, her emotional state had become Min's favorite discussion topic. Still, she would miss her roommate, and it wouldn't do to disappear without a note. Once her bag was packed, she sat down at the desk.

Minetta,

I'm off to Brazil to see my parents. Sorry for leaving so suddenly, but I'll be back before you know it. Do me a favor and fill in as the resident poet while I'm gone, will you? Remember: less is more when it comes to fortunes.

Love,

Jane

As she was folding the sheet of paper, a gleam of gold caught the lamplight. Sue's pendant, which she had taken off before the ill-fated dinner with Sutton's parents and never put back on. Scooping it up, she dropped it in the envelope and then added a postscript to her note:

P.S. When you next see Sue, could you give her back the necklace? I'll repay you in ice cream.

There. She had explained her absence and responsibly delegated her tasks. But what about the fellowship application? Its postmark deadline was only a few days away, and she still needed that last poem. Should she pull an all-nighter, or take everything with her to Brazil and pay an arm and a leg for international express postage?

But as she looked between the neat stack of papers on the desk corner and her poetry notebook on the nightstand, a wave of exhaustion came crashing down. Who was she kidding? Hundreds, if not thousands, of emerging poets would be applying for the award. It didn't matter that Anders would have wanted her to have it—he was dead, and the board would choose someone with real talent and potential.

Professor Ryan had been right. Sutton's father had been right. In this brave new world stripped clean of romance, it was time to face the truth. There were no spirits or magic or chi or luck. The facts were the facts. She had failed. She wasn't a real poet. She had no real prospects.

With one flick of her wrist, she swept the application off the desk and into the recycling bin below. The Sanitation Department would turn it into egg cartons or kitty litter or paper plates—infinitely more useful than poetry.

Wearily, Jane got to her feet, shut off the light, and slid into bed. Turning her back to her notebook, she closed her eyes and prayed for sleep to come.

CHAPTER NINETEEN

WHEN THE COMPUTER SCREEN began to blur in front of her eyes, Sutton rolled her taut shoulders and glanced at the clock. Just past nine on a Friday night. The rest of the lab was deserted, and a hush had fallen over the hallway outside. This was the time of day she liked the best—when none of her so-called friends were around to ask uncomfortable questions or shoot her pitying looks.

There had been even more of those since she had appeared at a press conference delivered by her father earlier in the week. She had stood by his side dressed in a navy Prada suit bought specifically for the occasion, publicly offering him her support as he apologized to his family, his profession, and the American people. As always, he had delivered the speech with eloquence, charisma, and that Southern-gentleman charm that had historically served him so well. It appeared to have worked this time, too— the surge of public sentiment against him seemed to be dying down ever since his remarks.

But while the nation's anger began to subside, Sutton remained conflicted. Her father hadn't made any more homophobic insinuations, thankfully, but he had begun talking as though her residency at Columbia was a fait accompli. And while she hadn't disabused him of that notion, she couldn't stop thinking of Jane's story about her mother. She wanted to find that balance between duty to her family and duty to herself, but how? Now that her own mother was showing signs of improvement, did she dare reconsider pursuing dreams? Or was that selfish and irresponsible?

In an effort to escape from both her father and her own indecision, Sutton had continued her workaholic ways—immersing herself in rounds and observations, and volunteering for even the most mundane surgical procedures. When the business of each day was over, she sought out the far corner of the computer lab to work on the changes Dr. Buehler had suggested to the latest draft of her next article.

She arrived early at the hospital each day of necessity, but she left late by choice. Where else did she have to go? The library was too social, coffee shops were too distracting, and Noodle Treasure was no longer an option. Every time she set foot in her apartment, she remembered being there with Jane. After a full week of insomnia, she had finally given in and started taking half a Xanax. Not a long-term solution, but she just needed to get through the next month without going insane from sleep deprivation.

Sutton powered down the computer and reached for her bag. There was always more to do, but she was quickly losing focus. She would go home, order in some kind of food that bore no relation to Chinese cuisine whatsoever, put on a mindless action movie, and try to recharge her batteries before spending most of the day in her mother's hospital room.

As she stood, her pager went off. Immediately on high alert, she glanced down expecting to see Tom's number, or maybe the ER's. But the digits were unfamiliar—an outside caller, not someone at the hospital. Her heart stuttered at the thought that it might be Jane . . . but no, it wasn't hers, either. Could it be someone from the press, trying to fool her into calling them back? Phone in hand, she hesitated before punching in the digits. She could always hang up. When the line connected and a female voice answered, Sutton mustered her best professional tone.

"This is Sutton St. James."

"Dr. St. James. Thank you for calling me back." The voice was soft but laced with tension. "I need to speak with you as soon as possible."

"Are you a patient at Langone Medical Center?"

"Not anymore. My name is Celeste. I'm one of the women who haven't come forward."

Sutton felt suddenly chilled. So many women had joined in the accusations about her father—many of whom, he protested, were simply jumping on the bandwagon for publicity. But this person wasn't among them? If she had something to say, why was she contacting Sutton, instead of the media?

"I need to speak with you," Celeste repeated.

"Go ahead."

"Not by phone. Are you willing to meet me? In a public place, of course."

Sutton's alarm at the suggestion was mitigated by Celeste's caveat. Her mind raced as she tried to decide how to answer. The longer this conversation went on, the more curious she became. But she had to be safe.

"Can you meet in an hour at Pegu Club, on Houston?" The famous bar was always busy, and by choosing the time and location herself, she could mostly guarantee this wasn't some sort of sting.

"I'll be coming from uptown. Depending on traffic . . ."

Sutton was tempted to remind her of the existence of the subway. "Call or text if you'll be late," she said instead, feeling as though she had slipped into a soap opera—albeit with a very polite and mild-mannered secret informant. "How will I recognize you?"

"I've seen you on television. I'll approach you."

After Celeste disconnected, Sutton hurried out of the hospital. The bar was near her apartment, but she wanted to change out of her scrubs and arrive early. As she walked quickly through the streets, she found herself wishing she could call someone who would accompany her and watch surreptitiously as she had this conversation with Celeste. Theresa would think she was crazy. Jane would have been perfect for the role, but Sutton didn't dare ask her for a favor after slamming the door in her face. She would have to do this alone.

An hour later, she sat facing the door at one of the high tables near the bar, taking the occasional, shallow sip from her martini. Each time the door opened, her heartbeat accelerated and her shoulders tensed. After a few minutes, she could feel the first tendrils of a headache beginning to creep toward her temples. Just as she reached up to massage the back of her neck, a woman stepped into the bar, pausing immediately to survey her surroundings. Dark, glossy hair brushed the shoulders of her navy coat, and her khaki slacks ended in a fashionable pair of high-heeled, brown boots. When her eyes met Sutton's, she immediately moved in her direction.

"Dr. St. James, I'm Celeste. Thank you for meeting me. I know my request is unorthodox."

Sutton felt her anxiety ease and her curiosity sharpen. Celeste didn't seem dangerous at all—no more dangerous than a younger version of her mother, anyway. "Please, call me Sutton."

"Sutton." Celeste looked around the bar furtively before she sat. "I saw the press conference you did with your father. I wanted to come to you earlier, but we . . . I wasn't certain of what to do."

Her pronoun slip—from "we" to "I"—didn't escape Sutton's notice. Was Celeste a part of some kind of group? Her wariness increased tenfold, and she kept her mouth shut, waiting for Celeste to elaborate.

"I know you have no reason to trust me. Hopefully, you'll feel differently after you hear what I have to say."

"Would you like to order a drink, ma'am?"

Celeste was startled by the sudden presence of the waiter. Visibly collecting herself, she ordered a gin and tonic, and looked furtively around the bar again as the man left.

"You were saying?" Sutton prompted.

"I'd prefer not to continue until he returns with my drink."

Sutton took another sip from her own glass, hoping to settle her spike of nerves. What was Celeste so afraid of? She studied her more closely as they waited in silence—the string of pearls gleaming iridescently against the fabric of her sweater; the diamond-studded bracelet that peeked out from beneath one cuff; the dark shadows beneath her eyes that even makeup couldn't entirely conceal; the worry lines creasing the skin around her mouth. Two things were clear: Celeste was very wealthy, and under a great deal of stress.

After the waiter set down her drink, Celeste took a long sip and leaned forward once more. "In some ways, my story is not all that different from those of the women who have spoken up in public. Three years ago, I was diagnosed with a brain tumor— benign, thankfully, but it still required surgery. At the time, my husband had just retired from his corporate position and was in the process of beginning a run for a seat in the Senate. He had met your father at some sort of event and insisted that I go to him for treatment."

"What happened then?" Sutton asked quietly when she paused to take another drink.

Celeste wouldn't meet her eyes. "I let myself get carried away. We struck up an affair, often meeting several times a week. I'm ashamed of how I behaved, Sutton. Ashamed, and deeply sorry for what I did to you and to your mother."

"Why haven't you come forward?"

"Because there's more." Celeste sighed, her well-manicured fingers curling around her glass. "I got pregnant. When I told your father, everything changed. He insisted I get an abortion."

Sutton felt the bottom drop out of her stomach. "Pardon me?"

"My husband and I had been trying, before I was diagnosed with the tumor. But then we stopped, and . . . it was almost certainly your father's baby." Her eyes filled. "But I wanted to keep it. I swore I would never tell. That I would raise it as my husband's."

Suttons fingers felt like ice, and she clasped her hands together for warmth. "What did he say then?"

"He wouldn't hear of me keeping it. He said that if I didn't get the abortion, he would lobby behind the scenes so that my husband would be certain not to win the primary."

"Oh my god." Heat rushed to Sutton's head, leaving her dizzy. Worst of all, beneath her disorientation, she wasn't surprised. Loathing welled up, twisting her insides, making it hard to speak.

"You can understand, now, why I didn't come forward." Celeste's voice was barely above a whisper. "And Sutton, I'm not the only one. Two other women that I know of were impregnated by your father, and blackmailed in similar ways."

Two more? Sutton swallowed hard, willing her autonomic nervous system to release its grip on her senses. She did not need to fight or flee. She needed to think.

"At first, I was the only one who wanted to tell you," Celeste continued. "But as more and more women spoke up, my—my associates began to soften. And when we saw you standing there, supporting him, caught up against your will in something you don't fully understand . . . we thought you deserve to know the truth."

"What are you planning to do?" Sutton managed to force the words out. Beneath the ringing in her ears, her voice sounded hoarse.

"Nothing. We—"

"Nothing?" Sutton leaned forward, incredulous. "You honestly expect me to believe that?"

Celeste was surprisingly unruffled by her vehemence. "If you don't believe me now, you will with time. I don't have an agenda. None of us can, by necessity. I will not be coming after your father with a lawsuit. I have no desire to risk my marriage or my husband's career. But neither could I stand to maintain my silence."

"Then what would you have *me* do?"

Celeste smiled ruefully, her eyes sad. "There's nothing you can do but keep our secret. None of us are judging you, of course. We understand what you need to do for your mother. But perhaps, now that you know the full story, you'll be better equipped to help her in the long run. And yourself, as well."

She glanced down at her watch. "I should go. My husband is returning home from D.C. tonight." Reaching across the table, she briefly touched Sutton's hand as she slipped a twenty dollar bill into her fingers. "For the drink. Thank you for listening."

As Celeste put on her coat, Sutton suddenly needed to know one thing. "Celeste . . . have you had any success? Getting pregnant since then?"

Her hands froze on the collar of her coat before moving down to fasten the buttons. "Not yet." She looked up to meet Sutton's eyes. "But we'll keep trying for a few more years. Good night, Sutton. Take care."

"Good night," Sutton said to her retreating back. She watched Celeste thread through the tables and hurry out into the night. As the door closed behind her, Sutton raised her glass to her lips and drained its contents, welcoming the warmth of the alcohol in her roiling stomach. Its burn echoed the anger sluggishly churning in the back of her brain.

What was she going to do, now that she knew the truth? How should she counsel her mother? And what about her own plans? Could she trust anything her father said? Should her priority be to maintain a united front with him for her mother's sake? Or should she try to get as far away from him and his lies as possible?

As she looked out the window toward the streaming headlights crisscrossing Houston, she missed Jane more than ever. Jane had been more than a lover—she had been a sounding board and confidante. She could have told Jane this news without ever fearing that it would come back to haunt her.

But no—she couldn't seek Jane out now without offering her something in return, and at this point, Sutton still had no idea what she was capable of giving. She had chosen to handle this alone, and now she would have to live with that choice.

CHAPTER TWENTY

SUTTON WATCHED HER MOTHER scrutinize the tray of hospital food, smothering a smile at the look of profound suspicion she was directing at the green Jell-O—as though it might jump out of the plastic cup and bite her.

"It probably tastes like lime," she said, only to find herself on the end of Priscilla's withering glance. She was getting testy. That was a good sign.

At that moment, the door opened to admit her father holding a large paper bag. "Don't touch that tray!" he exclaimed. "I had a real lunch delivered from Gramercy Tavern." With a flourish, he opened the bag and withdrew a plastic carton. "Your favorite, my love—the carrot soup."

"Oh, how wonderful."

Her full smile made her look so carefree, and Sutton's heart ached as she dutifully deposited the tray on the windowsill to make way for the feast her father had brought. He certainly was playing the part of the hero. As she watched him pull up a chair and begin to arrange the food, she resisted the urge to remove her glasses and rub her gritty eyes. She hadn't slept the night before. Every time she had started to drift off, Celeste's words had returned to jolt her back into wakefulness.

"I seem to recall you particularly enjoying the lamb, Sutton. Was that right?"

"It smells great. Thanks." She took the box and opened it. He had remembered well—the lamb was her favorite. But today the sight and smell of the food turned her stomach.

Reginald helped Priscilla fully elevate the back of her hospital bed so that she could lean forward to partake of the meal. Once she was settled, he tucked into his own. Between bites, he rambled on about the spring schedule at Lincoln Center, describing a new opera and wondering whether Priscilla might want to see it. Sutton, meanwhile, was having trouble believing what she was hearing. How could he be blithely chattering about the fine arts when he had blackmailed at least three women into having abortions? And in the next breath, he could rail against stem-cell research on his television program.

"Are you all right, Sutton?" His voice shattered her troubled introspection. "You've been quiet today."

"Just a little tired," she said, forcing her voice to not betray her mood.

"You should go home and sleep," Priscilla said. "I'm fine here with your father."

Sutton wanted to scream at her that she wasn't—really, she wasn't. But no. Celeste had confided in her. She had to honor that, and keep the secret with which she had been entrusted. "I'd like to stay for a little longer. It's great to see you doing so well."

"Speaking of which, shall we discuss tomorrow?" Reginald smiled at Priscilla. "It will be wonderful to have you home again. Maria has been absorbed in a cleaning frenzy as she prepares for your arrival."

Before her mother could respond, his pager sounded, its shrill tones echoing off the walls of the small room. He quickly silenced it and stood, his face apologetic. "A pediatrics consult. I'm so sorry."

"Of course, dear. I hope it goes well." Priscilla actually blew him a kiss.

"Good-bye, Dad." When the door closed behind him, Sutton moved into the seat he had vacated. "Are you finished, Mom?"

"Yes, I think so. It was very good. So kind of your father to provide such a delicious meal."

"Yes, that was nice of him." Sutton cleared all the containers and stuffed them back into the bag, wishing it were as easy to shove her anger and resentment down deep where it wouldn't have a chance to spill over.

Then again, maybe it should. She wouldn't betray Celeste's confidence, but maybe she could find a way to warn her mother. This might be her best chance—her only chance—to suggest to Priscilla that she had options other than burying her head in the sand. Summoning her courage, she took a deep breath.

"Mom, can I ask you something?" When Priscilla met her gaze, Sutton spoke before she could think better of it. "You know you don't have to just forgive and forget what Dad did, right? You can take legal action if you want. I'll help you."

"Legal action?" Priscilla paused in the act of reaching for the magazine on her nightstand.

"Divorce."

"Sutton." Her mother's tone was identical to the one she had used on the rare occasions when Sutton had misbehaved as a child. "I do not want a divorce from your father. Yes, he has made mistakes. But we all make mistakes. What's important is not what we did, but how we move forward."

"But what if there's more? What if we don't know the full extent of what happened? Do you really want to—"

"Sutton!" Her mother's voice was sharper than she'd ever heard it, and her mouth was pinched in clear anger. "Enough. This conversation is closed. Forever. Have I made myself clear?"

"Yes." Sutton gripped the armrests of the chair, silently squeezing out her frustration. "So . . . would you like me to read some of that magazine to you?"

Before she could move, Priscilla picked it up herself. "I can read it perfectly well on my own, thank you," she said frostily. "I'm sure you're very busy. Perhaps you should go attend to your own affairs."

That was as clear a dismissal as Sutton had ever heard. She stood, bent over the bed, and briefly kissed her mother's forehead. "I'll see you tomorrow, then."

As she left the room, she glanced over her shoulder. Priscilla held the magazine close to her face, a testament to her failing eyes. The sympathy Sutton felt at the sight was dwarfed by her irritation and hurt. Why couldn't her mother see that she was trying to help? Why didn't she want to know the truth? Why was she content to be manipulated and hoodwinked and deceived, repeatedly, when she deserved exactly the opposite from the man she had built a life with?

Sutton walked quickly down the corridor, opting for the stairs instead of waiting for the elevator. Her patience was in tatters and her mind in turmoil. She had tried so hard to make her peace with the fact that her mother needed her, and to stand by her family even though it meant sacrificing her dreams. She'd been convinced it was the right thing to do. But what if she had been wrong? Priscilla wanted an obedient, close-lipped version of her, and Reginald, by trying to bully her into doing what he wanted, was only employing a milder form of the coercion he had used so viciously against Celeste.

Jane had been right.

The realization stopped her in her tracks on the second floor landing. The stairwell was empty, and her quick breaths echoed noisily. As though it had been yesterday, she flashed back to their last conversation. *You don't have to give up what you want. You can follow your dreams.* Jane had been so passionate in her conviction, and so desperate to convince Sutton that she didn't have to abdicate her own desires for her family.

At the time, it had been easier for Sutton to convince herself that making those sacrifices was in everyone's best interest. But now, after she had watched her mother willingly step under the cover of her father's long shadow, she was certain of one thing: she didn't want to be a pawn in his game. Which meant her first priority was to go downtown, tell Jane she had been right all along, and apologize profusely for making such a mess of everything.

Suddenly invigorated, she hurried outside, already concocting her reconciliation speech. Jane wouldn't turn her away, would she? No. Jane had always been willing to listen. Jane would hear her out. And if groveling ended up being necessary . . . Sutton smiled at the thought of what that might entail. The stretching sensation in her cheeks made her realize just how long it had been since she had felt or expressed any kind of happiness.

Jane made her happy. That was the truth, pure and simple. Jane made her happy, and all Sutton had done in return was to string Jane along while weighing the pros and cons of their relationship against the other facets of her life—her career, her family, her perception in the public eye. Well, no more. Once she persuaded Jane to listen to her, she was going to make some clear promises about what Jane could expect from her: namely, behavior befitting a real girlfriend.

Girlfriend. She smiled again as she raced down the stairs into the subway. An elderly man walking up the other side looked at her in consternation. She didn't care. She was going downtown to confess to Jane that she had been wrong about her family, wrong about her priorities, wrong about what she needed. That she didn't want to live a stilted, atrophied life under her father's thumb. That she refused to let anyone dictate her choices. And that one of those choices was Jane herself.

The subway ride was interminable. To keep from going crazy, Sutton closed her eyes and visualized what she was about to do. She didn't want to call Jane or send her a text message—those could too easily be ignored. Instead, she would go to Confucius Fortunes and either find Jane there or discover her whereabouts. And if she came face-to-face with Jenny or Min . . . well, that conversation would be uncomfortable, but she would soldier through it and prove to Jane's family that she had her best interests at heart.

When the train pulled up at Spring Street, she was the first one out of the doors. The stairs were a blur beneath her feet, and she didn't stop to catch her breath upon emerging from the station. Instead, she darted across the next intersection before the flashing red hand could block her passage. Only when she turned on to Baxter did she slow her pace, not wanting to be out of breath when she greeted whomever was at home in the Chao apartment.

The lights in the windows of Noodle Treasure came on just as she drew level with the restaurant. Maybe, once she and Jane had properly made up, they could share a late dinner of soup and dumplings. Then again, they might be making up until long after Mei and Benny had closed for the night. That would be all right. They could return tomorrow. Or go back to Golden Unicorn for dim sum.

There it was—the front door of Confucius Fortunes. Feeling her palms begin to sweat, Sutton squared her shoulders, and pressed the buzzer marked CHAO. Her heart thudded erratically against her ribs as she waited for someone to respond.

"Hello?" The voice was slightly distorted by the speaker, but still recognizable. Min.

"Min, it's Sutton. Is Jane there?"

Silence. Sutton drummed her fingertips against her legs as she waited. After several seconds, she jammed her thumb against the buzzer again. Anger surged to the fore, trumping her nerves. In no universe was she going to let a petulant teenager stand between her and Jane.

"What do you want?" Min's voice reemerged from the speaker a moment later.

"Min, I know you're mad at me. But I really need to talk to Jane. Please."

"You can't."

"Don't you think you'd better let her be the judge of that?" Sutton knew she sounded testy, but she couldn't help herself.

"Don't talk down to me!" Min's disembodied voice fired back. "You broke her heart and then she left! It's your fault!"

"She left?" Sutton's mouth was suddenly dry. "Where did she go?"

"Brazil."

An instant of confusion gave way to understanding: Brazil, where Jane's parents were currently stationed. "Did she say when she's coming back?"

"Yes, but I'm not going to tell you."

"What? Min!" Sutton rang the bell a few more times, but to no avail. Finally, she let her hand fall. "Damn it."

For a moment, she looked longingly across the street. If she walked through that door, would Mei give her the cold shoulder? Suddenly unwilling to risk it, she turned back the way she had come, toward her apartment. Her chest felt like a deflated balloon. All that anticipation and all those plans, wiped out in the span of mere seconds.

Guilt filled the empty spaces pushing against her chest until it was hard to breathe. Jane had fled the city. She was clearly hurting—even worse than Sutton had thought. Her phone probably wasn't working in Brazil, so Sutton couldn't text her. And Jane had blocked her on social media, so she couldn't get in touch that way, either.

The only thing left to do was wait. She hated waiting, but at least it afforded her the opportunity to plan. Jane would return to New York—Min had been clear about that much. When she did, Sutton would be ready to fight to get her back. By whatever means necessary.

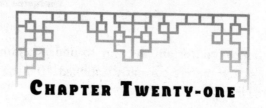

CHAPTER TWENTY-ONE

SUTTON WAS ABLE TO wait all of three days before impatience trumped her reluctance to return to Chinatown. Even the Xanax couldn't quell her anxiety anymore—every time she felt herself dozing off, a spike of panic would set her heart to racing, waking her up. The persistent insomnia had made her increasingly frustrated, exhausted, and emotional. No matter how she tried to distract herself, her brain wouldn't stop concocting plans for how to find Jane once she returned, and to convince her that her change of heart was sincere.

The problem was, without Jane's return date, every plan was vague and aimless. She needed information, and to get information she needed to have a real conversation with one of Jane's confidantes. Min was a lost cause, but surely Sue would hear her out. Wouldn't she?

After racing through her notes from the day's rounds, Sutton left the hospital and walked south and west toward Red Door Apothecary. A hot wave of shame flooded through her when she realized she hadn't been back to the store since the night she had broken off her relationship with Jane. She'd been so wrapped up in her own drama and misery that she had barely paid any mind to Sue's plight, despite having indirectly been the cause.

Her steps faltered as she realized just how much she had to apologize for. Maybe it would be a better idea to go and see Sue only when she was back in Jane's good graces. But that put her right back in purgatory, unless she dared to try her luck with one of Jane's other family members. Flashing back to Min's rejection, she shook her head and forced herself to continue moving forward. Regardless of what happened with Jane, she owed Sue an apology. And there was no time like the present.

But when she walked into the store, Sue was nowhere in sight. Giovanni stood behind the register, looking as gangly as ever in a button-down shirt whose sleeves were too short by an inch. Sutton wondered what he had heard about her, before she realized she was letting herself feel intimidated by the opinion of an eighteen-year-old. Resolutely, she marched across the room. He looked up at her approach, eyes going wide behind his glasses.

"Hi, Giovanni. Is Sue here?"

"Um. Well . . ." He looked around furtively, seeking out a distraction. Obviously, he was in the know about her treatment of Jane. Who was she kidding? This community was more close-knit than her own family. She was probably persona non grata in both Little Italy and Chinatown.

"Let me make this easy on you. I'd like to apologize to Sue, and I have a question to ask her. Now. Where is she?"

Ducking his head, he muttered, "In the back."

"Thank you." She pushed through the gate leading behind the counter. The hallway beyond opened into a cluttered office in which a desk, refrigerator, and bookshelf competed for space with stacks of boxes. Sue sat at the table, leafing through a pile of envelopes. When she raised her head, her lips drew down in an expression of clear disapproval. Sutton's throat tightened. No one thought well of her at the moment—including herself. But there was only one way to change that.

"Hi, Sue."

"Sutton." She sighed and put the papers aside. "Of course. I should have known you would come today."

Sutton wasn't sure she wanted to know anything more about

what Sue had seen in her daily horoscope. "I need to speak with you. Do you have a few minutes?"

Sue reached over and pulled out a chair. "Yes. But I must warn you—I'm quite angry with you."

"I deserve that." Sutton sat and laced her fingers together to stop herself from fidgeting. "First of all, I want to apologize for not making myself available to help when your store was broken into. Everything else notwithstanding, I could have found some time to pitch in, and I didn't."

Sue's face softened a little, and she reached over to touch Sutton's arm. "Please. We all knew what you were going through. You needed to tend to your family. How is your mother?"

"She's much better. She was finally released from the hospital on Sunday. And thank you for your kind words, but I'm still sorry for not lending a hand. Is there anything I can do now? Anything you still need?"

Sue raised an admonishing finger. "I need to know what you intend to do about Jane."

"I made a mistake. And now I want to make things right with her."

"You hurt her very badly. The ripples of her anguish destabilized the entire community."

Taken aback, Sutton covered her confusion by exhaling slowly. Destabilized the entire community? What on earth did that mean? "I know I've lost her trust," she ventured. "And yours as well. But I want to get it back. I want to get her back."

"That will not be easy."

"I know. I'm willing to do what it takes."

Sue leaned back in her chair and regarded Sutton thoughtfully. "What exactly do you think that will entail?"

After days of introspection, Sutton knew exactly how to answer this question. "I need to make her feel like she's an integral part of my life, instead of on the fringes."

"And how do you intend to do that?"

"Well, I was thinking about starting with a grand gesture. Something romantic." Sutton's nerves began to subside as Sue listened attentively. "I don't want her to have any doubt about how I feel. But I also know that a gesture isn't enough. I'll need to prove myself, every day, until she trusts me again."

"Yes." Sue was looking at her with a newfound respect that made Sutton feel better about herself than she had in weeks. "You will."

Mentally crossing her fingers, Sutton prayed Sue would divulge whatever she knew. "Did she tell you when she's coming back? I tried asking Min, but she wants nothing to do with me."

A touch of a smile curved Sue's lips. "Minetta is young and naïve and fiercely loyal. But she thinks the world of you. Give her time." Suddenly, she laughed. "Here I sit, counseling a Dragon to be patient. I know it isn't in your nature. But sometimes it is the only solution."

"I understand," Sutton said, even as she wondered whether that patience had to extend to learning the date of Jane's homecoming. "I'll do my best."

"Jane returns one week from today. Let me know if I can help as you plan your . . . grand gesture."

Relief sluiced through Sutton's body, a cool wave soothing the anxiety that had been her constant companion. "Thank you. So much. For everything."

When she stood, Sue did also and pulled her into a hug. Tears bounced into Sutton's eyes at the gesture, and she struggled to suppress the swell of emotion. This had to be the Platonic ideal of a grandmotherly embrace. Her own grandmother had only ever delivered air kisses.

And then Sue gasped. Her arms tightened momentarily before dropping away. Then she was hurrying across the room, and Sutton spun to see what was the matter. Giancarlo stood at the door, a large Band-Aid covering part of his neck. Sue paused a few feet away, hands fluttering at her sides.

"Are you—"

"I'm in the clear. The doctor just confirmed it."

Sue let out a small cry of delight and ran to him. As she watched them embrace, Sutton felt an unexpected twinge of jealousy. She watched one of his hands lightly caress Sue's lower back in small, comforting circles, and her own skin ached for Jane's touch. They made it look so easy to be together.

After a long moment, Giancarlo raised his head and met her gaze. "Hello, Dr. Sutton," he said gravely.

Sue pulled away, her cheeks tinged pink with embarrassment, as if she had just then remembered Sutton was in the room. "Forgive me. We haven't been able to see each other because of Giancarlo's illness."

"Are you all right?"

"Shingles." He shrugged. "It was more an annoyance than anything else."

"That can be painful. I'm glad you've recovered." Sutton suddenly felt like the third wheel, but before she could open her mouth to say good-bye, Giancarlo spoke again.

"How are you?" His tone was at once solicitous and wary.

"I'm . . ." Instead of finishing the sentence automatically, she forced herself to tell the truth. "I'm struggling, honestly."

"Sutton wants to make up with Jane," Sue explained.

"Ah." Giancarlo nodded. "Well. If I can be of any help, please let me know."

"Thank you." Sutton edged toward the exit, wanting to give them space to celebrate their reunion. "I will, once I have a plan."

"I'll see you out," Sue said preceding her down the hallway. "Stop by any time if you'd like a sounding board for your ideas."

She seemed almost gleeful at the prospect of scheming up a special event for Jane, and Sutton wished she could share her clear excitement. Her own enthusiasm was tempered by the high stakes. Whatever she did, it had to succeed. The alternative was unthinkable.

"What's this?" Sue asked as they emerged into the storefront where Giovanni was stacking several large boxes behind the counter. They bore the insignia of Confucius Fortunes, and Sutton's pulse jumped at the sight. She looked around for one of Jane's family members, but the only other people in the room were customers.

"Cornelia just delivered these," Giovanni said. "When I asked for the invoice, she said they were free."

Sue clucked her tongue. "They are being so kind to us."

Sutton watched as Giovanni opened one of the boxes and tore into the first bag of fortune cookies, emptying it into the large bowl next to the register. Jane's words were locked inside each of them. Each cookie was a message in a bottle, and after weeks without any communication, she was desperate to hear from her in some way—even if only in vaguely Confucian sentence fragments.

"I want to buy a bag from you."

Giovanni frowned. Sue looked confused for a moment before comprehension dawned on her face. "Don't be silly. They came to us at no charge."

"I'd really prefer to pay." Sutton extracted two twenty-dollar bills from her wallet and held them out to Giovanni, who took them automatically. She snatched up a bag of cookies and darted toward the exit. "Thanks. Must run!"

As she burst through the door, she almost bowled over an elderly Chinese man who was just turning to enter. Stammering an apology, she hurried to the corner and caught the tail end of the light. Tightening her grip on the bag, she walked north at a pace a professional speed-walker would have envied. When she finally entered her apartment, she kicked off her shoes, tripped over them, and almost faceplanted on her way to the kitchen table. She didn't even bother removing her coat before digging her fingernails into the plastic and prying the bag open. Fortune cookies spilled out onto the table, and she ripped through each individual wrapping like some sort of addict. Once she was finished, she perched in the nearest chair, gathered the cookies into a cluster, and began breaking them open. Each crack increased her anticipation, but she forced herself not to look at a single fortune until she had liberated them all.

But trepidation assailed her as she sat and stared at the small mound of paper. What kinds of messages would she find? Had Jane been thinking of her while writing any of these? Had she been angry? Upset? Sad? Or had she already begun to move on with her life?

"There's only one way to find out," she muttered, extracting a slip at random from the pile.

I miss you.

Sutton's breath caught in her throat. This one had to be about her, didn't it? How often had she wanted to write the exact same words to Jane? Each time, she had found a way to justify her reticence, when really, the explanation was simple. She hadn't had the courage to admit—to herself or anyone else—that the way she felt about Jane was far from casual.

"I miss you, too," she whispered as she reached for the next fortune.

Sleep left me when you did.

Sutton felt oddly comforted that Jane had shared her insomnia. The knowledge that they had lain awake together made her feel closer to Jane, somehow. Except, of course, that her distant behavior had been the direct cause of Jane's sleeplessness. Ashamed, she picked again from the pile.

It takes all my strength, every moment, not to go to you.

What would she have done if Jane had shown up at her doorstep? Her remorse intensified when Sutton realized that Jane had done exactly that. And she had reacted by insisting they break off their relationship. But there would be no more putting Jane's needs below those of her biological family. She wasn't going to live her life in fear of what anyone thought of her choices.

Every train station gapes as I pass, tempting me.

Sutton winced as she imagined Jane walking through the city, tormented by the sight of each subway entrance. What would the past month have been like, if Sutton had been more open to accepting Jane's help? She would have had someone to lean on—someone to share the burden and act as a sounding board. Someone who would have made her feel loved unconditionally, not contingently. Jane had offered that kind of love, and she had spurned it out of a misguided sense of duty and guilt. Her parents didn't care about what was truly best for her—they cared about what was best for them. She didn't want to be used anymore. She wanted to be loved. Pure and simple. Loved the way Jane loved her.

Every overheard conversation between lovers reminds me of us.

She flashed back to their adventure in Grand Central Station—to the way Jane's eyes gleamed and her hands gestured so expressively whenever she discussed her poetry. To the emotion that had saturated her voice when she spoke of her professor who had passed away. To the exuberance with which she had greeted Sutton's contributions to her work. Sutton had learned to see the city so differently through Jane's eyes—or, more accurately, hear it through her ears. Jane had taught her how to place her finger on the pulse of the multitudes—how to feel a part of something larger, instead of lost in the crowd. Simply by listening.

You think you have to carry your pain alone, but you don't.

Sutton lowered her head into her hands. Her eyes felt like sandpaper, and a dull throb was beginning in her temples. She was so weary, through and through. Could she accept that offer? Could she believe Jane was being sincere? What if Jane was wrong—what if, when she saw Sutton's baggage up close and personal, she wanted nothing whatsoever to do with it?

No. With a sharp shake of her head, Sutton resisted the urge to wallow in self-defeat. Jane had met her parents and weathered the storm of their bullying tactics. Jane had seen the skit, and read the newspapers, and cleaned up after the break-in at Sue's. Jane knew what she was getting into, and she wanted Sutton regardless. Or, at least, she *had*.

Sutton watched her fingers tremble as she reached for the next fortune.

Trust yourself. Trust me.

Tears pricked her eyes, and alone in the growing dark, she didn't try to hold them back. As they trickled down her cheeks, she thought about fate. It had always seemed like such a ludicrous concept, but when she thought back to the events of the past few months, her brain recognized a pattern that appeared—over the objections of her reason—providential. It almost seemed as though she had been driven out of the library and coffee shops, herded by destiny toward Noodle Treasure. That, having grown close with Benny and Mei over the course of a few weeks, she had been compelled to look out the window at the very moment Jane emerged from Confucius Fortunes. Coincidence? Maybe. But it felt planned, somehow. Orchestrated. And then Jane had proven irresistible, despite all of Sutton's efforts to be rational.

Suddenly feeling silly, she unfolded the next piece of paper. There was no need to turn to destiny and fate to explain what had happened. She had fallen in love with Jane, pure and simple. That was the truth. There was no denying it.

Trust yourself. Trust me.

Her first repeat. It was bound to happen sometime. She reached for the next.

Trust yourself. Trust me.

Sutton felt the nape of her neck prickle and made quick work of flipping over the remaining few fortunes. Like a refrain, or maybe a litany, the two simple sentences stared back at her over and over and over.

Trust yourself. Trust me.

Sitting back in her chair, she stared down at the papers scattered like tea leaves across the battered surface of the table. "Okay," she murmured, smiling through the tears that continued to trickle down her cheeks. "Okay, universe. I get it."

CURLING HER TOES INTO the sand, Jane hugged her knees as she gazed out into Guanabara Bay. The panorama before her belonged in most people's version of paradise: a pure white beach giving way to turquoise waves that curled like the necks of dressage horses before descending to break against the shore. The late afternoon sun warmed her back, and a light breeze cooled her face. She had been out here all day, not bothering with a towel or with any clothes other than her bikini, and there was time for one last dip before she needed to return to her parents' nearby condo to pack her bags.

Brushing a lock of hair across her forehead, Jane struggled not to look over her shoulder—north and west, in the direction of New York. She had found herself doing that so frequently, over the past two weeks—unconsciously angling her body to face Sutton, like some kind of pathetic pointer dog.

Scoffing at her own simile, she let her arms fall to the ground and pushed herself up. Longing after Sutton was pointless. Her brain had long since accepted that as fact. Now if only she could convince her heart. She had come here to escape Sutton's ghost, but she couldn't flee her own memories. Her mind wouldn't stop retracing them. She felt like the needle of her father's ancient record player, which never made it through an album without getting stuck in one groove.

At least her parents had been kind and sympathetic. Her mother had greeted her at the airport, immediately declared her to be too thin, and had started cooking up a storm the moment they'd walked in the door. Jane felt guilty for imposing, but at least she'd been able to bring along several cooking supplies from Chinatown that were nearly impossible to find in Brazil. As the kitchen filled with fragrant steam, her mother had pressed her for details about recent events. It didn't take long before Jane was surrendering—offering up the story of her aborted romance with Sutton. While she spoke, she had felt fortunate. Whom did Sutton have to turn to? Her parents were completely self-absorbed, and as far as she knew, Sutton wasn't close to anyone at the hospital. Where was she going for comfort and a friendly ear?

Jane dusted the sand off her hands, wishing it were as easy to rid herself of her lingering concern for Sutton. She couldn't stop asking herself those questions, even though she had no business doing so. Sutton wasn't hers to care about and worry over. She never had been. The sooner she accepted that, the better everything would be. Her priority now was to move on with her life—to focus on her own needs, instead of on the needs of someone who wanted nothing to do with her.

Twenty feet away, a wave began to gather offshore. Jane dug her toes into the sand before pushing off, sprinting as fast as she could toward the swath of cerulean blue. She raised her knees high as her toes met the ocean, barreling toward the looming wall of water that threatened to pound her body into the sand. As it began to crest she dove, escaping the clutches of the current to emerge victorious on the other side. Smiling broadly, she steadied herself against the undertow and waited for the next wave to take aim.

She loved the freedom of this—the sun beating down on her shoulders, the salt stinging her lips, the swirling eddies that clutched at her ankles. Last night, her parents had suggested that she return over the summer. Her father thought he could get her an internship at the embassy. If she enjoyed it, he had said, perhaps she should consider taking the Foreign Service exam before she was thirty.

It was a good idea. A solid plan. When she aced the exam, several careers would throw open their doors to her. She would finally be independent—finally able to provide for herself instead of having to rely on the clemency of her family. It was the right thing to do.

For all the wandering she'd done through the winding streets of Rio over the past several weeks, the city had yet to speak to her in poetry. Maybe she had left her muse behind in New York. And maybe that was for the best. With a twinge of shame, she thought of the fellowship, and Sophia's letter. When she returned to New York, she would write a real letter in reply, thanking her for her generosity in reaching out and explaining her decision not to apply. Anders might not have approved of the choices she was making, but she couldn't live her life for him. Or for anyone else.

Another wave began to rise, but Jane turned her back to it. This would be her last—instead of crashing through it, she would ride it in to shore. Sucking in a breath, she pushed off from the sand and began to swim. The water gathered beneath her, buoying her body instead of smashing it into the sand. Exhilaration sang through her veins as the shoreline hurtled closer.

Remember this, she told herself as she touched down again. *Remember this feeling.* She would return to New York triumphant—not bruised, not battered, not broken. She would be strong. She would be fine. The Atlantic had given her its benediction.

"ARE YOU OUT HERE, Mom?" Jane called as she stepped through the sliding doors and onto the patio. The distinctive hoots and whistles of a variety of indigenous birds greeted her approach. "Just wanted to let you know I'm home."

Shading her eyes with one hand, she finally spied her mother standing at the far end of their fenced-in yard, apparently taking a break from gardening by speaking with someone on the phone. The air was redolent with the spicy perfume of the exotic flowers she loved to cultivate, and Jane paused to watch the haphazard progress of a blue butterfly, its wingspan as broad as the length of her hand.

"Jane, come here!" Her mother beckoned with her free hand. "Minetta wants to speak with you."

"Can't she wait a day?" Jane said, even as she felt herself smile. "I'll see her tomorrow, after all."

"Just talk." Her mother held out the phone.

"Hey, Minnie," she said, anticipating the outraged squawk that would greet her use of Min's least-favorite nickname. "What's up?"

"This is no time to be cute." Min's syllables were clipped and rapid. "I just got off the phone with Sophia Niles."

Jane's good mood evaporated. She and Sophia hadn't actually spoken since Anders' funeral, and now she was calling her aunt and uncle's residence? "Oh man. Was she really upset that I didn't send in my application?"

A long pause greeted her question—so long that Jane checked the phone's display to ensure the call hadn't dropped. "Min?"

"Um . . . no? Because I sent it in for you?"

"You did what?" The sudden roar of blood in her ears drowned out the cacophonous birdsong. "Are you serious? You sent it in?"

"It was almost done," Min said defensively. "So I finished it for you and put it in the mail."

"You finished it *for* me? What the hell does that mean?"

"Aiyah," her mother scolded from where she was kneeling before a flower bed. "Language." But Jane barely heard her.

"You needed one more poem, so I typed up that one in your notebook." Min's tone was becoming almost as screechy as the birds.

"You looked in my notebook?"

"You left it on the nightstand!"

Jane clamped her lips together. She didn't want to say anything she'd regret, especially not to Minetta, but the knowledge that she had raided her private notebook—and then sent something in it to Anders' widow—made her head pound as though it were about to split open.

"Jane?" Min asked in a small voice, suddenly sounding very much like an eleven-year-old. "Are you really mad?"

Was she really? Surprised—yes. Terribly anxious about how her work would be received—yes. Frustrated that Min hadn't respected her privacy—yes. But Min had been motivated by generosity and selflessness. For some reason, Min believed in her work enough to take the time and make the effort to complete her application. Was she really going to let her fear of negative criticism stand in the way of showing her appreciation?

"No, kiddo. I'm not mad. You're the brave one, you know that? I need to learn to be more like you."

She could practically hear Min rolling her eyes. "You're only realizing this now?"

Jane let the gibe pass. "When you talked to Sophia . . . what did she say?"

"She wouldn't tell me anything. But she wants you to call her ASAP. You will, right?"

"I will."

Butterflies the size of the one she had seen in the garden began to terrorize Jane's stomach as she took down the number. After promising Min a full report in person tomorrow, she hung up and punched in the digits with trembling fingers, forestalling her mother's questions with a brisk shake of her head. If she didn't follow through on her promise and do this *right now*, she might lose her nerve.

The call took forever to connect, or maybe it was her imagination. But when Sophia finally answered, the sound of her voice brought with it a wash of memories—from the warmth of winter evenings spent discussing literature in front of their fireplace, to the dank chill of the morning when Anders' body had been lowered into his grave.

"Hello, Sophia," she said, unashamed of the snarl of tears behind her words.

"Jane? Is that you?"

"It's me. I'm in Brazil and calling from my mom's phone."

"I take it your charming little cousin delivered my message?"

Jane had to smile at her description of Minetta. "She did."

"I want to hear all about your adventures," Sophia said. "But before you say another word, I want to congratulate you on being the recipient of the first annual Anders Niles Memorial Fellowship." Her voice faltered as she spoke her husband's name.

Under the hot sun, Jane stood paralyzed as joy and grief ignited in the center of her chest. Only her tears ran free, coursing down her cheeks to drip, drip, drip onto the lush grass. Unlooked for, unhoped for, this moment was entirely overwhelming. Cradling the phone to her ear, she sank to her knees and looked up at the same blue sky that arced above the spires of New York City . . .

. . . and thought that perhaps she hadn't abandoned her muse, after all.

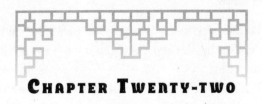

Chapter Twenty-two

THE TEXT FROM MINETTA came in as Jane was waiting in line at Immigration: *dont take train Sue & G will pick u up.* Jane blinked down at her phone and adjusted the strap of her messenger bag with her free hand. That was unexpected. And wholly unnecessary—she could have easily taken public transportation back into the city. At least their presence together meant Giancarlo had recovered from his shingles.

Still, she reflected as the line crept forward, it felt good to know she had been missed. It would be nice to have a welcoming committee who might be able to distract her from the trepidation she felt about returning to the city. The feeling had plagued her for the entire plane ride, making it impossible to concentrate on the in-flight movie. Each time she got distracted, she tried to manage her expectations. Yes, she was returning to the city in which Sutton lived. But they weren't going to see each other. Sutton had moved on. And so had she. End of story.

After showing her passport and answering the curt questions from the Immigration officer, she collected her duffle from the baggage carousel and walked toward Customs, mentally reciting the litany she had invented on the flight. *Don't think about her; don't look for her; don't go anywhere she's likely to be.* Instead of dwelling on her failure to maintain her relationship with Sutton, she needed to focus on her success. Not only was she a published, award-winning poet—she had also just won a distinguished fellowship.

The fact that she had done so despite her own idiocy was a warning she needed to heed. Next time, the universe—or Min—might not be so kind.

"Jane!" Sue's voice thankfully interrupted her ruminations. Jane looked up and saw her waving frantically from beyond the security barrier, Giancarlo beside her. Smiling, she raised one hand in acknowledgement and hurried toward them.

"Thanks for coming to get me," she said once Sue had embraced her and Giancarlo had thumped her on the back with an avuncular awkwardness.

"Welcome home," Sue said.

"We're glad you've returned safely," Giancarlo echoed. "The car is this way."

"How are you feeling?" Jane asked him as they followed the signs toward short-term parking.

"Good as new. The doctor said we caught it early enough for the antivirals to work quickly."

"I'm glad to hear it." Jane snuck a glance at Sue, hoping she had heard that last part about modern medicine. "Can we all agree now that shingles is caused by a virus? And not by anything else?"

"Of course it is." Giancarlo seemed confused. "A particularly nasty one."

Sue only shot her an admonishing look. At least she stayed quiet.

They stopped before a small red Fiat, and Giancarlo pulled out a key chain attached to a plastic gnome with bright pink hair. When Jane raised her eyebrows, he looked a little embarrassed. "The car belongs to my sister."

"It's cute," Jane said as she stuffed herself into the tiny backseat. "Must be easy to find parking."

As Giancarlo pulled out of the lot, Sue peppered Jane with questions about her parents, and about the culture of Rio de Janeiro. Jane had to pause her story several times while Sue scolded Giancarlo about his driving, and by the time she had satisfied Sue's curiosity, they were already speeding down the expressway.

"I have a book for you in my bag," Jane said, "about the medicinal practices of the South American *curanderos*. They use a lot of herbs as well. Maybe some even you've never heard of."

"Oh, how wonderful. Thank you!"

"How are things going at the store? How are the repairs coming along?"

"The insurance company paid the claim, and everything is almost back to normal. " Sue sounded relieved, and grateful. "I'm only waiting on a few of the more rare inventory items now."

"I'm glad to hear it. I'm sorry I wasn't there to help."

"Aiyah," Sue said sharply. "Don't you dare. You did so much. And you needed to get away."

For a while, they rode in silence. Jane watched the Manhattan skyline grow larger as they approached, its lofty spires glinting in the spring sunshine. It was an awe-inspiring sight, even for someone who had traveled the world. But for the first time, the city also inspired in her a sense of wariness. Somewhere in the midst of all that steel and glass, Sutton St. James was going about her daily business. Had she so much as spared Jane a thought, since their breakup?

Jane closed her eyes to block out the city. No. She was not going to indulge like this. They were over. *Don't think about her; don't look for her; don't go anywhere she's likely to be.* As she mentally repeated the refrain, she felt her strength and conviction return. Her heart might be bruised, but it wasn't broken. New York was her home. She had just as much right to the city as Sutton, and she wasn't going to allow the specter of their relationship to drive her away.

"Oh, Jane—your aunt asked for some of my homemade noodles," Giancarlo said as he turned the car onto the Williamsburg Bridge. "Do you mind stopping by the restaurant for a few minutes before we drop you off at home?"

"No problem." Jane smiled at the thought of Aunt Jenny making conventional spaghetti. "Have you convinced her to put tomato sauce on those noodles?"

"I'm not sure," he said with a laugh.

By some miracle traffic downtown wasn't heinous, but by the time they found a parking spot near Ciao Bella, the sun was beginning to set. As she walked into the restaurant behind Giancarlo and Sue, the scent of olive oil and garlic made her mouth water. But when she turned toward the kitchen, he shook his head and Sue reached for her elbow.

"This way, this way," he said cheerfully, leading her down a short flight of stairs. A thick, gold brocade curtain blocked their path, and Jane was just about to ask where on earth they were going, when Giancarlo swept the fabric aside to reveal a small dining room. Upstairs, the walls were covered by plaster boasting colorful murals of the Roman gods. But down here, the stone had been left untouched. Gas lamps were set into wall sconces at regular intervals, making the space feel like a grotto. A wrought iron chandelier had been set in the center of the ceiling, hanging directly above the lone table in the room . . . where Sutton was just rising from her chair.

Jane froze in her tracks, heart pounding so hard against her rib cage that she feared it might crack. The blood roared in her brain, making it impossible to string together a coherent thought. Sutton. She was there, a mere ten feet away, wearing a royal-blue sweater dress that clung to her curves. Dark stockings and elegant gray boots showed off the contours of her legs, and Jane felt her mouth go dry even as her palms began to sweat. Feeling suddenly claustrophobic, she turned around to look for the exit, only to find Sue and Giancarlo on their way out.

"We'll be upstairs," was all Sue said before they ducked behind the curtain. Leaving her and Sutton together. Alone.

"They tricked me." Jane could hear the hoarseness in her own voice.

"Only because I asked them to." Sutton moved forward slowly, as though Jane were some kind of half-feral animal. And maybe the analogy was apt. Conflicting emotions buffeted Jane's mind like hurricane winds—anger, desire, fear, resentment, pain. And love. Above all, love. Because, of course, two weeks and thousands of miles hadn't been enough to sever the connection she felt between them. The connection Sutton had rejected.

"Please don't be angry with them," she continued, taking another step closer.

"Stop." Jane held out one hand and summoned every remaining shred of fortitude. "Just . . . just stop. I don't have the strength for games. I need you to tell me, right now, what you're doing."

A flash of hurt crossed Sutton's face before it was replaced with determination. "I need to apologize to you."

Jane crossed her arms beneath her breasts, feeling stronger now that Sutton's advance had halted. "For what?"

"For a few things." When Sutton held up one finger, Jane tried—without success—not to flash back to memories of her touch. She swallowed convulsively.

"First, even when we were together, I never treated you well enough. I never gave us a real chance. I was too preoccupied and self-absorbed. You deserve better."

"Okay." Jane ignored the part of herself that already wanted to make excuses for Sutton. She was right to apologize. Yes, she had a high-powered career, but Jane deserved more than a casual relationship contingent on Sutton's whims. That was the truth. Forcing herself to remain impassive, she nodded sharply. "What else?"

"Second, I shouldn't have cut you out during the scandal, and when my mother got sick. Yes, I was going through a lot. But I should have let you help."

"I wanted to. So much." Jane hated the forlorn note that had seeped into her words. Immediately, she wished she could take them back.

"I know. I needed you." Sutton looked like she was on the verge of moving closer before she caught herself and stayed still. "I let my own pride and stubbornness get in the way."

Jane nodded. Hope bubbled up in her chest like a hot spring, but she tamped it down. She could feel her resistance melting, but she wasn't yet ready to surrender. Doubts continued to swarm inside her fevered brain. She wanted, so badly, to believe Sutton's words. But she had to be sure.

"Is there anything else?"

"Yes. A thousand times a day, I wish I hadn't reacted the way I did to the break-in at Sue's shop. I was frightened and overwhelmed and selfish. Again. I should have stayed and helped, instead of pushing you—and everyone—away."

Jane let her hands fall to her sides as the swell of emotion boiled over. "Now you're being too hard on yourself. You were going through an awful time. I understood that. We all did."

But Sutton shook her head. "You were always so open. So caring. And not only you, but the entire community. I turned my back on that, and I shouldn't have."

"Obviously you managed to prove yourself to Sue and Giancarlo."

Sutton smiled wanly. "Only because I showed them how much I wanted the chance to prove myself to you."

Jane swept her arm across the air. "Is that what this is?"

"This . . . this is a lot of things." Sutton ran one hand through her hair, clearly nervous. "An apology. A plea for a second chance. And . . . a declaration."

"A declaration?"

"I've fallen in love with you."

Dizziness swept over Jane, and she felt herself sway on her feet. Sutton was there an instant later, holding her tightly even as she steadied her. The fragrant scent of her skin, the gentle strength of her hands, the sensation of their bodies pressed together . . . Jane struggled to pull in a breath and blink away unwelcome tears. When her vision cleared, Sutton's eyes were locked with hers, silently beseeching.

"It's true. I love you. I love your compassion and your generosity and your sense of humor. I love how your mind perceives the beauty of language. I love your poetry." Freeing one hand, she reached up to brush two fingertips across Jane's lips. "I love your kisses. I love your touch. I love the way we fit together."

Jane felt herself trembling. Sutton's words were like a downpour onto the drought-stricken earth of her heart. After having given up hope, it felt completely surreal to be holding her this way and hearing her say these things. Had she fallen asleep on the plane? Was she dreaming?

"I love the way you love me," Sutton continued. "You make me feel strong. Cherished. Beautiful. I want to make you feel the same." Rising up onto her toes, she pressed a gentle kiss to Jane's dry lips. "I love you, Jane."

Slowly, Jane raised one hand and sifted her fingers through Sutton's long, golden tresses. When Sutton bit her lower lip in clear pleasure, Jane thought she might explode with emotion. Had she ever felt this much? Ever?

"I love you back," she whispered. "I never stopped. I tried, but I couldn't."

"I'm so glad. And so sorry for all the ways I hurt you."

Jane pulled her closer. When she lightly stroked her tingling fingertips down Sutton's back, joy burst through her chest, like the sun coming out from behind a cloud.

"I think you've apologized enough," she managed to say.

"I don't know about that." Sutton's eyes were bright. "But for now, would you like to have dinner with me?"

Jane smiled—her first unreserved smile in weeks. "I would love to."

"Oh, good." But instead of pulling away, Sutton began to play with the fine hairs on the back of Jane's neck. "I need to find Giancarlo and tell him you'll be staying. But I don't want to move."

"Me, neither." Dipping her head, Jane slid her lips slowly across Sutton's perfect mouth, contentment warming her from the inside out. "One more minute," she whispered. "Let's just stay like this for one more minute."

NIGHT HAD LONG SINCE fallen by the time Sutton stepped out onto the sidewalk in front of Ciao Bella. Immediately, Jane was behind her, holding her coat open. The display of chivalry made her flash back to the first day they had ever spent time together—Chinese New Year, when Jane had held open the bakery door. She had secretly enjoyed Jane's solicitousness then, but she openly loved it now. Murmuring her thanks, Sutton slid her arms into the sleeves. No one had ever made her feel so cherished. When Jane gently freed her hair from being trapped by her collar, Sutton shivered.

"Cold?"

"No." Sutton turned around, meeting Jane's eyes as she did up the buttons. "Not at all." She waited a moment for her words to sink in before turning back to face the door. Threading her fingers through Jane's, she raised her other hand to wave at Giancarlo and Sue. They stood just outside the restaurant, beaming.

"Thank you again for dinner," she called. "Your risotto is even better than the one at the Four Seasons."

"Yes, thanks," Jane echoed. "It was delicious."

"Our pleasure," said Giancarlo.

"Have a wonderful evening," said Sue.

With a light tug on their joined hands, Sutton directed Jane to turn north. They walked in silence for a while, and Sutton felt suddenly uncertain as she contemplated their next step. Ciao Bella's private dining room had been a romantic cocoon away from the rest of the world. Their discussion over dinner had been about the recent past—Jane's trip and the delightful news of her fellowship; Sutton's mother, Celeste's disturbing revelation, and the epiphany that had followed. Most of their conversation had flowed easily, though at times, Jane had seemed to retreat into herself. Their familiar verbal sparring had been wholly absent, but Sutton didn't want to tease Jane about anything until they were firmly on solid ground. Some of that footing would only be regained with time, but Sutton was convinced that what they really needed most was the chance to be alone together—to rediscover that deeper connection beyond language, where communication gave way to communion. Did Jane feel similarly?

Pressing their shoulders together, she spoke before she could lose her nerve. "I want you to come home with me."

Jane looked down at her, expressionless. "But I don't have a change of clothing. Giovanni took my bags to my aunt and uncle's."

Agitation joined her uncertainty. Had Jane changed her mind? Was she making excuses? But no—Sutton had only to remember how Jane had trembled in her arms to be certain of the truth. Jane loved her. Jane wanted her. Still, that didn't mean that she wanted her right this instant. Was Sutton moving too quickly? Every cell in her body urged her on, but was she following her instincts, or giving in to her impatience?

"I have a washing machine, remember?" she said, keeping her voice light. "You can throw in your clothes if you'd like."

"But then I'd be naked."

Sutton was debating whether or not to confess that that was exactly the point, when she caught the hint of a smile flickering at the corners of Jane's lips. The swell of relief that they had regained their customary banter quickly gave way to indignation. "You are the worst!"

"The worst?" Jane looked affronted. "I thought you said you loved me."

Sutton pulled her beneath the awning of a jewelry boutique, out of the way of pedestrian traffic. Jane deserved the truth from her—now and always. "I do love you. And I don't just want you to come home with me tonight. I need you to."

Even in the dim light of the nearest street lamp, she could tell that Jane's eyes had grown several shades darker. The sudden intensity of her expression made Sutton wish she had forgone her coat.

"Then let's go."

They walked quickly, and this time, the silence was anticipatory. As though by some unspoken agreement, Sutton kept her hands to herself and Jane did the same. By the time they reached the front door to her apartment building, Sutton's heart was racing and her skin felt hot and tight. In a matter of minutes, they would truly make love for the first time. Her brain couldn't seem to wrap itself around that fact, but her body ached for the moment when there would no longer be any barriers between them—physical or emotional.

The tense silence endured until they were finally standing outside of her apartment. Sutton gripped her key tightly between two fingers, not wanting to waste a single second by dropping it. Carefully, she slotted it into the lock, acutely aware of Jane hovering mere inches behind her. This was it, she thought as the tumblers shifted. Finally, they would be alone. She gestured for Jane to precede her, then stepped over the threshold and closed the door firmly behind her.

When Jane wasn't immediately there, pushing her up against the hard surface, Sutton's uncertainty came screaming back. She watched Jane cross the room to stare out the window that looked down onto Spring Street. Quashing her impatience, she removed her boots slowly, wanting to give Jane as much time as she needed.

"Are you okay?" she called softly when Jane still hadn't moved a few moments later.

"I'm . . . I'm a little nervous." Jane turned just enough so that her profile was visible. "I want you so much, but . . ."

"But?"

"But I don't want to fall back into the same rhythm as before."

Sutton thought she understood. "Because before, we weren't on solid ground."

Jane nodded, finally facing her. "I need—" Quite suddenly, she fell silent.

"What do you need?" Sutton asked into the hush, determined to provide whatever it was, by whatever means necessary.

But Jane was pointing to the table. "Wait, where did those come from?"

It took Sutton a moment to realize she had never cleared the fortunes from the tabletop. She had thrown away the cookie pieces and the wrappers, but in the interminable week that had transpired since her visit to Sue, she had often found comfort in rereading the tiny slips of paper. They reminded her of the depth of Jane's feelings. When she read them that way, even the most despairing of the fortunes had given her a roundabout hope that if she could prove herself to Jane, she might be able to get another chance. And now, here they were.

"I was desperate to hear your voice, but I couldn't talk to you. So I bought a bag of cookies from Sue last week." She moved across the room to stand next to Jane, who was hunched over the table and frowning. "They made me feel closer to you."

"But these—I never gave these to my aunt."

"You didn't write them?" Sutton couldn't believe it. "I was so sure—"

"I did, but . . ." Jane shifted back and forth on her feet, clearly uncomfortable. "It was while you were on Long Island with your mother. You were so distant, and I missed you so much, and I couldn't sleep. So one night, I started writing in my journal. Not arranging sound bites, just writing. Which is pretty rare for me."

"I remember you saying that." Sutton reached out to rub comforting circles across Jane's lower back. It hurt to hear the remembered pain in Jane's voice, and to know she had been the cause. But she wanted to hear this. She needed to. And then, she needed to convince Jane that they could move forward together. "So then, how did your poem end up in the cookies?"

"When I went to Brazil, I left my journal behind." Jane shot her a sidelong glance. "I was trying to escape."

"I understand."

"My aunt and uncle put Minetta in charge of the fortunes, and she freaked out." Jane smiled at a memory. "She was so nervous that she kept on calling me for advice. Uncle John's going to flip when he sees her phone bill with all those international charges."

"I bet." Sutton curled one arm around Jane's waist. "Were you able to talk her down off the cliff?"

"I finally suggested that if she couldn't come up with anything, she should use lines of poetry from the public domain."

Sutton wanted to laugh, but she bit down on her tongue to hold it back. She knew how sensitive Jane was to other people reading her work. "Looks like she took your suggestion to heart, in a manner of speaking."

"I think I'm going to have to explain that 'public domain' doesn't mean, 'your cousin's notebook that just so happens to be lying on the nightstand,'" Jane said dryly. "Though since her nosiness also resulted in my fellowship, I'm not sure I have a leg to stand on."

"Don't be too hard on her." Sutton leaned forward to press her lips to the soft skin just below Jane's ear, thrilling at the sharp intake of breath that greeted her kiss. "It's a beautiful poem. I'm glad I was able to see it."

Jane drew Sutton close. The gentle pressure of her hands made Her go molten inside. "That isn't all of it."

Overwhelmed by her body's reaction, Sutton struggled to focus. "Will you let me see the whole piece sometime?"

"If you really want."

"I want." Sutton reached up to brush her fingers through the hair at Jane's temple. She had let it grow out a little bit, and the shagginess was endearing. "I think you're brilliant. I love your work. I love you."

Jane's answering smile was completely unpremeditated, bursting across her features like a shooting star. In that moment, seeing how much joy those three words brought her, Sutton fell even more in love.

"Say it again."

"I love you."

Jane leaned down so their foreheads were touching. "Maybe just one more time?"

"I love you," Sutton murmured. "And I'll tell you as often as you like."

"Maybe you should tell me again in bed."

Sutton stepped back, reaching for Jane's hand as she moved. "I'll tell you wherever you like." She tugged gently. "But right now, there's nothing I want more than to show you. Say yes."

"Yes."

The syllable didn't waver. Jane's eyes had darkened into forest-green pools, broken only by the occasional fleck of gold, like a ray of sunshine filtering through the trees. Slowly, Sutton backed down the short hallway, never breaking her gaze.

"I know you've walked this stretch of floor a dozen times," she said as she reached her doorway, "and that the same holds true for being in my room." Pausing at the threshold, she reached up to cup Jane's face in her hands. "But this time is different. I need you to believe that."

"I do."

Jane dipped her head to claim Sutton's mouth in a fierce kiss that made Sutton's head spin and her nerves ignite. Cleaving to Jane, she surrendered control, glorying in the possessive clutch of those strong arms around her waist, bending her body back. Lost in the conflagration, Sutton whimpered involuntarily when Jane suddenly pulled away.

"I need to see you." Reaching down to caress Sutton's thigh, she rubbed the hem of the dress between her thumb and index finger.

"Then help me." Raising her arms, Sutton waited. A moment later, the dress was gone. Her lacy bra and bikini had been chosen with this very moment in mind, and she was gratified to see Jane's eyes widen. With a slow smile, Sutton smoothed her hands down her stomach until they encountered the waistband of her stockings. "These, too?"

"Everything." Jane's chest rose and fell rapidly, and Sutton could actually see the pulse in her neck.

"Only if you do, too."

In a surge of frenzied movement, Jane tore off her shirt and pushed down her pants, stepping nude out of the heap of clothes and stalking across the brief space that separated them. Seconds later their bellies were pressed together, hot and firm and already slick with sweat. When Jane's fingertips ghosted up along Sutton's spine, she shivered.

"Oh, please."

"Please what?"

Jane's eyes gleamed in the dim streetlight that filtered through the window. Gone were the shadows of her doubts, her sadness, her insecurities. In this moment, with nothing between them, they existed in perfect harmony.

"Make love to me," Sutton whispered.

"Yes. I will. Yes." Jane lowered her onto the bed, pressing her firmly into the mattress as her kisses stole Sutton's reason and seared her skin. This time there was no waiting, no teasing, as Jane staked her claim, one hand cupping Sutton's head as the other slid between their bodies. The confidence in Jane's touch sent a wave of dizziness through Sutton, and she dug her nails into the muscles at the base of Jane's neck.

Only when Jane's fingertips encountered the wetness at the juncture of her thighs, did she pause. Sutton couldn't suppress the sharp cry that left her throat. "Please," she gasped again. "I need you."

But Jane didn't move. "I don't just want you to love me," she said, the words choked with emotion. "I want you to be mine."

"I am. I am yours." Sutton captured Jane's lips with furious momentum. "Come inside," she whispered against her mouth. "Let me show you."

With a hoarse groan, Jane obeyed, swallowing Sutton's sharp gasp in a bruising kiss that went on and on in synchrony with her slow, twisting thrusts. "I love you," she murmured brokenly, over and over. "I love you, Sutton."

Immolating from within, Sutton barely had the presence of mind to reach for Jane, dipping into the exquisitely soft well between her legs as she felt her own body begin to spiral out of control. "L-love you back," she whispered, circling frantically. "Oh god, Jane, come with me, *please*—"

And then she was shattering from the inside out, surging up against Jane's body like a wave, muffling her cries in the hot curve of Jane's shoulder as Jane's fingers tightened in her hair and her hips thrust erratically and she breathed Sutton's name like a prayer, over and over and over.

When at last their bodies had quieted, Jane rolled to one side and gathered Sutton tenderly into her arms. Sutton buried her face in the crook of Jane's neck, feeling more at peace than she had in the past . . . ever. The thought made her smile.

"I can feel that." Jane nuzzled the top of her head. "What are you thinking?"

Sutton pulled back just enough to meet her gaze. "I'm thinking that I'm happy. Plain, old, uncomplicated happy. It's a new sensation for me."

Jane kissed her nose. "How can I keep you feeling this way? Because I'm already addicted to that smile."

The answer was suddenly so clear. "Come to Sweden with me."

Jane blinked owlishly. "Excuse me?"

"I mean it. Come with me."

Jane arched one eyebrow. "I thought I just did."

"Oh, stop." Sutton tried to frown, but dissolved into giggles instead. "You're impossible."

"You love this. Admit it. You love the way we are together."

Abruptly serious, Sutton nodded. "I do," she said quietly. "I really, really do. Which is why I want you to join me."

Jane frowned. "Are you sure you don't just want me for my language skills?"

Sutton couldn't believe her ears. "If you're asking whether I love you because you're a cunning linguist, then the answer is yes."

"Oh, hell. I blundered right into that one."

"You did." Sutton kissed her lightly. "So? What do you think?"

She watched indulgently as Jane made a big show of considering her request—frowning, sighing, squinting—opening one eye and then the other in an exaggerated performance of contemplation.

"I think I'd better," Jane said finally.

"Oh?"

"How will you survive, without me there to interpret the language and keep you warm during those long, arctic nights?"

"An excellent question." Shifting her weight, she pushed Jane down into the mattress and rolled completely on top of her. "Fortunately, you're now my prisoner. I'm never letting you go. So. End of discussion."

Jane's answering smile was incandescent, and she hummed softly in the back of her throat in a clear sign of contentment. "Okay. That works for me."

Sutton knew her heart wasn't really going to explode, but that's what it felt like. Smiling broadly, she surrendered herself to love and gravity.

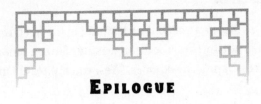

EPILOGUE

SUTTON SMOOTHED HER HAND down the left side of the poster, gave the adhesive at the corner an extra pat, and stepped back to admire her work. A baby penguin gazed back at her, black eyes bright in its fuzzy gray face. Sutton smiled. Her cheeks didn't feel tight anymore.

"I think this one's my favorite," she said, looking across the room to where Jane was stretched on her tiptoes, affixing a JUST SAY NO TO STYRO bumper sticker to the wall.

Jane glanced over her shoulder, laughed, and returned her concentration to the task at hand. "You said the same thing about the panda cub, not even five minutes ago."

"A woman's allowed to change her mind!" Sutton's protest sounded weak, even to her. Hands on her hips, she looked between the two posters that framed the window. The desk beneath it held a bubbling lava lamp, a brand new notebook, and a fountain pen. Outside, Noodle Treasure's sign winked merrily in the late morning sunlight. "They're both adorable."

With a satisfied sigh, Jane rocked back onto her heels and rolled her shoulders. "There. Done." She crossed the room and slid her arms around Sutton's waist. "And yes, they are—though not as adorable as you'll look in one of those floppy Ph.D. hats in just a few hours."

Sutton spun in Jane's arms and summoned her best skeptical expression. "I think the word you're looking for is 'ridiculous.'"

"You're giving *me* a vocabulary lesson? I'm the poet, remember?"

Suddenly not in the mood for teasing, Sutton smoothed her thumbs across Jane's cheekbones. "Yes, you are. And I'm so proud of you."

Thanks to her fellowship, Jane had managed to pull enough strings with Hunter's English Department to register late for an independent study with her advisor. She had spent the remainder of the spring hard at work on her senior thesis, and last weekend, the entire family had celebrated her commencement. Sutton couldn't help but smile as she remembered how nervous she had been to meet Jane's parents, but her anxiety had been unfounded. Jane's mother was warm and down to earth, and her father had an endless well of funny stories from all their time spent abroad. Unlike her own parents, Jane's were genuinely excited about their trip to Sweden and had shared the names of a few contacts they still had in Stockholm. They had even brought a few family photos along from their time there, most of which featured a gangly, adolescent version of Jane with braces and long, straight hair.

"What are you thinking about?" Jane leaned down to brush their lips together. "You just looked a million miles away."

"I was thinking about your graduation weekend. And meeting your parents. And those pictures of the last time you were in Sweden."

"Oh, God." Jane made a face and her arms dropped to her sides. "I'll never forgive them for exposing you to my awkward teenage self."

"Speaking of teenagers, do you think we should find Min? We're ready, right?" Sutton turned to survey the small space that had been Jane's office for the past year. Almost every available inch of wall was covered.

"I'll text her to come up."

While Jane bent over her phone, Sutton walked to the window and looked across the street. The sunlight illuminated the first row of tables in Noodle Treasure, and she watched fondly as Benny wiped down one of them with a cloth, while Mei refilled the teacup of a nearby customer. Benny and Mei, Sue, Giancarlo, Jane's family: she would miss them all. But fortunately, she was taking the best part of Chinatown with her.

"I stared at you out that window for . . . I don't even know how many hours." Jane had come up beside her, and now nudged her shoulder. "Do you forgive me for being a total creeper?"

Sutton felt herself blush. Even now, it was exhilarating to know just how much Jane had wanted her, and desired her still. "That depends. How do you plan to make it up to me?"

Jane's eyes darkened, and she opened her mouth to reply, only to close it again at the sound of hurried footsteps outside.

"Hellooooo? Jane? You know, you can't just *summon* me anytime you want. You're not the only writer in this family, and I was in the *zone* just now, and if this is some kind of joke—" Min appeared in the doorway, index finger raised in the mirror image of her sister Hester chiding her children.

"It's no joke," Jane said. "Welcome to your new office."

Min's shock was endearing. Her mouth fell open, and several seconds passed before she finally found her words. It was the first time Sutton had ever witnessed her speechless, and she bit her lower lip to keep from laughing.

"A lava lamp! And awww, look at that face!" She bounced on her toes, drinking in the brightly decorated space. "You—you guys did all this?"

"It was Jane's idea," Sutton said. "Since you're taking over writing the fortunes, she thought some inspiration might help."

"So you don't have to resort to hunting down all your sisters' old diaries." Jane's voice dripped with sarcasm.

Min stuck out her tongue. "You're not really mad."

Sutton glanced over at Jane and they shared a smile. More than once, they had laughed over Min's role in helping them find their way back to each other.

"No. I'm not." Jane stepped forward to ruffle her hair. "Have fun, okay? Who knows—maybe your chi will be even more powerful than mine."

"Obviously." Min perched on the folding chair, tapped experimentally on the surface of the lamp, and then flipped open the notebook. "Ooh, a fountain pen! I've always wanted one."

"We'll let you work," Sutton said, resting one hand on her shoulder and squeezing briefly. "It's time for me to go get ready, anyway."

But Min turned in her chair, her expression suddenly serious. "I'm going to miss you. Both of you."

Jane reached for Sutton's hand. "We'll miss you, too, kiddo. But you can come for a visit as soon as we're settled, okay?"

Min's eyes were brighter than usual, and she swallowed before nodding.

"Besides," Sutton chimed in, touched by her uncharacteristic display of emotion, "we still have the rest of the day to celebrate. You're coming to my graduation, right?"

"Of course!" Min directed a skeptical glance in Jane's direction. "It's going to be a classy event. Someone has to keep her out of trouble."

JANE STOOD AT THE appointed meeting place, holding a half-empty champagne flute in one hand and a bouquet of red roses in the other. She had considered getting something more exotic, but Minetta had convinced her to go with the classic arrangement. Having had several hours now to contemplate her choice, she was glad she had followed Min's advice. There was nothing ambiguous about a dozen red roses. They telegraphed exactly what she felt for Sutton.

She smiled as she looked out the windows onto the plaza of Lincoln Center, where the choreographed water jets of the fountain gave the illusion that they were dancing to some unheard music.

The day was perfect—clear and calm, warm without being too hot. A good omen, if you believed in that sort of thing. But Jane had had enough of astrology and fortunes. She and Sutton were going to make their own destiny now—starting tomorrow, when they would board a plane at JFK and begin their Swedish adventure.

"What's taking so long?" Min fidgeted at her side, torn between peering down at her phone and staring out into the crowd. A few graduates had already emerged in their purple robes and puffy black hats, but most of them were still inside the auditorium.

"She's probably talking to some of her friends and professors. Don't worry. She'll be here."

"I'm dying of boredom." Min, wearing a simple black dress that came down to her knees, might have looked older than her eleven years today, but she certainly wasn't acting like it. "I just want the party to start already."

Sutton's commencement celebration wasn't going to be in a swanky Midtown hotel, or even in her family's townhouse, but in Noodle Treasure. The decision had angered her parents, but Sutton had refused to budge. Jane could remember, with crystal clarity, the phone conversation between Sutton and her irate father several weeks before.

"It's my graduation and my decision, Dad. This is what I want." Sutton's voice had been strong and steady as she paced across the floor while Jane had watched from her bed. "You're welcome to come if you'd like, but I'm not going to debate this anymore."

Jane felt her smile widen at the memory. Sutton had been so certain, so self-possessed. Later, when they had curled up under the covers, she had told Jane that she wanted to spend the day of her graduation with the people who loved and respected her for who she was, not those who wanted to transform her into something else.

A waiter interrupted her introspection to proffer a tray of hors d'oeuvres. "Crab salad canapé?" he asked with a bland smile.

"Thank you," Jane said as both she and Min reached for the elegantly presented appetizer. Min sniffed it as he moved away, then took a small bite. Immediately, she made a face.

"I liked your graduation better."

Jane had to laugh. Her own commencement had been held last weekend at Radio City, and Minetta had taken the opportunity to stuff herself with popcorn. Jane was just relieved that she had been able to resolve her incomplete transcript and finally graduate. It had taken a lengthy conversation with the English Department chair, along with several less than enjoyable meetings with Professor Ryan, but ultimately he had accepted her senior thesis. She had Sutton to thank for both the inspiration and motivation to finish. The poem Min had dismembered for the fortune cookies had ended up being the centerpiece of her project.

Her lingering amusement faded as she caught sight of Sutton's parents approaching. Squaring her shoulders, she nudged Min with one elbow. "Look sharp."

Mrs. St. James clung to her husband's arm as they moved slowly through the crowd, and Jane wondered whether she ever felt a twinge of regret about her life decisions. Did she wish she had confronted her husband about his infidelities? Did she wish she had reached out to Sutton in compassion instead of in judgment?

"Hello, Dr. and Mrs. St. James." Jane spoke when they were still a few feet away, wanting the first word.

"Good afternoon," Priscilla said stiffly. Reginald said nothing.

"How did you enjoy the ceremony?"

"It was lovely," Priscilla said after a beat. Reginald remained silent.

At that moment, Jane's phone vibrated. Text from Sutton St. James. As always, her heart skipped a beat. *Heading to our meeting spot. See you soon. Love you.*

"That was Sutton," she said. "She'll be here soon."

An awkward silence fell between them then, and Jane was just about to make some asinine comment about the weather, when Reginald rounded on her. "I understand you'll be accompanying Sutton overseas."

Shocked that he'd brought it up, Jane needed a moment to muster an answer. "Yes, that's right. I lived in Stockholm for a few years as a teenager, and I'm eager to show her the city."

Reginald's face darkened. "Surely you can't believe this course of action is prudent. You live in completely different worlds, with completely different priorities. Your relationship is doomed to fail."

His words were meant to bait her, and only a few months ago, they would have found their mark. But not now. As she opened her mouth to respond, Jane caught sight of Sutton walking briskly toward them. She remembered waking up together this morning, one arm wrapped around Sutton's waist. She remembered the sense of accomplishment they had shared while decorating Min's office, and the excitement in Sutton's voice every time they imagined what their new apartment would be like. Her father couldn't have been more wrong on every count.

"Dr. St. James, you're wrong. And nothing you could say right now will change my mind."

When Reginald's mouth opened and closed silently, rather like a fish, Jane felt a surge of satisfaction that was trumped only by Sutton's arrival. She joined them in a rush of energy, cheeks flushed and eyes bright with joy, flaxen hair tumbling across her shoulders like spun gold. The floppy black hat didn't look ridiculous at all.

"Hi, Mom. Hi, Dad. Hi, Min." She had smiles for them all, but the broadest was for Jane. As their gazes locked, Sutton took one step forward, and then another, until they were separated by mere inches. "Hello, love," she said softly.

And then, in the sight of everyone, she curled one hand around Jane's neck, rose up onto her toes, and joined their lips together.

Conversation & Discussion Guide

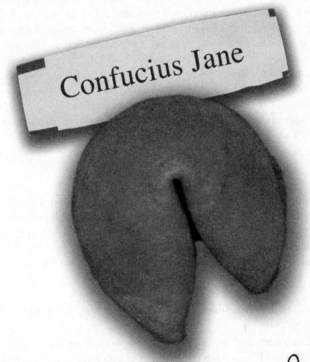

Confucius Jane

Katie Lynch

For more reading group suggestions,
visit readinggroupgold.com.

A Conversation with Katie Lynch

Where did the idea for *Confucius Jane* come from?

Confucius Jane emerges from my relationship with my wife, who is second-generation Chinese American. The process of falling in love and building a life together has involved amalgamating my northern European–derived traditions with aspects of her Chinese culture. From her and her family, I have learned so much about a part of the world I previously knew nothing about. For example, the scene where Sutton, Jane, and Min go out to dim sum together is lifted almost exactly from my first dim sum experience with my wife in Chinatown. Like Sutton, I was willing to try anything once, and Sutton's reactions to chicken feet and tripe are true to my own. This cultural intersection has informed all aspects of *Confucius Jane*, which tells the story of people who are defined both by the communities in which they participate and by the new connections they make with others. This theme plays out in the lives of primary and secondary characters within the novel.

How did you do your research for the novel?

While planning the book, I would make frequent visits to Chinatown. Often, I spent my time aimlessly walking the streets—observing, listening, and taking notes that would inform my descriptions of the setting. My family made a trip to the Museum of Chinese in America, where we went on a historical walking tour of the neighborhood. Since food is a central element of the story, we also made a point of dining in Chinatown frequently, which made the research process especially delicious!

As you mentioned, your wife is Chinese American, much like Jane. How did she influence Jane's character?

My wife was indispensable during the writing process, both as my muse and as my consultant on all things Chinese American. While she isn't hapa (multiracial), like Jane, her upbringing as a child of Chinese descent growing up in suburban America produced many of the cultural and generational insights that I integrated into the story. For example, I am always amazed at the way she seamlessly alternates between Mandarin Chinese and English when she talks with her parents. She has also introduced a range of herbal medicines into our winter germ-fighting routine. During my writing process, she helped me to imagine the cast of supporting characters around Jane derived from the "aunties" and "uncles" she grew up with in her community. My wife and her family were particularly useful resources when I had questions about Chinese-American cultural traditions surrounding the lunar new year.

What is the inspiration behind the elements of Chinese astrology in the story?

Connecting Sutton and Jane's romance to the symbolism of Chinese astrology made it possible to inject elements of magical realism into the book. My wife's family is sensitive to the guidelines provided by Chinese astrology, numerology, and feng shui. It seemed natural to not only integrate those beliefs and superstitions into the story, but to have them foreshadow and influence the plot and character development. And in a fortuitous twist of fate, *Confucius Jane* will be released at the same time the story opens: just prior to the lunar new year celebration inaugurating the Year of the Monkey, which will begin in February of 2016.

This book switches back and forth between Jane's and Sutton's perspectives. Did you find it difficult to write in both voices? Who do you relate to more closely?

Confucius Jane is the story of two very different women whose paths cross almost incidentally, but whose lives are changed as a result. I wanted to tell both sides of that story, and the most effective way to do so was to allow each woman's voice to be heard in equal proportion. Fortunately, Sutton and Jane are such unique characters that their voices sound distinct in my head. While I share attributes with both, I relate more closely to Sutton, who shares my academic ambition and neuroses. I wish I were more "zen" like Jane!

Why did you choose to write about LGBTQ characters?

One of the most powerful aspects of storytelling is its ability to hold up a mirror to society. When we see ourselves in that mirror, we become more invested in the narrative. As a lesbian, it has been historically difficult to see my reflection in literature—although happily, this is now changing for the better. LGBTQ-identified people are socially hapa by virtue of our sexuality: we stand at the intersection of multiple communities, endeavoring to make a space for ourselves in all of them. *Confucius Jane* takes up this theme.

In your day job, you are the head of the Honors program at SUNY Rockland Community College. Did any of your work life make it into your fiction? How does your job impact your writing?

Since I am now older than my characters, who are in their twenties and are exploring newfound independence, my students remind me of what it's like to be a "new adult" in the world, and they teach me about new trends, technologies, jargon, and philosophies that were not a part of my own "twentysomething" experience.

Where do you write?

Juggling a full-time job with writing can be a challenge, and I've learned to write in brief snatches of time that I can wrest away from the busyness of daily life. My commute from Manhattan to Rockland County is a lengthy one, and I do much of my writing on the train. I also spend a great deal of time writing at our kitchen table once our child is in bed and our dogs have been walked. But my favorite place to write is on the deck of our home in the Catskills, with a giant mug of coffee ready at hand and a canine curled up at my feet.

What other authors do you read, and how did they influence your story?

As a lifelong reader, I enjoy a broad range of literature. As a child, Tolkien's Lord of the Rings inspired both my passion for storytelling and my decision to become a medievalist. As a student, I fell in love with everything from *Beowulf* and *Paradise Lost* to *Mrs. Dalloway* and Stoppard's *Arcadia*. As a twentysomething, I gravitated toward the romances of Nora Roberts and Jennifer Crusie. When I came out as a lesbian, I was overjoyed to find lesbian romances by authors such as Katherine V. Forrest, Radclyffe, and Karin Kallmaker. As an English professor, I'm always curious to know what my students are reading, and their enthusiasm has led me to books such as *The Hunger Games* and *The Fault in Our Stars*. I think it's important to read constantly, and I don't have an agenda when I read—all I want is to enjoy a well-written story about characters with whom I can connect.

Discussion Questions

1. *Confucius Jane* is a story of two worlds: the tightly knit, middle-class community that is Jane's Chinatown and the wealthy, high-powered world that Sutton's family inhabits at New York's premier hospitals and on the Upper East Side. But the differences between these worlds go far beyond socioeconomic status. What are the prevailing values of each community? How are they reflected in Sutton and Jane?

2. Jane is "hapa" or multiracial—half Chinese and half Caucasian. How does she feel about her background, and what does it mean to her extended family and her friends? Where do we see her connections to her Chinese culture, and where do we see her remove from it? Do other characters represent or embrace mixtures of different cultures and different origins?

3. Jane's cousin Minetta establishes herself as a force to be reckoned with on the first page of *Confucius Jane*. What is her role in the story—matchmaker? Greek chorus? Intervening angel? Comic relief? What role does she play in Sutton and Jane's relationship? In the life of Sue's business? What can Jane learn from someone so young?

4. At its heart, *Confucius Jane* is about family. Yet the definitions of family, loyalty, and love shift between the book's two communities. What do Sutton and Jane each believe about the purpose of family at the start of the story and at its end? How do biological families and chosen families compare? What are the two women's loyalties and obligations to each? Is there chosen family in your own life story?

5. Both as their relationship begins and when it seems to end, Jane and Sutton each doubt themselves, often in heartbreaking ways. What pushes them to question their own motives? What parts of themselves do they never second-guess? How do you think their upbringings contribute to how they try to blame—or protect—themselves at various times?

6. Professional success is a theme that runs throughout the book, although it takes very different shapes for Sutton and for Jane. How is each woman's professional calling displayed in who she is and how she relates to the people around her? Is there a difference between plans and dreams? How does each woman evolve in her thinking about her work and her purpose in the world by the story's end?

7. Especially as her father's lies and betrayals come to public light, Sutton is torn by her sense of duty toward her mother. There is clearly love between mother and daughter, but who cares for whom in their relationship and in what ways? Who do you think knows what is best for Priscilla? What does Sutton ultimately discover about her own feelings of protectiveness and obligation toward her mother? Could their family story have unfolded differently if Priscilla had not had MS?

8. Fate, fortune, and destiny come up often in *Confucius Jane*. Which characters cling most tightly to a belief in fate? How does upbringing determine destiny, and what happens when some of the characters stray from the fortune set out for them? Do you believe that our future is already written? How important is free will in determining the paths that our lives take or the relationships that we enter into? Was Sutton and Jane's love "meant to be"—and what does each of them believe about that?

9. Katie Lynch explores ideas of belonging and otherness throughout the story, primarily through Sutton's journey. How does Sutton "fit in" in the Chinatown community, and how does she seem out of place? Indeed, how does she fit in within her biological family? What other characters begin as "outsiders" to various communities? What about Jane makes her able to be a bridge between Sutton and the world that Jane grew up in?

10. Sue makes what she feels is a crucial point about the connectedness of all people and all energies in their community when she tells both Jane and Sutton that Jane's pain is felt far beyond herself. Do you believe that one individual's experience can ripple through an entire community even when that community is not directly, tangibly affected by that person's situation? Are our energies connected to those of the people in our daily lives? How do those connections show themselves?

11. Sutton's ultimate discoveries about her parents lead her to make a radical shift in her plans and her loyalties. What are each of her parents' priorities, for themselves and for her? What do they want from her and for her, and what does she want for herself? What forms does love take in Sutton's biological family? How do you feel about the decisions she ultimately makes regarding her connection to them?

12. Sutton has been raised, all her life, to be a surgeon—focused, perfectionistic, driven, logical, and precise. Do you think that this was what she herself always wanted? As children, how much do we internalize our parents' desires for us to grow in certain directions? Sutton has dedicated her life to excelling as a surgeon, but what does her growing interest in research say about both her own desires and her personality? How do the two career paths differ, and which one do you think represents her most accurately?

tor-forge.com